To Craig

Enjoy!

# NOAH'S HEART

Neil Rowland

This edition published in 2014 by
Acorn Books
www.acornbooks.co.uk

Acorn Books is an imprint of
Andrews UK Limited
www.andrewsuk.com

# Contents

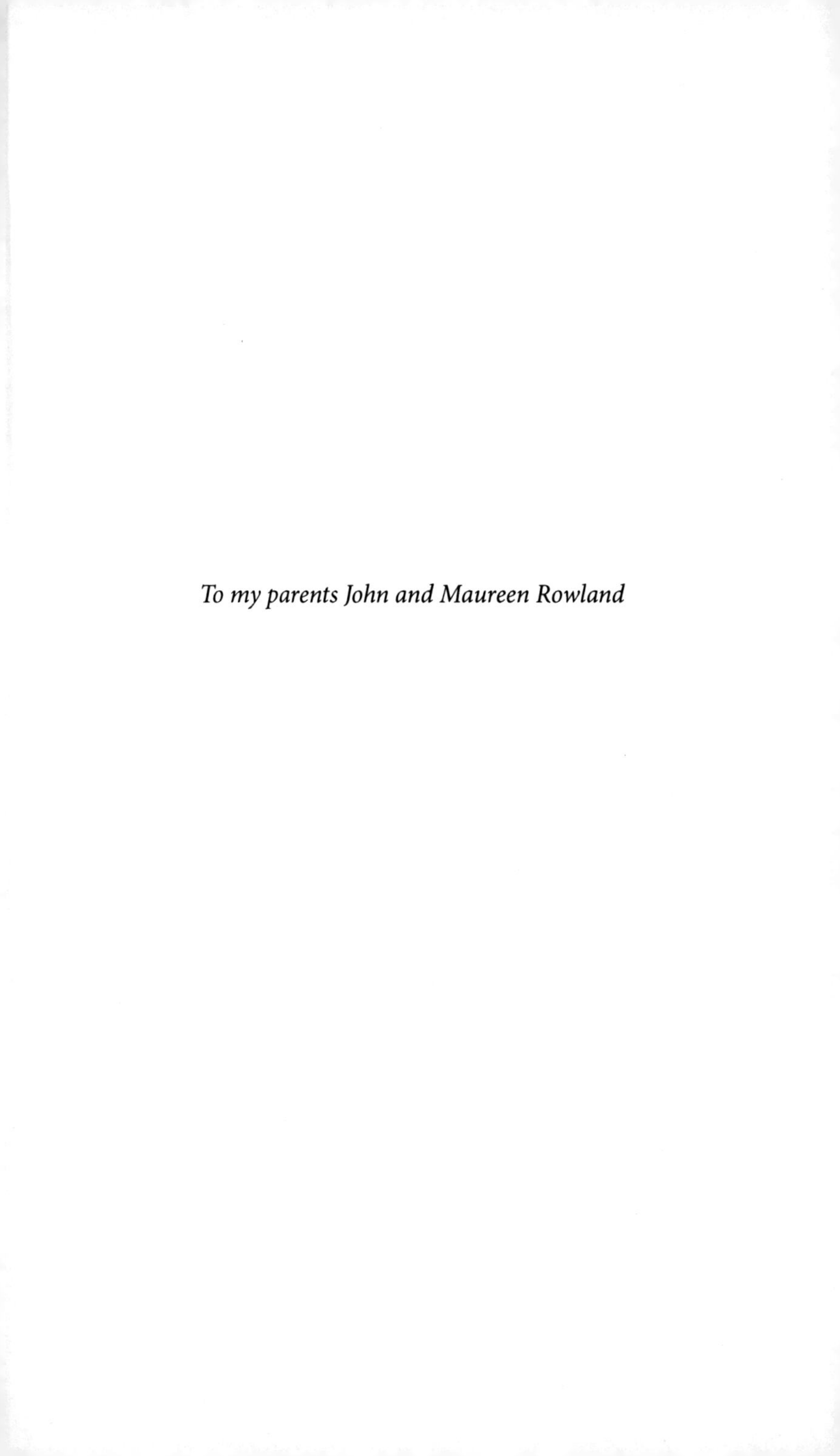

*To my parents John and Maureen Rowland*

Thanks due to Alex Colbourne for designing the cover.

My publisher Paul Andrews for backing this title.

To Elizabeth Grainger and Janet Davis for proofing. All 'first readers' of the script for their advice and comments.

To all those family members, friends and fellow writers who have offered their encouragement and camaraderie. I couldn't thank you enough.

Gratitude for the fantastic support and backing expressed by readers of The City Dealer.

# NOAH'S HEART

# All Tomorrow's Parties

## Part 1

# Chapter 1

**Bristol, England.**

I'm Noah Sheer, just shy of forty nine. I'm a kite maker, a champion balloonist, a former student radical, a devoted father and, contrary to all rumours, still in love with my wife. It's public knowledge that my private life is in bad shape.

But these details lost impact when my damaged heart put me into a grip. I believe that my own version of Bob Dylan's "Never ending tour" may be finally rumbling to a halt. My wife and I used to enjoy talking about individual destiny, yet lately I've just been riding my luck. You could say I've been struggling to keep myself to myself.

The other week I was going about my business, when there was a further heart incident. I hardly dared to breathe another. I collapsed against a wall holding my chest. I could feel moisture beginning to come out, bubbling up into each pore of my skin. My limbs turned to ice and began to break apart. My heart was sending out warnings about a complete meltdown. The novel of my life was coming to an end. There's something wrong with the pump again, I chastised myself; something lethally amiss, despite an allegedly successful major heart operation.

"You look much better. An amazing transformation," my best buddy had remarked, merely echoing the general reception of family and friends. "We can hardly recognise you," they said.

"From now or from then?" I enquired.

At the time of my hospital release I might have agreed with them. But my x-ray will soon be slapped back on to the lighted backdrop, after a relapse. I'm no more than a salacious image under the radiologist's red light.

I'd set off for town this morning to get a new pair of jeans: Which is the kind of optimistic freedom a guy in my position attempts to enjoy. The sun was bowling across the morning sky and the birds were whooping it up like Martha and the Vandellas circa 1967.

Our kids had apparently gone away for the weekend. They hadn't left any messages, or clues, behind. After getting back into the groove of life my idea was to get fixed for some new sounds, as well as find a party shirt to match my new pair of Levi's. When I say "new music" I mean the latest albums from Young and Dylan (note the importance of that 'and'). To quote Charles Mingus, mercurial jazz genius, it was time to let my children hear some music. They resist the idea of good taste but the terrible truth is hard to face.

Then, as I strolled along Broadgate, the breeze began to whip up, the sky blackened like the interior of a biker's jacket. To escape a drenching from a violent downpour I scrambled into the Old Galleries, one of our covered shopping malls here in Bristol.

The heart squeeze came on unexpectedly. When the symptoms began I became rigid with fear and shock. It forced me back against the shiny marble wall between shop fronts. I clutched my heart like Buster Keaton spotting the marshmallow face of his heroine. Shoppers continued to bustle along their course, perfectly in step with the rhythm-free shopping-mall musak. The tinkling melodies of the suburban Seventies amplified between my ears, in a jingle at the mouth of hell. No power on earth was capable of saving me.

"Are you all right, love?" trembled a female voice.

I just stared ahead, locked into a grimace.

"Are you sure?" asked the elderly lady.

"Don't worry," I wheezed.

"You poor boy, you look dreadful," she observed.

"Only need to catch my breath," I replied.

She examined me with sympathetic scepticism. "Can't I do anything for you?"

I groaned imploringly.

"Anything at all?" she urged.

"That's kind, but no." Everything was rocking and rolling; the final encore.

"Do you want me to call an ambulance?" she asked, pressing my arm.

"They can't help me," I replied.

"Then can I get you a cup of tea?" she wondered.

"*A cup of tea*?" I replied.

"Yes, there's a cafeteria next door."

Scrap the National Health Service, I thought, build a tea-urn the size of St Paul's Cathedral. Cure all.

Reluctantly the kindly lady left me. She thought that I was ungrateful and ignoring her. She took a grip of her deep handbag, gave me a hard critical look for rudeness and shuffled off. The other shoppers barely spared me a second look. I probably gave the impression of being a middle aged and middle class alcoholic, or even a drug addict. They had no intention of getting mixed up with a deranged idiot, slumped to the side. They didn't know there was a counter revolution going on in my beat box.

But thank god, I didn't pop my clogs. The squeezing grip began to slacken, the radiation of death to recede. Then I levered myself away from the marble surface that resembled an unaffordable gravestone. I was released again, even if I didn't know for what purpose. There was no desire for a cup of tea or anything stronger as, recuperating, I staggered away. I swallowed down the bitter oily residue of mortality and struggled to walk upright. I could feel mercury slowly withdrawing from my veins. I took out a wrinkled grey handkerchief and wiped my face.

Nevertheless my heart was gyrating like a cocktail shaker, shifting a mixture too bitter to drink. I was shaking; my legs wobbled; my head was scrambled. No doubt I didn't present such a wholesome sight to fellow citizens: even less the well-honed guy who used to bounce out of the gym every week.

How terrible the prospect of kicking the bucket in a shopping centre. Wounded pride didn't enter my thoughts at the time; just massive, overwhelming relief at having survived. So what the hell had gone wrong? What had triggered the latest malfunction? I had some leisure to consider these critical questions as I escaped the mall - my near final resting place. It couldn't have been the dash for cover out of the rain. I was supposed to be making a good recovery. Surely more than a jog was required to plunge me over the abyss, they'd insisted. Death had taken me to match point but I'd managed to fight back into the tie-break. To endure a heart attack at the age of forty-something had been the worst trip imaginable. You have to create some powerfully positive karma to survive that one. You can't afford to be negative and look back on terrible experiences. Therefore I was determined to encourage positive radiation.

The internal cardiology unit was all working quietly again, as I stepped off an escalator back to ground level. But there had been another coronary incident. The involuntary muscle had thrown another tantrum. That's a dangerous place to hesitate. So how close had I got to complete silence?

I drew the deep breaths of an escapologist who'd misjudged by a few seconds. I was bloody relieved, but I'd been terrifyingly close to a complete blackout, yet again. And according to the wise men and women, this was never supposed to happen. There was plenty of angst as I battled against the crowds, trying to find my car. My cheerful future evaporated like a drop of whiskey on the salt flats outside of Utah.

But maybe I'd just had another bad experience.

# Chapter 2

I'm not ready to talk about my life in the past tense.

Trouble with my heart first erupted while I was away on a last-minute break. My dream girl Corrina accompanied me on that anticipated holiday to Crete. The island had been already been devastated by a legendary earthquake tsunami in ancient times. That antique catastrophe, passed down through generations, should have served as a precautionary warning. Instead we surrendered deliriously to our romantic lust and visited the nearest branch of 'Cooked' holidays for a rapid getaway. In hindsight I know that something was bound to go wrong with the trip. But hindsight's like a successful career in show business.

After everything I've been through, I know that the ocean of my manhood is very different to the gentler sea of my youth, as far as I recall - at least by comparing the snaps.

"I need to blow out of town for a while," I told her. "Get some breathing space. What do you say?"

"Not sure if I have that much free time, Noah," she admitted.

"Come along, Corrina, we can make the time," I persuaded her.

My girlfriend squeezed her lips into an irritated reluctant pout.

There has to be a catch when you sign up to a money slashing scheme. There has to be a hitch when there are only hours remaining before take-off. But then some people say it was no more than I deserved. My divorce hadn't long gone through and not even the dust in England had properly settled. I had to leave our kids to fend for themselves, this was one issue. I couldn't always be watching over them: they were beginning to have their own lives. How were they ever going to discover themselves, if I never gave them any space? Corrina and I intended to get away from all my problems for a fortnight. But we barely escaped for a week. As it turned out, the near loss of my life had the effect of cutting the holiday short.

The resort airport resembled an isolated military outpost. I felt that if we walked too quickly from the aircraft steps we would be cut down by machine-gun fire. After a body search we picked up a hired motorbike; strapping two suitcases to the sides, as Corrina flipped her wrist again. That was a wise decision, to travel light, given the manner of my departure from the island. Corinna burnt a line down the roads leading to our rented vacation villa. She whipped that machine so fast that hot scented air scorched the interior of my nostrils. I gripped around her waist in neat role reversal; as she hurtled us forward on this Suzuki chariot, unaware that my own wings were about to be clipped.

"Hold tight, Noah!" she yelled, letting out a whoop as she slashed around another tight corner. By then I could feel dying insects congregating at the back of my throat. I was pulverising their external skeletons with every terrified swallow. I tried to imagine myself as Peter Fonda. I even had a new pair of azure wraparound shades for the trip: only slightly thinning hair streaming behind my ears. Don't tell me this was a clichéd male fantasy, as it was very real at the time. With a dangerous machine you need to keep a tight grip.

We'd rented a villa with superb Olympian views over the Aegean coastline. We even had a slice of the beach to ourselves, except for parties of local youths, as well as an academic German couple around the bay. Somebody offered us the use of a powerful launch at a reasonable rental, to dash us between the islands when we wished. Everything looked set for a great holiday: everything was in place. My only job was to learn how to take an afternoon siesta. After the holiday, I considered, I would feel rejuvenated with a new lease on life. There was no need to relive the horrors of a divorce; my regrets about a teenage marriage turned sour in middle age; or concern myself too much about teenage children of our own. Just lie back on the lounger and secure my eyes against solar flares.

By then I'd known Corrina for almost three months and she made me happy. She works for a world music company that has its HQ and recording studios at a large farm outside Bath. One fateful afternoon I drove over to the place, struggling with a local map and mental directions, bringing on destiny. I went there to sell them some of my balloons for an outdoor music festival. That's what we produce at my company - high-tech hot air balloons and competition standard kites. I've been keeping this business alive for over twenty years. On the whole we've done well, with a steady rise, if you'll excuse the pun; although we've had a number of uncomfortable zigzags in the accounts this year. Great timing, eh? So I drove over personally one day to talk dirigibles to this music company.

I'll never forget the first time I blew into Corrina. She emerged at reception holding out a delicate arm and introducing herself as company rep and guide for the day. She'd kept me waiting; I was sunk into a rush-woven sofa couch. She was wearing a Malaysian sarong, it was later explained. We freeze dried into our previous posture on sight of each other. It was one of those moments. Our encounter was supposed to be a formal business matter yet, though she didn't neglect her duties, she'd suffered this emotional collision with me. But I was my old self back then.

"Oh, hi! Noah Sheer?" Her smile was miraculous.

"How'd you do? That's right, that's me... pleased to meet you," I blabbed.

We spent a long interesting afternoon exploring the music complex. I gave her my pitch for aerostat fabrics and fuel efficient burner units. We drank down a whole urn of spice tea with suspicious aromas, to chill out the heat wave. There were panoramic views across the landscape, as we sat together in an eco-compound, which was constructed from sourced Congolese hardwood, I recall. Then, while she guided me around a converted oak barn, transformed into a hostel for overseas musicians (who came to put down tracks at the studio) she gave me a high bounce into the eiderdown. She was confident, assertive in her needs, but an intelligent princess, with mineral pink aureoles to her breasts, like the planet Mercury observed through a double telescope.

Corrina had been impressed by my authentic knowledge of music. Working for a music company she was the type of girl who was likely to be interested. I'd witnessed numerous legendary rock performances over the years, right from the Aeroplane, up to the Byrds and through to the Dead. I'm a Bob fan rather than a Dead-head though.

Her smile could have illuminated an entire rock festival - still could. So after we got straightened out again I invited her to a party the following week. I didn't waste any time, and at this point she wouldn't let me. Our relationship grew more intense and committed from there. She radiated beauty under the lights, a sparkling if teasing intelligence; she was a total Venus. She was the best thing to ever happen to me. She allowed me to find myself again, to think that life wasn't just one bad trip after another; just a helter-skelter slide to oblivion. She represented a new beginning, something brilliant in the future: you get the picture.

As you may suppose, we couldn't wait to fly off into our idyll in the Aegean. I didn't seem to have a worry in the world. Yet my world was already in peril; the clocks in my world had stopped ticking already. Before we set off on the journey I got the classic symptoms of coronary heart disease; tightness across my chest, unexpected aches and pains and inexplicable sweats. One morning, a few weeks before our flight, I dashed into the newsagents around the corner, only to feel that I had rowed across the Pacific, as I staggered back into the house.

"Where the hell've you been, Dad?" commented my daughter. "What's the matter with you?"

My arteries were clogged like old drains, my bloody thickening like cheap sausage meat, but I was still determined to make our quick getaway. We had booked a relaxing romantic holiday together, but actually I was living on the San Andreas Fault Line. I'd been living with disaster for months. I didn't have to look any further than the inside of my ribcage.

When did these symptoms begin to first show? Well, I've got to explain because events were extraordinary and, for the sake of other coronary victims, not typical. After rowing back across the Pacific, from the newsagents, I decided to make an appointment with my GP. After an examination and a line of probing questions, he put his earpiece back on my chest for a second listen.

"There's no need to worry too much about this, Noah. This is just a bit of wind, you're suffering from," he argued, taking away the device.

"Are you sure?" I asked, fastening my shirt and sinking into his club chair.

"Gave you a bit of a shock, didn't it," he returned.

Homer Timpson was the name of our original family doctor. The near namesake was a matter of hilarity for the kids. But the laughter soon died in my throat. His father, Douglas Timpson, had been an eminent scholar of ancient civilisations, well known at the university. Homer and I attended the same school together and sat many of the same exams too. Later we were students together at Bristol University, at the end of the Sixties. He was a medical student of course, while I was taking literature with history and philosophy. But it really should have been the other way round.

After I suffered that first coronary Homer was shaken by his misdiagnosis. Apparently he experienced bouts of depression in the weeks following. But I wasn't exactly on a high either. Our eldest boy, Luke, observed the man leaving the house, following his call. The good doctor was entirely dejected, understanding the implications of his blunder. His personal apology to me wasn't exactly cheerful, but in our house at least his demeanour remained professional.

"What can I say to you, Noah? There's nothing I can say or do that will make amends," he admitted. He'd grown dark patches under his eyes. But he still didn't look as dreadful as me, it has to be emphasised again.

This happened after I was flown back from Crete; with the sunny hills and orange groves of my life in ruins. Homer explained his mistake by referring to my previous spanking health. I'd been playing my regular game of squash, he reminded me; just the previous month winning another veteran championship at the club. I seemed active and I didn't overindulge the highly social vices; as far as he was aware. There was some truth in this, but did Timpson imagine that patients tell their doctor everything about their lives?

The initial symptoms of coronary disease don't hire a publicist. I was still bowling around the squash court, whacking that hard little ball as cunningly as ever. How could he know that I was potentially killing myself? Homer Timpson didn't want to restrict my normal social life or to frighten me with an alarmist diagnosis. He was aware that my marriage had broken up; that I was finally divorced the previous year; and that I am concerned about my business. Homer prescribed me a bottle of indigestion tablets, powerful ones, and gave me a brief lecture in chewing my food properly and the benefits of a good rest.

When I followed his advice the cradle of western civilisation as near as much became my grave. Corrina and I had only touched down on Cretan soil for an hour or two, before I began to feel a strange tingling at the top of my arms. This sensation couldn't be explained away as erotic excitement. I barely had energy to walk down to the sea that evening, never mind to smash my way through the warm waves as intended. I had trouble getting to sleep at night, despite gulping down fistfuls of Timpson's magic digestion pills. Certainly they should be named after him.

It was like physically disintegrating, getting out of breath, and with my vision blurred. The unaccustomed heat was the only alibi I could reach for. But only the Mojave Desert is as hot as that. Corrina began to think that I was really much older than she thought. To begin with she thought I was suffering a bit of male flu abroad. If only.

"It's obviously catching up with you, Noah," she remarked. "This is really a drag."

"Sorry, Corrie, I just need a good night's sleep, that's all," I assured her.

"Did you come all this way to have a good sleep?" she retorted.

"This is weird because I feel totally exhausted," I admitted.

"Well, Noah, you look it!"

Her speculation about this malady was no more exact than my GP's. I understood that something serious was going on, not connected with my eating regime or a male menopause, for that matter; the male menopause being a total myth anyway. I remained awake during the night, staring up at the ceiling, under my volcano. I dissolved in the heat of the day like an ice sculpture; neither the heat nor my illness giving any respect to a (relatively) trim and toned physique. I spread there wondering if I was the victim of a general nervous exhaustion, or was finally having a breakdown. Why should I suffer a breakdown while I was taking a great holiday with the beautiful girl of my dreams? This made no sense whatsoever.

"Why don't you pull yourself together?" Corrina rebuked me.

I was asking myself identical searching questions, but answers were harder to express.

I only truly grasped the problem when my heart kicked me, like a pack mule burnt by a stray cigarette butt. But I'd been no shrewder at interpreting the Oracle than Homer; even as I stared out from our villa into the dark cave of eternity. I wilfully ignored all the warning signs, because I didn't appreciate them. This despite a family history of heart disease. But I'm getting well ahead of myself here.

Not even the lovely vision of Corrina's bottom, flexing softly ahead of me, was any distraction from these symptoms. Simply to walk down that sweet little beach path to the shore below had become an ordeal, dreaded in anticipation. Not to mention that Corrina was eager to play beach tennis, to aquaplane following a light lunch. Why not, as we had itemised these activities beforehand?

"Come on, Noah! Stop dawdling. What's holding you up?" she would call back, as she got steadily further ahead of me: as her beautiful figure dissolved in a sheet of stinging perspiration.

"Give me strength!" I chastised myself.

We had planned an energetic sporting vacation. Until that moment I'd been a vigorous guy impatient with inactivity. This sudden leaden lethargy, as if I was carrying a mountain on my shoulders, was baffling and whimsical to her. She'd left on a jet plane with her dashingly mature lover only to land up with Grandfather Time.

In between times, we spread our bodies on the excruciatingly burning grit, in a semblance of sunbathing. I resembled a dehydrated jellyfish that had long lost its sting. I'd bury my head in the towel as I felt the sun cutting a groove across my neck, wondering if I'd ever see my children and my home again. There was an old guy who strolled along the grit every hour, his legs getting bandier, his moustache droopier, howling at us as he tried to flog local savouries. I allowed myself one glass of chilled beer daily, on the patio after dinner, thinking the refreshing alcohol would do me some good. But I felt like the Consul in Malcolm Lowry's novel, at the end of my last shot of mescaline, vaguely understanding my inevitable doom.

Talk between Corrina and I grew antagonistic, as neither of us understood what was happening. I guess that we should have referred quickly to a local doctor or health clinic, but I was in denial and it was a distracting idea. But that wasn't clever, as our groovy new love already resembled an archaeological dig. She would stay with me during the morning, after breakfast for a while, until the heat cranked up to laser intensity (as it felt to me) before she wandered away to the beach again, without me. Youth will have its way, I told myself, bitterly. I'd watch her beautiful figure blur into a biting haze.

On the Tuesday I did somehow drag myself after her. I had to watch her playing beach volleyball with a group of young local men. These glistening lads resembled bronzed spear throwers from the first Athens Olympics. They sounded like a bunch of young satyrs, laughing and exerting with her, but I was too strung out to offer any resistance, or any purposeful envy. However, Corrina attempted to rouse my body and spirits to join her, clinging to the idea of sharing these experiences.

"Come on, Noah! For goodness sake. Don't just lie there!"

I could merely raise a desperate hand, as if waving to her.

"Do let's try to have some fun," she told me.

"Sure, Corrina... I'll recover myself. Soon."

"You old lazy bones!" she called out, as if trying to shame me in front of the German party. "Can't you serve?"

I was busy empathising with those fish, dead and wide eyed, tossed on to the evening's barbecue. Corrina tucked into them voraciously after the afternoon's beach games. She suggested that I hold on to a giant kite behind a power boat. But even as a kite enthusiast I was reluctant to participate in this extreme fun; not any longer. Already I felt that I was flying extremely close to the sun.

The cool of our villa offered a chance for evening reflection. She and I were supposed to be crazy about each other. Before I felt ill she told me I was in great shape for a guy of my age, like a Peter Fonda, a Jeff Bridges, or some other ageing but handsome hero of mine. But I didn't resemble these alternative Hollywood idols any longer. As with our motorcycle trips back to the villa, my story line had veered off in a frightening direction. We had to go and buy some more groceries, fruit and vegetables, as we were looking after ourselves in the villa. Corrina wanted to buy some local artefacts as presents, as well as more hapless fish for the grill. On this errand we rode into the nearest village of note and began to stroll around the market there. I rode pillion to Corrina again as she snarled around the winding roads on a hired motorbike. I steeled myself to overcome this passing malady, or whatever it was bothering me, stopping me from enjoying the holiday and having fun with my girlfriend. Sadly I felt drained of energy as I staggered off her chrome horse, as if we'd torn up a thousand miles and burnt up the Easy Rider along the way.

We wandered around variegated stalls for an hour, for an eternity, in a crushing heat. Already my body language was drawing stares from healthier olive toned faces. We barged around this noisy market, dodging record temperatures, trying to make shrewd or surprising purchases. This was a special kind of torture as I approached meltdown point. I knew that my family and friends were out of reach. You could have offered me a tram ride down the Golden Mile, any day of the week.

The situation grew out of control suddenly; I couldn't get the better of this virus, or however I rationalised it. I had talked to her about feeling run down, so along came the ghostly juggernaut. I began to choke like one of the local mad dogs; tasted something oily, bitter, like nothing in this world. The tingles and aches intensified to a ruthless steel grasp. Despite her concern Corrina made involuntary noises of disgust. I was making a Jim Carrey of myself. It was a nightmare and before long I completely zonked out.

I battled to escape the crowded market, again like a dog that prefers to die alone. Such an aim was impossible as a large curious crowd followed us by this stage, as if I was some type of public entertainer, a juggler or even a medicine man. My legs collapsed under me like punctured water wings, so I didn't get very far away. I was dropping all the shopping I carried; spilling bags of fruit and vegetables around me, discarding the fish, which stared up at me from the baking dust.

Corrina managed to keep cool, so as to persuade an eager local guy to go off and find the nearest doctor. Can you imagine this?

"Excuse me. Do you understand English? Yes, well I suppose you live around here don't you," she was saying.

He widened his credulous eyes and mouth. Why did the lovely girl pick him out and talk to him specially?

"I wonder if you can help, by informing us if there's a good doctor in the village?"

He continued to stare at her in stage-struck amazement. He rattled a kind of hard sceptical ball stuck at the end of his throat. "Village?"

She was engaged in playing charades with this local guy, and he was mesmerised by her pure blue eyes and animated blonde beauty. She was trying hard to explain the cause and effect of my survival chances; but their minds were not focused on the same outcome. If he could've jumped her bones in his hillside goat herder's shack - or wherever he lived - he would gladly have forgotten all about me. Meanwhile, as they were trying to translate, I was writhing in the dust with the fish, and in retrospect I find this scene incredible.

The nearest available Cretan General Practitioner was a reasonable if thirsty guy. He had a few more home visits to make before he could get to me. His immediate assessment was that I shouldn't get back to my feet too quickly. He extended his arms and pumped his palms towards the ground, in a restraining gesture to me, as if to say "stay where you are". This was another medical genius. My confidence in the profession was sinking to seabed level, but to whom else could I turn? Fortunately the medics arrived to save me, as they had advanced driving skills, and speeds, around the hills. They slid me into the back of an ambulance. They whisked me away to the cooler. Or did I just had a bad experience?

Corrina didn't allow my heart attack to wreck her vacation. She continued to stay at the villa, and to join the morning beach games of that gang of bronzed heroes. She'd worked hard all year with her world musicians, the hyperactive percussionists and throat singers. I didn't question her holiday activities and erratic visiting times then, because I was too glad to escape. I already got the score, that she couldn't be crazy about me, as I originally believed.

The Cretan doctor instructed me to contact my own GP, as soon as I landed back in Avon. At least, that's what I think he was telling me. Homer Timpson. I would have to swallow a few more magic pills, until I could find another practitioner. I was strapped down in the back of the aircraft, like a celebrity whale going to a new water park. Looking back on the trip now, I wasn't in any immediate danger, but that wasn't my impression as my ears popped at altitude.

# Chapter 3

Following my return to a chilly Albion I had an appointment at the hospital in Bristol. I was falling to pieces but they passed me from hand to hand like some chunk of runic stone. At the local hospital I met some young guy called Doctor Hammel.

"Tell me everything you can about your experiences," he began.

Corrina probably had a few photographs to show him. I knew she was constantly taking snaps to illustrate her horror story back home. To Corrina I was no more than a giant octopus spilling ink on the quayside.

For the remainder of the consultation they put me through enough tests to dazzle a lab rat into submission. The medics explained that these were exploratory to begin with. Apart from confirming that I'd suffered a coronary, they couldn't tell me the immediate damage or consequences. But it was clear I would never win another veteran squash championship.

Anyway, after an anxious housebound wait, I received a letter from Hammel. He invited me back to the hospital for a conversation. This was his verdict:

"I have to level with you Noah, by explaining that your heart has been damaged. About a third of your heart was destroyed. We have also found that two of your arteries are blocked. There is some decay and malfunction to the heart valves," he told me.

These were not just a few mellow off-beats in the Jamaican style then. This was thumping to shake the whole house down, like the beats that emerge from my son's bedroom of an evening, when he's making a stopover.

"You will need to undergo surgery, to replace the valves, and to clear your arteries," Hammel continued. "In London they offer specialist techniques of particular help."

The surgeons were going to run a knife up my middle, as long suspected. I was so shaken by his verdict that I didn't hear everything. There was no choice other than to place my life into their gloved and razored hands. But trust is the word and you must place your trust somewhere, with somebody. Otherwise what are the alternatives? Where do you go?

Hammel pencilled me in as a priority. I would go into hospital as soon as they had a bed free. At this stage I didn't understand the significance of waiting for a bed to go free. It sounded as if I'd book myself on to an exclusive cruise. During my wait I felt my condition deteriorate. I was transformed from a fit guy into a creature that wheezed and whooshed in the effort of taking the stairs. I felt like the thousand year old man. I *was*. Clearly I might have checked out altogether without an intervention. I needed a surgeon to clean out my arteries, in the way Dad used to clean out the barrels of his shotgun. Death was waiting around the corner at all times. He was a simple over-exertion away. And he's been leering at me ever since.

Lots of people came by to visit then, including part time employees and obscure business associations. I was moved that so many people made the effort: including a few creditors. They kindly came to express their sympathy, their shock and their heart-felt sorrow. Also most likely to wish me goodbye, in case I never made it back from that high-tech London hospital. It was much cheaper than staying at the Dorchester, I jested with them, but I might never return from the bright lights. Noah Sheer was going into that long night under a general anaesthetic.

One day I received a letter telling me when to come to London. A bed was available for me and Elizabeth offered to take me there. Elizabeth is my ex-wife you understand. She came to my rescue at the last moment. To begin with our daughter Angela offered to drive me there.

"I can take you, Dad. No problem," she argued.

Angela had recently passed her driving test. To my relief she withdrew the offer on account of a head cold. She has a kaleidoscope of small yet niggling maladies. She's doing drugs of some type, she smokes and, to my way of thinking, she has life-style issues. For weeks she was celebrating her success with driving. Man, she throws that little hatchback around like a skateboard. When she first set off down the M4 her instructor thought he was in the cockpit of Bluebird. He was clutching the straps waiting for a back flip. Picture the Marx Brothers running that driving school. How the guy passed her I don't understand: it was either a matter of survival or he fancied her.

Then I wasn't inclined to ask Corrina Farlane to take me to hospital. She'd already driven me to hospital, you might conclude. However, it's easier to get through to the Bishop's private office, about some personal problem, than it is to contact Corrina during office hours. That's been my experience.

No, it was left to Elizabeth to run me up into the smoke. She wouldn't let me down in those circumstances. These days she runs an organic bakery and health products business. Arguably that's like Germaine Greer ditching her academic career to run a mobile burger bar. By profession she's a social psychologist. She's usually expensively dressed these days. She has a spanking new Merc coupe to whisk her between those dark satanic flour mills. She's become the real bread maker in this family. Lately I've been struggling to gather up the crumbs into a mouthful.

She tried to interest me in herbal remedies and alternative medicines. This was before we finally split. For a period she succeeded in bringing down my blood pressure and stabilised my stress levels. Then she told me that she wanted a divorce. Nowadays I have a more detached attitude towards healthy living. Liz argued about the potency of alternative medicine, but it would have taken a bucket of St John's Wort to improve my mood that day. She holds supplies in her health boutiques to keep the entire 'new age' population of Bristol high, until the Mayan end of the world. That place is a bouncy castle of tofu. But I'm running ahead of myself again - or bouncing ahead.

My ex-wife dropped business for the day to collect me. Then we set off to the metropolis together in her brand new coupe. This was our first prolonged encounter for months, if not forever, and the atmosphere was tense for a while. No doubt my health situation softened her attitude a jot. Our break and divorce had been acrimonious, even though I told myself there was no real conflict and that I was completely in the right about everything. Even in the courthouse, stood up in the legal chariot trying to defend myself, Elizabeth's side of the story, her account of my character, was hard to fathom. But I knew she'd stopped listening to my version. There was never going to be another eureka moment for us. Perhaps only when our marriage had been dissolved, as the legal beaks put it, and the divorce decree was final and absolute; and how more final can you get?

Liz and I managed to survive an M5 gridlock together. Although she had brought our youngest son Timothy, aged eight, along for the journey, to save herself. She had allowed him the day off school, as if she didn't trust the home help to skim his organic pizza into the oven. The trip to London was an adventure to him, although we didn't drop into the official London Dungeon. Tim's presence served the same function as a noisy fruit machine in a pub full of alienated strangers. It's bloody miserable that such an image occurs to me.

Elizabeth said to me, while we were teenagers together, that I was her "whole soul in life". No doubt you can hear young lover hyperbole in these declarations. But you tend to remember such beautiful things throughout your life. I remember thinking something very similar about her too. What a shame that the spell had to be broken. You may describe this as fancy thinking from a past day and age: old hippie daydreams as stale as last week's rock cake. Certainly she gets claustrophobic and anxious that I am still living in the same city. She doesn't enjoy the idea that I am only a short drive away; that I occupy the wreck of our old life, when she's set about embarking on a new life. She would move back to her native Somerset, if it wasn't for our kids, to be closer to her parents, in their quasi-military camp, if she could.

It took an emergency to make her share my company again. Yet we found a friendly vibe on the road, trapped in the congestion; we got along tolerably well. Obviously this was a genuine emergency, to which she responded with typical alacrity. I almost imagined us together in the past again, maybe going up to London for a big concert or a demo. I felt that our divorce had been thrown into the recycle bin. I could imagine that we still loved each other, that I was still her whole soul in life. But if you imagine life as a movie, then the past is hard to reshoot, too painful to view again, even as a *nouveau vague* kind of movie. We're the same cast, with the same experiences, but we're estranged. There's no emotion that vanishes as absolutely as a woman's love, I've found. Women's love will always be a mystery to us. Do we have any influence over their feelings at all? Better try to move mountains.

She tackled the challenge of London's road system, faced the labyrinth of the capital city, to take me to the east end hospital. Small wonder then, after these stresses, that I arrived at the entrance of the institution like an ashen spectre. What sensible, still healthy person would have rated my chances?

"Almost there," she assured me.

I wheezed. I saw grey all around me; sky, fog, concrete; invading every sense.

"Step carefully," she advised.

This was an exhausting hike. Forty three yards had turned into a marathon. I was ready to blow out of here.

My ex-wife supported me to a chair and then to a trolley, left me there as she negotiated with the receptionist about my stay. If I didn't yet want to knock on heaven's door, I was doing a fine impression as a visitor. But I still remember Elizabeth's touch. She pretty much held me under the armpits at one stage. It's been a long time. We've been through a lot together over the years. Not even *she* can forget that.

Liz watched philosophically, balancing on a toe with her arms crossed, as I changed into a pair of pyjamas. These were standard issue, undersized stripy PJs, leaving an area of calf and forearm to view: except who was looking or bothering. Suitably or otherwise attired, they lifted me over on to a steel frame bed. My ex-wife was not obligated to keep me company during these uncertain minutes. I thought this would be a strict porch-to-porch driving job for her. Outside the ward window, another London rush hour was apparently gathering, like a finale at the coliseum. But she decided to stick around for my benefit, rather than to make a quick getaway, as I'd assumed. She realised that her supporting presence was worth more than a course of treatment. She didn't have to say anything. You can't erase all the good memories from a life together. Time seemed to slip away peacefully. Bad memories felt trivial in the drift net of eternity. She could have walked out then. She could have headed back west. She might have returned immediately to her new life. After all, she's a big girl now.

She stuck around because she felt sorry for me; she even pitied me; this drained and breathless shell of a man. Not because she was still my girl, after all. She wanted to see that I was properly cared for; tucked up in bed. But that didn't infer any renewed affection or love. In that regard the lights had already been switched off. But were those bad motives? I can't accuse her of stitching me up, can I? Cynical self-interest is hardly likely to get a man into the heart hospital, if you see where I'm coming from.

What about Timothy? How was my youngest son coping with this trip? Quickly his excitement at new adventure turned to fear. What was his Daddy doing in the hospital? We had tried to explain something to him along the way. This was a real hospital after all. This proved that Daddy was really sick. His sensations were complex, but the overall signal was difficult to misread. Even at his age.

"How long you staying, Daddy?" he enquired.

"That will depend," I said.

"The doctor will try to make Daddy better," Liz added.

"So when you getting out of here?" Tim returned.

"When they finish my check up," I assured him.

"After the nurses help Daddy to feel better again."

"Can you watch telly in here?" Tim wanted to know.

"Sure," I said.

"There's a football match today," he informed me.

"Should be a good game."

"Daddy needs to rest."

Liz meanwhile was looking for a second opinion about my health. Didn't she notice all those junior doctors already sharpening their pencils and knives?

But I wasn't anxious for a quick prognosis. I'm not a complete hypochondriac. They explained to me that my heart was messed up. Was I able to conduct an operation on myself? I would venture into that night and hope that it was just a temporary occlusion of the sun.

Liz had to leave me to the surgeon's nimble fingers. 'Visiting hour' is no longer so strict, but the evening was drawing on. The artificial lighting on the ward grew harsher. The nurses propped me up against hard pillows; folded frayed sheets across my lap.

No doubt I was a pathetic sight and my family was not unaffected. Tim threw his arms around my neck at the last and refused to leave. Liz had been looking out of the window at the traffic; she checked her watch, walked over and kissed me on the forehead. They had to go. I felt a dreadful sinking sorrow at this moment. I felt more desolate than I had ever done. When she pulled Tim back, found his hand and they walked out of the ward. She didn't look back.

My guard was down. Hospitals, especially the old models, are not joyful institutions. You don't go there to have a good time. They are not holiday centres under a dome. I considered a private room, but finally that wasn't a smart idea. In grave danger you have to establish relationships: especially divorcees. That's what is important in a perilous situation, in the face of a sharp or blunt instrument. Call me a sad hippie who sings along to *All You Need is Love*, but trying to insulate yourself from a life threatening situation only makes the experience worse.

Having said that, I soon found the dangers of taking a brotherly loving approach to life, within this environment of frail health, physical weakness and - we should be honest - people taking their last breaths. You still have to look out for yourself in the end.

I made friends with the guy in the next bed to mine. Our amiable alliance developed after I had settled in: except you can never settle in or wish to. The chap was bursting to talk with me, to share his burden. He was a retired head teacher from Swansea. To my mind he was a smashing guy. I was glad to share the hospital experience with him; to go shoulder to shoulder in the battle against coronary disease and an early bath. Owen was twenty years my senior, but acute angina is a powerful equaliser. It has the potential to bring generations together, like many serious conditions or afflictions. I can see this guy vividly right now: Owen Hopkins, a gangling bony man, upright in the bed, with a thin, trim moustache and sharply parted hair; every inch the traditional headmaster. The kind of man I would have rebelled against as a youth, except that disease had turned us into comrades: we were transformed into socialist skinny dippers.

"Apply yourself, boy. You'll come out smiling," he told me.

This became his encouraging catch phrase to me, even as he came back from another gloomy interview.

Over those days we became friends and neighbours. In our real lives, carrying our individual briefcases, we might not have got along. In this dismal place (for all the fresh paint and flowers) we had to sleep side by side, wake side by side and take our medicine together. We allowed ourselves to be lulled into this routine. During the long days we would chat, reminisce; at night time we became conscious of our mutual fear; as we heard each other's awkward breathing and unhappy bodily grumblings, in the brittle half-dark silence; infringed upon by the street lighting and the capital's never-stopping traffic hum (as if the angels or the devils were busy preparing to take us).

Until one afternoon they wheeled him away into the operating theatre. This was to be his day - his big hour. But he died during surgery. A particularly worn out heart, apparently.

That evening I blubbered myself to sleep. Just as if I'd lost my own father again. I got back in touch with my inner child. Owen hadn't been a well man, I should have realised, with that ghostly pallor and untimely atmosphere. Maybe I really had been thinking about my own father. But then we cardiac patients were "all in the same boat," as Owen kept reminding me.

Through this acquaintance I learnt that it's risky to get too friendly with them. The cardiacs I mean. You may grow to feel a lot for them, to soften the feelings of isolation, but the danger of sudden loss is increased. In the end it was like losing a mate in battle. You're bringing more down on your own head. You can only learn through experience, but there are some you should avoid. I had to follow Owen Hopkins into the operating theatre a few days later. Would this be a recurring nightmare? I could be attached to the same machinery, with the same surgeon. The nurses coaxed me out of this depression, aggravated by the empty bed to my side; until some other guy came along to take the head teacher's place.

My turn came around. They gouged tubes of sugary liquid into my arms. Enough dope to make Hendrix's eyes bulge. Then they wheeled me out to the carving table, as they made private jokes.

My surgeon stepped forward out of the lights to re-introduce himself. His voice was full of brandy and Havana cigars even under the bandana over his mouth. But would I ever experience such luxuries again myself? But he tried to make me feel like a privileged passenger, invited to look around the cockpit; until he snapped thin rubber gloves over his long fingers.

As they prepared knock-out drops I was terrified; witless. Even the lovely faces of the nurses seemed as remote as lost love. This was to be my first trip to the theatre. I was following the muffled conversation, their quiet rustling movements around the space, with the small clatter of preparing instruments and equipment; ready for the operation; which was to be a triple bypass. As the show got on the road they dropped me they dropped the house lights into darkness.

The girl was rubbing my wrist; watching me kindly, saying: "You only need to relax. You only need to..."

I returned from this state, you might guess. Consciousness shakily returned like a rainbow across a soap bubble. They'd shut my brain off for a few hours; put the old grey matter on ice.

There were tubes up the nose, tubes down my throat, tubes from my stomach to drain away excess blood and other detritus. Sever a man at the chest, hew out a couple of his ribs, tear out veins from his arms and legs, then you're going to leave him in a sore mess; even if you have repaired and unblocked main arteries and valves in his heart. It's still the main approach to chronic disease - you smash a person to pieces to replace a broken component. I couldn't jump up and shake their hands to thank them, even if I'd wanted to.

For all this discomfort - which increased and gathered as the anaesthetic diminished - my operation was declared a success. Gradually I set about the process of trying to recover from this trauma. Post operational agonies began to touch me, in cunning sword points. I had the agony of soreness, around torso, cicatrised by surgical cuts; aches and pains, pulled stitches, clicking ribs snuck out of place and then rubbed back together again.

But if life is just a temporary trial, then the vacation had been extended. I could breathe again, if not very freely. I'd got my second wind. The specialist couldn't tell me how many years were left. But that wasn't my first thought.

Angela came to collect me for the return trip. Maybe Liz couldn't afford to lose another day. Therefore our daughter tore up the motorway in her idiosyncratic Renault Clio that I'd purchased for her as a birthday present. After a few weeks at Big Pink (that's what we call our house in Bristol) I was beginning to take the stairs again; contemplate a walk along the street, do a bit of gardening. At first I took up residence in my leather armchair, listened to album after album, and caught up with my paperwork; but I could stretch myself and felt more comfortable with every passing day.

Big Pink was a total heap, though Angela finally dragged a bath towel over the grimy windowsills and made other hasty tidying actions. My mate Bob had come around to do some gardening in my absence. That's Huntingdon, not Dylan.

Even my complexion began to recuperate. I would no longer get a character part in *Doctor Who*. Everybody was happy to see me back in circulation, including (at first) Lizzie; fussing over me, panicking when I made any exertion. The off-beat had been corrected and I could return to the regular thump of my life, private or otherwise.

My kids' ideal of personal liberty dates from that hospital stay. My holiday getaway with Corrina was also an encouragement. When I returned from hospital I was more or less housebound for weeks. But they were exploring the boundaries of independence away from their parents. I recovered from my own type of degeneration, and the young generation was flourishing.

I was so relieved to be alive that my family radar was switched off - at least, at first. For that period I was not so anxious about checking up on my kids, finding out where they were going. I didn't try to seek Corrina out. The house became my own again. I had enough time and room to recover from my op. I was alone then except for visits from the doctor and my business partner.

# Chapter 4

But there I was battling against the crowds like a released statue. How can that latest episode be explained away as trivial, so that I could sleep with myself tonight? If my heart surgery hadn't been a success, where else could I turn? What were my other options? They might ask me back for another heavy gig at the theatre; a five hour Springsteen type of epic. The thought of being cut again is hard to accept. I want to believe that I've been born again.

Then I've never been prone to anxiety or panic attacks. Most likely those experiences are distressing enough, yet my experience in the mall was different. My heart had kicked into full gallop like a spooked mustang. I didn't know if my nag would keep running until it was exhausted or dropped death from shock. So I was forced to go along for the ride and find out.

While my heart was bucking, herds of healthy people were breaking around me. This was worse than getting trapped in a crowd of football fans, while attempting to leave the stadium after a capacity game. Most likely my face is bloodless and perspiring, so that I resemble a crazed zombie, out of doors at the wrong time of day. I don't take any notice of angry words or expressions as, in my desperation, I crush toes and push. I'm no longer in the same reality zone as these guys. I've been put back into the cardiology department waiting room. How in hell did I get here?

There's a *history* of heart trouble in our family. That's what the GP often enquires about isn't it? So there's a history in *my* family, such as A J P Taylor might have written, or even Gibbon. The assessment of blocked arteries and damaged valves didn't arrive as a complete surprise. At least I was still alive to hear the diagnosis. Really I should have recognised the symptoms earlier and not allowed death to leave even an autograph. After my fortieth birthday I became more conscious of the risks, recalling my notorious family history. In response though I just decided to run harder, thwack the ball harder, even as it returned from younger opponents with extra speed and cunning.

My parents came from the same Wiltshire village. Dad collapsed while he was chopping wood in the yard; whack, split, whack, split, until his heart did the same. A fork of inner lightning struck him down in front of our eyes. Although at the time we thought it may have been a joke. He subsided into the mud and puddles and we stood around him; huddled, calling to him, patting his cheek and hands as we tried to revive him from the stony fit. We couldn't pull him back, we could only watch as his limbs turned to lead. Doctors and nurses were not closely located to our village. There was nobody to save his life on the bumpy road to the hospital. They had the benefits of a traditional community, but family friends and neighbours couldn't save him. I always want to look to the future, although there are drawbacks. Sometimes we fail.

When Dad suffered that coronary I was eight; which is the age of our youngest boy today. Dad passed away in the back of our next-door neighbours' Morris. Mum was there to keep him company, on the way. Unfortunately he ran out of the road. Grandma was looking after me, while I waited for my parents to return. She chatted without looking at me, as she made and baked an apple pie. I was lucky to survive my heart attack, recalling that experience. After all I got a reprieve; another chapter, or maybe just a rewind.

I was edging towards peril as I entered those middle years. As the decades went by, like some poor guy clinging to a log, the river of life plunging to a fall. You don't listen to these stories while you are fit and young. I should have demanded regular check-ups from Homer. I informed him about my father and my grandfather. But I was as taken-in as the doctor, that a regular busted gut in the squash court was proof against a dodgy pump. I gave up smoking French cigarettes and fat cigars in my early twenties. I drink only moderately most of the time. Yes, I played those racquet sports, I joined a running club (half marathons along the Avon every summer month), I launch up in my hot air balloons... but still I was squeezed to the point of death.

Following the scare I get back to my car. I drive a Citroen DS 23 circa 1964. Man, they can see me coming in Bristol, as if I'm wrapped from head to foot in surgical bandages. My infatuation with this car began with the French new wave cinema. I used to yearn for Anna Karenin or Jeanne Moreau. I would pose with a Galloises on my bottom lip. My accountant has advised me to get rid of this monster. My wife always had the same advice. Plus she was embarrassed to be seen in the thing. She loathed the ugly-beautiful machine, more outdated with every passing year. But as long as my heart puts one beat in front of another, I'm not going to sacrifice my identity. She will never convince me that Dylan is not a great artist, by emphasising his musical shortcomings: As long as I'm living and breathing that old Citroen's safe from the auto-graveyard.

The engine fires and I'm cushioned on the suspension. The machine is still in remarkable condition. Home is in Clifton, that elegant, historic and most expensive area of our city (let's be upfront). The rows and crescents reach to the rocky gorge edge and lean apprehensively over the rim. As a young guy originally from a rougher part of the city, I wasn't against jeering at people who lived in this district. Not only were they unreachably better off, but they seemed very comfortable and dull subjects. I'd turn my nose up above an unfiltered cigarette. I required a good education and decades of hard work before I was one among them; strange where your passions and enthusiasms will take you. Nowadays I'm clinging to the cliff face with my fingernails, from both a financial and health viewpoint. I'm not so ready to sneer at my neighbours, but I'm at risk of plunging down into fizzy lager territory. My brother has always lived there, by the way; with no appetite for change or movement.

As soon as I return to Big Pink I call up the new doctor. I want to get his take on my heart stopping experience. Could he reassure and chase away the after-images of my latest scare? Or am I doomed to wander middle earth?

This is a shame, because I hadn't spoken to my doctor for weeks. He practises his trade under the name of Voerdung. But I was almost eager to forget him. I got through to his surgery, checking that Luke, our eldest son, is out of ear shot. He's oiling the wheels of his skateboard on the kitchen table.

I related to Voerdung what had happened to me in the shopping centre. I made it sound a punishment for spending too much on music and clothes. That is, I tried to describe the experience, but I am baffled by what took place, except for the sensation of being kicked around the sternum. Listening to me, responding with some manly throat sounds, he promises to fix an appointment at the hospital. If there's another episode over the weekend then I should call an emergency number.

"You all right now, Noah?"

"As we speak," I concede.

"Sit tight and relax over the weekend. Right?"

I'm grateful for the lifeline, but am I losing my grip?

This could be described as the long weekend. Hard liquor had a powerful draw - it had an action hero appeal to the thirst. I'm afraid of another heart attack, collapsing at home; the problems it would cause, the scene provoked, the lasting family impact. Why couldn't Voerdung put me safely back into a hospital ward? He was spilling the ball as Timpson used to do at rugby. They wouldn't even allow that guy to carry the bucket and sponge, to be frank. You could say he's been unfortunate, but then what about me?

I kept my date with love-interest Rachael that evening. She invited me to a Tibetan barbecue held by some friends in Totterdown; animators of children's books. I didn't want to pour cold water over the Tibetan charcoal. I met this woman at the squash club. She's dark, with some French ancestry; slightly plump (despite the running around) enveloped in a bitter sweet mist of perfumed sophistication.

Now and again Rach's younger sister, Marcia, would show up at the club. Marcia is an England squash squad member, so it turned out. She insisted on having a game with me and, inevitably, trouncing me; like Federer having fun with the lower ranks. Apparently she liked to put herself up against the guys. Man, she whipped me around that court like a wet towel, while she barely shuffled her toes. From then on I was apprehensive that Marcia would show up at the club. I still had the picture of her flexing her knees in preparation of our game, putting on entirely redundant sweatbands and checking that her laces were tied. The memory of that thrashing put me off the idea of squash and any other hard sports.

Marcia was hot looking though; dark haired and coltish as Lizzie Taylor on Black Beauty, or whatever they called the nag. She was definitely too hot to handle though, not only when the door of the squash court was locked behind us. Man, that was a very lonely place; no man's land would look better. I was trapped in there like a dog belonging to a single yuppie. I anticipated a knock up with Miss Sabatini, only to find Miss Navratilova there instead. Marcia was hard and humourless on the court and every point was a matter of life and death, even at fourteen nil.

But I was determined not to be a loser with Rachael. I could see her as more of a double's partner. So I tried to take that demolition of my sporting prowess gracefully. I was storing up my rewards in heaven. They considered me a great sport and never let me buy the drinks afterwards, even when I ordered more than one; doubles too.

Thank god, this summer Marcia is away backpacking in the Himalayas, with her fire service chums. Rachael remains cheerfully and pleasantly plump on the British Isles. She runs an antiques shop and auction house in Clifton; ageing beauties being her passion in life. She's also a divorcee, from an American hotelier who couldn't stay out of his guest rooms. She's the best listener I've encountered since Elizabeth shut her ears to my complaints forever.

"I thought you were going to buy a new shirt today, Noah. What happened then? Did it explode?"

"Not exactly," I demurred.

"Then where's your jeans? The Levi's? Haven't they shrunk down in the bath to your shape yet?"

I kept the painful truth close to my chest.

But I didn't say anything at the barbecue that evening. There were no fish on the grill, but it brought back memories of Crete. I picked out a folding chair and stayed under a passion flower. Painful memories returned with interest and, most likely, I didn't look so great either, despite all efforts. I didn't enjoy taking probing questions about my erratic ticker; not until the doctor looked up the appropriate page in the manual. There were a handful of local BBC celebrities there, but they didn't come forward to interview me. Rachael was the only woman who even looked at me.

After the Totterdown party I invited her back for coffee. My kids were out experimenting for the evening. Unfortunately my sexual appetite deserted me, even as she was in the mood for a bedroom killing. She thought I was more comfortable in the squash court than on a mattress; which was obviously a subjective opinion. I didn't confide my own bedroom secrets to her. I knew that she wanted to spend the night with me. Her blood's always bubbling away like a Jacuzzi. Of course she wanted a lasting and meaningful relationship. Obviously she had the wrong guy there.

Troublingly she drove off in tears, adding me to her list of snubs and disappointments. Should I have been more open about my situation? Maybe this was the final nail in the coffin of our relationship. I thought how I appeared through her warm brown eyes. One moment my squash shorts were around my ankles, the next I was filling my hot water bottle. At times my heart gets too full and I can't part with the truth.

In the small hours Angela returned home, with her posse of friends and hangers-on. Waking with a start I heard them around the house. But I stayed there and waited for them all to leave. It was hard to deal with more than several invisible dangers at the same time.

# Chapter 5

The consultant in Bristol wasn't able to explain the reading on my Richter scale. She was equally as baffled that the organ had tried to beat me up again. She directed me back towards London; more state of the art equipment, tests, light shows and psychedelic effects. This was turning into the ultimate bad trip. But would I recognise the encore?

I decided to make this second trip by myself, without bothering family and friends. They would be upset, confused and anxious at my recall. I made numerous business trips to London by train; at least the journey was nothing strange or new.

Part of me didn't want to learn the truth. What was the chance of returning home again with a positive attitude? As I faced the crush-hour I resembled an official warning on the dangers of a stressful life. Except that I have not lived a particularly stressful life. But I looked as unsavoury as a vampire who'd lost his nerve and the will to bite.

A distressing *deja-vu* came on me, as I made my way about 'Little Britain' in London. Hadn't I already undergone that drawn-out, terrifying and excruciating surgical procedure? Would they insist on putting me through the same performance again? They would need to take another reading, until they gained a deeper impression of my scars, to say what had gone wrong.

There was no ex-wife and living woman to hold my hand this time. Everything was too recognisable from before. I was taken into Cardiology and re-introduced. Meanwhile there was time to kill until my appointment. I gazed about at the new set of cardiac patients and their companions. They looked out of sorts, laughing nervously, flushing, twitching, hands wringing. If you caught their eye momentarily then they would look away. They were mostly beginners at this game. Few of them had faced surgery, or knew what to expect. They'd hardly smelt any sterilising fluid or seen a powerful lamp on the ceiling. I'd already been through it all. Now I was back for some reason.

I drifted away, making up for lost sleep, when I was roused by the sound of my name. I was being summoned. I shook myself and took my number. From this point a friendly nurse led me to the office of Anthony Wickham. This was another gentleman of the heart. But appearances can be deceptive. Call me paranoid.

"Come in, come in, dear chap," he told me.

This sounds generous, but the greeting was uttered with monotonous routine. The sound of his voice was like a sticky door forced open.

I tried to look vigorous and fearless. As if I could brush off any bad news. Heart conditions just require a tough attitude, rather like Afghan tribesmen. Then I managed to slam the door behind me. This noise ricocheted around the whole building. Somebody had applied a few drops of oil recently. This had the effect of shattering my nerves. I carried my broken nerves behind me, as I stumbled into the guy's office, like a sack of pebbled glass. Mr Wickham hadn't even flinched. Yet he was inconvenienced by my floundering posture.

"Don't worry about the blessed door," he told me.

The place wouldn't have overshadowed a prison isolation cell. There I was trapped inside with a dusty white coat, which owned the power and authority to pronounce a death sentence. No wonder I was nervous.

"Come along, please take a seat," he told me, stretching out a long bony arm while avoiding eye contact.

He was scratching some arcane script on to a papyrus scroll with some quill gifted to him by a great grandfather.

"So here I am again," I offered.

Mr Wickham cleared the dust from his throat and gazed up in surprise from my medical records. Or at least I assumed they were my medical records.

"Excellent, Mr Sheer, sit back and relax for a minute, can't you?"

I speculated whether his sense of humour was generally very dark. Meanwhile he was scratching, interpreting, leaving me to shift on the knuckles of my backside. Perhaps noticing my discomfort he attempted small talk on the perils of modern public transport. Only some kind of primitive noise worked up from my diaphragm in response. The subversive heart was smashing away to its own tune. I was wondering what he would come up with next.

Wickham was an extremely tall, bony and craggy guy. He was a Geralde Scarfe caricature peeled off the page. He was gaunt and shadowy in the face, as if emulating his patients. His eyes spotted me over half-moon lenses and under long spiky eyebrows. His voice sounded exhausted, but became incisive when interrupted.

The hands were enormous and fidgety as if they were tempted to chop something. Probably he was never more content than when cutting a dash in the operating theatre. But frankly I wouldn't trust him with the back of my television set.

"As I understand the situation, in your own words, you suffered another coronary incident," he remarked. "Can you describe the particulars of the event?" His bedside patter was decidedly lukewarm.

"I'll do my best. I went out to town the other Saturday afternoon. I was going to bring my CD collection up to date, with the latest Dylan... and there's always good stuff coming out of the archives... official release of bootlegs, you know. Then suddenly I got this terrible sharp pain in my chest. Knocked me backwards," I recalled. I coughed, as if to illustrate, but it was the dingy ambience of the room.

"I understand," he said. He was scrawling more esoteric symbols across my record again. Already this was shaping up like another biography of Brian Wilson and his brothers.

"A definite heart pain," I added. So that he couldn't make any mistake.

"Ah ha. Did you recognise the symptoms?"

"Most of all it was the pain."

"Pain?"

"Extremely."

"Ah ha. This wasn't some kind of anxiety attack, Mr Sheer?" His yellowed eyes turned up briefly over the cut spectacles.

"It made me anxious, but that wasn't the cause," I argued.

His gaze held me uncomfortably and he made a small hole of his mouth. The longest hairs of his eyebrows fluttered in a secret draft.

"Therefore you have convinced yourself, have you, that you suffered another heart attack?"

Had it really been another heart attack? I thought again about that incident around the shops, as I'd been doing over the days and weeks following. I could design kites and make balloons, but I couldn't pinpoint my own faults.

"This was different," I offered.

"Then you wouldn't say that it was a heart attack?" he challenged.

"It didn't feel the same as the first time."

"Can you be more specific?"

I shifted my bones. "The pain was more centred," I explained. "It was more intense and focused."

"Ah ha. Is that really the case?" Wickham intoned across the space.

"I could have reached inside my own chest, if that had been possible...and even pointed to where the pain was coming from."

"Towards your heart, do you mean?" he declared.

Constant aches across my shoulders, neck, displaced pain, tingling along the arm; a feeling of breathlessness, exhaustion, that is.

"No, this time I felt something different."

"Can you be more exact?" he commented.

"I'm not the consultant," I pointed out. "It was just as if somebody put a knife into my heart, to be honest with you."

"Oh really," he mumbled, note taking. "A knife."

"So what do you think?" I appealed.

He raised his spidery writing hand for a moment with a groan. "After we have concluded a few tests, we may be able to locate some more specific factors," he told me.

Sure enough I underwent these 'tests'; questions, probing, analysis, during the rest of the day. I was connected to tape, needles, stickers and electrodes, the works. They subjected me to another angiogram, yet another ECG (electrocardiogram). All the contours of a bad trip relived, in other words. As if they hadn't made a strong enough impression on me first time.

To finish up the gig they took another set of x-rays of my chest. The radiologists expended a lot of time and effort with me. This puzzled me because it was a new approach and didn't seem connected to the heart. Their fondness for my company rightly roused my suspicions. I was beginning to feel like a revolutionary new drug. All this was enough to give Tim Leary a queasy stomach. This was the mother of all bad radiation. There were reasons for being paranoid.

I was prepared to stay in hospital overnight; even longer. Wasn't this the usual deal? I'd brought along my toiletries and a change of clothes. My test results would have to be processed and then the medics would study them closely. Then I'd have to wait for Mr Wickham and his cronies to hit on some smart ideas. This is what I came to expect of a hospital visit. They would put me back into ill-fitting pyjamas.

Anyway, a few more hours went painfully by. They called me back into Wickham's office. I was getting a rush from all the instant tea and factory made Battenburg cake, that I'd been taking in the waiting room. I didn't know what the consultant's verdict was going to be, but the nurse said I would not be staying in the ward. Obviously they offered a one-hour service in this hospital.

"Come in then, come in," Mr Wickham summoned. He was still perched on that creaky chair behind his battered desk, as if he hadn't moved all day. He looked even more fatigued than before though, as if he'd examined a dozen wards during our pause. He was taking another sortie through my paperwork; as if it could be more positive in a different combination, or would eventually disintegrate. The rims of his eyes had turned iodine violet; the eyes of an all-night horror movie fanatic.

"Please sit yourself down, Mr Sheer," he offered, with a strange and recondite gesture.

I nodded like a grateful peasant as I edged towards him and ducked on to the chair.

"With luck," he began, "you will be catching your early train back to Bristol."

"Oh really?" I said. And an early bath too?

"You may even be home for a reasonable bedtime."

"You don't know my house," I replied, attempting levity.

"Ah ha, yes."

So I wasn't comforted by his approach. Take drugs, drop out, as I should have done years ago. Now my daughter seems to be following that example.

"Yes, so, we have enough test data back to say what may have malfunctioned with you," he said, "back there, when you were out shopping in Bristol that day."

He shook a fresh pile of documents alarmingly, as if trying to rearrange the sense of them.

"Your surgery was a complete success," he stated.

"Oh?"

"The angiogram today did not reveal any further problem with your heart. No hardening or constriction of the arteries... no further damage to the tissue of the muscle... This was not another episode of angina pectoris. It's as you originally surmised," he said, as if to praise me.

"Is that right?"

"I examined the video screen myself... I read through all this information."

"You didn't find another blockage?" I wondered. "You don't need to unplug the veins?" I felt like a pretentious plumber.

"No even non-invasive procedures are relevant. Your heart appears a trifle swollen, yet it is in remarkably good condition."

"Good condition?" I said.

"We were really pleased with it," he told me. His glance rushed towards me, as if noticing a spot of colour in my cheeks. "That's right, the swelling was caused by the recent trauma, not through any mistakes during the surgical procedure."

"That's good news then," I remarked. But his voice and expression was sending me a different message. I couldn't avoid the negative vibrations. There was a dread over his elongated stiffness, like a black rag draped over a judge's head.

"Your heart remains in satisfactory shape," he repeated.

"Something hit me very hard," I protested.

"Yes, no doubt you have that idea after the incident. I don't wish to confuse you, Mr Sheer," he argued, "or to obscure our justifiable concern, but..."

He rattled on.

I was uneasy, losing his reason as I once lost consciousness. His eyes avoided me as a fly avoids a rolled newspaper. His fringe tumbled down from his forehead in a moment of anxiety. The hair style was a classic Bobby Charlton in reverse; the sweep back. It would be extremely fortunate if I ever lost that much hair.

"So what's wrong? Don't you know?" I interrupted.

"Of course we are confident that we know," he replied. This came as a disgruntled parenthesis.

"Then why don't you come right out and tell me?"

Finally he was treating me to full eye contact. His expression communicated 'you are not going to like this'. How entirely correct he was with that diagnosis.

"The problem you experienced has been isolated to a minor surgical component," Wickham said.

"You didn't leave a scalpel inside me, did you?" I exclaimed in horror.

The consultant studied me in surprise. "No, this was not an implement left behind post operatively."

"Then what are you telling me is wrong? There's something wrong, isn't there." Was it ethical to keep me guessing? A new wave of anxiety didn't unglue me from the plastic seat.

"Yes, yes, well. The hospital cannot take direct responsibility for what is outside its jurisdiction," he began. "This matter has been fully presented to our insurance claims board. They assure me that there is no culpability or obligation on this hospital's part."

"I'm losing you. Which part?"

"We are fully covered in these eventualities."

"In what way are you not to blame?" He was pushing me into the territory of empirical philosophy. But I was no longer a gullible eighteen year old.

"Blame would be an inappropriate word in this case," he replied; he lifted and hardened his tone.

"What exactly did you screw up?" Nails were more appropriate than screws.

"We treated you in an entirely professional and competent way. I just have to explain a few technical points to you before..."

"Are you saying I am to blame for this?" It was as bad as divorce. The ultimate weapon still disturbs my dreams.

"Any blame can be attached to the company." He registered my bafflement. "The particular company that manufactured these components."

"Which components are you talking about?"

"These devices; these artificial plastic heart valves."

I felt my chin wobble and my lips twitching, as I mumbled over a response to this. These wretched plastic heart valves made their first appearance in my imagination (if not in my body). Cold horror invaded, as if my body had shrunk down to protect my besieged heart.

"This is shocking," I managed.

"Are you perfectly all right, Mr Sheer?"

"Why of course I'm not all right," I told him.

"You are aware of technological advances in treatment."

"What were you trying to do to me?"

"Artificial devices were inserted to replace the diseased natural heart valves," he explained, shrugging.

"They've gone wrong these devices? That you put inside me?"

"There's nothing intrinsically sinister about this product."

"Excuse me, but is that the issue here? Just tell me what's gone wrong, can you?" Suddenly my voice had broken up. I was back into puberty. I wasn't fully in control of myself, if I ever had been.

"It's fractured," he told me.

I made a helpless drowned noise at the bottom of my throat. "Fractured?"

"According to our reports there was a manufacturing flaw... in some of the valves at least. It clearly broke after your successful surgery. That is what you experienced the other day."

"What are you planning to do about this problem?" I said. "Are you thinking of helping me? Do you suggest another operation?"

"We are considering very hard, corrective measures. Allow me to explain further," he said. His huge hands chopped at the desktop. "These little chaps are tested thoroughly during the manufacturing process." He was growing fond of them.

"I'm sorry. You're telling me I've got a bit of cracked plastic stuck in my heart."

"I wouldn't put it like that."

"That speaks wonders for the miracles of medical science," I remarked.

"If you would allow me?" He drew himself up in the chair, as if dealing with a heckler during a medical lecture. He couldn't extract the component, but he could deal with the rude rabble. "The chance of anyone in this country being affected is so many millions to one."

"Well, it looks as if I'm the lucky one," I argued.

"Ah yes, my dear chap, a few of these damaged parts were exported."

"That's no excuse for leaving me in the dark," I objected.

"No, we were almost as much the victims as you. That may be small consolation, but we were equally as unsuspecting. I'm sorry you are upset by this. It is simply terribly bad luck, Mr Sheer."

"I thought I was finally at the end of the run," I explained.

From the way his big hands collapsed on my paperwork, I knew he wanted to finish the meeting.

"If you will now excuse me," he began. He'd chewed the fat enough for one day. He sought more action. There were more cardiac patients on his workbench.

"I hope you are going to remove this faulty component," I said. Terrible as was it was better than nothing. But:

"It cannot be removed," he said. "There you have it."

"What do you mean? How exactly?"

"We had to cut away a section of the aorta. The placement of the valve had to be secure. It has to stay there, reinforced with..."

"You can't get the little bugger out," I concluded.

"Clearly such an operation is not possible to reverse. There is an inevitability of damaging the artery."

"I'm simply confined to the reject pile," I concluded.

"Now, Mr Sheer..."

"You don't want to see me again."

Wickham shook his hands bizarrely in front of himself. "Certainly not, you should keep in touch with your GP. Otherwise I don't wish to waste your time and resources."

"What's going to happen to me...from here on in?" I asked.

"Some of the patients in California didn't even survive the first crack of the valve. From what I have read... You are an extremely fortunate man, Mr Sheer, to be sat here today talking to us."

"Fortune has a crooked smile," I remarked.

"To be honest I am staggered that you survived."

"Is that right?"

"If you will forgive such a bold personal statement," he said.

"Flattery will get you nowhere," I replied.

"But you may be lucky in the future as well. Who am I to tell you that you, you know... that you *won't* be?"

"Then the component may break up altogether?"

Wickham examined his hands for a moment, then shook them violently, as if the wretched scalpel wouldn't unstick from his fingers.

"We hope that you may lead a full natural life," he told me. He really did possess a black sense of humour.

"When is this going to happen? This evening? Tomorrow? Next week? Or *any* time?"

I was beginning to lose my cool at this stage.

"Obviously it helps to take jolly good care of yourself," he replied.

"No smoking then?" I remarked.

"You could think about retiring early, if you can afford to do so."

"I'm just shy of forty nine, with my own business to run... with a full and happy life. Why should I have any plans to retire early?"

"That's for you to decide, Mr Sheer. You must be conscious of your medical condition, in how you choose to conduct your life."

"Is that your advice?" I felt despair come over me, like the fluey symptoms of angina pectoris.

"You must ensure that your family know about your condition...the risks you now face."

"Cheers."

But did I want my friends and family to modify their behaviour and their attitude towards me? To be treated as a medical freak, with twisted wires and cracked valves? Not likely.

"You risk fatal outcomes," he informed me.

"Are you trying to scare me, or what?"

"I would advise you to get in touch with your solicitor."

"Does this always happen with your patients?"

"This case is extremely rare. Presuming the suit in America against the manufacturer succeeds you may be entitled to compensation. Unfortunately I am not able to inform you of the exact details. Although there will be somebody in the hospital who will be able to," he explained.

"I've already been too familiar with lawyers," I said.

The ultimate weapon had already been launched, with catastrophic effects.

# Chapter 6

As if I had put my football boot into the calf of an Argentinian opponent, I took an early return home. Rather than becoming bedridden again, I became reintegrated into the national transportation network.

The heart hospital had lost all interest in me. I was out of fashion, as far as the medical establishment was concerned. The consultant was embarrassed by my style of cardiac operation; the stitches were all wrong and I didn't know how to combine a new valve with an artery. They'd rather expose themselves to a new flesh-eating tropical disease than to see my face around the ward again. They didn't listen to the faint murmur, that the heart attack machine was still strapped across my shoulders.

The force of London's traffic and population knocked me back, as I struggled on the underground with my kit bag. There was something sinister when I thought about going 'underground' again, however routine for Londoners and commuters. My self-confidence shattered down there like a snow house in the path of an ice-breaker.

On the way home from Paddington I sat in a carriage that grew empty. I wasn't conscious of the journey, as I reflected on Wickham's verdict on my medical outcome. I struggled to get my head around the idea of a damaged medical component, having come through radical surgery. The idea of some piece of plastic threatening my existence was too much for a former hippie to contemplate.

The towns and cities glided by. I realised how weird this world can look, when fear clamps down. Between the small lights of human interaction there was a gathering night. Now and again I caught myself reflected in the window glass, startling myself with my own appearance, like a painter attempting a portrait at the end of their time. How did I intend to explain my situation to friends and family?

Until I stepped off at Temple Meads station and hauled myself to my automobile. The familiarity of returning to Bristol lifted my spirits, as did the deep cracked upholstery of my veteran car; which is almost another country to me; it's an insulated haven, such as Luxembourg or San Marino or some place; it has its own architecture and climate. I got back into an upbeat mood as the ignition fired and the suspension lifted me from the dirt. You can find well-being in mechanics.

On the drive back I thought about hooking up with Rachael, or even with Corrina. There was a big party at my friends to look forward to. There's still plenty of action to be found in this city. The reaper would have to catch me first, if he was thinking of pushing down my eyelids with his thumb. I'm not about to slip into the past tense yet. I'm not checking out until the house lights come back.

Big Pink seemed empty as I approached. As I let myself back in, there was no obvious human presence, just a mountain of shoes and coats in the hallway. The place was in complete darkness, until I fired my path. I clumped upstairs to pack away the contents of my overnight bag. There were no other distractions. I had plenty of preoccupations. Then I returned downstairs, watching out for loose tacks on the boards, running my hand along our Bates' Motel balustrade. I wandered into the kitchen to fix myself a rock 'n' roll milky drink before bedtime. There was no elixir of life to be found in the cupboards, even though I examined all the labels. Ovaltine hasn't got a miracle ingredient. Still preoccupied by the day's drama I wander into the living room. There, much to my surprise, I discover Angela: bunched up into an armchair, reading under lamplight, with a mug of tea balanced on the arm. A novel - she must have raided my bookshelf out of curiosity. Liz had taken a truckload of possessions, but she lifted a bare handful of books. She's got different titles on her reading list these days.

Angela's presence arouses my curiosity, because she's just not been herself recently. She rarely stays indoors all evening. That isn't her contemporary style of living. I watch her for a while, my senses taking her in; but there's no smell from the other type of tea that she smokes. She knew I had walked into the room; something at the corner of her eye. Even arriving in stocking feet,

I made her jump. But she chose not to look up, as she kept her concentration.

If you need a description of my daughter, she is small, delicately constructed, dark, secretive and gregarious. Those two contradictory qualities can be a volatile combination. See the effect if shaken. Despite her fast lifestyle her character is as tough as an old tractor; although every father knows his daughter's vulnerable side. I don't want to cause an explosion, for lack of sensitivity, but there's a lot of unexploded powder between us. Angela has problems to sort, issues to face; a crowd of bombarding atoms in her mind.

"Hi Dad," she says finally, voice brightly cracked, as if long internalised. "Just reading." When she does pick up a book she can read through the night.

"Hi. Didn't know you were here."

"Do now," she pipes.

"Something interesting?"

Her eyes lift with a brief smile. Black, dilated, agleam with stimulation.

"Kind of."

"Don't mind me."

"Where you come from?" she insists.

"Me? Where? From London," I reply. The Doctor Marten's on the other foot, much to my discomfort.

"So what were you doing there, then? Up in London."

"Not a lot. Talking to a client."

"For real?"

"Why not?"

I gaze around our musty living room without pleasure. My dressing gown is threadbare, a gift from Christmases past; my eyes red rimmed over the steaming milk. My silvery blonde hair is flying from my scalp. I look a sight.

"Which client?" she probes.

"You interested?" I object. Then considering as her gaze holds me. "Just some company, Angie. Some medical company, matter of fact."

"So they made you travel all the way up there?"

"It isn't so far," I assure her.

"You haven't been that well," she reminds me. She returns her eyes to the page, but is listening for a reply. You can feel the emotional vibe between us.

Angela connects trips to London with the heart hospital; with Zorro leaving his mark across my chest. She's a sensitive girl, neurotically attuned to nuance, I might say. She's able to receive any ionospheric change triggered by casual remarks. Certainly there's no simple remedy for my dysmorphic condition. Not even head to toes plastic surgery would transform me back. So should I try to smuggle the truth past my daughter?

"Don't want to worry you with my problems," I say.

"You're joking aren't you, Dad?" She looks up at me again, although I'm practically in darkness.

"You're already crowded out with problems."

"You think I'm too young and naïve to get my head around them?"

"You're not interested in my work. Why should you be?" I add.

I try to avoid the critical truths with my cup of hot milk and brandy. I didn't mention the brandy before, but you always add it afterwards.

"What are you saying?" Angela protests. "I've always been interested in your work."

"Are you sure?" I say. "Never heard you express it."

"You hardly ever invite me to the factory," she says. "I can't remember when you last asked me to fly kites. As for your hot air balloons, I've never had a ride in one... not in my whole bloody life."

"Right." I shrug my shoulders. Sometimes kids can cramp your style.

"I've never been up in one!"

I descend stiffly into a Rhino-hide leather armchair, which has also seen better days. If you ran a finger around this room the dust ball might turn into an avalanche down the hill. My friends offered to redecorate and to repair, but I haven't taken up the offer. You don't see kids with a pot of paint these days, except maybe under the subway.

Angela is cosy in the armchair; sitting within an arc of reading light, with the darkness surrounding and me in the further half shadows. It doesn't look as if negative or evil forces can reach her there. She's intellectually at peace. I don't envy that quality as much as crave it - our youthful ideals. It stirs recollections of our university days, when Elizabeth and I fell in love and began the adventure of life together; although we'd known each other at primary school.

But I'd be living on my nerves in future, not on my intellect. I'd be lingering, waiting for another letter from the hospital, telling me, informing me, of god knew what. Not meeting friends at the café to share plans and enthusiasms.

Everything that I most enjoyed and valued was in danger; since my life is in danger. Maybe that process began some time ago, without me noticing. I'd reached a landmark crossroads in my life, like seminal blues-player Robert Johnson: But the paths are wearing out to vanishing point.

I study my daughter as she sits reading, pausing, breathing; so youthful, so healthy, so intoxicated with possibility. I am lulled by the contemplative atmosphere she has created, as she turns pages and repositions. I'll never plug my psyche back into the optimism again. I'm brimming with love, despair and confusion towards her. My future has been imperilled by a technical fault; meaning that the movie of my life could stop at any point. My cares cling to me as the outside cold was trapped in my overcoat. What can all this mean to her?

"Are all the pubs and clubs trying to save on electricity tonight?" I remark.

"You're bloody annoying, all of a sudden... aren't you!"

"Tonight I couldn't have the energy to re-read my own will."

She darts her eyes up at me. "What the hell do you mean by that?"

I stare back, startled at my indiscretion. Why is it hard to be entirely honest, even if the truth is an SF horror?

"Ah, nothing, just came from the top of my head..."

"What a thing to say?" she tells me.

"Yes. Bloody ridiculous, if you ask me. Can you forgive me? It's been a terrible day, to be straight up. Business, that is. I must be going bananas. Gaga."

Such adolescent jocularity fails to impress, but she subsides to quiet again and jumps back into the book.

I'm disgusted at my blabbermouth. I cut myself disgusted expressions as a warning. Maybe my brain is still working. Hopefully there's no obstruction in the artery leading to my head. So why did I face my daughter in this evasive way? They'd already been through the original trauma of my heart complaint and visit to hospital, not to mention the upheavals in their family life. Did I want to put them through anymore? They'd seen me as a total physical wreck, but not as a kind of laughing stock on a short fuse.

I don't want to cast this bizarre shadow of their lives. People say that time is a healer, but that depends on the wounds. My best mate suggested that I open my heart to my kids, as well as to everybody. Don't hide the truth from them, allow them to sympathise and give strength. But if I don't have a better explanation, I may as well nail my tongue to the roof of my mouth. Better if family and friends think my heart could stop by itself, than asking them to image some Californian toggle trying to top itself, from the beach hut of my right ventricle. Even Dylan couldn't put that into a rhyming couplet.

How can I keep these secrets, bizarre and isolating, while trying to be the good guy and a decent father? Should I be forced to share my secrets and my new view on the universe? At some moment I will need to tell them the exact truth, like a murderer bragging to his mate in the pub.

"You look a tiny bit disgusting, to be totally honest with you, Dad."

"How do I look disgusting?" I reply. But she's become used to my new image.

"You look like that jar of lemon curd... that we left in the fridge for six months."

"Thanks love.

"You're welcome."

It's here that my eyes focus on a bracelet. She has a new gold bracelet, with a type of yin yang whirly design. I look at this heavy thing glinting in the lamplight from her arm, trying to explain where it came from. Has she broken into her savings account?

"Where did your new bracelet come from?" I wonder.

She snatches at the metal, disconcerted; but did she think I could miss it?

"Oh, this! Do you like it?" She fondles and admires.

"So who's buying you expensive jewellery these days?"

She holds it up, blushing, chestnut brown eyes flashing. "I bought this all by myself. Why should anybody have bought this for me?"

My suspicions are aroused like a detective finger-searching a murder scene. "That didn't just drop out of a tree. Can you afford to buy yourself something like that?"

She extended her delicate arm to offer a closer look.

"Isn't it totally lush?"

I reach out and grasp her tiny wrist to see. How could anything be more beautiful? "Is that your name engraved there?" I ask, straining my eyes.

"Did you *forget* my name?" she rebukes.

"Somebody bought this for you. Some guy."

"No." She makes a juggle with dryly-ironical laughter. "Which guy is gonna buy me something like this, eh? I wouldn't let 'em anyway. I bought this with my own money," she insists. Well, it makes a contrast to her ragged jeans and crumpled shirt.

"We don't have bottomless funds," I warn.

She laughs at this information. "Do you think I stole it, then? Is that what you're telling me?"

I am staring at her with a perplexed helpless expression.

Her dark eyes smoulder at me, although she evades contact. She makes repeated efforts to tuck a section of straight dark hair behind an elfin ear.

"I'm happy that you take some pride in your name, Angela," I say.

"I'm earning money these days, Dad. I can buy myself a little bracelet can't I? Is that more than I deserve? to treat myself?"

"Do you earn enough to buy these kind of treats?"

"It's a high tipping place," she assures me.

"What kind of people are tipping you there?"

"Then sometimes you get talking to guys."

"Here we are."

"You get to know them, and they ask you to do little jobs for them."

"Oh really, Angie? What kind of little jobs you referring to? What kind of guys are you getting talking to?" This was ringing alarm bells even before her mother got hold of it.

"Well, you know, all kind of people come into the café. He doesn't mind us talking to them, when we're quiet. Do you know what I'm saying? They'll ask you to do jobs for them. I don't mind if they keep back a few queenies. It's only fair."

"So aren't you meant to be serving tea and sponge cake?" I wonder.

"You're well behind it, Dad. Nothing too radical."

"I guess you need to save for the future now."

"Of course I do, Dad, straight up."

"That might be for university. That's what we passionately hope for, your mother and I. We're not putting any pressure on you. But you haven't been drawing on that special university account, have you?" I said, horrified.

"Why should I want to do that? Even if I wanted to go to uni?"

I expel breath in relief. "We've all worked too hard over the years... for you to go and blow that fund."

"Don't sweat about it, Dad," she advises. She makes a big demonstration of finding her place in the book.

"So who's your big infatuation?" I speculate.

She's exasperated. "What are you talking about now? Leave me alone, will you?"

"Aren't you going to share his name?"

"Would I? When you talk about your own infatuation," she argues.

"I don't have a girlfriend at the moment."

"Do you think I was born yesterday?" she answers. "Not even that pushy cow? You know that nasty snob who works for the music company? The one you took on holiday but came back by yourself?"

"Especially not," I assure her.

"You don't give yourself any peace. Not even at your age."

"What's that supposed to mean. At my age? I'm in charge of my own destiny. I'm the only guy around here who can deal with it," I explain.

"Obviously you've had a bad day. You should go to bed. Tuck yourself up."

"Look who's telling me to go to bed," I repost.

"Don't forget to take all your tablets," she reminds me, more gently.

"Don't worry, I know the medicine I'm expected to take."

"Better do as you're told, Dad," she warns.

I take another survey of the chiaroscuro living room. "Anyway, where's your brother this evening? He in bed already?" I wonder.

"Luke's around Jahinder's place," she informs me, as if his absence after midnight is unremarkable. This is definitely out of our routine.

"What's he doing there at this time of night?"

"Working on another computer programme."

"Right, so who said that was acceptable?"

"What's the big problem?" She gives the book another shake of impatience.

"I'd just like to see Luke from time to time, that's all."

"Bloody hell Dad, you must have taken a knock to the head," she tells me.

"We've always been a close family. We're all fond of each other," I insist.

She laughs dryly and deeply. "Right."

I have to touch base, to make sure the kids are happy: to ensure they are more real than me. Possibly my sentimental mood alerts her to changed circumstances. They should be getting used to change as a permanent principle. But my loose talk has made her suspicious about my health battle.

If you check out of life early, there's some comfort in the idea of continuity. That's it: the idea of leaving behind people who loved me is important. The thought that however low Liz and I have become in each other's estimation (or anyway I in hers) we've still given a lot back to the world. Life is divisible by life. We've got something to show.

Or maybe it was just getting too late.

# Chapter 7

How can I influence my daughter, if she doesn't trust me? How can I share her dreams if she has no ideas about the future? Aren't I the type of open-minded, tolerant and progressive father that any girl would envy? Any contemporary girl, trying to find herself in this mad violent world, would be thrilled to get me as a parent. Why isn't she able to open up about all her problems? What's a father for?

Angela's on some risky trip of her own. I don't know which direction she's heading in, but I know she has set off on the journey. At least medical drugs have known effects or side-effects. When you have treatment at the hospital for your troubles, there are results and conclusions. In relationships we have to make our own conclusions. In life other people often leave us to find our own; to join together the blanks.

Lately I speculate if I have the persuasive or - I must face this - the *physical* powers to bring her back. Elizabeth insists that Angela is determined to ruin her future, as hastily as a bride throwing her bouquet. Angie's mixed up with a set of bad characters, keeping unsociable hours and habits; although *they* seem to think it's *very* sociable; intimately flirting with future cancers and psychological problems. Although I take Liz's criticisms of my parenting in bad part, I can't deny that my ex-wife (and still present person) is justified in worrying. I can't entirely dismiss her concerns as an expression of her new go-get identity, even if I've voiced that phrase a number of times. Liz reads our daughter's life-style like an anonymous warning letter. You can't say there's nothing to it.

I like to think that Angie's too smart to put her life through the scrap-yard shredder. She raves around the clock, but she hasn't switched off the lights. She's following her own logic, I argue, which will find an answer. How may I convince Liz? She says that we have to intervene as parents, to stop and correct, to change Angela's life for the better. That's always been her line on parenthood, saying that I am too laid-back and easy going: or I used to be. To me that's like saying I'm too good looking; which is something I never heard Lizzie say. When she's at the top of a rage she will accuse me of being a negligent and terrible father. Which hurts; which has some impact. No use denying it.

So we don't enjoy how Angie spends her leisure hours. The girl is neither the champion sports woman or domestic goddess her mother thought about. We don't approve of her boyfriends, who make Nirvana look like a boy band. She's in no hurry to hammer together a confession box to apologise to us. Whatever my ex-wife and living breathing woman tells me, I'm not going to put my big feet or mouth where it isn't appreciated. Even though such vows haven't always restrained me.

Sometimes you can grow so sick with worry that it knocks you out like traffic fumes.

After the appointment in London I was too shattered to remain awake. Instead of waiting for family to come together, I dropped into that uneasy kind of sleep. I was soaked in sweat, restaging the interview with the consultant, thinking back on Wickham's dreadful prognosis. I could hear my own heart thumping into the mattress like an argumentative talking drum; like those stocked in towers at an African shop in town.

I tried to dismiss the idea of a faulty coronary valve; a flaw in the artery. How could a cracked piece of plastic be allowed to dominate my life? my future and my fears? I could beat this. The body can fight back against such ridiculous intrusion, as to fight an invasive scouting group. There was no reason to hold the pillows down over my own face; I wasn't about to surrender my life.

I wasn't able to play strenuous sports like squash or tennis again. But nothing stopped me from taking up comparatively gentler activities, like sex or, to get real, other interests. Therefore I investigated what evening classes were on offer in the city. Of course there was nothing like sex; unless you mean anonymous disease clinics. At the local leisure centre, there was bowling and line dancing I noticed; assuming I would have any time away from friends, girlfriends and family. I would even try to get out some nights, take up a gentler art for the mind and body. Again this didn't include sex, although I couldn't stop thinking about it.

Fair play, the *Shin Ga Do* class was definitely off limits, the *Taekwondo* Academy a complete impossibility: despite adverts relating the therapeutic benefits of smashing crockery or even bricks; the satisfaction of jumping reverse side kicks, and such manoeuvres. For me there's no obvious advantage to flying through the air screaming with a foot raised. So in the end I settled for a weekly yoga class. This would be as good as spiritual sex.

Previously; you know, when the heart was in tune; I wouldn't have the patience for yoga. Now I'm in no hurry for a last rash move, so I can sit in my own spiritual bubble of mild suppleness. There's a whole class filled with beautiful women in the lotus position. They're just waiting with relaxed diaphragms for the right guy. I first noted the yoga class on our way out of the squash courts. I was taking my raw joints and torn muscles towards the bar, allowing Rachael and Marcia to slug it out until the death. Even before my aorta and aleatory tactics failed me, yoga looked like a clever alternative.

Heart disease has made me a wiser, better balanced guy. Serious illness can have this effect on the victim, of putting him back in touch with himself. It was making me confront life adversities, not only to overcome health obstacles. I took strength from this, even if I am more dented and scarred than an old punch bag.

Radical surgery had been brutally invasive, that is fair to say. I couldn't stop thinking that my integrity as a human being had been wrecked. My soul, if you want to talk about it, was smashed and trampled, like the skinny kid's wire glasses in the hands of a bullying crowd. But I don't want to sound ungrateful.

As I dropped off that night I thought that I should have told Angie the truth. I hadn't set out to lie and deceive, but I had made the wrong decision, in the fear of a moment, by choosing to conceal. I resolved to explain myself when the right moment came along. Problem was that this evening *was* a good moment - I'd fluffed my lines. Now I'd have to wait for another opportunity, to be alone with her in the right mood.

Going by her questions she knows something's up. Would she be as interested if she knew the ridiculous truth? It's easier for her to ask caring questions than to hear honest answers. After missing the moment of fearful truth, I might be kept waiting forever.

Rousing myself from oblivion next morning, I heard Angela running down the staircase, then pulling the front door after herself. Where was she heading, after fleeing the scene again, before I could ask about her pastimes? I had woken with a determination to confess all my dark secrets to her. That's typical of her schedule these days, if that's the right word. It's like taking a ride on the last bloody metro around here some times.

While I am brooding about this, Luke turns up into the kitchen. Not from the direction of his bedroom, as you might expect, but from the front door. Most likely he passed his sister in the street on his way. He's come back from an illicit graveyard shift at his mate's computer lab. Looks like he didn't get any sleep at all last night. How's he going to grow and strengthen like that? Or maybe he catches up during lesson time. Hair up in a rough and quill; a pilot's jacket and silk tee have been thrown on. My heroes were rebels too, but at least they had a sense of style and fashion. Elizabeth purchased these clothes for him, in protest against the Woody Guthrie donkey jacket and checked shirt that I bought for him. Why does she protest against the style that Dylan adopted when he first began to play around the Village?

I like the idea of bringing Luke into my business one day. The plan is becoming more urgent as bad luck begins to outpace me. That's assuming that I can keep my kites and balloons in the air, by juggling with the balance sheet. Luke never looks impressed with the idea, and it's optimistic to believe he is yet capable.

Luke's our eldest boy, so how am I expected to think? There's nobody else to take over the controls, after I've thrown away the guide rope. He could still develop a passion for our kites and balloons after I fly into the heavens. But I can't quite see it at the moment.

Luke's not our 'little' boy any longer. Best to clear up any misconceptions. He's just a shade under six feet and not quite sixteen. Takes after his mother's uncle; Teddy, the civil servant who couldn't get his knees under the table. There's been a lot of lanky bastards on her side of the family. With the exception of her parents, who cut themselves back to regulation size and took out a chainsaw on me. Fortunately I always kept them at a conversational distance. Student politics and the folk music scene taught me how to verbally defend myself. Though I've never been a street fighting man. I've never been a bar brawler as my brother used to be.

Luke strikingly resembles his mother physically. I hope that his heart was turned out of the same maternal jelly mould. He's wired up in the same way she is too. That's why she isn't angry or upset that he chooses to live with me. He's supposed to be torturing me with his mere presence, reminding me of what I lost. But does his mother care what I think and feel anymore? To her I've always been flying above the clouds. Once Bob Dylan was the poet of our experiences, not the adenoidal fraud she now claims him to be. That was calculated to wound me. She put her knee into my soul.

Luke's living here out of habit, I sometimes believe. Kids don't measure or quantify love, according to my family thesis. So does he take our love for granted, even as it has forked out? There have to be a few questions in that mental processor of his. Even his would-be step father, Frank, doesn't have enough hard disk capacity to resolve those equations. Most human codes are beyond Frank's reach, if you want my opinion.

Luke doesn't play his parents off against each other. That's more than you can say about the gaggle of lawyers and accountants. He has a smaller and less experienced heart, in better condition. It's able to cope, to function, and to keep going. In fact his heart is beating away contentedly, despite lack of sleep and revision work. Final school exams loom through his wet dreams like Godzilla. That's my role.

Feels sometimes as if Luke and I merely exist under the same roof. The kid's moody and remote, spending hours on the computer, locked away in his control centre. That's a top of the range model, suggested by Frank. The Edible Woman got her magazine husband at last. So what could be more perfect?

I'd be surprised if Luke didn't feel any anger. You have to feel something when your world ends. Even when you have the chance to build a new one. I feel like mother bloody goose buttering up his slices of toast and pouring out a mug of tea. Can I really imagine him taking over my business one day? How can I wait around until he gains enough experience?

"Hey, Luke!"

He grunts like a troglodyte that's taken the wrong exit.

"So you coming to the footie match this afternoon?"

The next rough noise indicates a negative. There's none of his computer wizardry on display for me.

"Your little brother's coming along," I explain.

Luke collapses on to the chair and swipes away his cereal bowl. "I already told you. Tim's just a little kid, aint 'e. How many more times?"

"You've lost all interest in football now?" I reply.

"Yeah."

"Cool," I comment.

He rests is chin on his forearms. "I'm going in to town," he explains.

"Who you going in to town with?"

"My mates!"

"What you doing in town all day?"

"What do you think?" He treats me to a roll of eyes into the back of his head.

There's nothing out of the ordinary about this, I understand. But he's not going to get any cuddlier either. I've noticed a gang of youths skulking about the town centre lately. He's familiar with them at weekends and some evenings. Elizabeth has some logic by dazzling him with technological boxes of tricks.

What draws them to the most god-forsaken spaces of the city? The isolated walkways, concrete expanses, graffiti smeared underpasses and vandalised benches and shelters? These are useful surfaces for skateboarding, but they are often just hanging about. Why do they laugh like loons, or simply scowl, when they notice me walking by looking at them? They don't need to escape from my generation of enlightened parents. There's no way they can satirise us as a bunch of squares or green monsters. When are they going to appreciate what we did and emulate us?

I could hardly concentrate on reading my newspaper. Luke's dead fortunate to have a father tuned into youth culture.

I still have a decent knowledge of what's going down with contemporary music. He's into the hip hop and crap music. He doesn't even appreciate the more melodic and fashionable bands of today. Liz is right to worry that extreme volume will ruin his IQ. In a few years he won't be able to find the volume control, or even the power switch of his computer. Although his mother and I should have brains like dried peas in an oil drum by now, if that theory is correct. Although she was originally a big fan of Joan Baez. You could only hear Joan's voice and acoustic guitar if the whole festival was keeping a hush. So Liz has frontal lobes of alien proportions obviously, hardly able to tolerate my presence any longer.

"So who are these new mates of yours?" I wonder.

"Nobody 'oo wan's to know about you, Noah!"

"I'm your father," I remind him. "Don't refer to me by my first name."

"Lay off me, will yer?"

"So who are your mates? Where are you going... And how long will you be?"

Luke hurls his chair aside and stomps out of our kitchen. The illuminated heels of his pricey sneakers flash like airport semaphores. Now it looks as if he's hopping mad, with a pair of Liz's luxury cheesecakes tied above his ankles.

"You suck!" he shouts back.

I don't respond to his movie Americanism. "These guys are more important than your own brother?" I fire off towards his back, helplessly.

All right, he's unpredictable and I always say the wrong thing. He's a volatile teenager in a broken home. He's developing an after-hours life style to rival his sister's. I begin to wonder if brother and sister know more about each other than I do; if they have more confidence and trust in each other; if they conspire to keep their secrets from their parents.

Luke spends two nights at his mother's new place: at the show home. From time to time he manages to get out of those dates. But he has a more harmonious relationship with his mother lately. They're more attuned to each other. He gets along with her new husband no worse than with any other horny old dinosaur. Prehistoric beasts enjoy a certain vogue with the very young.

The high tech attractions of the Noggins household are losing their power. He's losing his morbid fascination for the fat-wad techno-Dino. I guess he's grown up in this house and it will always be our home. I wish I understood exactly what's happening with Luke. I agreed to purchase all that expensive computer stuff, as Liz told me it was educational. Why blast off for a new planet, when the old planet is comfortable? Why risk a strange atmosphere with unknown occupants? That sums up Luke's attitude, when he chose a house to live in. Liz may regret allowing him to stay here with me at Big Pink. Now the dinosaur and she are trying to renegotiate. She doesn't want to trust a 'failed father' to watch over him. All they require is a good legal technicality or evidence of paternal neglect and failure. Our goalkeeper doesn't have to stay as watchful and nimble toed as I do.

While I try to read a feature article and polish off my egg, I am disturbed by the thumping of Luke's feet over the boards above. When this storm concludes I hear him bouncing down the staircase and slamming the door after him; in the style of his sister before. He's abandoned the good ship Enterprise to leave me alone on the bridge. A great Earth day this is turning out. Doesn't his attitude show psychotic tendencies? Or is this another episode of space warp paranoia?

Wickham should understand how difficult it is to lead a peaceful life. I can join a yoga club, but how can I regulate my breathing in between? How to keep a count of my heart rate, when our kids are going off in every direction? Against my peaceful principles I'm tempted to fall on my own sword sometimes.

Giving up on any family style breakfast, I tidy away dishes and go to tidy up the living room. John Lennon took a nurturing role for many years, didn't he? I wonder if he was frustrated with the tasks of a house husband. I don't believe his sons were ever the victims of this pubescent psychosis however. But what do I know?

The place is neglected and turning into a pigsty. Even the moth balls are getting dusty. Angie never does any work around the house, while Luke only vacuums his own space. He's got a sudden mania for keeping his bedroom spotless. Perhaps this is a symptom of missing his mother. You could describe me as an abandoned house husband.

Elizabeth grew intolerant of any disorder or dirt. I thought we'd get through that 'bad patch' in our marriage but, man, it just kept spreading and spreading. It was a sign of the future that I chose to misinterpret. A pebble hit me on the head one day, and this was no mistake, it was danger of rock fall on the road ahead.

Liz would be horrified if she could see the house today. Not that I have any plans to invite her back. God no. You never know how far the lawyers are behind her; those black riders of the marital row. I don't approve of the mess either, but I've got tubes in my body to worry about; and the untidiness does remind me of our student days. But even my mother has a more exciting home life these days. My social diary shrinks in proportion to my lung capacity. Though believe me, I'm still trying, I haven't given up on a great gig yet.

# Chapter 8

By the following Saturday I'm in better spirits. I slap on a bit of expensive stench - some mix of whale musk and stag sperm - pull on a new pair of posh jeans, cowboy boots, a peacock waistcoat and velveteen jacket. Then I confront myself again in the shaving mirror, inspecting the signs of waste, smoothing back my fringe, before stepping out into town.

If you know Bristol you can see that Park Street isn't very kind to cardiac patients. It has a gradient to daunt Edmund Hillary and Tenzing Norgay. I feel like making a camp half way up the hill, to boil up a kettle and catch some gasps of thin air. Liz and I would bounce up there as students, but that was a whole different epoch. Light years back.

Fortunately I am going downhill - if that's the right way to put it. My idea is to call at a place called Mike's Café at the bottom of the street. That's where Angela works and I decide to say hello to her, whether she wants my greeting or not. She stands about in the café in a blue uniform, rather similar to a school uniform, except for the white pinafore apron and legitimate cigarette breaks.

The café has an airy bohemian ambience. Where have all the artists and intellectuals gone? I can't help wondering. These people's trivial conversations just make my head ring. Man, the times have changed. It isn't cool to be clever or even want to understand anything.

Not that Angie is rushed off her feet as a waitress. When I spot her she's relaxing under the outside awning with friends. She has an impressive number of friends; hedonistic bat people who watch the world labour by. Mike's Café is a perfect bolthole for them to regroup and recover from the night before. Unless, like me, the body clock has gone crazy. I have to settle back into Zen-like emptiness. There's no ready cure for dysmorphia.

The chat staggers to a halt when they realise who's coming to lunch. Angela spots my approach and she makes signals. What's this all about? She would be happier if I waved and just kept walking by. At first I thought my trendy threads would be sure to impress these youths. They would be in respect and awe of a hep-cat guy. I've seen many of the greats in the flesh. But on the contrary, they are not impressed or intimidated: they regard me as a teetotal magistrate on a field trip.

"Hey, Angela! You don't mind if I hang out with you for a bit, do you?"

I peel off my sunglasses and try to grin winningly. They are not impressed, but somebody jumps up and offers me a seat, as if I need one.

"Sit yourself down, Noah," the guy says.

"Thanks boy. That's kind of you," I agree.

"Comfortable?"

"No need to fuss."

Stuck with me, the group look about at each other awkwardly. Despite my expensive aftershave there is a bad smell around here. It's a beautiful morning but suddenly there are rain clouds in their view. But I'm not to be discouraged so easily. I always take along my own nuclear umbrella.

"Having a good day, Angie? Busy?" I venture.

She manages to grumble darkly through her fingers.

"So how're you doin' anyway, Mr Sheer?" one lad asks.

"Couldn't be better," I reply.

"Are you sure?" he says.

"Try that one on me again?" I say.

They give the impression that they don't know where to look. They haven't bumped into Angela's Dad for a while. I've dropped into their group like an unwelcome gargoyle. They only remember the guy who was once going away on a romantic holiday. It's hard for them to grasp that I now stay away from travel agents at all costs.

"This is a cool little café," I tell them. "I enjoy coming here with my friends as well."

"Lennon and McCartney," Angie comments.

"Your mother and I used to come here," I correct her.

"Did it exist in those days?" a girl asks.

"D'you know there used to be groups and artists performing in here?"

"Music in a café?"

"A folk club. Those were some talented guys. Great times."

They remain unimpressed, distracted.

"What would you like?" This from the waitress still on duty. The girl stands eagerly next to me, notepad ready.

"Double espresso. Something to jab the life back into me."

The chick scribbles this down into her little book.

The group continue to exchange ironic and impatient glances. Or they resume their nonchalant gestures of drinking and smoking; while cutting out any chat. I may resemble the thousand year old man, but I'm still interesting and attractive, don't they realise?

"No thanks, I don't smoke. That's a lethal blend of tar and 'monoxide," I tell him.

"You used to smoke, didn't you Dad," Angie rebukes.

"Used to," I retort. "You might as well start sucking on exhaust pipes. Gonna do you just as much good."

"Thanks for the advice, mate."

"Anyway, what's happening here?" I persist.

"Happening?"

"Going on."

"Nothing much," comes the laconic reply.

"So what's hip this week?" I pursue.

"Why don't you keep quiet and relax, Dad," Angela advises.

I notice a jittery quality to Angela, extra to embarrassment. She couldn't be more relaxed than here, 'working' with her friends, but somehow she's tense. There's a constant underlying anxiety, a negative charge that sets off her mental alertness. Something is definitely going on, even if she refuses to share her secrets.

Gradually their conversation begins to pick up again. Like an old folkie at a psychedelic séance, I grow accustomed to sitting mutely in the background. Meanwhile the double espresso goes to my head. I speculate if any of the young men are my daughter's latest beau. There's more than a heavy gold bracelet hanging off her these days. There's a sense of happiness and exaltation about her lately, despite or because of the late nights. She isn't going to sneak this new boy past me, even if she thinks I was born yesterday. Life as it is, you don't need to experiment with drugs.

The mystery guy is having a powerful effect on her. If she's a natural romantic she is taking after me. I have noticed the signs of a party atmosphere around her tropical island. Like a hint of absinthe, her falling in love hasn't escaped me.

I decide that the new boyfriend isn't present. I keep an eye on her as she looks around the table of faces. It's hard to determine what her taste in boys may be. Except that she's had a few already. But it wouldn't be cool to express any opposition. All I can do is keep my ears flapping like the wings of a condor. While I am between them her friends stick studiously to neutral topics.

I'm trying to persuade her to enrol at the university. Liz and I have been conducting this campaign since Angie decided to take that gap year or two. It isn't as if the girl isn't clever enough to get a decent degree: she passed her A Levels with a few stars. She wouldn't have to leave Bristol to attend university. That would satisfy her mother.

So far Angie has taken three years away from education. She doesn't have any desire to work for charities or to go backpacking around the globe. She's a student of experience, that girl. Not necessarily wasted time, as I try to argue to Liz. But I still hope that she chooses a course before long. There's no better way to meet a free thinking boyfriend, with good taste in music and sound sense in life. Don't plant seeds in the garden and go digging around to try to find them. The girl will flower.

Talking about myself, I have a talent for getting along with the young. I have to be the envy of her friends' parents. The trick is, I retain my youthful spirit and curiosity. Obviously you tend to fall behind in the operating theatre. But my mind and spirit burn brightly as ever. I wore my hair long until my thirty fifth birthday. I can't quite remember what happened to me on my thirty fifth birthday.

Kites and balloons are an expression of idealism. They keep me in harmony with the world, as seen from above. They're the epitome of peacefulness. Get me away from the noise and craziness of this world. I feel happiest up there in my balloon, to be honest: Enjoying a sport that does no harm to the earth or to any other human being. We all need to take some spiritual time out. This world is a beautiful if scary place.

I'm telling Angela's friends as much, once I get an entrée.

"Yeah, that's really cool, Noah," somebody remarks, sarcastically.

Angie continues to cringe and to keep checking the heavens, as if to see if I am going to return there in a balloon.

"Yeah, for the Chinese kites have religious significance. They even used them in warfare... to help them gain advantage in battle."

There's no positive response.

"Yes, kites spread across the rest of Asia. In India kite flying is considered to be a sport of the gods. Did you know that? The practise has powerful symbolism, you see, within the Hindu religion. Do any of you know anything about Hinduism?"

"That interesting, Noah, like *fascinating*!"

"Sure it is, because the Japanese were flying kites a century before Christ showed up," I explain, "or thereabouts."

"Amazing, man!"

"We sold some of our kites into China and Japan. That was pretty amazing, let me tell you. Did you know that our fighter kites are among the quickest in the world."

"Amazing!"

I relate my legendary, notorious business trip to Tokyo. This adventure almost claimed my earthbound existence, before a coronary got hold of me. That was my only significant long haul trip out of the country. When I showed my currency to the wrong bar friend and got chased along back alleys by the thief's friends. As yet I haven't visited China, although we have representatives in Shanghai. There's a chance of setting up a factory there one day, as the dragon economy begins to breathe fire. I'm practically rubbing my hands together. In a few years' time I could be bringing home the pandas.

"Thanks for the life story, again."

Even my denims had the wrong cut and label. They'd never seen me in a crushed velvet jacket before, yet it failed to impress. They'd no idea what was hip. So I didn't pick up any news items about my daughter, or any clues about her new boyfriend. Angie had to return to her serving duties, with her private diary locked and hidden. It was her turn to stand behind the cash register, looking pretty and numerate. Maybe this was a positive image of her life that I could report back to Liz.

I stood up from my chair, somewhat stiff, breathless and awkward. *Bout de Souffle*, indeed. There was hard proof that my youthful charm had worn away. I managed to swap polite farewells. From there I tackled the hill back to home, as casually as I knew how. My jacket was hooked over my shoulder, sunglasses repositioned. This didn't fool them or disguise my own unease.

I rediscovered the security of my big nosed French car. I was back behind the wheel and gear stick, feeling in control. Then I set off towards Redland: not the socialist utopia it sounds, but that district in the north of Bristol, where my ex-wife Elizabeth now lives with our youngest son. With any luck the horny dinosaur might be out, hunting for his lunch.

# Chapter 9

"What time do you call this?"

"Only a few minutes," I insist.

To escape her derision I already tucked away my sunglasses. Her censorious look cannot so easily be deflected. But I'm completely out of phase in this era.

"Why are you so early? every time you call around here?"

"Don't know, maybe I'm excited to see my son," I counter.

"What happened to the navigational wristwatch?" That was a Christmas present from her; a last souvenir.

"That's why I'm here on your doorstep. That watch is far too efficient," I bluff.

She masks an exasperated look.

"Would you prefer me to be late?"

"You were never so generous with your time," she replies.

"Am I interrupting something, by any chance?" I wonder.

"That's no longer possible," she remarks.

She takes in my dishevelled weekend image; the faded denims, the curly image of Dylan under a floral shirt and waistcoat. There's still no sign of access, as Liz looks down on me from the doorstep, as a cat watches passers-by from a window ledge.

"Why can't you wait in your car for ten minutes?"

"I have the legal right to see Tim whenever I choose," I retort. I am forced to resort to standard dirty tricks, or I will be banished to an alternative reality. It's essential to control the feeling of panic and outrage, as my heart threatens to bolt, with a danger of plummeting over that cliff edge.

Liz casts a repelled look at my car, which is moored to the opposite kerb of her street, like an old monster from a tormented realm.

"You'd better come inside to wait," she relents.

Avoid neighbourly spying. She never used to care what other people thought. The front door jolts and rattles as she springs back. Or she claimed not to care; when the children ran about the garden, shoeless, naked with their hair long down their backs; Liz holding her generous bust in a flimsy halter-top, generous gourds containing the spices and substances of the east.

The hallway has a newly decorated look, with the smell of carpets and furniture polish. There is the mellow, regular beat of the new grandfather clock. The clock was a wedding present from Frank Noggins's parents. Otherwise I could recognise Liz's taste, in the Art Nouveau pottery and engravings. I'd learnt *something* about furniture and art from dating Rachael. A pair of Luke's boots were under the stairway - a spare set for his visits. A stack of Frank's computers were piled in a corner; obsolete props from an old science fiction movie. Like people over fifty, machines over five are judged surplus to the economy.

Mrs Noggins leads me through. She's a tall, robust woman, with a blaze of thick copper hair. Quite Amazonian, she might have lead a Celtic tribe to chase away Roman legions. The hair colour isn't natural any more, but she allows the ropes and coils to fall down to her waist, in a burnished mane. I remember her dashing around Bristol as a student, in a characteristic red duffle coat, burnished locks flowing from the hood. She has powerful green eyes that can turn men into columns of smoke.

"You just came here from town, did you?" she asks.

"Didn't think you were interested in my movements."

"Out spending your money again, are you?"

People admire her integrity and determination, albeit with a touch of steel like the doors of a high security bank vault. She doesn't have the kind of mind that you can change back. But she loved me with the delicate poetry of an elf princess.

Unfortunately she rooted out all her happy-go-lucky ways, in favour of something harder and more chic. Her Indian cottons, silks and hand-made jewellery went on a bonfire. She wanted to up the ante, and the rot set in from there.

She argued that she was growing, moving on, leaving the past behind; implying that I wasn't doing the same. When the roof collapsed on our marriage she didn't appear much damaged. I get a recurring nightmare on this theme: the cathedral collapses on our heads, during our wedding ceremony, burying us in rubble. Then, finding that I have, incredibly, survived, I begin to search frantically for my new wife, throwing aside stones and masonry.

There's an arm extended from the debris, but when I reach and hold on to the hand, I only drag out a rotting corpse instead, not much more than a skeleton. Man, you don't need to be R. D Laing.

Can any man be essential to a woman anymore? Does any intelligent woman rehearse those vows in these contemporary times? Is it any life, being a wife? We were children in the Sixties; I say *children.*

Liz gives clues away about her second marriage some times; at least a flavour of her life with Bristol's version of Darth Invader. But there's no spy in this particular house of love, to overhear their conversations, the true life drama, apart from a heavy sleeping eight year old in a strongly fortified house.

"Where's Tim?" I say.

"He's still upstairs getting changed," she explains.

"Shall I go up and see how he's getting along?" I offer.

"Look, you're really far too early."

I have the standard weekend contact with my youngest. Now that the football season has begun I take him to Ashton Gate for every home game. Those goal posts never move.

Elizabeth advances into her kitchen, that's been extended to boost business; not to accommodate me. Already you can't keep the lid on her fruit pies. Palpably she's been in the middle of a baking session this morning. There is a warm exotic aroma and her fingers are still floury. She had no intention of shaking hands with me, so there was no need to wipe her hands. She's making dough - lots of it.

She goes to church every Sunday now. She refuses to break anything but holy bread on the day of rest. She even goes out on weekend Christian picnics, listening to sermons and those Jesus cats twanging guitars and crooning in a high pitched evangelical style.

"Didn't Luke want to join you for the match today?" she wonders.

"Football isn't an exciting fixture for him," I report.

"Then what will he be getting up to today?" She fixes her arms resolutely under those firm and separated inter-continentals.

Despite trying on a mature if genial expression, I'm pushed into the uncertainty of an awkward corner.

"I dunno, Liz, he might be going into town... to meet some school friends of his. You know what those lads are like about fashion these days," I chuckle, tugging on my flowery shirt cuffs.

"I thought you told me he was coming to the football... to keep Tim company."

The fingers of my left hand take a sweep on the brush aluminium work surface and return with a sprinkle of icing sugar.

"So you allow him to roam the city centre?" she assumes.

"Have you tried talking to him lately?" I challenge.

"Certainly I have. You bet. He's my son."

Liz and I haven't had an argument for days, but the new Luke issue is breaking the peace.

"The guy's nearly sixteen, Liz. We can't tie a rope around his waist and haul him in, can we?"

"He would be better off living here, in a family." This scheme is on her mind, like a poisoned tart.

"With Mr and Mrs Noggins, do you mean? Moving him here? Luke?"

"Why certainly, Noah. His behaviour is getting more unpredictable by the week. How much effort is he putting into revision?"

"He's burning the midnight candles, I can assure you."

"Aren't you worried about him?"

"How is it going to help him? moving here?"

Another piece of my family was at risk.

"How does Luke behave around your place? I often wonder," she tells me. "Shut up in that dull old place of yours, over the hill."

I'm stunned for a few seconds by her charming depiction. "Doesn't the boy deserve a bit of freedom?"

"Freedom? What are you talking about?"

"So you require a definition these days, do you?"

Her spotlights hold me in their cold intensity, like Walt Disney in his chest freezer. "What does your idea of freedom mean?" she asks. "It doesn't have any significance for me."

"We already agreed that Luke lives with me."

"You're self-centred."

"If Luke agrees to hang out with me, that's his choice," I explain.

"Why don't you put him first?" she fumes.

"The boy goes nowhere unless he wants to." That's unless medical science fails during the interim.

"You know he'd be better off with us. Consider it," she suggests. "Luke has an aptitude for computer science. Frank is only too pleased to help him."

"You should realise that I'm determined to keep Luke with us...at Big Pink... at any cost. That's not negotiable."

"We'll see about that," she says. She examines me from a sardonic angle. "You're not fit."

"In what sense are you talking about?" She's not going to label me as a failed father.

"Luke and you are always fighting. He turns up here complaining about you."

"Luke and I need to get our heads around a few issues," I concede.

"He can't do anything right, as far as you're concerned. Just because he doesn't enjoy kite flying, or balloon flying, like you do," she objects. "What normal boy is interested in those ridiculous hobbies of yours?" she says fiercely.

"Why shouldn't he be?" No mention of inheriting my business.

Elizabeth slips into resonant silence, sharpening her focus.

"Better than messing about with those computer chips," I say. "That can't be very healthy, can it?"

"You're always critical of him. Why shouldn't he be interested in computers? You are only hostile because my husband works in the IT business."

"Remember the eight-track cartridge machine your Dad used to have in his Ford Capri?" I tell her.

"Don't be ridiculous, Noah."

"Trust me, I'm more in touch with the zeitgeist than most. There's no point scoffing, because I see a massive pile of discarded boxes in the future... that nobody's interested in anymore."

"You're ridiculous, Noah. I don't want to hear this."

"Maybe you're thinking that he will help the dino...help Frank with the business one day. Is that what you're scheming about with the computers?"

Plainly this scheme hadn't yet occurred to her. I was putting brilliant ideas into her head. "You promote your set of redundant ideals. Don't you want Luke to make a success of his life?"

"He has everything he needs at our house," I argue.

"He doesn't have Frank to teach him about computers."

"I think Frank knows what he should go and do."

"Unlikely my husband is ever going to follow your advice," she tells me.

"That depends on the quality of the advice," I say.

"You might as well face the truth. Leave him out of your plans, Noah."

"That's for me to decide," I reply.

"Exactly," she says. "Mug up."

"He has more space to develop around our place." *My* place that is.

"Look, you might as well drink a cup of tea, while you're waiting," Liz offers.

"I just came from Angie's café," I explain. In fact, after that double espresso, my eyes are like flying saucers.

"How would you like a slice of cake?"

I bang my rib cage. "Bad for the old pump."

"Then can I get you something else?"

"I wouldn't turn down a nice cold beer."

Elizabeth heads over to her gigantic refrigerator without comment and extracts a chilled beer for me. One of her husband's, Frank's, chilled beers. She twists off the cap without hesitation, plucks out a fancy glass and pushes the whole arrangement over.

"Careful, it's lively." She claims a high stool next to mine at the breakfast bar. She's transforming the interior of her house into a Hollywood film set. Archie Leach would be perfectly at ease here. She poses on the high stool like a sexy college kid.

I pour the beer carefully; keeping tabs on the tremble; and then sip. "This isn't too bad at all, Elizabeth."

"At last you found something in common with him."

"Tastes good," I admit.
"So how is Angela today? What's she getting up to?"
"You need *me* to tell you?" I goad.
"She lives with you, doesn't she?"
"Doesn't she pop around to catch up?" I wonder.
"I haven't seen her in weeks," Liz admits.
So how *is* Angela? "Thriving. You know what the girl's like. She leads an amazingly busy and sociable life." I can see every sign that Liz's new life is demonstrably busy and full.
"You saw her earlier? Did you say?"
"Just to check out that she's all right," I say. I'm enjoying the icy fizzle of beer on my lips.
"So does she manage to get to work on time, lately?"
I put a little spin into the beer bottle. "Most times, she does."
"What about her love life? Does she have another boyfriend?"
"Could be. Not sure."
"Better if she doesn't have her head turned. I'd rather she was focussed and independent," she argues.
"I don't expect any introduction soon," I assure her.
"You suspect she's going out with another boy then?" she surmises.
"Technically she's already classified as a 'mature student,'" I lament.
"She was never like this as a little girl," Liz recalls, wistfully. Like what?
"Come on, Liz, ease up on the girl, she's just finding her feet." She didn't want to stay in Kansas. Would she grow homesick?
"You're far too soft and easy going with her. She's completely wild, or so it looks to me."
"Well, I can't always work as private detective."
"Oh yes, that would suit you, wouldn't it. Playing Philip Marlowe," she tells me.
"Angela just has a complicated existence right now. But she isn't the only one," I add.
"What's complicated about working at a café?" she wants to know.
"It's surprising."
"We were too busy studying, to take jobs."

"That isn't all we were up to," I have to remind her.

"But we managed to study... and there were too many books to read, too many new movies and ideas to discuss."

"Angie reads a lot of books. I found her last night. I believe she goes to the cinema."

"Not towards her exams," Liz reminds me. "That is different to doing those things for pleasure. But they need to be done."

"Yes. I take your point. Though she has to make some money, to help pay for university studies. She was working hard in the café today. Working the cash register. Looking responsible and grown up."

My former partner doesn't look convinced. "There's no sign of her getting back to study. Is that the kind of future we want for her?"

First I take another gulp of Frank's well-brewed beer, then I put my foot into my mouth. "What do you do? In that cake shop? If you don't wait on people?" I gag.

There's enough flame in her eyes to roast several sacks of nuts.

"I offer employment to people. I have four shops around the city, with expansion plans for other cities. Why should I both to explain the difference to you?"

It was true, Frank put up the initial capital, but after that she expanded due to her own hard work and acumen.

"Forgive me," I say. Unfortunately she doesn't sell any humble pie. You can't easily get the better of Liz, try as hard as you like.

"Angela's an intelligent girl, in her own way. Why don't we help her to become a success?"

"There's no reason why not, Lizzie," I agree.

"Don't call me Lizzie," she tells me.

"What's the problem? Hook up with Angie some time."

At University people called Lizzie 'Witchy'.

"You have more chance to talk to her these days," she admits.

"I'm trying my hardest. She's been an elusive character, to be honest with you. I know because I lie awake some nights worrying about her." I instantly regretted this discouraging insight.

She looks at me with more sympathy. She has beautiful eyes, sharpened by her intelligence. They have a mesmerising mineral complexity. "Angela's well on the way to becoming a drop out."

"She doesn't know what she wants from life yet. She's a student of experience," I argue. "She wants to get some experience outside of student circles."

"She's never been *inside* student circles." Elizabeth's jungle eyes swirl and harden. "Unless you count compulsory education."

"She has research to conduct on the real world."

"That's ridiculous, Noah. Research? She has little experience of what you call the real world. When is she going to submit her paper?"

"In the end you decided to drop out of academia... and it never held you back."

This argument doesn't impress her, for reasons I have yet to explain. "If you allow the girl too much liberty, well, she'll be working in that café for the rest of her life."

"Nonsense, the girl just has to find herself first."

"I'm appalled to hear you spout that twaddle," she retorts.

"What do you mean?" I object.

"If she doesn't get herself directed soon, she will miss out entirely."

"No point going anywhere or doing anything," I say, "if you don't understand yourself first."

"That's just the kind of liberal nonsense I expect to hear from you."

"You can't change me," I vow.

"I wouldn't want to change you for the world, Noah."

We glare at one another, propped uncomfortably close on her tall stools. This is how I watch my memories of her, unending and silent, drowned in the lonely darkness.

I manage to swallow down the insult and she prises away her powerful eyes. But at least I have a chance to relax again.

She's justified in some of her concerns about Angie. There's more than a lick of pain and confusion for me too, in the struggle with our daughter.

Angie's whole existence is tangled up in her parents' history. This is because Lizzie got pregnant while she was studying at university. I agreed that she should have an abortion, given the circumstances. Instead Elizabeth decided to have the child and to marry me. Despite the problems involved, we were ecstatically happy and the future seemed to slot into place. The outside world hadn't caught up with our way of thinking, but we didn't calculate parental and societal attitudes. Not for nine months.

It's agony to understand that Liz and I are irreconcilable. She's a determined woman and she knows her own mind. Obviously I have a lot of admiration for those qualities, even though she can be as tough as tough. Why did she drop me in the middle of our life journey, half way across the ocean?

Although I know she has a few ideas about *me* too.

"I suffered another heart incident," I confess.

"Another?" She's clearly shocked. "What does that signify?"

I'm still more comfortable discussing my life and death adventures with her. We've known each other since school days; although we didn't undress each other until we reached university. She didn't allow me to touch her until I proved myself smart enough in a seminar, or had made my first significant political protest. That's how we used to impress a girl. These days they go out and shoot all their classmates.

Unlike your record and book collection, you can't take back a store of shared memories: all the parties, the gigs, the festivals and holidays. She and I were married in our final year at university and she gave birth to Angie while I was taking my finals. We had no reason to post Angie off to be second marked.

We're not marching on the same side any more. Even in your personal life you're either a unilateral disarmer or not. I'm not exactly in a position of strength. If I can't share my terrible secrets with her..? But I have to be more discrete with my medical files. I can't throw myself on Elizabeth's charity any longer. They say that a diamond lasts forever, but not under a sledgehammer.

"What exactly did the consultant mean? A complication?" she enquires.

"He didn't offer the exact details," I say. How could I explain the freak component in the aorta artery? My heart's under siege but I have to keep up some defences. They'd already reserved a cloud for me, but I had to keep a reality check.

"The hospital is liable if they messed up your operation," Liz reminds me.

"I can't claim to be the expert," I reply. I'm backtracking already, because I know the one technical detail that counts.

"You must be devastated by this setback," she argues.

"I'm trying to carry on with my life, as per normal," I claim.

"So you are in decent shape? Mentally, I mean?"

"Let's just say, I'm trying to stay in one piece."

"Right, Noah, so you have to change your life style."

"How come?"

"Have you looked at your diet recently? You don't eat properly these days."

I absorb the suggestion. "There are plenty of nuts and berries in my diet, I can assure you. The demands of my new life situation aren't helping," I blab.

"What's that supposed to mean?" she wonders, shifting her bottom.

"You know, the people who are close to us, the people who are no longer so close to us."

"Shouldn't you be getting over that episode, at least?"

"Pulling us in one direction, and then in another direction..."

"Isn't that your own affair or, should I say, your *affairs*?"

"How can we be saved, unless we choose to cut them out of life altogether?"

"Sometimes it is necessary," she told me.

"How civilised that is. How comforting to reach an agreement," I comment.

"You don't want to be left behind, do you Noah?"

"I suppose that we need other people... otherwise we wouldn't bother, would we?"

"Change is hard to accept," she says. I heard the deliberate echoes.

"Do we lose interest in someone, or is it really our own self that we become disillusioned with?" I consider.

"Either way we have to adjust," she argues.

"Or we go back to square one," I suggest.

"We have difficult decisions to make."

"While we still have enough time and money," I remark.

"Why certainly Noah, because what would be the point? What would be the purpose of change and self-discovery otherwise?"

We gaze into the barrel of another futile argument; as if trying to break the private images that had already been shattered.

"Is there something very wrong with your heart, Noah?"

The change of tack catches me by surprise, with one set of thoughts adjusting to another like cross-cutting waves.

"How's that? Very wrong with my heart?"

"That's right. What do you know?"

She waits expectantly from the stool, with her gorgeous eyes wide, her long legs, so intimate and familiar to me, gently crossed. Even if I survive I have been cut out forever.

"This is something I'll just have to live with," I argue.

"Can't they make good their mistake?"

"I told you already."

"You must be worried out of your wits," she concludes.

"I shan't go out to celebrate," I admit.

She stares as if she can't believe the man she sees or imagines I will vanish in a moment. "What's happened? You can't tell me or you don't want to?" She drops any hint of expression from her face.

"What I mean to say is... that the specialist explained... that one of my heart valves is wrecked."

Her eyes flicker over me and she gently shakes her head.

"It's quite serious, to be honest with you," I say. As she had driven me to the heart hospital that day a little honesty was not out of place.

"Is it life threatening?" she wondered.

"To me, it is," I reply.

She puts hands on her hips and leans back on the stool, just not to quite imperil herself. "Aren't you devastated?"

"I'm worried."

"What's to be done about this, Noah?"

"I've taken up yoga," I tell her.

"Yoga? Is that enough?"

"Not really."

"Yoga's never been one of your interests," she says.

"Not when you find yourself single again...and you're just shy of forty nine... as I am."

I want to forget all my troubles by tying myself up in even more knots.

"I'm surprised you can find the time... even if you're able to relax enough to begin to..."

"You shouldn't under-estimate the gentler arts. Not until you try them yourself," I retort.

"No, well, if you think that may help. You're not joking, are you?"

"Would I pull your leg, Liz?"

"You look so much better than you did," she informs me.

"I'd turned into a skeleton, before I went in for the op, hadn't I?"

"I don't know why they pump people full of drugs these days. We have powerful natural alternatives," she says. "But you shouldn't disregard medical advice entirely. That isn't what I am saying."

The specialist more or less told me to go jump in a lake. If you listen hard, you can almost hear a splash. My ex's words were appreciated, yet it was difficult to hear the concern in her voice, without picking up an underlying emotion. We're way past love Elizabeth and I. Love looks like a dot in the Pacific Ocean from this vantage point. She prefers to remember our married life as a nightmare. This kind of sympathy is hardly worth feeling. It's only a tormented sketch of the original painting.

"Did you have another heart attack?" She doesn't give up the investigation. The marbled green orbs hypnotise me.

"No, no, it wasn't another heart attack. There's an artificial valve inserted into the artery. Inserted when I had the bypass. This moved about inside me, apparently, and that caused me pain." I was too close to the truth here. I didn't like it.

"I understand. Oh, yes, I see."

She gazed at me along her cute nose, still bumped and freckled after all these years. It got broken when she was ten years old, on a Guides' trip to the New Forest.

"Do you? Do you really see?" I returned.

She ran straight into a low lying branch at full tilt. Before I came along.

Her intense eyes began without emotion, then tightened focus. "So what is the hospital intending to do about your valve?"

No doubt I stare mysteriously back. "They can't do anything about the valve."

"What do we have a health service for?" she wonders.

"I don't know," I admit.

By this stage everything is being processed by the left side of my brain.

"Can't you get another opinion?"

"Why should I need another opinion, Liz? Do you think this is election time?"

"Can't they offer you another operation?"

"Only to further reduce my weight," I observe.

"You're telling me that the doctors can't put this mistake right?"

"The body isn't a collection of nuts and bolts," I argue. That's precisely what my body has become; like one of those put-it-together-yourself vintage sports car kits.

"The surgeon had better do something about this," she warns.

She'll have her finger back on my pulse soon.

I gulp back the final inches of Frank's speciality beer.

"The specialist promised to write to me again." I make the guy sound like Boswell. "I'll get regular check-ups. Hospital appointments as required. Learn how to take better care of myself." Take care of my effects would be more accurate.

"My god."

"I know."

She observes me with some anguish. "This is disturbing. We noticed such a huge improvement. You really had your puff back, didn't you."

"What can I say? *C'est la vie*," I tell her.

Previous rancour falls away from her eyes. If I'd said something good then I didn't object.

Timothy Sheer bounces downstairs to join us. He's prepared for the big kick off in his Bristol City shirt. "Hiya, Dad!" Thick glowing copper hair like his mother's, how it used to be, clashing a bit with the red colour of the football strip.

"Hello boy," I exclaim, ruffling his hair up, giving him a hug. "What position you playing in today?"

"Striker!"

"Centre forward. Did I really need to ask?" I respond.

My terrors that Darth Invader would steal his love has proved farfetched. You always worry that the second husband will become substitute super-hero. But I've acquired a bit of superstar status myself in the role of distant parent, absent Dad.

"Are you sure you're well enough, Noah?" enquires his mother.

"Well enough, *are you joking?*"

"No even you are joking about this," she replies.

"Much better to be off out in the fresh air, than to skulk about the four walls of your cave." Like any old flat-footed dinosaur glued to the screen.

"Then you know what you're doing, do you?"

"Totally."

"So long as you don't get caught out," she warns.

"Don't worry."

Suddenly I am intolerant of non-sporting males. I've noticed Noggins' snooker table in the front room. Liz used to enjoy going to the football with me. Now it is a rowdy outlet for sociopath barbarians.

"We have to be off," I announce, grasping Tim's hand. "Kick off time is nigh." I sound like the match referee in the sky.

She gives me a sceptical and doubting look. "If you really must. Let me know about any problems."

"See you later, Mum."

"See you then, Timmy." At which she treats him to a litany of don't and dos.

Our son swivels between our two expressions. He surveys the opposing shores of the Gibraltar straits. What a disaster it's been for him, as for everyone else. We used to take him for a regular Sunday morning kick about. The guy stole my wife from me, but he refuses to deal with the consequences. Even a thief should have a thought. A person has to be rounded in life; and that includes some physical exercise, not just with other blokes' wives.

We walk back through together from the kitchen. Liz watches us out into the front garden, still displaying that hideous Cupid statue, in the middle of a water feature, that springs a capricious arrow. I can't even bear to look at the mischievous little guy.

Frank has his own computer company: Computer Links Appointments. Works six days and the best part of seven. What did she ever see in him?

"See you later Tim. Don't get over excited."

This is my last year at Marienbad. I'm stranded in the middle of an overgrown, blocked off maze. I'm the amnesiac killer.

You don't want to go there. You're lost if you do.

# Chapter 10

Through the eyes of an eight year old Ashton Gate football stadium looms as an heroic amphitheatre. A few light-year centuries ago I was a boy the same age as my son, with similar impressions. I can tell that he's almost overcome by awe and anticipation, as we close on the ground, from our riverside walk.

After we push through turnstiles I get Tim a match programme; a home game souvenir to add to his bulging collection. We scan the Bristol City team sheet quickly, decrying the inclusion of one player to the omission of another, while anticipating the brilliance of a new signing.

We greet familiar faces among home support, as we navigate towards our seats. Immediately we try to impress with match omens and up to date news briefs. Sometimes I sound like a studio pundit in the making. My brother's always been a Bristol Rovers boy, disgusted by my allegiance to 'the pirates'. As a result he's reluctant to talk about football with me, unless Rovers have a recent triumph to gloat over. This could have been a shared passion between brothers, as books and films never were.

Timothy grows restless at my elbow, pulling and complaining. I am trying to keep that recent conversation with Liz to the back of my mind. Yet she is striking at my frontal lobes, which are the most influential, according to brain boffins. I am also concerned about Angela since she crashed out this morning. Liz used to discuss the idea of Angie becoming a lawyer, defending women's rights, championing human rights around the world in international law. Maybe this put undue pressure on the girl. She'd have our full support in any job or profession she chose. We'd shell out our last penny or brain cell to get her through legal school up in London, or wherever they hang out. Not that I have any appetite for lawyers.

"University would only ruin my life," Angela insists.

I can't say she doesn't read interesting books or doesn't take any interest in the world.

I'm paranoid about Luke prowling the pedestrianized city centre. He probably stood on a skate board, careering over concrete surfaces; assuming he doesn't tumble over his flares or fringe. Some of his stunts on the board are impressive - they *look* impressive - I have to admit. What's the harm in this off the wall behaviour? My former wife and her team of crack lawyers are less impressed by the sport. Should he mess up with a tricky move, perhaps a skim along the railings, Luke will be back to his mother's house, as fast as the plaster may set. Then he'll be climbing the walls of that freshly papered prison instead. Then I wouldn't have a leg to stand on, would I. He'd be rolled out in front of the magistrate again, faster than he could whiz around a drained swimming pool.

How can I molly-coddle a six feet sixteen year old? When I was his age I was studying James Dean; the shy troubled gaze, quicksilver charisma, and the gently hurt voice. In the contemporary era I have been recast in the father's role, like Vanessa Redgrave going through Chekov's. I'm all cardigan and blood pressure, even though I still own a leather jacket. These modern kids are equally as tough as our generation. Except that we can never predict the direction of their rebellion. We'd have more luck trying to predict the next big technological breakthrough; like growing new hearts or something. But I can't afford to just stand idly by, with my eyes closed, as I feel him swish past: Especially when love has turned to rivalry.

I direct Tim along an aisle towards our pair of reserved plastic seats. After settling, we stare about at the filling stadium around, as red plastic transforms, piece by piece, into a multi-coloured weave of humanity. Season ticket prices have shot up considerably. Next year I'll have to donate one of my organs to pay for them. That's not including the appendix, which is the most detached organ.

There's a crescendo of cheers as our players jog out for their warm up. You will never catch me doing that intense physical stuff these days, I remind myself: apart from occasional sex, when there's a chance. Obviously the thousand year old man is sensitive to vigorous exercise.

The stadium announcer reads out the team sheets, before reading out special announcements and other football info. There's a definite feeling of community as well as rivalry to football; which you re-join at every match attended. Our team captain throws up a coin - it was probably a brass farthing when I attended as a lad - and 'we' appear to have won the toss. Let's hope this isn't our only victory at the final whistle. Teams have to change ends. So this arrangement takes time to complete, to the ref's satisfaction.

Then, as the players take up their positions of readiness, the speaker music is switched off. A roar of anticipation and excitement swirls around the tinny stadium, filling the atmosphere within seconds. The match ball balances on the centre-circle spot, as if culturally confused. The referee raises a hand up, as if consulting with the top referee in the sky, sends the split pea in his whistle to a frenzy, and so he starts the game off.

My mind tends to wander. Not that I'm bored by the match or sleepy. My senses are following the action. But my thoughts and feelings are going elsewhere, following the terrain of my past life. This may be a way to clear my head, or to cleanse the old wounds, as when I play a board game while listening to instrumental music.

Watching football isn't equivalent to challenging Kasparov, I guess. There's nobody here to ask me awkward questions. Though I am not exactly alone with my thoughts either. The experts at the hospital already warned me. I'm trying hard to follow Wickham's advice how to live. I gave up all robust physical sports, including my squash games and tournaments, and even signed up for yoga classes. There's no incense or lotus position here, only a chilly atmosphere needling into my bones. What type of stress-free and relaxed life is possible for any contemporary person? It kills many people just trying to get to work in the morning. Does family life allow these luxuries of time and space, talking of the contemporary period?

According to Wickham's advice, too many emotional pile-ups will have a fatal impact. How can I protect myself in the immediate future? Then also a calm mind and life isn't necessarily going to save me, or extend my time here on Earth. As Dylan wrote, Time's an ocean, but it ends on the shore.

I have to transform myself into a west country Confucius, just to stay sane. Then again Leonard Cohen decided to become a Buddhist monk. I could root out the old texts, get myself into the garb, follow Cohen's footsteps. The Chinese don't scare me.

The faulty plastic valve broke in my heart, like a snapped crab's claw. The surgeon fitted this ingenious component to save and extend my life, but somehow it was sub-standard, causing it to split and move, while inserted in my body. That's what caused the intense pain that day, followed by shock. Somehow the component didn't break up entirely, so it was not lethal. That's why I have a memory about it; why I can think about what happened. This artificial valve could disintegrate at some unspecified moment. Then it will be curtains and floral tributes. You get a new car with a faulty breaking system or a prematurely exploding airbag, something negligent like that, then the manufacturer will recall it for replacement. But men are irreplaceable, often, it would seem.

There I was about town, enjoying the sensation of being a new man. I had that fresh lease of life. But my heart's working out again; pumping away. The wise guys say that my heart was swollen, but the swelling will disappear. The heart is just a big muscle of course. It doesn't feel anything! It doesn't have any nerves! There's a cracked plastic valve in the artery wall. They certainly have a bloody cheek. The mechanism that cleverly opens and shuts, opens and shuts, like the doors into your hypermarket; ad infinitum; allowing the blood to flow, oxygen to oxygenate, but which harbours a potential catastrophe. Causes me to wake up in the middle of the night, going through cold sweats, gasping, frightened to death. But I don't want to frighten the people who are nearest and dearest. Maybe I just had a bad experience. Nobody gets out of here alive, as Hank Williams wrote, and it always gets you in the end.

"When is our striker gonna kick on the goal?" Timothy objects.

"What's happened to our approach play?" I return.

He's noticed that I don't put as much of myself into the match as usual. He's becoming a passionate supporter of City. He's learning to stand up from his seat to curse. But you can't stay terrified for a whole ninety minutes. Life continues.

The surgeon explained that heart failure can happen at any time. It could be while I am tucked up in bed, either with Rachael or with a wretched mug of malty drink. I could be in the garden clipping my roses, or I could be sitting here at Ashton Gate football stadium. Death ain't fussy.

"We're all in the same leaky boat," Owen Hopkins said.

Not anymore, am I. I'm the captain of my own boat now, which is a type of holed rusty hulk, dropped to the bottom; worse than the Great Britain when they first towed her back up the river, dragged the ship from its graveyard and began to patch her up for tourists.

The feeling of peril makes me sweat; the weird calamity of collapsing and dying within seconds, right in front of my boy's eyes. Such a terrible memory would be branded onto his mind forever. Although I still wanted to take him to the game today didn't I, and insisted to his mother. Who's going to take him to the football otherwise?

We're sat together in this noisy, unpredictable place; my son and I and twenty one thousand other souls, men, women and children. Everyman's sporting wisdom is reverberating in our ears. I have no choice other than to sit tight, a tempting target for fate, until the game is over.

Crowd noise whips up. The ball is struck long down field. It's laid off to our centre forward, whose quick pass leaves the Grimsby defence like a tattered fishing net. The ball is driven low and hard into the left hand corner of the net. The Bristol City crowd rises to their feet in expectation of a certain goal.

Unfortunately the Grimsby goalie manages to scamper across his goal line. Doubling back he manages to nudge the ball away, in a miraculous last ditch fingertip save. The crowd's fever dies back to a rumble of muttered disappointment, banished by a round of thunderous, encouraging applause. This vigorous excitement beats off the cold, although it might cause the stadium to collapse.

I have to get on with my life, don't I. I have to persist with all my normal activities at home and work. It would be daft to turn inwards and live like a terrified recluse. I understand how hard it is not to brood about the past, when the future's as unpredictable as nitro-glycerine. I still have responsibilities - wardrobes full of them. Meanwhile I'll take a few pints of best bitter, keep up with the local music scene and keep half an eye open for the ladies.

The Grimsby 'keeper kicks long, creating a two on two situation at the other end. Our defenders try to force their second striker out wide, but somehow he manages a jinx and cuts back inside, towards the area, throwing a dummy pass. At the end of a strong run he manages to get a shot in, that swerves beautifully through the air, right into the top corner. Our goalkeeper stares back over his shoulder, gormlessly up towards the corner of his own net, where the ball was stuck for a few seconds, more like a basketball. A cracking goal; a real sizzling banana kick. Ronaldo would have been proud of that one. But it wasn't for the City team. We're a goal down to Grimsby already and we're sick. You couldn't get a parrot from Brazil that's sicker than we are at this moment.

"Jammy bloody bums!" Tim squeals.

If only Elizabeth could be here to enjoy his word play. The guy next to me is even less equivocal.

I cast a determined stoic glance towards the celebrating 'Mariners'. "Don't get into a depression yet, Tim boy. There's loads of time to roll 'em over," I tell him.

How's Lizzie going to feel about my demise? It would require a grotesque effort to be smug about it; even if acrimony has taken the place of matrimony. I can't say how she is going to be affected. But I can't help being curious, or hoping for the big tearful goodbye. How do you mourn an ex-husband, while you resent their intellect and good looks? I guess she'll be upset to receive the news, if only for old time's sake.

She may have more tender feelings towards me, when I stop putting in personal appearances. They say that absence is a brilliant aphrodisiac to dead marriages. I'm not going through this evil trip just to make her feel bad. I've had to reconsider my legacy. I've had to reappraise my character, if only through the glass darkly of a broken marriage and a damaged heart.

"I had to tell you, Noah. I really had. That my feelings have changed," she explained. She reached for a formulaic phrase. But I already knew the score. I hadn't objected to previous formulaic phrases. She made this confession while getting undressed for bed.

"What does this mean?" I said.

"I'm going to have to leave you."

"Leave me? Why?"

"The plan is to move out."

She laid this on me without warning, although she cried every night for days after that. She stifled her sobs into her pillows and soaked her tears into my pyjamas. What should I do to console her? How was I ever going to sleep peacefully again myself? My heart just freezes at these memories. These memories circulate through me like cobra venom. I put my arms around her and tried to comfort her. What else could I do? She wouldn't like to talk about this now. There are intimacies that she chooses to forget. She disappeared from my life, while I sit tight for the end of the line.

They went out for a drink together after a lecture. She and Frank. I realised that. They started going out for lunch together. That was more suspicious and alerted me. He'd pull up outside Big Pink, in that armoured personnel carrier of his, and let her back out. What had they been up to after their sorbet? They were following a Master's Degree in business studies. I didn't realise they would go to town on that.

Lizzie finally got the free time and motivation to return to Uni. She resumed her studies, changing her subject. Frank Noggins offered her the support and advice to be a student and to write an essay again. She went to the pub with a group of fellow students after evening lectures. There was nothing harmful about that, until she claimed to love the guy.

All right, his business had been performing well. But you have to ask, where's the soul in high tech? How could she sacrifice our ideals? Forget about our struggles in the past? Why couldn't she sleep with the dinosaur, if she really fancied him, without wanting to marry him? Why did she have to jump ship in mid ocean? Why not have a sordid affair? Her fling with the dinosaur had to be pure and principled: Like the struggle against apartheid.

"Noah, it's finished... We're finished." These weird dreadful words from the woman I loved. I looked at her in horror, as if she was the double of herself. It shook me, how a relationship can take on an entirely new spin. Our emotions are actors with the insufferable versatility of an Olivier, after he blacked up and mugged up as a Jamaican busboy for *Othello*. No longer was I an incorrigible original, but an insufferable old fool and hopeless case. Amazing. The times they were a'changin'.

Shaken, blind-sided, I considered the disintegration of our relationship. What was marriage? It was our love and friendship, our being together and being happy, that mattered. I can't help being a left brained guy in a right brained world. I hadn't fully realised how unhappy and discontented she was; although she'd become more disgruntled and awkward. It was like finding a set of tree roots had grown under our house, so much ruining the foundations that it required demolition. I lost my peace of mind watching these changes in Elizabeth. I didn't know how to respond to her evenings away, or the uncharacteristic excuses. We were going nowhere fast, and I couldn't see any mutual escape route.

It was never the idea to get married, in the first place. I've never seen the charm of churches, to be honest with you. But Elizabeth was a once in a lifetime girl, and how could I let her get away? Anyway her family's Christian morals were offended; when they found out she was pregnant. But I surrendered willingly at the time. I was waiting there at the end of the aisle, as expected. They insisted on a grand wedding, at Bristol cathedral; where they'd been praying for years. I was hiding in a morning suit. I had this image of myself as a peacock, on his big day. But I was just a turkey in ribbons. They had to sew a few extra hoops into Lizzie's dress.

We lost our freedom. We gave our lives up for the baby, and Liz dropped out of Uni. Dylan married Sara and still managed to write all those great songs, I explained to my lovely new pregnant wife. We didn't have to compromise. It was just hard to avoid.

We tasted poverty. We were trapped in our small flat. But we were as tight as the ring on an anchor. That's how we were during those days, with a screaming baby. We knew the dangers we faced, but we had a strong grip.

The referee blew for half time. Timothy nags me for a can of coke and a chocolate bar. So we leave our seats for a while.

"We're going to lose," Tim moans.

"Give them time."

"We're hopeless."

"No, we're playing some good football. Set your team formation, get the right tactics. Allow the team to play well... the goals will follow."

The boy's not convinced, on the first half performance. But he'll carry some great memories of attending football matches with me. My grandfather first took me to games. I easily recollect the flavour of his pipe tobacco, aromatic on the frozen air. He'd press Everton mints into my gloved hands, which I would unwrap with difficulty, rather than to risk frostbite. He had great wiry white eyebrows, leathery skin over sharp cheek bones that seemed imperishable. He kept my hands warm by knocking them together with his. He'd utter phlegmatic criticism of the action, without any cursing, as the beautiful game was frustrated again.

Tim's old enough to keep some impressions for the future. We take them along to the game to mould them, to bring them up right; to offer the same chances and excitements as we had: we fathers, I mean. I like to think that Tim and I are good friends, as well as father and son, as his young heart patters along after mine. I know he spends more time with his stepfather on balance, but I'm still the sporting super hero. He can't be that close to Frank Noggins, despite an armoury of electronic games and toys, trying so hard to show their love and to impress. But what's going to happen after I'm substituted?

The refreshment queue dwindles, allowing us to reach the counter. Then we take our tea, coke and chocolate bars back to our seats. There are grumbles as we pass back along our row. These guys can scream and whine like a gang of hard bitten alley cats. The masochistic joy of supporting a comparatively small club is unbeatable. Though I can't say it beats topping leagues, or getting promotion or lifting trophies.

The referee gazes up into the sky, as if summoning the elusive gods of entertainment: he checks the moment from his watch and gets the second half underway.

How can Liz tolerate a swap of fathers? How can you permit a stranger like him to bring up our son, rather than to keep faith with the natural father? I've reason to resent the influence of Frank Noggins. She put me through that whole custody struggle and added heart break to insult. He never impressed me with his fat cigars and games of bar bloody billiards.

There was a photograph of them stepping out of a white Cadillac; no expense or ritual spared. He was flashing his radiator grill of caps, while Liz was looking radiant as a girl. I didn't attempt to gate-crash their happy day, second time around. I try to keep with the good vibrations of life. Most of the time.

There was just *one* time, when I failed to keep negative vibrations in check. For some reason I had the crazy idea of going around there, with the intention of killing him. I don't know what got into me, I know it was stupid and a mistake. I could have dug up a concrete road with the bad vibrations. I didn't rationally consider the chances of killing a big bloke like Frank with my bare hands. After all he's an erstwhile member of the Territorials. He's got a rib cage that wouldn't shame a shire horse: hands like medicine balls. Somehow the facts of Noggins's physical capabilities escaped me. I wasn't prepared to sit at home feeling sorry for myself. I'd go around there and let him know how I felt.

So I jumped into my big nosed Gallic automobile and made their business my own. On the way I cruised through red lights; I mounted a pavement along Colston Avenue, causing panic and escaping lethal collision by millimetres. As it was a Friday evening the centre was crowded with relaxing punters, strolling between clubs and bars. I managed to scatter a big crowd of smart people, waiting for an opera to begin, outside Colston Hall.

They had to physically toss themselves out of the way, many of them. There was a small column in the next evening's newspaper about me, or the antics of a mad driver. Luckily the police had something about an old foreign car, but nobody could give an accurate model type or a full registration. But I'm a champion balloonist, not a psychopath.

Amazingly in one piece, I pulled up outside his place. After grinding up into the kerb and falling out into the road, I strode out towards her new home. I ripped aside the wooden gate, lunged up a front path and smashed my hand on the bell.

"Let's be having you, Frank boy. Come and show your face!" I shouted.

But I was answered only by a long suburban silence.

A hallway light illuminated the coloured glass of their door. They were inside hiding. I pictured them sheltering behind their sofa; whispering to each other in panic about what to do. Calling the police was an obvious tactic. But that easy option didn't come into my mind. I wasn't thinking straight or cool. Frank had his contacts in this city and his police mates would turn up in rapid time. Faster than an ambulance. But I would get to him faster than even they could.

It happens that Frank has a hideous, kitsch statue in the middle of his front garden. He's proud of it and even had it transplanted between properties, as he's climbed the ladder, like an overweight Jack. It's what you'd describe as a Cupid figure, balancing on one foot at the edge of a marble bowl, with a bow pointed at the moon, with water dribbling from his mouth.

So I strode out into the middle of his front lawn and managed to pick this statue up in my arms. I felt every vein popping, every sinew ripping. Having achieved this lift, I struggled back to the winding path with it. With all my strength I staggered back towards the house and heaved it through their living room window.

There was an almighty crashing and splintering. But as I looked into the recesses of their exposed living room, I began to understand that they really weren't at home. They were not hiding, attempting to wind me up, they were simply not indoors. But it was too late to be ashamed and disown the guy I'd been, just a few minutes beforehand. I couldn't turn back the clock, no matter how I disliked myself. They wouldn't hear about it, even if I hadn't been myself. In fact I was more out of character than ever. If there's something that women don't like it is masculine stress and aggravation.

The little god of love was wedged inside their living room. Only the rough bottoms of his feet were sticking out, as they'd broken off from the base. His face was pressed into their rug, as if after a night out on the town. He may have looked a light fellow, as he was floating off the grass, but he was only made of concrete after all. A thin jet of water shot up into the night sky, dousing Liz's new convertible.

They were not going to be happy with my contribution. What else could I do, other than to escape the situation? There was no point staring mournfully at the spot, waiting for the couple to return. Maybe they'd bought tickets for the opera that evening.

I might have been charged. I could have been banged up. Fortunately the neighbours didn't hear or see anything of the assault. The Noggins pad is detached and surrounded by thick shrubs. I'd arrived in the area like Steve McQueen. I had to touch up the body work after that and fill a small hole in the side panel. There was a scrape of paint along the kerbstone; and a lot more forensic evidence. Surely there aren't that many cool people in this city?

So I made a remarkable escape. Or they chose not to let on. Surely they didn't think that some freak event or alien being from space had tossed that statue into their living space. No, it wasn't only a matter of calling in the glaziers, because they required a frame and repairs to the brick work at the front of the house. I was a bit sheepish when I had to call around again, to claim my contact with Tim. But she didn't refer to the subject. Cupid didn't enter the conversation. That was the whole point, she chose to ignore it, as I ignored the lorry load of workers who were drinking mugs of fair-trade Kenyan tea on the lawn, between times of fitting new aluminium frames, state of the art, as well as mixing a bag of cement and moving around a pallet of fresh bricks. I pretended not to see them and didn't ask. I hoped that she would think I was jealous.

If they sought any revenge, it was when they put that dreadful statue back. The little bastard was still in one piece.

Grimsby's defence is at sixes and sevens, scurrying about like ballerinas with a mouse on the stage. A miskick looks as if it is going out, yet the ball takes a wicked deflection and finishes in the back of the net.

A goal! We've equalled the scoring. The whole stadium, with Tim and I, erupts into joyful relief. The passage of a plastic sphere over a white line can release this euphoria. We are up on our feet, shaking clenched fingers towards the sky, with renewed belief in divine creation. The City team congregate for quick hugs and kisses, before trotting back to their own half ready to restart. The away team loses its spring, as the match resumes with extra intensity; the home team seeking a winner.

By half past four the sky is closing over us; a bloodless late-afternoon light drawing in, bringing the influence of a shivery mist from the close-by Avon and gorge. Floodlights come on, intensifying as darkness gathers; casting starry shadows around each dancing player on the pitch below.

Tim has settled back in dejection, in the popular belief that another score draw is probable. Grimsby might even steal it in injury time, given our luck this season. But I'm glad to be here and look forward to our next home game. As the clock winds down my attention wanders to the crowd around us; and I gaze over at those hundreds of faces in the opposite stand. I wonder if I - my distracted or worried expression - has been picked out by anybody over there, like a still head at a tennis match? Paranoia, most likely.

I notice that a full moon has emerged in the sky. I gaze up to a smoking moon and I am reminded of love, the past and of course about death. These ideas are not as romantic as they used to be. Gravity is failing me and negativity won't pull me through, as Bob Dylan remarked. He has an even drier sense of humour.

The referee blows for full time. Following our row out I hold Tim's shoulders, to prevent the danger of getting crushed. Even if City will be fortunate to reach mid-table this season, I'll be happy to see them to the end. The years of comparative cup and league glory feel long distant. I hope the team give Tim something to really cheer about in the future.

When we turn up at the Noggins' street I notice that Frank's tank is re-occupying the driveway. The dinosaur is back in his lair, after a Saturday afternoon trouble shooting session. I hold Tim's hand as if I'm never going to let him go, as we wander up their garden path. I set off the chimes of Canterbury and wait for Liz to crack open her watch gates again, to receive back her prisoner.

Tim is aware of my helter-skelter health history. After that bad trip to the London hospital he tends to cling. There's no doubt about it, he wants his real mother and father back. He wants this nonsense sorted out and to get life back to normal; our kind of 'normal'.

His new mother finally responds and pulls him tensely indoors, with barely an exchange of eye contact. Is she afraid that Frank and I might go cheek to cheek? Maybe she has some rear windows to replace.

This is definitely the worst moment of the week. Until I find the strength to point myself back around, stride past Cupid without so much as a side glance; then to let myself through the garden gate and climb back into the spotless automobile.

Whatever happened to the girl I loved?

# Chapter 11

Bob, Susan, Lizzie and me; we've been friends for ages. For about three light centuries I'd guess, since student days. And we've stayed friends ever since, come hell or high water as it often was. The Huntingdon marriage is still an unbroken rock; they're as crazy about one another as during student evenings, crammed into a snug of a quayside pub, smoking *Disc Bleu* and sharing a jug of real ale, while yakking about music and movies.

The only time I ever saw them suffer a fall out was after a Donovan gig. The singer/songwriter kissed Susan on request after he gave her his autograph. Bless her mellow yellow cotton socks, she told him to write his autograph on her lacy ladies handkerchief. Bob took exception and seriously lost it. To rebuff Bob's accusations she pointedly blew her nose on the handkerchief and threw it away. Then Bob, unable to retrieve the situation, felt as bad as Pablo Picasso eyeing young girls along the Parisian left bank.

Bob is still embarrassed by the memory, when it recurs. But I wouldn't hold Donovan responsible for the one serious row. I wouldn't criticise him for kissing Susan after his concert at the folk club that evening. 'Flower Power' holds a different meaning for Bob these days, as a keen gardener. That isn't a bad record after twenty years of marriage. More than you can say about Donovan's recordings. Bob and Susan still spin in the same groove. Whereas Liz and I had regular rows and crises. We were always the thermonuclear couple.

Would I have been forgiving if Lizzie had smooched George Harrison over a peace pipe, for instance? She was constantly singing the mantra of the quiet one. I found this passion out, when she showed me her bedroom, and its many rock star pictures on the walls, for the first time. As an amorous undergrad it can be hard to compete with Harrison even when he was a poster.

During our Uni days Lizzie and I were part of the 'in' crowd there. We were the stellar couple, much talked about on campus.

Student life is formative for many of us, but I can't underestimate the impact for us. When there was a demo in the Students' Union or a sit-down protest at the Chancellor's office, you could bet your bottom anti-dollar that Lizzie and I would be at the heart of it.

Our fresh passionate faces, legs crossed and fists in the air, captured in dots in alternative newspapers. The media always loved a young good-looking photogenic revolution. The cops frog-marched me down to the station to issue me with a warning. I took the caution, then got a letter from the university telling me that I was officially suspended. In response to this, our fellow students went on strike; and they set their banners out on the green; forcing them to reinstate me. Even to this day there are people, with longer memories and more conservative attitudes, who despise me for taking those radical stances. Although I've mellowed, considerably, of course I have.

Lizzie and I were never exactly the 'ring leaders' of these demonstrations, but we played our part. In contrast Susan and Bob were more inconspicuous. They restricted themselves to friendly debates. They hardly got their glasses steamed up. They agreed with many of our views and actions, but refrained from shaking their fists. Liz and I had the potential to be first class students as well as troublemakers. We were snarled up in radical politics and that crazy social scene. But then we had a marriage certificate before I was handed my degree certificate. How's that for double honours?

At the end of our last year Bob and Sue decided to go backpacking around the world. This was not then so much a predictable rite of passage, as for youth in the present era.

"Let's go, before we have responsibilities," Bob argued.

"In theory, that's wild," Lizzie admitted.

We had to pull out because Lizzie was already throwing up. Since we hadn't left the country yet, this couldn't be put down to travel sickness. She wasn't going to sail oceans, merely break water. Heart breaking for her.

"Maybe another time," I came back.

They were hitching across the States, while we were moving into our first rented flat. It should have been illegal to keep pets in a box that size.

We were preparing for the baby's arrival, as they went from San Diego to Los Angeles. I remember because I made the word association between babies and angels. I was busy painting the bambino's room, trying to make one pot spread over four walls. As Lizzie was booking her bed in the maternity ward, we got a card from the beatnik couple, that Bob had scrawled from the bed of a truck, while the pair of them crossed the Great Basin from Salt Lake City. Man, as teenagers we dreamed of making such a journey.

Meanwhile the new married couple was festering in that pokey flat, rubbing their pennies together. On their return Bob and Sue decided to go off on yet further travels; this time doing good. They taught English in Malaysia and undertook charity work in the poorer districts of Kuala Lumpur. We had black fungi and mildew spreading from the walls of our main bedroom, as if a scrofulous devil had coughed blood there. We'd been idealistic students, but we didn't imagine poverty. Not our own poverty, that is.

This wasn't a glamorous kind of poverty, such as I'd heard in songs or read about in literature. At least Woody Guthrie got to hitch a few rides, to hobo a few train lines and to hustle some action, to see a bit of his continent. In contrast I couldn't play two notes on a guitar or even sing down my nose.

"One day," Lizzie warned, "I'm going to release that scream pent up inside me."

I'd wince with shame, embarrassment and frustration. But as I already said, we had a strong grip in those days.

We never got far with our talk of seeing the world, though arguably we were the more adventurous couple.

More positively I was making my first move into running a business. I rented out an old work shed on the quayside. Grandad used to take me flying kites at the weekend and, curiously, the hobby always caught hold with me. I remember the evening my wife and I went out to celebrate our first 'product'. We made our premier kite, to my own design and colours. Every day Liz came down to the workshop to help out. We cut, sewed and packed our first order. This wasn't great art by any stretch of the imagination, but Lizzie was my muse.

Otherwise we were unemployable hippies, already married with a child, living in virtual poverty, relying on hand-outs from her parents. But I'll tell more about my kites and balloons later in the story, as I'm getting blown off course.

We still got out to the summer music festivals, despite the simple twists of fate. This included the Isle of Wight, big demos in London, with the infant Angie strapped to Lizzie's back, like a free cherub of the loving universe.

What was Bob and Susan's next move, on their return from Lumpur? They rented a couple of rooms above a Chinese restaurant in Clifton for the summer; and packed the place out with their spoils from the East, such as forest fetishes, blow pipes, penis sheaths, and the latest electronic gadgets. They had another five years of travelling and fun before they finally tied the knot. No wonder we were choked.

As far as I recall, they made their vows during a stop-over in Vegas. They stood before a 'minister' in a tartan suit, he told me, with a soft drinks salesman as a witness. They had a toast in Mango juice and drove all the way to Niagara Falls on their honeymoon. Figuratively speaking Bob cast aside his penis sheath as Sue got pregnant with their first child. At least it was more memorable than our own experience, when we conceived our first kid in a damp student bed-sit, rather drunk and not fully understanding what we were getting in to. They'd planned it all out, whereas we had a splitting condom under a scratchy blanket.

"They're following the original script," I observed.

I was stunned at our bad luck and stupidity. Somehow the spermatozoa had wisecracked their way through my prophylactic barrier. When you create a couple of cells they won't stop dividing. Then Liz refused to stop them.

I think it was only love and hurt and rage that got us through. We tended to keep our disappointments to ourselves. We knew that my business was beginning to work out by then. At first we were missing payments on the mortgage of our first house. I'd be damned if we relied on her parents. These changes of fortune didn't impact with our friends, Bob and Susan Huntingdon. They didn't have any snippets or snipes ready for us, or treat us to any pieces of the worldly wisdom, that they must have acquired from their travels and work. They're genuinely gentle people, not quick to judge. Though the temptation must have been there.

That's a rare thing.

Next weekend, on Saturday evening, the Huntingdons have invited me to their party. They're holding their annual double-celebration, for her birthday and their wedding anniversary. I'm ready to congratulate Bob for having killed two birds with one stone. I don't intend to let them down by staying away, despite a troubled mind.

Susan has a startled expression when she answers my call. The sight of me forces her to make an uncomfortable triple-take. Yes, this really is my new image. She gazes into my pallor as if wandering around a room dedicated to Rothko. Her face has the outlines of a speech bubble; I could guess what she was saying. Am I blind to a common sense that is obvious to her and everybody else? Should I have stayed at home for an early night with a hot drink?

"Hi, Sue!" I'm looking as if the post service just dropped me.

"You made it here after all," she tells me; smiling down from the tall doorway, trying to adjust to the change in my universe.

"Happy Birthday!" I declare, handing over the card and gift. "Congratulations!"

"Thanks, Noah, won't you join us?" she invites.

There's no running away. I convinced myself to get back into the swing of things.

It's a relief to get off the dangerous street, as any expedition is dangerous for a coronary sufferer. I luxuriate in the relief of their warm and familiar home; even if they have a Maori spear and a Japanese warrior helmet on display, to add menace to the traditional mirror and hat stand. Fortunately the original owners of these trophies aren't pursuing them in revenge.

"How are you, Noah? I can't believe you made it," Susan coos.

"Oh, I made it through," I explain, eyeing their Pacific paintings. "Back on my feet."

"I can see that. Are you out of breath?" she observes.

"No, out of breath, not in the least. You know about the steep hills of Clifton."

"Really like the jacket, Noah. Really cool."

"Thanks, Sue. Found this at the back of the wardrobe."

Essential Seventies Zimmerman. Swimming a bit in this black velvet jacket, against a white ruffled shirt, over black jeans: street illegal. The fringe is having to work hard though, on triple time. Then my toes are funnelled into a favourite pair of ankle boots, with decorative silver work from Toledo. Only my closest friends and I know that these boots were a precious gift from Liz: *'My true love, your boots of Spanish leather - Witchy xxx*

I was delighted that Susan had appreciated my togs and got all the references. I always make an effort for their double celebration. She can't help checking on my pallid visage again. My arm and leg muscles have decided to get wasted; while I'm getting used to holding myself together in the middle.

"The last time we saw you, when was that? Must have been when you first got home from the hospital," she considers. "That must have been some..."

This will be a constant theme of the hoot. A constant harping. Just when I imagine I'm getting towards the end of the labyrinth I lose the piece of string, and there seems to be another abrupt turning ahead.

Susan's perceptive enough to understand that I am not ironing my tennis shorts for next summer. She has memory traces about my angina, and those symptoms that left me permanently under the weather. These ailments have cleared up. So I no longer have to keep a weather eye, or resemble that thousand year old guy. But Susan's sensitive enough to know that I'm not back into the rose garden. Somehow I don't look so great or send a positive message. I haven't lost the negative vibe, or been able to eradicate a sense of anxiety, either from my face or my limbs. She is shocked and tries to work out the problem. She's worried and knows that I haven't returned to normal life, as they expect, or even my own version of normal life.

Even if surgery was successful at first glance, the dangerous fault-line has not gone away. The broken valve is lodged in my mind as well as my chest. I tell Susan as much as I can about my health, while being vague about the exact truth. That wouldn't do much for the party mood.

"No, we're glad you came along. We've invited a lot of familiar faces. You'll see. There's Rupert coming along later. Melanie and Damion are already here. There are plenty of interesting new people for you to meet," she says.

I wonder if I count as an interesting new person.

"How about Liz? You didn't invite her, did you? Along with King Snake?"

"Can't you bear to be in the same room as them?"

"I tried it once," I tell her.

"Oh, come on, Noah."

"Did she give you any reason for not coming?" I wonder.

"Not really, but it sounded a bit enigmatic. She asked me if you would be invited and then if I needed any old windows replacing."

"Why's she speaking in riddles these days?" I turn cold inside.

"Yes, quite a riddle. Couldn't get to the bottom of that one? Did she add a new skill to her business?"

"I no longer have the ability to read her mind," I argue. "Cupid pulled back his little bow and she's been unable to talk plainly since."

"We were a bit hurt," Sue admits.

"You know how young love is," I remark.

"There are plenty of lovely people this year." Was she trying to fix me up? "You may notice a lot of strange faces as well tonight."

"Oh?"

"Bob went and invited many of his work colleagues and even some of his customers down at the garden festival."

"You do seem to have a crowded house," I observe. Indeed we are squeezed and the air has become warm and close as we edge down their hallway.

"He doesn't understand the concept of limiting the numbers."

"Where *is* Bob?" I ask.

"You know what he's like at these parties, Noah. Plans them the year round, then shrinks away at the first call. Presently he's hiding in the kitchen, trying to ration the booze. You could try to prise him away from there, for me. There's always something for you to do in this house."

I promise to do my best, and get Bob away from the kitchen at his own party. Susan disengages her shy smile; her amber eyes crinkling with warmth, the soul of discretion. I feel a healing suffusion pass into my dry bones, like the squeeze of lemon to a scurvy suffering sailor. It was great to come across my true friends again. This was good radiation.

But I grew more nervous with every step. Not so much a party animal myself these days, as a whipped mutt; despite the pompous togs.

This is my first social outing since a cyclone hit my health chart. My first real hoot since Lizzie put her best frocks into cellophane and ran away with the guy she mussed up. I was a confident and adventurous young guy, back in the day. I was regarded as charming and easy in my style. It's a long time since I've been at the centre of any party. Not that I've come out looking for sympathy. When did I last pray for the less fortunate?

Elizabeth was always popular at parties of course. Her radiant intelligence captivated and drew people to her, like sparks from an Iron Age copper forge. I was really much shyer and less assured, which I made up for with bluster and controversy. For many shy or hesitant people Lizzie *was* the kitchen at a party. That's unless you crossed her because, believe me, she could turn up the heat, as she wouldn't dissemble any disapproval. She always made an impact at parties with her burnished virago beauty. People didn't know that she disliked her own appearance. She knew how to carry herself in a crowd, even while she felt differently. That's why I'd lose my mind.

Obviously she hasn't come to light up this party, or to control her paradoxical lack of physical self-love. Instead she chose to stay away and only leave an ironical calling card about replacing windows. She knew that Sue would keep hold of this *bon mot* and pass it on to me later, assuming I was in any shape to call. This year I have the uncomfortable sense of attending the Huntingdon party alone. I am left gazing nervously at fellow guests, while wandering into a crowded reception room. There was no chance to rustle up any trophy girlfriend this time. The cabinet is empty and it's just me and my cardiovascular system. How am I going to handle myself in company again?

Susan senses a lack of confidence and sticks by my side. She's really a sweet and thoughtful woman. She talks to me about work and children. She became a mother in her thirties. She and Bob have two boys; stocky and robust as badgers, like their father; who are with a hired baby-sitter at their grandparents' this evening. Susan never gave the feeling of being an instinctive parent. She required time to adjust and to gain knowledge, slowly and painfully. God knows you require nerves as strong as electricity pylons. It was Liz who was the earth mother never in doubt.

The Huntingdon couple show symptoms of restlessness, as opium pipes and palm wine gourds indicate. I don't mention that my own kids are flying away, even without leaving the country. It's a beautiful but scary world out there. Bob registered one of his roses under the name of Susan Amber Huntingdon. Despite such poetry, some women are incomparable, even within the beauties of horticulture. Look at a woman like Susan and you really curse death. And she's not alone.

"Find yourself a drink and mingle, Noah."

"There are a lot of new cats in your house tonight," I say.

"I don't recognise many of them, as they are friends or colleagues of Bob."

"Is Bob trying to create his own Python sketch?" I wonder.

"He's always afraid that nobody will turn up."

"Looks as if his fears are ungrounded, Susan."

"He was on a sponsored walk last weekend, in Bath. So he just invited along everyone he met...along the way."

"You'll just have to put your foot down," I reply.

"Bob and I are going out for a quiet celebratory dinner tomorrow. Tonight's party is as much for friends as for us. We've hired a baby sitter for the boys." A sumo wrestler?

At which point her gaze is distracted by something happening past my shoulder.

"What's up, Sue?" I ask.

"Somebody's trying to get your attention, Noah," she explains.

"My attention?"

"Behind you."

# Chapter 12

A foghorn is blasting across the room at me. "Noah! Noah! We're over here old bud." My ship's coming in?

"I'll leave you for a while," Susan says.

"Must you?"

"You'll be all right, Noah."

"Catch you later then."

Her smile flares above her shoulder as she turns and goes.

"Noah! Good to see you again old bud."

I turn about stiffly, to stare at close range into another middle-aged male face. A gleamingly buffed face, with sharp blue eyes and a range of teeth like the interior of Iceland.

"Ross. Long time no see," I say.

"Couldn't be better. Top condition. So how're you, bud?"

I can feel my teeth gritting again, as if back on the Cretan shore.

Ross grins as if about to bite my head off. His face is as deeply tanned as the flanks of an old donkey.

"Top condition, top condition. How's the missus, Noah?" He leans forward and cocks his head.

Ross isn't a subtle guy. He has a bad reputation, although all bad reputations are bad in a different way.

He creaks a brown leather jacket across his shoulder blades, trying to make room for himself. He and I have known each other since school days, though we never sat next to each other. He was a notorious 'long hair' in his youth; a rocker that is. Now he couldn't muster a single long hair to save his own skin. Ross and the gang used to intimidate my older brother, who himself had a tough guy reputation. They'd pull up alongside him in the Stapleton Road. Now *neither* of them would be caught dead there.

"I'm breathing free again Ross, cos Liz and I had our divorce through last year," I bluff.

He taps the side of his puffy nose. "Clever boy!"

"She moved in with some software dummy and married him instead. I'm not going to have anything more to do with her, if I can help it."

"Best shot of her, bud," he confides.

"That's what I keep trying to tell myself," I grumble, trying not to lose face.

"There isn't one dame in this world that isn't replaceable."

I process the stale air at speed, but he doesn't take the hint.

"Did you ever meet my fiancée?"

"Seriously?"

He nudges a twenty something blonde, who must have won a shopping trolley of free cosmetics. "Noah, this is Shirley. My 'Shirley Valentine'!" he beams.

"Well done."

"Isn't it."

"Pleasure to meet you, Miss Valentine," I say. Must give the old lothario some credit however.

Ross is discomforted for a split second. "Shirley sugar, this is Noah Sheer. One of the big wheels of Bristol industry and commerce. One of the most respected businessmen in the city."

"Glad to meet you!"

"Really, Ross, that's a very generous introduction but..." Makes me sound like Al Capone.

"When Noah first began his business, he and his missus were practically eating off the floor."

"Yes but the wife'd wipe it over first. Look, Ross, there's no need to..."

"But don't worry, sugar, cos he's got a lot more in the bank vault these days."

Shows how much he knows.

Ross sets his sizeable lower jaw like a prehistoric aquatic carnivore. You could rest your pint glass in there when he opens his mouth.

"Got away on your holidays this year, Noah?" he asks, chattily.

"Holiday?" I retort. The negatives come back to haunt me.

"Yeah, holiday."

"That's a long story," I bluster.

"Shirley and me went to the Windward Isles on a practice honeymoon. We wanted to get a taste of somewhere exotically different. It was extremely pleasant."

"Is that a US Air Force base?" I wonder.

"What is?" His penetrating eyes search me in bafflement.

"The Windward Isles?"

Perhaps I was thinking of Cuba. In truth I'm not the best travelled guy. Much of my world knowledge comes from television documentaries.

Ross looks shocked at my ignorance. "No, Noah, they're St. Lucia, Trinidad, Grenada... *The West Indies*. Where have you been?" he teases.

"Now you come to mention it... How bloody stupid of me."

Ross gloats politely. "We had a gorgeous little vacation in the Caribbean. Didn't we, sugar? So why don't you tell Noah something about your experiences there?"

"Yes, lovely, thanks!"

"Superb. You've never seen so much luxury in all your life," he assures me.

Years ago he'd bike down to Weston over the weekend, to do battle with the Mods. After scattering pensioners from the sands, they'd all have fish and chips before roaring back home.

"Glad you had a nice time...there in the lap of luxury."

"Very interesting," Shirley says, "because most of the time I didn't understand a word they were saying."

"Did you say you'd been on holiday this year, Noah?"

"It's a bit of a sore subject with me, to be honest with you."

"Oh?"

"You don't look very brown," Shirley Valentine remarks. She narrows her eyes suspiciously and disapprovingly.

"Maybe he went on a skiing break, love," Ross concludes. "Have you been on the piste?" he asks, without irony.

"Not consciously," I admit.

He bends at the knees to relieve the clasp of new jeans. "So where have you been then?"

"At first I went to Crete."

"They invented the first running toilets, yeah?"

"We bought ourselves a last minute ordeal," I explain.

"Beg your pardon?" says the dumb painted stick.

"Hotel all right?"

"We hired out a villa."

"Cheap?"

"But then I felt unwell and had to come home early." Best to keep these memories to myself.

"I did hear rumours about you getting a massive coronary," he says, sucking air and wincing.

"Rumours?"

"That you'd been knocking on the door, bud."

"I had a mild heart attack while I was out there."

"Then you will not be competing in the veterans' championship this year?" he concludes.

"Unlikely. Next year," I concede.

"Nobody expected you to have a massive heart attack out of the blue."

I struggle over his heartless description. "It came as quite a shock to me as well, Ross. At least it didn't kill me outright. My father also had coronary problems. Runs in the family. Family history," I say.

"You poor thing," remarks Shirley, widening her eyes alarmingly.

"Did they have to cut you open in the hospital then?" he pursues.

"That's the long and short of it," I admit. "I had a successful triple by-pass operation. Then they stitched me up again," I add pointedly.

"Then I guess you're almost back in top condition," he replies, laughing in relief.

"Exactly. Look, good knocking into you again, Ross, but I really have to circulate." I move away.

"It was a thrill," Ross concludes. "Family well?"

"Very well, thanks."

"Your little Angela's a bit of a tearaway though, isn't she?" he fires over.

"How do you mean?" I cut back.

"A pleasure to meet you," Shirley adds.

"Noah, boy, where did you get that outfit from?" he winces.

"What about my outfit?" I want to know.

"No comment!"

Always the long hair, although in contemporary times Shirley Valentine could adjust her cosmetics in his smooth pate.

Ross isn't such a bad guy. I think his heart's in the right place.

# Chapter 13

The evening is yet young and there are still sponsored walkers to meet. A lot of these chaps are growing impatient, not to say dehydrated, around the feeding tables, as beverages are slow to arrive or in short supply. It's my task to discover the reason and look for Bob Huntingdon; our host, our innkeeper, our brewer.

I'm not reduced to lurking in shadowy corners. But the walls are more alluring than ever. I cannot predict the horrors in store for me. The idea was to go out, relax, meet old friends and enjoy myself. Trying to be at the centre of attention is no longer so appealing. They have a bead on me as the social misfit in the room. There's no use trying to disguise the truth, that I'm divorced and solitary and making up an expedient threesome with Burke and Hare.

The soft room lighting becomes as glaring as a rock festival stage rig. My personal angst, ganged up with this party atmosphere, makes me feel intensely uncomfortable, decentred. It's like I've been thrown out on stage, after losing my singing voice, without even a flying V to cover as a fig leaf. So do they expect me to shuffle off stage left?

Edging my way back to the hallway, looking for Susan, I finally catch up with Bob. I get a glimpse of his stocky, pudgy body, and of his bearded and harried countenance. He's apparently making excuses for keeping a dry house, between the cheery guzzlers and joggers. I expected the Huntingdon couple to be more relaxed about their annual double celebration. You'd think they've had enough practice by now. But no, they get out their butler and maid uniforms, and turn their house into Fawlty Towers (maybe while Basil is on vacation). Apparently Bob and Sue were more relaxed in that Malaysian rain forest (before the bastards cut it all down); with sex-starved Maoist guerrillas nosing about the undergrowth, ready to kill a man for the stub of an American cigarette.

Bob vanishes from sight, but I understand he is making camp in his cellar-kitchen where he is guarding vital supplies. I wonder if *Sainsbury's* could offer him an armed guard for this bulk order of alcohol? He's so anxious that he doesn't notice me following in his tracks down the wooden twist of stairs. Until I get his attention by putting my hand on the wall in front of him.

"Excuse me, would you mind not...!"

"Hey, Bob!"

"Noah. Glad to see you, mate!"

"You going to kill all this beer on your own?"

The stress overcomes him like a sudden waterfall. "Ah, yes, it's a massive responsibility. At this rate of consumption its going to..."

"You've got enough booze here to keep the army going over Christmas...overseas," I tell him.

"Do you reckon? Anyway, thrilled you made it. We wanted to leave the decision to you."

"Couldn't let you down," I say.

"Well, great, glad to see you," he grins.

"Wouldn't miss your party for the world."

"Great get up," he remarks, casting a gaze over my threads.

"Cheers, Bob. I haven't compromised yet."

"No, so it would appear... Glad somebody's holding the torch for our generation."

"In safe hands," I reply, ignoring reality.

"Your wardrobe's your own choice," he assures me.

"May I ask for a beer? Or is that too forward?" I suggest.

"Certainly mate, you can, but at the present rate of consumption... the house will be dry in two hours...if those guys don't stop throwing back the booze as they are."

"What do you expect, most of them are athletes," I say. "They're not satisfied with half a shandy."

"Sponsored runners," he corrects.

"All right, but they're going to be thirsty, given those daily training routines."

Bob's perplexed. "You may be right. Do I have enough?"

"Will you let me join in myself?" I urge.

"These all have to be shared," he insists.

"Anarchism is complete froth. It's complete Kropotkin. I'm sure that beer is excluded from duty," I banter.

"Noah, I'm amazingly occupied at this moment."

"You can't let those marathon men suffer, Bob. You invited them after all."

"What was I thinking?"

"Cool down, man. Let the people serve their own juice. Look, I'm going to help myself to one of these beauties," I comment, picking myself a Czech brand. "What can be so stressful about something so lovely?" Brewed from the purest mountain water to replenish a man's well spring.

"How many guys are there upstairs?" he urges. "Can you help me to make that simple calculation? How many beers will it take to satisfy them?" he stresses.

"How deep is the ocean?"

"Go on, help yourself to a beer, Noah. When it's gone it's gone," he relents.

"That's a wise attitude," I tell him. "You are liberated. What are you doing here in the kitchen anyway? Isn't this your anniversary? You've got to get yourself away from the sink."

"What the hell's going on here?" He colours beneath his bristles. Maybe he's plugged into his memories of Donovan.

"Keep your cool, Bob."

"Susan is chatting away to people up there, without a care in the world. It's left to me to keep a watch on the booze and organise everything."

"You should be up there mixing and enjoying yourself too," I remind him. Where was his tuxedo? He had one for our wedding.

"So you decided to accept our invitation," he remarks, cutting back to cool down.

"Thanks for the warm welcome," I say.

"It's great to see you," he emphasises, breaking out into a grin.

Like a GI with the last two hand-grenades in each hand, he's still holding on to his imported lagers. He does bear a certain resemblance to Che Guevara, if he wasn't a stocky bearded pacifist instead. Then there's his work as a skilled horticulturalist. Rather than hunting down capitalists in the jungle Bob is more taken with new orchid specimens. Flower power went to his head, as Brigitte Bardot to Roger Vadim.

"You planning to stay the course this evening?" he wonders.

"You bet, Robert. Until the fat lady sings," I assure him. "In fact I am the fat lady this evening."

His dark bristly eyebrows rise, as he takes note of my drawn features and pudgy belly, these classic hallmarks of the coronary patient.

"You look a lot better than you did," he tells me quickly. "As you did after you returned after your surgery? Better to put on a little weight, than to be as skinny as a rake, like..."

"Yeah, like Keith Richards," I say. "Do you think this is anything to worry about? My body has changed so much over the past year." I'm dysmorphic man. "One time I'm fat, the next I'm losing weight again."

"Don't worry too much about it, Noah. Only about getting well again."

"I'm dysmorphic man," I tell him.

"You were practically a skeleton," he recalls.

"Almost as thin as a model. Though I doubt they'd take me for the slimming industry," I conclude.

"Maybe so. You were unable to catch your breath. You couldn't take the stairs or leave the house at all. You were house bound."

"I'm glad to be back on the roustabout. Man, it's just like old times. I'm freewheelin' again."

"That's the spirit."

"Thanks for looking after the garden for me. While I was away," I tell him. "I plan to start gardening again soon."

"Did you notice I put some hardy plants in your front borders?" he presses.

"Unless our son's rabbit died, then I noticed."

"You wanted perennials to come back for the spring."

"Everything looks a lot better, thanks Bob."

"Any time, mate. And you should cut your fruit trees back next year."

"Right, thanks for the advice. I'll get around to that. Man, you're smarter than my GP."

He narrows an eye and rubs his luxuriant chin. "Then how's your health, Noah? Sue and I put the mower over your back lawn as well. You should get one of the kids to do that next time," he suggests. "Until you heal up."

"You're joking, aren't you?" I reply.

"Getting back to regular now?" Bob enquires. "As fast as you can?"

"I'm getting into yoga," I say. "Yes, I picked up all the literature from the leisure centre. It's a new world of contemplation and peace, both physical and spiritual. No more whacking balls or smashing the concrete," I argue. "After my experiences I have to adapt to a new life. Only gentle physical stuff." Perhaps I was thinking about sex again, after an absence.

"Sounds as if you're back on firmer footing," he returns.

While I consider this image, Bob casts another anxious glance at his alcohol collection. He's thinking about the soon-to-be dry party above our heads. There could be a riot among the charity workers before long. He's like a guerrilla who loves his weapons so much he's too upset to fire them.

"Do you know how much this drink cost me? Do they appreciate what they are drinking?"

Then, as he returns his gaze, he picks up an alarming vibe from my face. A feeling about my general disposition disconcerts him. I have offered him an accidental insight into my psyche; I offer him the idea that I'm really not well yet or getting better; and that my crazy sorrow continues. His shock is just enough to crack my façade, my party features, like a fissure opening up across Frankenstein's forehead. A perceptive guy, Bob, I should have been warned.

"Sure everything's cool, Noah?"

"Don't worry," I say. But I can feel my cheeks sagging.

"Something's up," he observes.

"It's just the old ticker again," I concede.

"I thought you'd healed up, man."

"Yes, well I was, but they called me back into hospital."

"Yes?"

"There's been some kind of cock up following surgery."

"You're kidding!" Suddenly conscious of the two beers he puts them back down.

"They'd taken out my stitches, I didn't feel so sore, but there's been a mistake."

"But you got here this evening," he says.

"To the best of my knowledge," I tell him.

"You were like a ghost, Noah."

"The thousand year old man. But I do feel a lot better. I feel much better."

"Then what's the problem...the mistake?"

"Where should I begin? How far back should I go?"

"Take your time," he reassures. What would his thirsty guests say to that idea?

We can hear muffled conversations and footballs going above our heads; signs of the restless drinkers, shuffling like Van Gogh's convicts around the prison yard. Bob's staring at me, craning forward eagerly for my health info: dark brown eyes rounded, shoulders squared, bristling for the absolute truth.

So I describe that painful episode in the shopping mall, about the second consultation in the smoke, and of the damaged plastic valve lodged in my chest cavity. But I don't offer him the manufacturer's trademark or product history. I confess that there's been a serious setback to my rehabilitation, without saying that my child support payments are under threat.

"I didn't see this coming," I tell him.

"You don't deserve this," he states.

Bob's shocked when he gets all the dope. If I'm prepared to admit that my life is at risk, what must the *whole* truth be? "What were the medics doing with you? I know that it's legitimate to interfere with nature, to cure and heal... but this looks like an intervention too far," he argues.

"Don't ask me."

"Did they inform you about potential risks?" he wonders.

"You have to put your faith into the future, I guess."

"They shouldn't experiment on people."

"It wasn't an experiment; at least not on their side," I say.

"There's only so much that's acceptable. Did they explain fully? The risks? The likely outcomes? Why don't they take more care?" he agonises. But it isn't *his* ticker.

Now that Bob has the low-down on my heart, I'm afraid to have ruined his party. I can tell people about my predicament, but I shouldn't spread anxiety like a bush fire. Scaring people isn't going to make me better. I have to sit down with Angela, and the others, and tell her the exact truth. When? How can I do that, when it's hard to accept and to explain to myself? Talk about a bad trip - this truly is.

Is it better to cut them out of the loop? This dilemma rattles around my head all the time, like the cocktail of tablets I am daily obliged to swallow. Wouldn't have been so enthusiastic about illegal drugs, had I known about the lethal legals ones, which I must take, to give a chance to survive. Not self-destructive tendencies, but self-preserving necessities. Glad we couldn't look into the future that belonged to us.

"Take care, Noah. Take life easy from now on," Bob implores.

"It's a beautiful but scary world, Bob."

"Give yourself enough time, Noah."

"I'm getting into the garden when I can. Taking on a few modest home improvements, you know. I've even subscribed to an oriental art."

"Noah Sheer? There couldn't be a healthier or happier guy. We thought there had to be some mistake. Now you're having some more bad luck," he laments.

"Looks like I used up all my luck," I suggest.

"No, you can always turn luck around," he insists.

"How can I make my own luck? Do you know the secret formula?"

Robert may be right with his notion of luck. It's as convincing as any explanation. More attractive than thoughts about fate, destiny or foul play.

"You can't go around blaming yourself, Noah. I know you're not going to feel sorry for yourself or blame others. I've known other guys in your position, after having a heart attack, who blame themselves. But you can't escape by changing the factors, such as diet, or exercise, or transformation of lifestyle."

"I don't know, because luck's not giving me any living space," I say.

"Not all the factors for any disease are within the individual's grasp," he argues. He was getting close to a genetic explanation for my heart problems.

"I didn't always keep an eye on my case," I admit.

"You have to focus your powers of healing," he advises. "You shouldn't put your system under any more pressure or interference."

"Can you tell me how to avoid it?" I reply. "Did we succeed in solving all the world's problems? Was I looking the other way?"

"You say you're out of luck, old friend, but I'm sure that things will look up. I know you well enough by now, Noah, and you never give in. Don't try to turn that into a witticism. At some point you're going to pull around," he decides. "We need you around, Noah."

He puts a hand on my shoulder and gives it a squeeze. I find myself moved at his show of solidarity. "Thanks Bob. Great to get some encouragement."

Despite this Bob's anxiety about the party soon returns. He has the haunted look of Dylan Thomas locked in a chapel during opening time.

"Leave me to take care of the booze situation," he instructs. "You go back upstairs with our others guests...and enjoy yourself."

# Chapter 14

At my ascent I spot the terrible couple. Melanie and Damion were friends of ours before Liz and I became estranged. Now they wouldn't touch me socially with a toasted tofu fork. At least not with an unheated one, while Lizzie was watching. I shimmy around a wall in an effort to avoid their spying on me. He's a freelance journalist on social policy and community relations issues; or as far as I understand. She writes such self-righteous books on capital punishment (against) and liquid castration (in favour) that even an ageing liberal like me would happily see her strung up on moral grounds. I'd let the category one prisoners do the job for me, before they returned to their cells to watch more television.

She also commandeers a crèche, for radical fem parents; a laboratory of infant psychology and behaviour, that makes that Summerhill place look like a boot camp. As a couple Melanie and Damion are the Kray Twins of rainbow politics. They are still close to Liz and the dinosaur. They share all the latest dope on me, by that route. Gossip runs around these parts like a paper boat in the gutter, believe me. It's as much as I can do to keep my back turned to them.

In the decade after university they invited Liz and me to join their commune. They had this ambition to establish that big shared household. It really happened too, as they bought some farm buildings from her father, concealed in the countryside outside Bristol. Lizzie thought it was an exciting concept. She would have had our kids running about in the buff with these flabby free love hippies. Speaking for myself I didn't even want to shower with those guys. Did that make me a fascist? Then they had Melanie's timetable of daily chores around the free love farm, ranging from cooking our collective potatoes to shovelling the pig pen and hosing out the communal latrine. Man, individually speaking, I preferred our pokey flat. Lizzie couldn't understand my mind set.

I'd rather that Melanie throttled me in the straps of her dungarees, with one of her boots on my throat, than agree to endless evenings debating with them. If Liz had insisted on going to their commune, I couldn't have separated from her. But I knew that I might be heading off into the woods alone.

"Noah. Is that you?" Damion declares.

"Who else?" I offer.

"You're still peaky," Melanie says. She scrunches her face as if changing a messy nappy.

"Neither did I!"

"No, he doesn't look so great," Damion remarks.

"I couldn't agree more," I say.

Damion runs me through a complete body scan. He takes a few seconds to bring himself up to date. Certainly the results are fascinating and alarming. "We haven't noticed you knocking about for months," he comments.

"Who's counting?" I say.

"So where you been hiding out recently. Keeping yourself out of view?"

"I had other appointments," I explain.

"Oh?" he returns, studying me.

"You don't look as if you're exactly thriving," Melanie observes.

"Thanks for that."

They notice that I'm on the emotional and physical ropes. They're moving in for the killer punch. No point trying to dodge away. It's like a scene from *Raging Bull*, except in this version he's being pounded on the ropes by bitter sister Melanie, not Sugar Ray Leonard.

"We understood that you were supposed to be feeling better," Damion says.

"So why aren't you keeping Mr and Mrs Noggins company this evening? Aren't they feeling a bit lost without you?"

"Do you think she could be relaxed? Knowing that you are at the party?" Melanie accuses.

"Liz and Frank thought it would be sensible to avoid you this evening," explains her partner.

"Right? Why's that?" I wonder.

"Ask a stupid question!"

"As a new couple they don't know if enough time has gone by. For you to be accepting of the new situation," he suggests, nodding.

"That's bloody thoughtful of them," I reply. It's hard to mask the hurt of Lizzie avoiding me out of embarrassment, or fearing the consequences. Maybe the concrete cupid really got to her.

"Liz knows how close you are to Bob and Sue who, apparently, are sympathetic to your attitude," Damion says.

"What did you say to them?" Melanie wants to know.

"I can understand if the newly marrieds are ashamed to show their faces tonight."

"They're very happy together," Damion coolly assures me.

"They have no earthly reason to feel any shame, whatsoever, in regard to you. How do you compare yourself to Liz? She has nothing to criticise herself for. Certainly next to you - some ageing menopausal man, absolutely lacking in any self-awareness over your behaviour and ethics, assuming you had any personal ethics in the beginning."

"There's no need to stick your neck out," I observe.

"It must have been a rather bitter pill for you, Noah, to lose a woman like that."

"It's amazing what a guy can get used to," I argue. The guy should understand that I'm the expert on taking bitter pills.

Melanie checks out my fresh complexion. "We noticed you lurking around here, all by yourself," she gloats. "Enjoying the consequences of your behaviour."

"You're the girl to feel a man's pain," I remark.

"What's that supposed to mean?" she retorts, colouring.

"So how are you coping with your life, all on your own?" Damion wonders.

"Fantastic."

"You can't fool us, since Elizabeth told us everything. She confided in us," Melanie tells me.

"Don't believe everything you hear," I advise.

"You're lucky she didn't punch you on the nose," she returns. She has a girlish face, with apple cheeks and even plaits or pigtails. There's a warrior queen waiting to split my skull, if I bumped into her by mistake. I find her as grim as the rope she affects to revile, to be straight with you.

"You telling us you enjoy your life as a single guy?" Damion comments.

"Did you notice any talent at this party?" I ask.

"What's he saying?" Melanie says. "There's something creepy about him."

"I think that Noah understands very well...what we are sensitively trying to suggest about his new life."

Damion takes a sociable sip from his glass and waves the glass significantly around my face. Under a halo of fine blonde curls he looks like a cross between Martin Luther and Art Garfunkel.

"Make no mistake about whose side we're taking. It wouldn't be to give any solace to a man like you," she states.

"How devastated must you feel now, to have lost your soul mate in this life?"

"I never take any trouble to analyse my feelings. So where are the good looking women at this party?" I wonder. "No disrespect, Melanie."

"He didn't lose his soul mate, Damion," says the crèche commander. "Liz finally got wise and outgrew him in an instant. As Liz readily admits, she should have recognised him for what he is and left him years ago."

"She's lucky to have a girlfriend like you," I tell her.

"You have to admit you're in a miserable place right now," Damion adds.

"Not in the least, mate, 'cause I've never been happier. Sorry to disappoint you, but I've been given a new lease on life."

"Don't listen to him," she says disgustedly. "You know how he treated Liz."

"I couldn't survive without my soul partner. Goodness, no. In my life situation I'm lucky to cohabit with my perfect counterpart. A masculine element to interchange with the feminine... social and economic construct though it may be."

"Talking for myself, man, I'm well shot of her."

Damion's scrubbed yet stubbly pink cheeks stir; though not with anger or resentment, oh no. "Your reaction comes from a defensive masculine attitude. Excuse me, but the truth about your marriage, and your relationship with Liz, is merely offending your crude macho defences," he argues. "So you put up a sturdy defensive barrier to repel any sensitive or accurate explanation."

"Do you have any more ideas from the top of your head?" I ask. He makes my love life sound like the Paris Commune.

"Leave the brute to his misery," Melanie suggests.

"Noah is just upset because he's lost what's most important to him. He's lost the feminine, both of his own personality and literally... so he compensates by emphasising the more unpleasant male traits."

"What was it you read at university?"

Damion considers me dispassionately. "Noah, I believe you know very well what I took at uni."

"Urban architecture?"

"No, it was not..."

"Damion, don't bother to even listen, or to take his arrogance seriously. He's too arrogant and unreconstructed to take in a word of your advice. And the truth of what you say strikes him directly to the heart."

"Wouldn't you be furious with Melanie, Damion, if she ran off with another guy?" I ask.

"Melanie? Run off?" he retorts.

"Wouldn't you be annoyed with the little lady, if she went and absconded with some... some body building type, say?"

"Don't be ridiculous!" The blood has coagulated in her cheeks. Fine strands of fair hair are flying away from her scalp, with the build-up of static.

Damion attempts to consider my flippant idea seriously. After all you never know what life is going to throw at you next. "No, I hope that I would respect her decision," he tells me.

He succeeds in provoking me, though not deliberately. "Would you hell," I tell him.

"How do you know that?" he protests.

"Don't take the slightest bit of notice of him," she insists.

"Don't get personal," I warn.

She twists her neck to scoff at my dress sense. "There's something louche and revolting about him, Damion."

"Noah, I would ask myself a few searching questions, if Melanie ever informed me that she wished to leave. The female has always represented the life instinct for me. I must respect her movements. She turns towards the creative, away from the destructive," he argues.

"You don't have to be a woman to be a feminist," Melanie proclaims, triumphantly. Not for the first time.

"So you don't care if she runs away with a body builder?" I facetiously pursue.

"I would *not* run away with a body builder," she maintains, bunching her fists.

"But let's just consider, for the sake of interest, that you did," I reply.

"Why should I be interested in any other guy?" Teeth grind, eyes glint, cheeks burn; weight on the front of her feet, ready for the killer punch.

"Melanie and I are very happy," he assures me.

"Can't you accept the idea of an open minded man and a passionate woman being in a happy and equal relationship?"

"Are you for real?" I tell her.

"Are you suggesting that we are not?" she returns, scrolling up her bottom lip.

"I have no hesitation in declaring myself her feminist soul mate," Damion tells me.

His wife drills him with an awesome tenderness.

"Still a good idea to keep your body in shape," I suggest.

"You seedy old lecher," she snarls. She rolls up the sleeves of her rainbow coloured goats' hair sweater.

"Oh yes, she is, Noah." He raises his dulcet voice a notch, as well as a thick finger. "They cope better than we do. We're still grunting cave men in that area. We indulge in these chest thumping displays of anger and inadequacy," he argues calmly.

"You're wasting your breathe on him," Melanie argues.

"Why bring up gender, to avoid the consequences of our actions?" I challenge.

"Take Liz for example."

"What about her?"

"She took a hard look at her life situation and decided to change. Didn't you always admire women who decided on change?"

"You have to admire her strength of mind," Melanie adds.

"I got an idea about that," I admit.

"You had to be more aware of her frustrations," he suggests.

"I completely share them," I tell him.

"You're still bitter and twisted."

"I hope that I never get to that place, when Melanie has to leave me. We're both in touch with her emotions and we're not going to lose that."

"I don't give a shit about Melanie's emotions, honestly," I say.

Damion narrows his eyes at me. "Both parties in a relationship should know when it is going wrong. It's not very credible to deny the obvious," he argues.

"It's never been obvious to me," I say.

"Your sexual politics are the most segregated I have ever come across," Melanie tells me.

"Then you haven't lived," I repost.

"You're completely off the map," she insists.

"You may find some humour in your situation, but you're asking for neuroses."

"Oh, what neuroses can you offer me?"

"*You weak man.*"

"Even now when it's too late for your relationship, you refuse to listen to your wife. That is your former wife." His baby blue eyes twinkle submissive empathy and irony.

"Is there any better time?" I wonder.

"When are you ever going to understand Liz's problems with the marriage?"

"Listen, Damion, let's just have a few sociable drinks together, shall we? Let's relax at this party and forget about our problems for a little while. What's the use of all this fussing and fighting my friends?" I ask, in a lyrical mood.

"What's he blithering about now?" Melanie wants to know, screwing up her girlish features.

"Why don't you loosen up a bit, Mel?" I suggest.

"How would you like your balls smashed?" she returns.

"You're over compensating again, Noah."

"He never deserved such a clever and loving girl as Liz."

"We're lucky enough to stay in contact with her," Damion admits. So he allows me to overhear and confirm my parnaoia.

"So I understand."

"She's made a remarkable transformation in her fortunes," he argues.

"Is that the case?"

"You could learn something from her."

"She could end up in one of her own cup cakes."

"You're revolting," Melanie declares.

"From the chains," I comment.

Damion tests a patient smile, concluding that, after all, I must be jesting on the subject, to some extent. "That's a depressing confession, Noah. Yes, because your psyche is obviously vulnerable."

"Perhaps my mother was to blame."

"You're only talking in that offensive way because you miss Liz."

"I don't miss her. I wish she would emigrate."

"You should think about attending my men's group," he says.

"I'm too busy trying to pull," I assure him.

"I would go through some soul searching, if I was in your position."

"You'd tell Liz all my secrets," I conclude.

"Not that my wife is ever going to leave me. As I already explained, I don't ignore her essential needs or disregard the psychic messages she gives off."

"My husband's a remarkable man," Melanie informs me.

"There's no question," I say. Then as she kisses his forehead, I take the chance to get away.

For all those harsh and pompous words, I can't help thinking they scored a few direct hits. She didn't knock me out, but she won on points. Didn't Elizabeth's choice expose my failure to understand? I certainly failed to anticipate. I squandered a megaton of emotional and legal fuel in the process. It's hard not to speculate about female sides, emotional competence and, even, psychic intuitions.

# Chapter 15

I resolve to limit my topics of conversation at this party; to restrict myself to discussing my garden, recent political scandals and the weather. It's safer to chat about kites and balloons, with no mention of hearts and marriages.

After taking that emotional bruising I attach myself to the group, clutching my beer, catching up with other people's gossip. I'm content if nobody takes a blind bit of notice. I breathe easily when their eyes pass over me without delay. I've become a bit of a sight. What would my teenage incarnation say about that?

We all go on a youthful ego trip, which lasts about a decade. Everybody would be famous for fifteen minutes, according to Warhol. Every radical kid would have his day in the water cannon. This was the stuff of idealism or just optimism: which is much better than the alternatives.

We discoursed about the inevitable decline of late capitalism, the transformation of western society. We couldn't foresee how chance would shape us too, as representatives of the individual. We knew we were part of Life, this bigger thing. But we didn't talk about our futures, the terrible surprises. We got high. Fearlessly we gave our utopia to the world. You can look back on history. But we upped the ante - and the anti.

I lost my father when I was eight years old. Lizzie and I lost our closest old university friend when he was just twenty three. Those experiences of loss have always been at the back of that big Life thing. That was going on, even during our wildly happy, free wheelin' days.

Later in the evening Bob and Susan cut into their anniversary or birthday cake. In the contemporary era this cake is a proper expensive model, in commemoration of the Las Vegas original, which was two pancakes in cream and blueberry sauce. The Sheer wedding cake was a leaning tower of Pisa, with replicas of Liz and I on the roof. Lizzie's stomach was too delicate for her to blow out the candles on her birthday cake that year. So I queasily recall.

The Huntingdons press the knife again. The guests are noisily appreciative. My friends can't help blushing and stumbling, with all guests' eyes turned on them. Why do they put themselves through this matrimonial ordeal? They must find some good radiation out of this somewhere.

Bottles of champagne crack open, froth, pour, flow into pyramids of fluted glasses, before the sparkly is passed around, and the structure is steadily, carefully dismantled.

The Huntingdon's living room has the mood of a crowded country inn at harvest time. The atmosphere is close and claustrophobic under reduced lights. Yet this is a happy and united family, under the same roof, and what's the price of that? A toast is proposed and everybody teeters into a few verses of Happy Birthday, watching each other's merrily frightened eyes with merrily frightened eyes. Their party is proving a great success again this year, although it isn't the wildest happening since Keith Richards last came to town.

Nuptial rituals complete, we disperse back around the house: we return to our previous conversations. There wouldn't be a lack of audience to hear about my holiday experiences. Shrewdly I'm not sharing my memories around. I'm keeping that particular box of confetti in my jacket pocket. They don't entirely understand what private nightmare they could stumble into. It was a kind of garbage dump at the side of a luxury new hotel. Not since that guy decided on a day trip to Pompeii, has any holiday plan so badly backfired. They believe that the Cretan vacation has ended all my romantic inspirations. I got my comeuppance with a clownish pratfall. I'm ready to play along with their views. I don't offer any latest twists.

As I continue to roustabout I find Rupert Lloyd. I haven't seen this guy for, oh, five years, since he's been living in east Africa. Now he's got himself hitched rather than ditched.

A sculpturally featured Kenyan girl, slim, elegant, bosomy. A smile sweeter than a boat of ice-cream. Rupert's another of these well-travelled guys. His wide experience of the world leaves me far behind. Not including my one lost weekend in Japan, when

I was hunting for fish and chips around downtown Tokyo. They had my guts for sushi.

I'm afraid that he'll be shocked to recognise me again. What can I tell you about Rupert? He was another fellow student of ours, part of the Students' Union. He was a high-prestige Marxist intellectual, big league public speaker and formidable agitator. During the first year we admired mutually, *agitated* together. But we soon began to eat each other, with more relish than the brothers Grimm.

We disguised a radical personality clash with political fall outs. He was in favour of direct political action, whereas I was opposed. Studies disrupted, we soon began to fall out. Antipathy and argument got us, like a Stalinist meeting with one chair short on the platform for the politburo. Rupert didn't approve of my lecture room demo against the arms trade, without asking his permission. When the university tried to expel me and fellow students prevented this, Rupert was envious. For a serious finger pointer, he didn't raise one to save me.

The situationist antics of our friend, Stuart Maybridge, particularly annoyed him. He was glad when security guards escorted Stuart from the premises. The rumour had it that Rupert had given the Chancellor's office a tip off. There were emergency meetings and motions all over the campus. Lloyd was deeply resentful and contemptuous of Stuart's madcap strategy. All right, the grim reaper got the last laugh there, although a hollow one.

The chicks at Bristol were not misty eyed. They were not excited by Rup's brand of visionary dialectic. Apparently Rup's become more attractive in maturity; which is the opposite of my own experience. You could grate a policeman's baton on those high cheekbones of his. His fiery politics put off the most hep university females. From his angle I was merely an attention seeker and an irremediable skirt chaser. I was the guy who refused to throw a petrol bomb into the science lab. I was the inauthentic man, having a good time out of the protest movement. Looking back he wasn't too far off the mark. What's the point of arguing?

When Lizzie and I became a regular fixture, he resented it. He went so far as to denounce Bob Dylan in front of fellow students. This was long after Dylan had recovered his blues roots and went on electric tours with the Hawks. But Rupert had a long memory in music, as in politics and romantic rivalry. At a committee meeting he denounced our hero as a traitor to the movement. He described Zimmerman as a "cultural dandy and parvenu". Who can forget a description like that? To this day I hear him shouting out in a cracked voice across the canteen. I'm sure that I was his true target, stood right behind our hero, too much of a straw man in Rup's eyes to be named. He truly despised Liz for going out with me, when I was clearly not worth the trouble. He never forgave her for falling in love with me, then deciding to have my child and get married; even though Lizzie and I had known each other for years, since school. Dylan wasn't there to defend himself.

One day we came to blows. We had to be physically separated by a student mob. This fight happened in the humanities coffee bar one lazy afternoon. He threw himself at me across the table, from nowhere. I must have said something off that he disapproved of. Like "I love my girlfriend and I believe that killing anybody is wrong." He launched himself, grabbing a weapon along the way, which happened to be a bottle of tomato sauce. The tomato was an embarrassing mess, but it was the glass bottle that was most dangerous.

Maybe the tomato sauce bottle was the ultimate proletarian weapon. Obviously from Rup's background it was borrowed and symbolic. I couldn't tell if he was for the masses or against them, in this particular battle. My mother had worked in a factory canteen, so I had to be in the working class corner, don't you think? Quickly there was sauce all over my face. The sight caused instant panic among fellow students. I've never like the taste, surprisingly enough. Luckily Rup didn't succeed in smashing the bottle across my temple. That's what he intended to do.

The battle had more to do with testosterone than ideology. His step would falter, and he'd look away, redder than red, whenever Lizzie and I walked along the corridor to pass. Plenty of testosterone has ebbed and flowed since those days. Man, some events are too painful and embarrassing to remember.

"You're back in circulation, Noah?" he remarks. A different kind of party has brought us back together. "How are you?"

So I make my excuses again, give hint of the scars. Rupert may be older and wiser too, as he doesn't take my new look too badly.

"Nobody gave me any clue about your health problems," he explains. "What a dreadful surprise. So are you on the mend?"

I make some positive noises.

"I can see you've been through some traumatic experiences."

Not nearly as traumatic as being assailed by a ketchup bottle.

"How's business, Noah?"

Another sore topic. "Keeping my head up above the crowds," I say.

"Right, glad to hear that. You still think that barrage balloons can still be the first choice for commuters? Is that going to happen any time soon?" he recalls.

"Still not beyond the realms of imagination," I claim.

"You're still clinging on to the imagination?"

"I haven't given up my youthful hopes and ideas," I assure him.

Rupert smiles ironically at me. His ruddy visage is marked by characterful cracks and creases. He's aged as nicely as a Puritan cottage. "I've been searching for new ideas, based on respect for values and traditions," he suggests. "What we singularly lacked as young men."

"I haven't entirely given up on the young men we were."

"You still dare to dream of peace and equality, Noah? Still putting up your utopian slogans around the Sorbonne?"

"That's your territory," I remind him.

"Used to be."

"Anyway, I gave up on all that guff years ago. It makes me squirm when I think about it. When we thought that Bob Dylan was a talented musician," he echoes. His claret drinker's eyes take in my dress sense. I'm glad if he thinks that's the only wrong aspect about me.

The infamous coffee bar assault was still running at the back of my mind. Apparently Rup had wiped that from his memory, along with everything else.

"If you ask me the whole period was shameful. Our radical left student years. Looking back I hardly recognise myself. And I don't want to even try."

"So you don't hold anything against me, any more?" I wonder.

"Why should I, Noah?" He puts his mind through reverse gears. "We failed to agree, but it was never personal."

"Not even when we were on first name terms?" I say.

He squints a bit at me and laughs. "No, no, certainly not. All right, I admit a few errors of judgement as a young man. Didn't you make any mistakes yourself?"

"Best to keep them to myself," I reply.

He exchanges a look with his wife. She smiles back ironically, leaving this to us. "I heard you've got a few business troubles at the moment. Anything in those rumours, Noah?"

"You're still got your ear to the ground, Rupert. There are the usual pains...interest rates, regulation, late payment from clients... that kind of stuff."

"When are we going to have a positive business climate in this country?"

I rifle the retrospective files of my mind. But he's got me on that one.

I'm curious about his aloof girlfriend. She's the kind of lady to cause a nuclear reaction at a party. In our youthful years black people were less familiar, despite the terrible epochs of Bristol's history in slavery and capitalism. We had a patronisingly provincial view during those decades. Rupert's outfitted in a yellow African trouser suit himself. My bohemian peacock look is mundane by comparison. He's in great shape and as imposing as an African prince. I raise my hand to smooth a phantom quiff. Some roads are rougher than others, as Robert Johnson would attest. You just don't understand *how* rough, when you first set off.

"Excuse me, I didn't introduce my wife, Sheila," he says.

"Your *wife*? No! Hi!" I crumple. Looks as if the Cuban heel is on the other foot. Of course I'm now barefoot, doing penance over a hot gritted beach.

"I'm so delighted to meet you, Noah. Heard so much about you."

She holds out a long delicate arm to shake my hand.

"Not all that bad, thanks," I reply.

My health has faded like the wedding day carnation I still keep pressed between the pages of *On the Road*.

"Your attire is *distinctive*," she tells me.

"Do you really think so?" I goof.

"Do you mean that as a compliment though, darling?" Rupert laughs.

"Can you tell me if all these garments belong to you?" she asks, earnestly.

"They've been in the wardrobe for years," I admit.

"I heard people saying that you're divorced from Elizabeth," Rup says.

"Gossip never wears out," I remark.

"At least not gossip then," he replies.

"Tho' it can get a bit thin, after constant repetition and white washes," I suggest.

"There's no sign of her this evening. Has she come to the party? Wasn't she invited?"

"No and yes," I say.

"To be honest it's hard to believe that you're divorced."

"Don't worry Rupert, it isn't a fresh wound." But the first cut is the deepest.

"Such a beautiful girl." He's half addressing his wife. "I remember when I first saw her at university. Such a vivid memory for me." Should I thank him for the compliment?

"I still think about her," I admit.

"How could we ever forget her?" he tells me.

Maybe he'd really forgiven and forgotten our bad experiences. He'd been through a succession of failed relationships, bad relationships, during his twenties and thirties. He was sending off for prospectuses from the best monasteries. He was engaged to a female racing stable owner once; a kind of horse trainer of the revolutionary left. It's amazing that such people can exist. She kicked him out eventually. Maturity suits Rupert. He's taken a hard ride since his university days.

Lately he runs an import and export business in African goods. He started out with a small shop in Bristol but has moved on to bigger premises.

"Sheila and I met at a party in Mombasa," Rupert explains.

"A bit different to this one, then," I assume.

"I suppose so," he admits, gracefully.

"We've always enjoyed a good party," Sheila teases.

"We did all the social rounds together in Mombasa, didn't we darling. Eventually I found the courage to pop the question, during drinks at the Ambassador's reception."

"Good for you," I say.

"He was shouting at me over the band," Sheila recalls.

"Well, well, you're putting on a brave face," he observes.

"Do you really think so?" The idea disconcerts me, as I picture covering my real face with a ritual African mask. Are the spirits about to depart in wrath?

"Sheila's the perfect woman for me, Noah. Really she's perfect."

"The second time around for Rupert," she reminds us.

"Took me long enough, didn't it," he admits.

"There could be hope for you yet, Noah," she says.

"I could never have predicted Sheila coming into my life."

"We don't succeed in many predictions," I agree.

Who am I talking to? I think about Bob Huntingdon and our earlier conversation. Or is it all just another simple twist of fate? *Like a freight train!*

"Our wedding was one of the social occasions of the year. We were in all the magazines there...on television...everywhere."

"Rupert had to leave me in Kenya, shortly after our honeymoon, to return to England. What do you think about that?"

"Of course we kept in touch, but it was frustrating. I began to wonder if we'd ever live together as man and wife. I had reason not to believe my good fortune."

"My youngest brother was sent back to Nairobi from Heathrow airport you know. The immigration officers decided that his papers were not in order."

"Officially Sheila remains on a tourist visa to this country. It's all a dreadful headache."

"Caught up in a heartless bureaucratic machine," I suggest.

"Ah ha. Exactly. They certainly lack any sentiment." This time the smile is more like a grimace.

"I must return home, when my permit runs out. Rupert is going to join me in October and we will stay in Mombasa until further notice."

"So you're about to emigrate, Rupert!"

"Yes, it could be. I shall come back here on business."

"We may not meet again."

"Don't say you're going to miss me," he remarks.

You would think I was sorry about it.

"My family is doing everything they can for us," Sheila tells me.

"You should visit us in Kenya one day, Noah. To actually see the country for yourself. I'm tremendously moved and impressed by the people there," he tells me.

"Not sure that I will ever get the chance," I inform him.

"You're not one for travel?"

"Not for the long haul."

He's looking around the room again, restless. They want to move politely on. "Why don't you call round the house one evening? We've got a dinner party in a few weeks. Join us. Wish us bon voyage, while we're still here in Bristol," he suggests.

"Why not?" Social invitations haven't exactly been racking up.

"Excellent, Noah. Then, if we don't catch you later, we'll be in touch."

Even the recollection of a fire bombing in the science block has cooled. I almost vanished from sight altogether, back there in the student refectory. He left me with tomato sauce on my face. But I still got the girl.

Bob emerges to repeat his refrain of the evening:

"Find yourself a beer, Noah, before they're all downed. I never realised that these chaps would sup so much."

"They must be rehydrating!"

I decide to follow him; the prophet of the tankard; down the characterful winding wooden stair, back down into the kitchen (or beer strong-room). There's a cluster of revellers already gathered. Susan is entertaining friends around a large oak table at the other end.

I'm still choking on envy after meeting the new Mr and Mrs Lloyd. He's managed to outmanoeuvre me after all these years, by jumping back on the love train. I get the idea that Rupert has enjoyed the last laugh. But how do we know when to laugh 'last'?

The other guy could sneak-in their jubilation at the last moment. No, you just can't predict anything in this beautiful but scary world. How can you ever tell what's going to happen next? I don't have smoke signals or talking drums at my disposal.

The next moment, while attempting to circulate, I experience another jolt. It's another shock at this party, as I see Corrina Farlane. She's here. She's been invited. She's one of that group talking to Susan. I feel as if somebody's just fired a champagne cork down my throat. Who's responsible for shaking this old bottle? This could be another bad trip, and we've only just returned from the last. A revolution is building in my chest, even as I resist another uprising. But do I have enough determination to counter attack? Corrina has the lead role in my personal nightmare movie. She looks great, I can't help checking her out. But how can she have the effrontery to turn up at this party?

What's she doing here? Obviously she came to feel my pulse; to check how my health chart is coming along. She must think it's safe to put her pretty face above the sand dunes again. Take another look at my good looking corpse. We didn't repair our fault-lines in that smelting pot. She's curious about my public appearance, to see if I have defected to another time dimension. You don't need to drop any acid in this life.

"What's she doing here? Corrina?" I stammer.

"Take it easy, Noah. Why shouldn't she be here?"

"We just got back from purgatory together."

"There are a lot of people here tonight," he reminds me.

"D'you see that nail between her teeth? That's the last one for my coffin," I complain.

She's a lot of woman, Corrina - whatever I think of her ethics. I need to hold on to Bob's arm for support. She's wearing a type of silk shift, tied at the middle with a cord, as translucently and ideally sky blue as a Greek isle is supposed to be; revealing black knickers and brassiere beneath - cups as large as coal shovels - making no concession to anyone's feelings.

"Pull yourself together, Noah. It isn't another heart rumour, is it?"

"She told me she was well shot," I bitched.

"She just turned up on her motorbike a few minutes ago," Bob said. "Susan took her helmet and leathers up into the spare bedroom."

"Can't you throw her out?" I declare.

My friend is disconcerted by such an idea. Not on his life. "We can't very well do that."

Corrina's serpentine figure demonstrates that the sands of sexuality are running out.

"Susan did mention that you might be coming along. She thought that would put her off."

"Thanks for the vote of confidence."

Or were they trying to revive my love life, at a minute to midnight?

Corrina looked toned, trim and healthy as healthy. She still had that golden tan from our Cretan break. No, the tan hadn't worn off - it went with the memories. When she shook her hair it had a scintillating effect, against her diaphanous dress. The flame of bleached hair was the only reminder she would take. My second coming is of no significance to her.

What's she doing at the Huntingdons' hoot? This isn't her crowd or even her generation. All right, so she made her entrance on the Triumph Trident, that has pipes like a donkey on the pull. But that's where the sparks stop, because I'm stalled with engine failure. Why try to revive a clapped out old hippie like Noah Sheer? Why, she could take her pick from the rich handsome guys, hanging about the trendy waterfront bars and restaurants of this city. She doesn't in any way resemble me these days, as I sit at the theatre bar alone, staring into my drink, down on my luck.

"Sure you're all right?" Bob says.

"Cool. How do you think?"

"Don't let her get to you. Don't take any notice of her," he tells me.

"Has that ever been effective advice?" I reply.

"Can I look out another beer for you?"

"Yeah, you know, I could drink another beer."

"Join them at the table, if you'd like. You should give yourself a chance to recuperate, after all your terrible experiences."

"That's what they told the South Vietnamese," I repost.

"Corrina may be here to make peace," he suggests. "Anyway, you were stretching yourself to go on holiday with her."

"I'm stretched now," I agree. "Don't be long with my beer. Don't go and *count* them all again, will you?" I implore.

"Handle with care, but don't set up a bad vibe."

But he hasn't rescued me from 'Nam yet. Rotor blades are still whirring significantly above my head. Bob leaves me and makes for the fridge, searching for more liquid ammunition. But where's Miss South Vietnam gone to?

Maybe she gave her spare crash helmet to a different guy. This other guy could be riding pillion with her tonight. Sure enough, I pick out this younger man; this dumb jock ready for the high jump. Certainly he's less scary looking than me: less likely to plunge from the back of her bike at the first hairpin. Nevertheless, going by the body language, he isn't sending out a message of complete confidence. The poor sap.

# Chapter 16

I just stand there swallowing more champagne corks. I gawp like a moron as if waiting for the Über-organ to kick-in again. My fellow party animals are too preoccupied to notice any strange behaviour. I too lose track of present company and surroundings. Not only am I staring at Corrina: My mind has refocused on her and our vacation adventures. My dream girl has returned, despite our trip to hell. Maybe the other revellers believe that I am going mad - something has got into me. I've had a reputation for strange and unpredictable behaviour following my divorce. This may be the kind of thing they're talking about.

I assumed that Corrina would avoid me, to the ends of the earth. Or she thought that I would do everything to avoid her as well, even as far as to snub my best friends' celebration. There was a careless double invitation to take into account. Susan told her that I could make a surprise guest appearance; there was a warning out. So what kind of game is Corrina playing with us? How does she think I fit into her life at all, in contemporary times?

I don't do the wise thing; I don't just walk away, keeping a feel on my pulse. She sits at the table making small talk, pretending that she hasn't noticed me. But she must have done by this stage. She has 20/20 vision: she can read off an optician's chart from the reverse side. On holiday I had to wear my glasses down to the beach (as grit is not helpful for contact lenses) while she rattled off Greek alphabet in small print to show off. You can immediately tell the charm of this April to September romance.

Bob gestures for me to sit down, so I try to lighten my load. My legs turn to spaghetti; my palms are melting and I have lost sensation up to my armpits. She doesn't look at me, but her colour has risen. I can feel the indignant beat of her resentment against me, as if it is *her* heart that's pushing my blood around. She shakes out her burnt blonde hair, as a mountain torrent.

*Where did you show up from? Why are you looking at me like that? What are you trying to pull this time? I've got nothing to be ashamed about!*

"Fancy meeting you here, Corrina," I comment.

"Not really," she retorts. "No, I didn't, actually."

There's mixed radiation between us.

"You look well," I tell her. Like great.

"I'm going to Canada this Christmas, with a boyfriend."

"I didn't think you liked the cold," I say.

"More than you can imagine."

"Don't want to think of you alone...at that special time of the year."

"Don't worry."

"I've moved into a more solitary period of my life...when I enjoy my own company." I make myself sound like Jack Kerouac at his mountain retreat.

"Glad you are at a happy place," she replies.

"I wouldn't be that positive, at this phase of existence."

"That's your problem, Noah." Her facial expressions take account of other people around the table. I believe they are desperately filtering us out; all except her new boyfriend.

"I'm a more reflective kind of guy now," I argue.

"Glad you manage to get out and about," she observes.

"Into the back garden, mostly."

She closes up and I have to compose myself.

I haven't seen nor heard from her since I was packaged back like a skewed kebab. Gossip was her way of discovering if I was dead or alive: and she didn't want me either way. She turned up to this double-hoot to verify the facts for herself. She's cutting another back-wheel groove into my imagination. I didn't expect to see her again for dust.

Elizabeth revised her ideas about me, when I first hooked up with this girl. I could still pull and Lizzie had better watch out. I was rejuvenated, despite the risk of this new relationship coming apart like an old bone shaker.

I have that memory of encountering Corrina Farlane for the first time; meeting her at the reception of Whig Wham Music. I still hold that picture in my mind, like a delicate flame in the cup of my hand - the flame of life. My future was clarified in those moments - or so I fooled myself. There's still a flame between us; if not an idealistic type. I hope she hasn't deleted that memorable day from her organiser.

*Who do you think you're looking at? Do you really think I'm interested in you any longer? How dare you get so close to me again?*

She keeps up a sheet of cold detachment, but she's surprised too, going by the sunset glow spreading around her neck. We didn't see anything like that on holiday.

She's talking to our fellow guests with too much emphasis. She refuses to meet my gaze or acknowledge me directly. Midnight blue, the colour of her eyes, almost black sometimes, as if the lights are going out. I hadn't forgotten them, but I couldn't exactly remember them either. She came here to prove something. I can sense her physical excitement running under the surface with mine. You have to take the bitter with the sweet, or buttery skin with a sharp tongue.

Corrina's new squeeze is desperate to regain her attention. Her attention wanders back to him for a split second, but then her mind gets away at a hundred miles an hour. Ashley her boyfriend is called. A square shouldered, Aga-jawed kind of guy; only relaxed in contact sports. Put him into a ruck with fifteen thugs and he's more socially at ease. He's solidly handsome, but he has to be handsome if anybody is going to pay him any attention. He's taking a public flogging right now; serving up his spineless back to Corrina like a real trooper.

"All my cousins go to the same school together, that my father and I went to," he is telling us. "They are all right tough little buggers, I can assure you. They're constantly getting into punch ups on the school team. Each and every one returned home with shiners this summer," he brags.

Sadly for him his girlfriend doesn't take the slightest interest in his pugnacious cousins. The delights of childhood interest her as much as the antics of pot-bellied Vietnamese pigs. The poor sap. Although I've been there. The village stocks, rotten fruit, ritual romantic humiliation that is, not 'Nam.

My foot taps her shin by accident. This startles her, but she calms the reflex, despite hectic splashes across her cheeks. Ashley knocks my shin as he attempts to get nearer to her. I presume it is then Ashley's knee, going by his shocked jump. No wonder she can wind this guy around her little finger like a money spider. He'll be down on all fours cleaning out the barrels of her Triumph soon.

Bob returns holding a beer for us both. He's out of breath and grimacing as if having unloaded barrels off the lorry. He hands a foamy tankard to me as if beer can restore my powers. It's certainly worth a try. He plunges back into a chair in relief.

"Here you are at last," Susan chastises.

"What do you expect me to do?" he says, recovering his breath. "There must be near to a hundred people here tonight."

"They are all your invitations, and you'd better look after them," she suggests.

"I'm aware of that, Suze."

"Everybody's having a great hoot this year," I assure them.

"There could be a riot before the end of the night," Bob warned.

"You would prefer to do some gardening, wouldn't you," Susan objected.

"You're just as shy as I am," he tells her.

"Some shy people enjoy throwing a party," Corrina said.

"Do you think so?" Susan returned.

"You may overcome your inhibitions at a party."

"Are you talking about yourself, Corrina?" I wonder.

"You'd put anybody off going to a party," she answers coolly.

"I don't think of you as being shy," I insist.

"There you are, Noah, you've learnt something about her," Susan argues.

"Birthdays are just numbers to me," Ross contributes.

"Just too big these days," Susan laughs.

"When you're in top condition, you're in top condition," Ross beams.

Everyone treats him to a quick examination. Like an iguana in a bottle of Jamaican Rum, he is very well preserved. Shirley Valentine keeps him in trim as well.

"You hired a cruise ship for your last birthday, didn't you, Ross?" Bob recalls.

"Only to please the girlfriend's relatives," Ross admits. The pair of new jeans pinches his scrotum suddenly.

"You don't suffer any melancholy thoughts at all," Susan wonders, "as you approach the autumn of your years?"

He holds an overwhelming grin. "None of those, whatsoever, Sue, love."

"I don't want to get a day older than now," Corrina discloses.

"Are you afraid of ageing already?" Bob says.

"I'm terrified of wrinkles."

"Anywhere in particular?" I wonder.

"Most of us around this table should be terrified then," Bob remarks, easing his shoulders.

I don't know if 'wrinkles' is a reference to me.

"Why should a beautiful young woman worry about wrinkles yet?" Susan says. "We used to be lovely too. I have to warn you there."

"You're always lovely to me, Susan," her husband says. "I wouldn't have named that rose after you, otherwise."

"What's your attitude to ageing, Noah?" Corrina quizzes.

"Me? My attitude?" The thousand year old man with a shot of eternal youth? "I'm not so very old, am I?"

"What does everyone think?" she asks.

"What is this?" I complain.

"Do you look far into the future?"

"No more last minute deals," I tell her.

"You're a pessimist then," she concludes.

"I don't presume that I will live to a ripe old age," I say. "I can't make any assumptions about my future...how it is going to shape up...or who with."

"Yet who can really tell," Bob comes back, "what they should expect in the future?"

"I'm just grateful to wake up in the morning," I tell them.

"You can thank the medics for that," Corrina reminds me. For my second coming in life, she means.

"Live fast, die young. That's always been my motto," Ross explains. His pebbly eyes sink into contented laughter lines.

"I'm glad you're only speaking for yourself," Susan says.

"Fast and dangerous is the only way," Corrina argues.

"I don't mind the idea of fading away," I admit.

"You don't do so badly. You have a good life. From what I can see. Why are you always complaining?" asks the caring bike girl.

"Thanks for you undying concern," I return.

"Fading away sounds reasonable to me," Bob admits

"Wouldn't you like all the clocks to stop, Noah? Now... For time to stop at precisely this moment?" Corrina challenges. She exposes me to the shimmering surface of her swimming pools. Either I drown or I dive in.

"I don't have an overwhelming desire to race ahead," I concede. A lap of honour is better than the *last* lap maybe.

Bob Huntingdon scratches his bristled chin and squints questioningly.

"You're in a more positive frame of mind, Noah," Susan tells me. "You only needed to get out of the house to enjoy our party. Do you see?"

"Your party has worked wonders for Noah," Corrina remarks.

"What are you talking about?" Bob asks, turning to her directly.

"Why look at the little smile on his face," Corrina suggests. This chick is a strange cookie. "It's as if something's turned up."

"Shirley and I always enjoy a good knees up," Ross asserts.

Which remark provokes further puzzlement and stifled laughter around the table.

"You're a remarkably positive man," Susan praises, to rescue everyone. "We're thrilled that Noah could make it this evening as well. He definitely seems more like his old self."

"Noah's always in the mood for a good knees up," Corrina tells them.

"Not since I came back from holiday," I remark, enigmatically.

"As Sue said, we're delighted to see you, Noah. We're glad you came to say hello to everyone, and enjoy yourself," Bob tells me, squeezing the top of my arm.

"He knows how to enjoy himself all right, Bob. Noah's the world authority on enjoying himself." The cold vodka is racing to her head.

The Huntingdons stare back, as if exposed to another indecipherable dialect among the remote hill tribes of New Guinea.

"That was sun stroke," I tell her.

"Noah can be down for a while, but then he bounces back again, as big and strong as ever. Isn't that the idea, Noah?"

Susan gazes at her not innocently. Bob pulls a wry face of discomfort and heaves a deep breath. Corrina's new boyfriend, Ashley, coughs and colours. Ross's fiancée giggles outrageously, then shuts herself up in a second. A jogging couple are out of breath at the end of the table. Finally it is left to Ross to break the deadlock of stymied embarrassment.

"So you heard rumours about my little birthday bash on the boat, Robert?"

"It was his dream party come true," Shirley adds.

"Yes, yes Ross, quite a lot about your party. Sorry that we couldn't make it."

"It was an incredibly enjoyable little celebration," Ross explains.

"That's right, we ordered fourteen crates of pink champagne, two hundred thousand rounds of sandwiches and we held a beautiful bottom competition. Which I won."

"Which she won!" Ross adds proudly.

"Do you have anything to prove it?" Bob jokes. Laughter unites the varied company.

What does Corrina make of me now? Last thing she knew I was a broken down wreck, like a bike that's hit rocks on the descent; a warning to humanity in the Alps. They wheeled me through the terminal like a set of buckled golf clubs. Could anything much have changed? I bear all the gouges and marks of a triple heart bypass operation. With Wickham's little added extra. Not that I any longer resemble death warmed up, but I don't look like Johnny Depp in his swimming trunks either; or even Burt Lancaster in his.

She kicks my shin under the table again; another gentle erotic protest. So I offer her a friendly tap in response. A nanosecond afterwards Ashley explodes into agony.

*"AArrhh! Whatever made you?"* This was more devastating than 'the wall'.

"*Ashley?* Ashley, I'm really so terribly sorry. How very clumsy of me."

"Bloody hurt! Look at the bump there," he suggests.

She attends to him. She struck at the wrong target. Ashley had been playing footsie with her too. Masculine feet had been attacking her from all angles, like war planes. Ashley rolls up the leg of his trouser and begins to rub a bump, as she bends down to investigate her work.

"Can I go and fetch anyone another drink?" I offer. "Corrina?"

"What?"

"Can I fix you up?"

She stares at me in hostile amazement. *"Thanks all the same."*

"Yes, go on Corrina, have another drink," Bob tells her. "While there's still a few bottles left," he suggests.

Reluctantly Corrina gets to her feet and scrapes back her chair.

"Well, perhaps one more vodka, just for the road," she concedes.

I exchange a few ironic glances with my friends and their guests. If her looks could kill me, as they say. Undoubtedly she's already had a few shots over the limit. Sober or drunk she will flirt with the speed limits. That isn't a good idea when you refuse to wear body leather and you're returning home on a reconditioned antique Triumph. She's extremely fond of that ageing but characterful machine.

To the amazement of Bob and Sue it seems we're reunited again. Ashley isn't alone in questioning our intentions or our sanity, as we head towards Bob's cache of beers and spirits. You just don't need to drop any acid in this life.

It's a beautiful and scary world, and appearances can deceive.

# Chapter 17

But Corrina looks as sober as the vodka: clear, sharp, fierce and icy; like the expression of the county court judge, who couldn't help but share his ideas as he dissolved my marriage.

"So you're leaving already?" I ask.

"That's a safe assumption," she tells me.

"Didn't we have this conversation somewhere before? Lemon?" I ask.

She takes a grip of a ferocious serrated knife: the centre piece of an expensive set. In a second she is seduced by the wide glinting blade and holds it up between us. She wasn't seriously thinking of putting that between my ribs, was she?

Talk has resumed around the table behind us. They are relieved to escape our sexual animosity and debts; with the exception of Ashley, who dashes desperate glances towards us, between rubbing his shin. Where did she pick him up from?

"Enough for you?" I say, holding up the little glass.

She signals and takes it away from me. "You seem to be on the mend, Noah. Aren't you? No more heart shocks I assume."

"No, nothing to get excited about," I inform her. But she's still trying to work out the new features in my face. Only the landscape of Iceland changes so much.

"You were definitely frightened when you had that attack," she recalls.

"True," I admit.

"Not the kind of excitement you were looking for."

"Definitely not."

"Your surgery was a complete success though?" she queries.

"Disappointed?"

"You must be glad that it's all over with." There's brightness in her voice, like relief.

"I'm here, aren't I?"

I'm uneasy about my appearance, as I try to keep a firm voice and a straight face. The warning signs are flagged up, despite my self-confident get up. The exact malady is hard to identify, just a lack of good health and a troubled mind. My daughter said I looked like an old cheese sandwich. I continue to avoid hot lights.

"So Corrina, where have you been hiding all these weeks?"

"I've just been extremely busy," she tells me.

"With what?"

"Did you forget? There's the Whig Wham festival to organise. So we're busy attracting top musicians and performers from around the world to play."

"Did you invite those throat singers and nose flautists back?" I wonder.

"We bought enough of those silly balloons from you. Don't you want our order this year?"

"Don't worry, you'll get everything in time," I say.

"Perhaps this will tip you back into profit again," she suggests, looking sardonically through her soft lashes.

"You'll fall in love with them," I insist.

"Hopefully that will do something for your share price."

She'd been watching that at least. "I didn't come to this party to *think* about business, never mind to *talk* about it," I argue, loosening the epaulettes of my jacket.

"You do know that your company is going down like...like a burst balloon?"

"Like a Lead Zeppelin. That's been said before? You don't know that?"

"Take a look at your ex-wife's business. Elizabeth. Her company is absolutely roaring ahead, it seems. Didn't you notice that?"

"Never look back," I suggest.

"She's known as Elizabeth *Noggins* now, isn't she?" Corrina leans forward on her toes to get my response to the situation.

"Hilarious isn't it?"

"He's really quite a big handsome, charming sort of chap, it would seem, isn't he? Frank Noggins?"

"How do you say that with a straight face?" I reply.

"However you may scoff, Frank certainly knows how to run a dynamic business."

"They make a nice couple then, don't they," I say.

"They must be worth something between the two of them. She with the baking business and he with his computer company."

"Do you think so?" I tell her.

"Your ex certainly landed on her feet," Corrina argues. "You have to admire her for making such a success of her life."

"You're going to buy yourself an apron, are you?"

"She also manufactures herbal medicines. Health products, doesn't she?"

"I obviously broke up with her too soon," I comment.

"I bumped into her the other day."

"Who?" I declare. "Where?"

"Your ex. She didn't have much time for me. You'd hardly expect her to though, would you?" Corrina says. "Yes, she was in town with her son. The eldest one, I believe."

"Luke. He's my son too, you know."

"Though he exactly resembles her."

"Physically."

"They look lovely together," she remarks.

I stare into her midnight blue vortices, trying to pull out a splinter of sympathy. The vodka just sharpens her tongue to an arrow. As Marvin Gaye said: *only love can conquer hate.*

"Did you miss me?"

"Not a great deal," she admits. "Perhaps in the early hours, if I was very restless."

"Right, well, that's a start I suppose."

I feel my anger and excitement, like a double aggravation.

"I've no intention of listening to your erotic complaints," she informs me.

"Not even after our romantic escape?"

"That was the worst experience of my whole life," she says.

"Women can be so bloody sentimental," I remark. "Too much feeling."

"Look Noah, why take me away on holiday, if you had a blasted heart condition?" she wants to know.

"Why didn't you visit me? In hospital?" I ask her.

"Did you want me at your bed side, crying?"

"What's wrong with that?" I tell her.

"I was afraid you were going to die," she admits.

"Well, I'm feeling much better these days," I say.

"Are you sure?" she wonders.

"Yes, I'm sure. I'm back in great shape. I feel like making love to you. At this very moment, as a matter of fact."

"Don't be ridiculous Noah. With all these people around?"

But her eyes flicker to the bridge of her nose: the outrageous idea excites her.

"We can go upstairs," I suggest. What's wrong with me? If I have to prove I am a teenager again?

"Don't try to get us hitched again, Noah, will you. Upstairs is full of guests."

The hallway is crowded, the stairway is congested, the living room is packed. As a friend of the owners I know the secrets of their house. There's a back room at the end of the dining room which leads to a hidden room. An underworld made for two.

We steal kisses between bitter tasting drinks. I fool myself that our romance is starting over. I'm searching for that new life again, that second youth. How can this be when I'm shy of forty nine? What can she give me other than a final humiliation?

"This doesn't mean I want to marry you, or anything. Or to spend the rest of my life with you... as you once talked about," she insists.

"Haven't we been through all this before?" I tell her.

"I don't want you to have any illusions," she says.

I support myself with a sturdy posture. "We've been through a bad trip, but that's all behind us."

"Are you sure? You have a rumpled type of charm. I like older guys. But I have my own life."

"I'm in a good place now too," I say. "You don't think so?"

"Why should I get myself involved with you again?" She shakes her head of abundant hair - gold from an emperor's hands.

"I'm fully restored. You can see for yourself?" Deliberately missing the point. I have an arm around her shoulder pulling her into me.

Corrina gazes at me with anxious doubt.

"They just opened up the old fire box and made sure it sparked properly."

"They obviously didn't mess around with you too much."

"You're still a very beautiful and special girl to me," I assure her.

"To be honest, you're not my ideal man," she confesses.

I absorb the blow. "Tell me something I don't know."

*Sister, am I not a brother to you? Deserving of affection*?

"That didn't matter to me on Crete, but it makes a difference now...somehow."

"You put my 'ideal' into the shade," I tell her. I've plunged back into the ocean, regardless of the potential sharks.

"You don't want me to lead you on, do you?" she tells me. "You're still a good looking guy. So long as you understand where you stand," she jokes, pushing me in the stomach.

I need Dylan to write me another protest song. But the hard truth doesn't restrain me. She falls into my arms again, in the half darkness of the confined room, with party noises dim and distant. I couldn't resist her.

No flashbulbs pop, no crowd waits to greet us at barriers, on our return. Perhaps we did manage to slip away unseen this time, as if we are back from holidaying together, in the Sahara. This hope is dashed when I understand that Damon and Melanie have noticed us. They stare at me with a round 'caught you' expression on their ruddy angelic faces, as if they spotted a high court judge nicking tea towels in Oxfam. They are stood in one corner of the dining room with home-made fair-trade fruit juice each. Almost as if they followed us here to enjoy the post-coital moment. Or was I just being paranoid? I know they're on very friendly terms with Liz and the Dino. Will they report back on my party antics? Did they string up Hanratty or stand Gary Gilmore in front of a firing squad?

Just as Corrina is determined to make a fast getaway, Bob reappears on the scene. It's our scene, but it's his party. His friendship offers up these incidents - he's like a war reporter. He's the guy doing fatalistic interviews, through the noise of a helicopter above his head, while clearing personnel from the roof of the American embassy in Saigon.

In typical party pose he's reduced to waiter's duties, holding out a couple of foaming beers. A glimpse between Corrina and I informs of the new situation on the ground. He's a shrewd enough guy. We're caught in our tracks.

"Did you finish your drink?" Bob asks her.

"Thanks Bob."

There are these carnations in her cheeks to make any man wonder.

"You're leaving after all?"

"You've got another great hoot on your hands this year, mate," I assure him. "It's a proper roustabout."

Bob gives me a dubious look. He isn't impressed with me. Long suffering. "Your friend left half an hour ago," Bob informs her.

"There or thereabouts," I say.

"Your young companion, that is."

"Ashley? Did he say why?"

"No, but he was upset."

"I hope he remembered his crash helmet," I say. "Not to worry, Corrina, he'll get over it."

"That's all very well for you to say, Noah Sheer. We have to work together at Whig Wham. I can't afford to upset a colleague like that."

"You're doing well so far."

"I just gave him a lift here on my bike, that's all."

"He called for a taxi. I guess he was impatient," Bob observes.

My friend holds up a beer in each hand, like a water carrier or a moral measure.

"Damn, I suppose I'll be eating humble pie on Monday," she complains.

"Best to cut your losses," I advise. "Is one of those beers for me, Bob?"

"No, not these." He pulls the tankards out of reach.

"That's a pity, because I always get a good thirst after... after a swinging party," I say reluctantly, pulling my eyes away.

"Yes, Noah, I'm aware of that," Bob tells me, before he marches off.

"I'm leaving," Corrina clarifies.

"Story of my life." But the party isn't over until I start singing.

Bob is struggling through the hordes of guests he invited, clinging on to his pitchers of ale, his bacchanalian scales of justice. Apparently the beer is intended for Lloyd, so it's not just the last laugh he'll enjoy.

In his current serving apron Bob resembles a Bavarian barmaid, albeit one with prodigious facial growth. If Jimmy Page could see him now, he'd never offer an autograph.

I hear Susan's voice nearby, as she cuts a path through. She's offering to fetch someone's coat. Best to get away before Damon insists on genetic fingerprinting. He'll force some kind of swab into my mouth.

There's certainly going to be plenty of health food for thought.

"Another night cap, Corrina?"

"I'm going to make tracks," she tells me. "Some friends and I are going to Bath tomorrow."

"More clubbing?"

"We're not going clubbing, Noah. We're working."

"Another time then?" I wonder.

"We'll see."

"You should move in with me. That would make life much easier."

"You have to be joking," she retorts.

"So maybe you need to sleep on the idea." To smother it to death perhaps.

"I wouldn't hold your breath," she warns.

No, I've already tried that. "What's so bad about the idea? Of you and I shacking up together? We discussed it once," I remind her. "Afraid of being happy?"

"I already have somewhere perfectly decent to live, thank you."

"Oh? Where exactly is that?" I press.

"You're definitely not getting my address," she says.

"You want to preserve your privacy?"

"Something like that."

"But don't you owe me an apology at least?"

"An apology?" she challenges. "Why should I ever apologise to you, Noah?"

"You haven't knocked on my door, since I was discharged."

"You had the bosom of your family to return to, didn't you?" she argues.

I consider the pleasant image. "That's right, my wife stopped everything to be with me, to drive me up to the hospital."

"Then what on earth are you grumbling about?" she wonders.

"I don't know. We're divorced," I protest.

"So that makes you a better proposition for the future, does it?"

"It may help," I say. "Why should a near fatal coronary come between a man and a woman?"

"Don't you have three children? I assume they're yours."

"Whose do you think?" I object. At least I am confident there.

"The eldest one is a grown woman. I bumped into her the other night as well."

"You meet my family more than I do," I tell her. "What was she doing this time?"

"She was out with her friends."

"Clubbing?"

"That's right."

"Oh?" Again Angela. She keeps turning up, but only in other people's anecdotes.

"Quite a girl, that one." She could talk. "Then I bumped into her outside the pub last week. They look a funny bunch, her friends. High as kites, all of them."

"My daughter doesn't interfere with my life, or who I choose to see," I argue.

"Why should I invite you back?" Corrina argues. "Do you think I need you?"

"Seeing another guy?"

"I'm concentrated on my job, to be honest. Next year I aim to become a director. If I want to go out clubbing or to a concert, then I go with someone at the studios."

"Ashley?"

"No, not bloody Ashley," she scoffs. "Look, Noah, I want to get home."

"I said something similar on the Aegean," I recall.

"That was all your idea," she comments.

"I didn't know I was knocking on heaven's door."

"There's never a perfect time for making an exit," she argues.

"So you are going to stay, after all?"

"Look, I'm pleased that you are still around, Noah. Let's catch up with each other, if that's what happens. But that doesn't imply any commitment or feeling on my part."

I'm encouraged. "Meet me out on the Down one Sunday morning? If you're free? I'm usually over there, enjoying my sport."

"Flying your kites, do you mean?"

"That's right. A relaxing and inspiring *sport*," I emphasise.

"Not a hobby or a pastime?"

"Definitely, not just those things," I say.

"Whatever turns you on then, Noah."

"That's always been my philosophy."

"Such as it is."

"Right."

"I'm pleased you are back to something like yourself, at least."

"Something for us to share," I say.

"But I have to dash." All my hopes?

"So what is your new address?" I add.

"Not known to you?"

She collects her crash helmet, encases her cranium, fastens the strap. She's always kept faith with that infernal machine, if not the ghost contained. Her obsessions are as intense as my own, I have to concede. She loved Robert M Pirsig's great book, that I loaned out to her: which is the closest we get spiritually, when it comes to the subject of motorbikes. Certainly not the case, when I was gripping hold of her waist for dear life.

Your life gets written up into your face eventually. You definitely get the kind of snook you deserve. Will she ever want to look at me again? In full day light? I may struggle to keep up with her in the future, even riding pillion. Contemporary times are just leaving me further and further behind. Would she tolerate my dilapidated shape among her friends? How would she introduce me? As her pervy taste in affairs? Screwing about with a sick older man? That's really going to build up my esteem and improve my health affairs. But desire can be stronger than sense

- or even perception. Is it stronger than public opinion? Peer opinion? Can I feel comfortable with the general prognosis? Is she?

Can she tolerate my degeneration? The marks of mutiliation? She has an old motorcycle accident scar herself. It's from the middle of her rib cab, squiggling along to her belly button; starting from beneath her right breast. But does this compare to my own scars? On both sides of the fence. Is she hiding her disgust? I don't get that idea.

I'm never going to encounter another woman like Corrina. I'm convinced she is the last throw in my love game, here on the planet. I'm still energetic, with cool musical tastes, up to date attitudes. I have something to offer a young woman. Corrina gets that.

The surgeon didn't screw up in that regard. The surgeon didn't make a complete mess. At least he knew how to make neat stitches.

# A Family Affair

# Chapter 18

On a Sunday morning - a few weeks on - I am back out on Clifton Down, flying my kites. More than ever, this should be the traditional day of rest, but typically I'm back out in the open; reverting to a comforting childhood pursuit, as Lizzie puts it.

In theory my business partner and I are testing some new model kites; innovations in construction, design or materials; variations of our ideas and fancies; before we put them on the kite market. Often though this becomes a type of free exhibition of kites to the public; children and their parents stand, hands on hips to stare, who also happen to be out on the Down, enjoying a leisurely family Sunday. It's great to be on the Down: plenty of space and fresh air on this breezy plateau; I'm certainly boosting a good vibe, building up positive karma, as if trying to gain reincarnation as an axe hero. It's a lovely morning for flying kites, with a moderate fourteen mile per hour wind and a bit of cloud protection.

Romantic bedrooms are off limits but the skyways are always available. Obviously kite flying is quite spiritual and doesn't imply any extreme pain or risk. At least you'd think so, that there's no better way to relax. Nobody likes to be proved wrong, but this particular Sunday it just doesn't turn out like that. There were a few incidents and somebody turned up from nowhere.

I'm testing kites with my number-two and financial guru, James Nairn. He's been living in Bristol for more than twenty years but originally came from Edinburgh. James hammered at the portals of Big Pink that morning at the premature hour of six, having pulled up in our solitary company van. I still was sunk into a hung-over type of doze, with the bed clothes rucked up to my eyebrows, having fallen into the hollow on Lizzie's old side of the bed. Like Dracula hearing the knocker on his castle door (allegedly) I was forced to climb out of my box to investigate. The little Scottish explorer forced me to get out of doors and into the sunlight.

What more can I say about this Nairn guy and I? If you could imagine the Marx Brothers running a factory you'd get an idea. No, really, he needs to bring me back to terra firma, should I start to light up my cigar and strut around like Isambard Kingdom Brunel; putting my thumbs into the loops of my Levi's. I'm fortunate in regard to my business, because undergraduate daydreams turned into reality. I was a type of hippie entrepreneur, if not as successful as others. I've never grinned as broadly as Branson but I've done all right. When you're developing kites and balloons you don't have to invest into finding eco-fuels. To me it was an idealistic and peaceful enterprise from the beginning: I've never intended to hurt anybody in my life - even if I fall short in my personal life. I created my company in partnership with my best friend from university. That's a guy called Stuart who's sadly no longer with us, God rest him. I'll say more about Stuart later, if I'm able. The business was a principle to me, an exemplar, as much as it was fun. Did my twenty year old self know how hard it is to live up to?

In modern times the business employs fifteen people. With Stuart gone we'll always be one man short, but that includes designers, builders, sales people, packers and comedians. I floated the business - so to speak - and distributed shares to family, friends and small investors, as well as to myself and to the Ex of course. I have a majority holding, but that may change if that Chief Exec in the sky calls me to account. I like to believe that my original dream will survive after me. The idea is for Luke to take over the business afterwards. I wish him to guide our Enterprise through the relative time of distant galaxies. That's after Liz has encouraged him to gain his MBA, after he passes some school exams; although I didn't have any formal qualifications in business myself.

In this era the business hasn't been doing so well. According to James Nairn we face a number of harsh financial decisions. This could even involve sacking people who - many of them - have been with us for years. I was trying to put these off, and my heart attack came to my assistance. Personally I find this to be harsh medicine - invasive surgery. Believe me I am the expert on invasive, painful and questionable surgery. Didn't we find anything more sophisticated to overcome our problems than cutting and hacking? Just as a balloon may scythe through a storm, I plan to grip tightly to my rigging and survive this turbulence. What will Luke think if he loses my company before he can even leave school? What kind of image is that going to leave him of the old man? No longer one of the savvy hipster.

Lizzie's business is going up-hill, so he will never be deprived of designer clothes, electronics or roller blades. But that's hardly the point.

The first kite I'm flying this Sunday is the Eddy kite, named after its inventor, who struck on the idea in 1891. This design was a breakthrough because it got rid of a kite's typical swishy tail. We've made a few technical adjustments to our version. It bobs about in its window of sky, simple to control. As I'm not back to peak fitness I don't want to wrench any strings. Not until I'm sitting comfortably in a lotus position, surrounded by princesses in leotards. I dig my Cuban heels into the turf, as the breeze finds a piece of my hair to ruffle, losing my hangover with the invigorating morning; with the city of Bristol vibrant and lovely below and around us.

James senses my happiness and absorption, while he's busy flying a Delta kite. According to the wind the pilot can change the wing angle of this model. This Delta has an impressive, colourful effect; a sail of rainbow colours breathtakingly, far above us. It's hard to meet demand in the US, as this is our best-selling and best reviewed kite in North America. James is deciding if this version meets design standards. Satisfied, he concentrates on gradually winding the machine back to earth. The breeze has picked up to generate strenuous pull on the line. I wind back a Pear Top and afterwards push up an Arch Top; which has a polyester skin and graphite frame.

James sends up a Hyper kite; which is an exceptionally fast, sensitive and tricky number, requiring alert piloting skills, through double lines. He requires all the sensitivity of his skilful fingers and the strength in his knotty arms. He succeeds in drawing a pattern of spectacular dashes and swishes across the wide sky, much to the appreciation of by-standers. Already people are gathering to watch us; including impatient dogs and one particular Labrador who once ate a box kite. The kids' little fibreglass models are waving about like handkerchiefs. This can be painful for me, as it reminds me of the man I used to be; the father and husband.

The Hyper kite is a stunt kite with a high tensile surface that responds sharply to commands, as well as to errors; requiring James to jig as nimbly as for a family reunion back in Edinburgh.

It's no wonder that we attract an audience. Some visitors are kite enthusiasts who know that I am going to be around, as usual. I chat to some of them, as they're keen to get any technical advice or even to place orders, as well as to enjoy Nairn's flying skills. Often we send people to the Bristol Kitestore, or other excellent specialists in the city who stock our models. For some time I stand akimbo admiring my partner's manoeuvres, sharing observations and ideas.

Liz and I always brought a picnic up here on Sundays. She could put up with kite flying more than my hot air balloons; she always refused to accompany me. We'd shake out our blanket and set out our lunch, as the kids ran around having fun, with their box kites, or sometimes a bird kite. I encouraged them, although kites didn't pull on their imagination for long. Even then Angela was in the habit of slipping away, going out of sight, reach and call, leading us into desperate searches. You got that desire for independence, for individuality - crazy kid. Even though my concentration has wandered, I always intended to return. Did she want to put my eyes out?

In our thirties we'd hit the highway in our orange VW Caravanette - complete with peace signs, flower symbols, smiley face and zebra patterned seat cushions; like hippies on safari maybe. We'd pack our gear in the vehicle and set out with the kids to Weston or beyond, for marvellous family holidays between the dunes.

After all Lizzie and I had been married at the nozzle of a smoking gun, for all that we were crazy about each other. A Russian roulette with happiness? I kept my eyes open all the time.

Even though we only had two barrels to play with. How could she decide to jump ship in mid ocean? What was the big draw of Captain Hook?

What a flawless afternoon. The crowds gather. Avoid airports, dogs and power lines. James is challenging himself with an ultra-light sport kite, that I have been tinkering with for months. He's thinking ahead to the annual international kite festival. The idea is to show off our wares and to sell.

Not to be outshone I assemble our best fighting kite, a fantastically curved shape, our Nagasaki Hata. The design of this kite originated in China, moving to Japan during the seventeenth century, due to Dutch seamen. This kite depends on accurate symmetry, as well as delicate balance - which has to be just-so.

Funny that they called those diaphragm things Dutch Caps. How did Liz and I allow the happy times to escape? Are all those good and happy memories recorded somewhere, like Nirvana at the back of the Cosmos, or pictures on the retina after you close your eyes? God knows. Or maybe all those old family movies just went up in a bonfire, under the heat of an arc lamp. Man, it's a beautiful but scary world.

I control my kite well, as I follow it bobbing about in the sky, like watching my son in the swimming pool in a bright rubber ring. But I allow my concentration to wander with my thoughts. There's too much slack in the line. Such a small mistake is enough to create problems with a performance kite. Consequently the Hata plunges towards the ground. Only at the last moment do I rescue the situation. There's a first round of applause as spectators gasp at my trick. I know how much care was put into the construction of this kite. I couldn't look my staff in the eyes over a pile of sticks. One more false move and the kite will crash. For the time being it circles and swerves, confident and graceful as an angel. I begin to feel as if the Hata has a living force; animated. I suffer a type of stir-crazy sensation, even an hallucination, that the kite is flying by itself, or even manipulating the flyer. It is a child controlling the parent. It is looping, darting and plunging, escaping the snares of my gloved hands. I struggle to describe beautiful patterns across the sky, as is the intention, to delight the passers-by. It should have been graceful, exciting and inspiring, but it's turning into an embarrassing disaster, like a love affair gone wrong. The turns are quicker, the drops are deeper, the ascents steeper, the descents sharper, than ever could be intended. How can I ever escape while keeping face and saving my soul, such as it is?

James turns his head to investigate, after his own kite has been reeled back to terra firma. As long as they don't stamp a spade into the grass, I don't mind. We all think about that from time to time. I don't wish to be morbid. There's the big interested crowd, pointing and discussing. I twist myself around, pulling hard on the right line, battling to avoid calamity. I succeed with only centimetres and a split second to spare. Fantastic flying, partner: a startling round of applause, like a sudden crackling in the ears. Somebody's turned up the volume. I feel as if my mind is going up in flames.

"Keep her tight!" James barks. "Don't let her go with every waff of wind!" He's flapping around like one of those guys with lollipops at Heathrow airport years ago.

There are *oohs* and *ahs* from the audience.

Next moment I experience physical discomfort: the too familiar symptoms. Unpleasant sensations of heat and constriction. Not so much pins and needles, as nails and bolts. I realise that I'm losing the battle to fly. Another round of applause is dead static in my head. I know that my heart is playing up again. I can feel the strings breaking on an out of tune guitar. There's no other explanation for this conflict. There's no easy cure for dysmorphia. The damaged heart valve may disintegrate, so taking me out of Einstein's equation. Or is it just shifting position again? Moving with excruciating effects? Your guess is as good as mine.

The Hata kite plucks and tears my nerves as it dashes about the sky. Not even Fidel Castro in his prime could seize control here. As the precious kite goes on the razzle, I'm caught in a despairing gesture, with all eyes on me. This could be my last turn. My final flying show on the Down. I raise my arms into the air and let go of the reels; abandoning hope. There's gasping and groaning from the gods. Line rips through my gloved hands, as the kite escapes, jettisons across the sky. The Nagasaki Hata snaps towards the horizon at full pelt and vanishes forever. Like a teenage daughter who isn't going to listen. The pilot has made a complete naked ape of himself.

James scurries angrily in my direction, intending the hairdryer treatment. Why did I fly our precious little machine in such a cavalier way? But he realises that I'm not responsible for a crass piloting error. I tumble back on to the grass, as my heart thumps like a kettle drum and my legs snap. No, not unless I take failure badly. I press down on my ribcage in an effort to stop this pain. It looks as if a sniper has put a bullet into my chest, in this posture. But if I'm apparently lying lifeless, it is more out of terror. This is a passive-aggressive strategy against the Reaper. You don't need to drop acid to get a view on unreality.

I try to gather my thoughts, trying to understand what the hell, as I stare up into the sky. Just as I used to lie back on the sand dunes, during those family holidays. Waiting for the heart valve to break up, anticipating the flood of oblivion. This time I wasn't day dreaming. The children were occupied making sand castles, complete with flags and moat. Liz and I had hammered in the windbreak, played a game of beach tennis, before stretching out on our towels to recover. I remembered the moment I knew that I was in love with Elizabeth; that I would make her my own and probably spend the rest of our lives together. It was as she came down the staircase between classes. She recognised the feeling from my look as she stepped towards me. This was the moment of realisation, for both of us. It was the electric moment in our relationship; a friendship that had begun when she joined my class at school. This was like God breathing life into the world.

But as far as oblivion goes, the tide was still out. This is the proof: James is kneeling at my side, holding my head from the ground, talking to me - in words that are at first badly distorted. So I must have checked out for a while. My senses gradually arrange as I tune back into station. Slowly I regain consciousness, gazing into his sharp anxious features. I'm spread out in the middle of a worried crowd. Maybe they thought this was part of our show. It's the escapologist jumping out of his barrel of water again. But I just had another bad experience.

"We'd better call an ambulance, Noah," my friend insists.

"No, there's no point?" I reply. "Where's my kite?"

"How do you mean - there's no point?" he wonders.

"They can't help," I insist.

"Why not?"

I raised myself from a spread-eagled position on to my elbows. "They've done all they can for me, James. The doctors, the surgeons. All that and a bit extra too."

"What's the matter with you, Noah?" he pursues.

"Something's gone wrong with the compressor."

"I thought you're feeling well again," he says.

"They tried," I say, forced to spit. James is perplexed at this and a few onlookers disgusted. But I'm provoked by the radiation of mortality.

"Are you all right?" he asks again.

"Just a few side effects," I tell him, coughing and spluttering now. But really I don't understand these side effects, or symptoms; where they come from, or where they lead. I'm still floating in some distant space, like a diver with the bends. "Sod it," I complain. Who can prise out the invisible sniper's bullet?

James scampers across the field to fetch my medication, like Lassie on acid. This gives more time to pull myself together, find a peaceful or reassuring expression. I sit up and fend off shocked questions from the public, incredulous at still being alive. Gradually the audience begins to disperse. Are they disappointed, or what?

James comes trundling back, carrying my personal bag, complaining about the cancelled ambulance. Which hospital are they going to take me to? What procedure are they likely to follow? I've tried all the hospitals. I've been through the 'good hospitals guide'. Maybe I need to share my case history with other people. Not only is my secrecy dangerous and isolating, but it scares the life out of others too.

I pull out some propranolol tablets from the bag. I could swallow down the whole bottle. These are of zero medical benefit in my case. In *my* case they threw out the medical rule book. I wash down some pills with a nip of brandy from Granddad's flask. It's a beautiful object, with swans engraved into silver, rubbed black with time, taking off from water. I always thought of Elizabeth.

The sunlight has an edge, slicing across my eyes like a scalpel. Finally I attempt to defy gravity again. James puts his hands under my armpits to help. My limbs are still like over-boiled pasta. I force myself to take breaths and declare myself fit again. But there's nothing to be given for a botched heart operation, other than a clown's nose and the collected works of Kierkegaard.

# Chapter 19

I recognise the last person I wanted to see, coming towards me: Striding, across the common towards me, with apparent purpose. Not the grim reaper, but his young and pretty assistant, his deceiving foil, like Charlie Manson's female disciples, youthful and beautiful, yet besotted, brainwashed by evil charisma. Corrina Farlane. Surely I have to be hallucinating in this time warp. Just when you get to the end of one bad trip, you reach the beginning of another. Sometimes I want the path that's *most* travelled. Does Corrina know what she's letting herself in for? Has she noticed the hooded guy with a sickle behind her shoulder?

I need to take another look, struggling to refocus my vision after that fall, to ascertain if it really is her. *It really is her.* Somebody must have slipped something into my hip flask.

"See that woman coming towards us?" I tell James.

"The brassy blonde?" he observes.

"She's my girlfriend... or my ex-girlfriend," I say (living and breathing all the same).

"What about her?"

"Don't mention what's happened to me, will you? No, she mustn't hear about this. She'd only worry herself sick."

James looks at me sideways as he untangles lines and dismantles kites. "Then you should look after yourself better," he urges.

My own logic has been turned upside down lately; James struggles to make head or tail of my remarks.

Corrina checks my logistics as she progresses to our flying spot. She's definitely the last person I expected to meet here. I'm conscious of my physical shortcomings at this moment - *tangled up in blue*. The Earth must have hurtled millions of miles since Corrina and I collided into each other at the Huntingdon's double celebration. *Time goes so fast, like a jet plane*. What thought or desire made her fly off in my direction? Hadn't she already seen me transform into an old man? finding heart trouble in demi-paradise? What sort of catch does Noah Sheer represent any longer, to such a dynamic young woman, with her job, her looks, her energy? Man, we've already gone all the way to the end of the line. Can there really be another fork in the story? Another corkscrew to the heart?

I recall inviting her to join me one Sunday morning, to fly my kites on the Down. Several weeks had gone by since that evening, so I hadn't expected her to pick up the invitation. Any roads, I was practicing my party rhetoric and like my party shirt, the suggestion was desperate and half-winded. In truth I believed we'd been separated forever in the departure lounge. I was convinced we'd said our farewells in that terminus. Nevertheless, my dodgy heart rejoices at the sight of her; skips the proverbial beat. I can't afford to skip too many beats. What brings her out here, to take another free wheel through my life, as I get up on my last legs? As I balance on my hind-legs like that Minotaur fatally wounded?

For here she comes, kicking through the rough grass. Not exactly smiling with anticipation but certainly decided in her actions. She must have parked the bike somewhere, as she's holding her helmet. She's also wearing motorcycle boots. Not any other form of protective clothing. Why doesn't she take precautions after having that serious accident in France? I thought that full leathers are requisite for the road. Sunlight hurts my eyes as it glints off her. Good fortune that she showed up at this moment. A beautiful relationship would have folded with the kite and its pilot. Who am I kidding?

"Hi, Corrina!" I put up my hand and arm. I form this image of strength and unflappable joviality.

I put myself through breathing and stretching exercises. This is what nurse Ratchet instructed. The gentle sport of kiting has become too strenuous for me. A brisk wind might dislodge the mickey-mouse valve. I thought I was safe out on the down. But then the down was pulled out from under me. Corrina will notice how shaken or groggy I am. James shares an uneasy look, as I fight to pull myself around, to look instantly happy and healthy, as my gentle sport would suggest. In the struggle to conceal myself from Corrina, I am revealed to James. He changes his attitude. But not in the way she has.

"I decided to come to see you," she tells me. "I saw your kites in the air."

"The show's over," I explain.

"Is it? I'm really out of breath..." she explains. "Walking all that way over the down, just to meet you."

"You're getting out of shape?" I say.

"I need to get off the bike more often."

She fills her lungs deeply and expels forcefully, a number of times. Her rude animal vitality shocks me. Am I so far out of touch?

"I thought I might catch you," she adds.

My smile is troubled as I meet her look, afraid that she's noticed the alarm signals. My hearing is partly blocked by high pressure. Heavy metals swirl around my gums. There's a radiation of death once again, in the background, like the disturbing noise of her motorbike on a peaceful day.

"We're packing up now," I explain.

"You're leaving already?" she exclaims.

"I'm afraid so." All bets are closed.

"How unlucky," she remarks, staring inquisitively. "Couldn't you fly a kite just for me?" she wonders. She takes a big step towards me, hands on hips, flicking her mane, 'filthy healthy'. The wind bellows her soft dress as if persuading me to fly again.

"My colleague here and I have completed all test flights. We have made all technical calculations to our machines...and now it's time to go home," I say.

"Your kites, do you mean?"

"Yes," I retort. "My kites. What else?"

"You've never liked to disappoint me, have you, Noah?" she tells me outright.

"Jim and I may call into the pub for Sunday lunch. Mayn't we, Jim? On our way back home?"

He grunts back without committing himself. James is trying hard not to hear or see what is unpleasant or confusing. It's unlikely that my ex is going to interrogate him on the matter.

"At the Huntingdon's party you invited me to watch you fly," she objects.

"That must have been weeks ago now. Anyway, I'm exhausted now."

"You can't be tired out already. What have you been doing?" she wonders. She shakes mellow sunshine out of her hair.

"I just had another incident. You know, with the organ."

"Which organ?" she replies.

I stare back trying to decipher her meaning. She's stood close and I'm lost in the hypnotic ripples of her eyes, as if making a low approach across the Indian ocean.

"Around the equator or..."

"What are you talking about, Noah? There's always something happening with you, isn't there. I can never predict what could happen next." She straightens her posture and gives her hair another vigorous shake.

"Another heart pain," I admit.

"What, another one?"

"There's been another explosion in the carburettor," I tell her. I slipped into a language she could understand - motor mechanics. I didn't fancy stringing up another kite to show off for her. Times had definitely changed again.

"You're pulling my leg, aren't you?" she smiles.

"Not for a long time," I assure her.

I don't have a pocket mirror, but I must look a sight, as her eyes puzzle over my remote features. "You do look pale and sticky," she observes.

"Pale and sticky?" I return.

"You didn't have another coronary, did you, or something like that?"

"No."

"What do you have against me, flying one of your little kites?" she says.

I'm not flexible enough to oppose her. Better if she's distracted until I'm fully re-oxygenated. "Fair enough then, Corrina, if you really want to," I offer.

"Oh, how lovely." She almost jumps up and down.

"You can fly by yourself today."

She tosses her motorcycle helmet to the ground and prepares. She's wearing a light summery dress and, going by exposed bra straps, lacy black lingerie. A hell of a combination. I'd have to be embedded in a tomb of frozen nitrogen, not to notice or to resist. But does she *want* to break my resistance?

James grumpily puts together a simple diamond kite for her and hands across the reel and line. To start her off he holds the edges of the kite and gives it a gentle push into the air. Eagerly and gracefully it takes to the sky, joining the hundreds of kites that are still being flown around the common. People have lost all interest in my demonstration. They must have thought I was some kind of showman, pulling a stunt like that. It's frightening when it happens; when you have a coronary incident. You feel like an escape artist hammering on the inside of the fish tank, observers thinking it is a comical part of the performance; with you pulling funny faces of panic and fear; although you really are trapped and panicking. Definitely that's a scary place to be.

Her flowing hair forms a lower tail for the kite. She lets out a squeal of delight as it ascends and circles. It beats a fistful of uppers any day. James looks between us and returns to cataloguing his equipment.

"How are you finding it?" I call to her.

"Lovely! Wonderful!" she returns.

She has confidence and control, as the simple structure moves smoothly across the heavens, with a flurry of long beribboned tail. Watching her has a calming effect. I lean back into the shadows of a beech tree to watch her and to gain time. I'm the only guy for whom kiting represents an 'extreme' sport now. Last year Corrina jumped off the suspension bridge on an elastic band, for charity. While we were together in Crete she tried kite surfing. She was there cruising across the sky like a bat, while I was below, sprawled on the beach; her wing span crossing over me in a chilly shadow. She wouldn't persuade me to get up there *with* the kite, not even at my peak.

"Noah, can you tell me something?"

"Go ahead, what's that?"

"Why did Bob Dylan decide to be born again?" she wonders.

"Born again?" Didn't see this one coming.

"Yes, whatever made him?"

"Corrina, that isn't something that you choose," I argue. "Being born again is something that you don't recognise or see coming."

When she asks me these questions, she's trying to get around me. Why is she trying to get around me?

"Don't you know the answer to my question?"

I stay to consider. "Who does?" I retort. "Dylan received a lot of heavy criticism around the time of Slow Train," I recall. She's turning me into Lester Bangs, putting me aboard the Greil Marcus *Mystery Train*.

"So don't you know why he was born again?" she objects, with a peevish dip of the shoulder. She's working the line and staring up at the sky, as if for a direct answer.

I've never been one for the firmaments or the abysses, myself. Typically I've kept my eyes on the horizon; maybe not covered my back well enough.

"Who are we to judge? Because as an artist he had spiritual reach? There was always Christian imagery in his songs... though he was Jewish. As a genius he had to discover, to strive, to aspire to a higher condition," I argue.

"That's your explanation?" she calls.

"Yes. Why not?" I scrutinise her profile for any criticism.

"You are saying it was merely an artistic choice? A type of pose?"

"As an artist he needed to exist in a spiritual state. Maybe the Christian vibe was congenial... and the spirit really did touch him," I tell her. "Have you thought about that, Corrina? Jesus spoke to him. Why not?"

"Has Jesus ever spoken to you?" she challenges.

She goads me into laughing, dryly, out loud. "Are you serious? I might not have been listening. Who knows?"

"You must have thought about this, Noah. After your heart attack."

"Sure, I'm a spiritual kind of guy," I tell her. "Straight up. But I'll never be a cash donator."

"It would have transformed your life. Don't you think? Being born again?"

"I can hardly imagine it. What I'd be like," I laugh. "Unrecognisable."

"Isn't that the point though, Noah...of being born again? To be changed? Renewed?"

"You can get that nonsense out of your head," I insist. Drinking a pint of beer without choking, walking to the park without gasping - that's the point for me.

"Not even while you were lying in a hospital bed? The condition of your soul?" she calls out. "Didn't you want to think over the big religious questions?" Without breaking her concentration on the kite.

"Never. There were other calls on my attention." Not least of which was her. Her motives. Her whereabouts.

"Why not talk to God?"

"You try," I suggest. "I didn't feel the spirit."

"So you don't have any time for the Christians then, despite Bob Dylan?"

"I wouldn't throw them to the lions," I tell her.

"Isn't Elizabeth Noggins a Christian?"

"You'd better ask *her* about that," I answer.

"I believe that her new husband is also a Christian."

"He's a prehistoric pagan," I assure myself.

"What's that?"

"Can you say that again?"

"I heard that your former partner is a regular church goer lately." Was she trying to torment me with this? Did Marilyn marry more than one man? Liz and Dick get back together? Terry and Julie cross over the river?

"Is it any wonder?" I remark.

"Sunday service, evensong, choir practice and fund raising fetes," Corrina elaborates.

"Like she doesn't want to be alone with him," I argue.

"Who do you mean? Frank Noggins? They attend church together, as I understand it."

"I respect Liz for her Christian faith. I respect Dylan." Just not Frank.

"But don't you find her beliefs objectionable?" she challenges.

"Why should I. That's her trip. It helped her to cope with divorce. Maybe. I don't know."

"Does that make you feel vulnerable?" Corrina suggests.

"Vulnerable? How?"

"You don't understand or share her faith. Isn't that the most important part of her?"

"I didn't understand her fully. Including her faith. I thought I did. But I was wrong. I was wrong about her. Finally she lost patience and cut me off."

"What great fun this is!" she declares.

Again my attention is returned to the diamond-shaped handkerchief above her head. "Is that dangerous enough for you?"

"This is a well-kept secret," she comments.

"I have others."

"But your business is in trouble?" she blurts out.

"No more than anything else in my life, I can assure you."

"I suppose that's true," she tells me.

I consider from under the shade, with my back to the cool smooth bark. "Everybody thought we were crazy to begin a business like that. Kites and balloons. They didn't look ahead... and see that people would have more free time. You just can't predict, so you need to keep a wide horizon."

"You always have a pithy philosophical thought ready."

"That's how you see it?"

"But a good idea doesn't belong to one person, does it? Not even the person who first thought it up? Even if it was original once," she remarks.

"Sounds a bit too philosophical to me," I reply. "Anyway, I told you. My kites are no secret. You can see me flying them most Sunday mornings. So what took you so long to get here?"

"I already explained, Noah, that I noticed you on the down.... with your kites. They stand out and you were giving an exhibition. There's no need to be so jumpy," she admonishes.

"We were about to pack up. What took you?"

"I went to call on an old boyfriend of mine." She speaks disjointedly. "But he was out."

"Did you try dredging up the bottom of a lake," I suggest.

"This is tremendous fun, Noah."

"My youngest lad likes that kite as well."

"Does he? How lovely. Can I buy some kites off you? For myself, that is, not professionally speaking, as last year."

"You can buy as many as you like. Do you turn away customers? When they want another album of your nose flautists?" I comment.

"Can you demonstrate some other models? I can't buy your products without learning about them."

"Don't pull so hard on the line," I advise. "That little kite almost flies by itself. You can keep that one, if you like. Try not to mess it around."

"That's really sweet of you. Then I'll take this one back home with me."

She stares up delightedly into the puffy blue sky, digging her biking boots into the silky grass, delicate hands weaving into the air. Much of the negative radiation between us has evaporated, in this rush of tenderness that a shared interest provokes.

I re-convince myself that she's my last chance for happiness. But I just had a bad experience.

"How am I doing with this?"

"Keep a hold."

"Feeling better now, Noah?" she calls over.

"Much." Her presence was putting my head into a more positive warp.

She pretty much vanished from the action and turned up again from nowhere - like a girl in a David Lynch movie: One of the later Lynch films in which the viewer needs a psychogenic substance to create any sense out of the drama before their eyes. But has Corrina Farlane come back to heal my wounds or to rend them? When it comes to matters of the heart she's difficult to pin down. My future's a blank cheque.

Corrina used to be employed by an insurance company, 'til she quit to work for the Whig Wham music people. She heard their pitch and began a more creative career. She's been adding her own lick to the world music scene. This is where I came in, as the dishy older guy, with his dirigibles and, unknown to either, a broken heart.

"Why didn't you come out to see me before?"

"We didn't make a firm date, did we?"

"Did you get a terrible hang over after that party?" I wonder.

"Not particularly, if you must ask."

"I've never seen a girl nip back so many beakers of vodka," I say.

"I wasn't particularly yucky... although I did have a bit of a sore head, if I can remember."

"Did you ruin your position in the office?"

She turns to look at me. "I shouldn't say so."

"Why not?"

"Are you interested?"

"Then this other guy at the studio isn't anybody special? No, I don't mean bloody Ashley either."

I listen to myself utter these juvenile questions. This is what happens when you are back on the singles market, just shy of forty nine, following a huge coronary. But should I stay home nursing my memories? My memories are unravelling like stitches. But I don't want her sympathy. No, not her *sympathy*.

"Are you serious about this new boyfriend of yours?" I say.

"Who do you think was the old one?" she asks. A neat thrust.

"Nobody special then."

"There are a lot of interesting and attractive guys in Bristol."

"Happy news for Bristol," I say.

"You know what I mean."

"Has there ever been any special guy in your life?" I ask. It's rare that I get this close and personal to her in conversation.

She doesn't give anything away. You could write down what I know about her personal life on the back of a postage stamp.

"I prefer to keep my distance," she admits.

"Oh, why is that?" I reply.

"I don't know, Noah, but if you get hurt or they let you down, or anything like that... then your life is suddenly dictated by this guy. You offer that man the chance to take over your life."

"Isn't that a danger we all have to run?" I comment.

"Just months, or weeks before you didn't know this person. Suddenly you can't exist or function without him. I'm never going to expose myself to that."

"You're pretty tough, aren't you?"

"Am I?"

"So you keep all your emotions in check?"

"That's about it."

"So you are a complete person already."

"I keep my feelings to myself."

"You don't want to grow? You don't want to absorb new experiences?"

"I'm not going to allow any guy to stay on board."

"Didn't you ever allow me on board?" Only for a ride to the shops, apparently.

"If you don't mind, Noah...I don't enjoy phishing about for my individual profile," she objects. "There are places you don't go."

"Tell me about it," I reply.

I get echoes from her inner life, but she cuts them off. I don't have to be holed up in the Chelsea Hotel to feel the underlying melancholy of this young woman. I've become sensitive in that way. Maybe she's justified in not revealing her deepest thoughts and feelings to me or to any guy. But I never know where she's coming from.

"I'm getting cabin fever, aren't you?" she says.

"Here on the down?"

"Let's go off somewhere."

# Chapter 20

Even if her heart is clamped shut, Corrina has explored some of the secrets of kite flying.

James is disgusted and baffled by our reunion. He's content with Classic FM on a Sunday evening, along with his meteorological charts and his two neutered tabbies. After scraping his fish dinner out of a can he'll set off on a long walk along the towpath. He has a lovely house on the loch of the canal. Sometimes I envy him. No wife, no kids, no worries. But he can't smooth my mind of Corrina. He thinks I've completely lost it over her. I help James to finish clearing away and taking our gear back to the company van. In the process of doing these jobs I regain confidence on my feet.

I told myself that I had only over exerted. Forgot about my condition for an hour or two. The chainsaw massacre. Otherwise I'm fit and sturdy, I convinced myself, as I got back on to my Cuban heels. Determined that she wouldn't notice anything wrong, further to what she'd already seen in my face. Somehow I found enough willpower to wash over the scenes of horror again. To prove that I was back to match winning fitness.

Maybe the kites put her into a more cheerful phase, as she agrees to visit the pub with me. My pleasure at this made me forget about our mode of transport. She invited me to climb on to the back of her Triumph. I was holding on to her waist, but I didn't have a helmet. It wasn't the first time she'd asked me to take such a big risk. Again it could have been my last.

Her take on the highway-code is unconventional. She's colour blind for starters. She doesn't always see the red light. Her road manners are not impeccable. She wouldn't have persuaded Dylan to ride on a motorbike with her.

As she catapults across the face of Bristol, I hold on grimly. Kites are no longer uppermost in my thoughts. Getting from A to B, without reaching Z, is roughly the idea. I have to be more careful about risking everything. She swept me up on her chrome horse and thundered back into the tunnel of love. It's long and dark. It could be a blind alley.

This is just like old times. Fortunately we get there in one piece. We're still in one piece; or at least she is. She snorts and snarls into the closed harbour and pulls up in front of her favourite pub. There are muscled guys windsurfing across the water. Apparently she is drawn to wherever they congregate. Like a dire warning on a cigarette pack, they jump to my attention. She's got an infallible instinct for hunks doing their exercise. Why take me along for the ride? Even in my racquet sports days I was never quite the bronzed god. Love and beauty was mostly in the head for my generation. The evening is drawing in and these rippled guys are finding something risky and strenuous. They're balancing on the water, pushing their sails into the wind. Apparently she finds them irresistible.

Shakily I dismount her iron horse; I unhook myself stiffly from the leather seat and find the ground, engine heat collected between my thighs. I experience euphoria to be still alive. She'd hurtled through Bristol like Satan's child spat out from fiery hell. Luckily the cops could no more recognise me on this occasion, than when I scattered the opera crowd that night. They wouldn't have been able to focus properly.

Corrina Farlane leads me into the ancient pub, as everywhere else. I'm glad to let the bar prop me up. We decide to nurse our drinks outside. There's an evening chill, but Corrina doesn't mind. She's impervious to extremes. But it's far too late to listen to advice now. We watch the sun set like an atomic test. I discover a string of hot air balloons in the sky, threading a route between the ideal kite flying hills, into the flaming dusk. Wishing I was up there in a balloon too, gazing down at creation from a height, where I am happiest; getting a grip on the fret-board of the great Stratocaster.

But I don't look away for long. Corrina is a hypnotic presence. Her voice is easy on the inner ear - its fricative timbre. The final rays of Sunday gild her fluttering hair, illuminate her lapis lazuli eyes, which ravish my heart effortlessly. She could strip the pain of Casanova. I still adhere to the powerful illusion that love can save my life. Why bother living otherwise?

Taking me by surprise she invites me back to her place. Trying to discover where she lived was like trying to get the secret ingredient of coca bloody cola. As autumnal darkness falls we shoot back into the centre, rapid as one of those bullet trains that nearly ran me over in Tokyo. Man, I don't want to go back there. I'm holding on for dear life again. She's ready to invite me back for cocoa on her own terms. She's shacked up in a house share in Clifton, I discover, only a few streets away from Big Pink. She chains up that infernal machine after I jump off on to wobbly legs. She explains that the house is owned by one of her bosses at Whig Wham. That megalomaniac music exec with a synthesised piano. Was she dating the guy? Who can say. Best advice is to keep cool and say nothing at this stage. What's the reward of being competitive? She shares with three other women.

Looking at the unpacked boxes she hasn't been here long. All her personal stuff, half unwrapped, not quite finding its home. Our dreams of independence can be disappointed, I know from my own experience, when Liz and I began to set up home together. Corrina's in the upmarket part of the city, but the property hasn't been well maintained, in either fabric or decoration. She must be in contact with our landlord during his twilight years. Full of character detail, the estate agent would no doubt wax. The parade of empty shops begins at the end of the world mews.

"I have my ambitions," Corrina tells me.

"Got to start from somewhere," I reply.

"Saving for a better place, if you want to know."

"Sensible."

"You're not in any hurry are you? Stay for some dinner?"

No, I tell her, as the internal compass begins to whir like Nairn's meteorological instruments, through a gale. She's not working up to getting laid, is she? I feel hungry after all that activity from running about the down; and from lying on the grass of the down. Corrina leads me through into their shared kitchen, dusty, crammed and aromatic as a herb and spices shop in a North African souk; offering a view into a long and tangled back garden.

"You ought to trim back those apple trees," I suggest. "For the autumn. Have a word with Bob. I would come around myself to... He'll be able to help."

"I'm sure we can snip a few branches," she assures me.

That image of a souk is inspired only by friends' travels. As I sip my wine at the table Corrina rifles through a shelf of curled, stained cookery books.

"I'll try one of my favourite North African dishes," she decides.

"I guess you learned all about them at Whig Wham."

"This job has exposed me to all kinds of influences, actually. It's been very exciting," she says.

This dish consists of couscous, roasted vegetables and a type of lamb casserole in an orangey sauce. She cooks with speed and verve. The meat has been prepared in advance. I chop up some vegetables, while she offers instructions. I'm enjoying myself; we seem to be compatible. This is how I might have imagined our life together, until a coronary interrupted our courtship.

We eventually sit down to our succulent, pungent meal, tossing out mutual compliments, not only to the dead sheep. This could have worked, I tell myself. But our recent history still doesn't look very appealing, however we serve it up. Our taste buds may be luxuriating in Morocco or Tunisia or wherever, but our thoughts still go back to Crete. No offence to that island of course, but that's where it happened, isn't it; that's where the fuse hit the explosive powder.

"Oh yes, this is amazing, isn't it. Fabulous," she announces, waving a spoon around.

I'm conscious of eating too much lately. I am trying to fill the empty space. Many evenings I have to combat boredom at home, whenever my kids are out on the town, or perhaps raving in a field or an empty warehouse somewhere or - in Luke's case - bolted into his room. Inevitably I raid the fridge; while I'm watching a movie; I have a Truffaut boxed set at the moment; accumulating another couple of pounds around my middle, which doesn't sit pretty on my overall skinny cardiac's body. At least you've got a healthy appetite, I tell myself. But if I imagine that a healthy appetite is going to save me, or even make me feel better the next day, then I'll just fall flat on my stomach.

"Open another bottle of wine, Noah."

"Thanks, honey," I reply, reaching over to her rack.

"Paul Jacob offered me a dozen bottles of Pinot Noir off his chateau. He has another recording studio over there. It's absolutely fantastic... *The sound.* Some of the biggest names in world music have recorded there."

Paul Jacob is one of her bosses: an egomaniac rocker who has served on United Nations special missions. I try to keep authority in my voice. "Every recording studio has its own sound. Sun Studio? Stax?"

"He's invited me there over Christmas. While they're remixing the Whig Wham sampler album."

"Impressive. But I stay clear of remixes," I insist, knocking back another wine lake.

"That would depend on the producer," she tells me. "Paul's the best."

"Fine," I remark. "You know, this has been really great... spending the afternoon with you. Calling into the pub... *This,*" I elaborate, indicating the meal with a fork. "We should definitely do this more often." I try on the charming, affable mug of a settled and experienced guy, whose company is to be enjoyed and accepted.

"That would spoil it," she says.

This has a stunning effect on my grin. "How? How would it?"

"If we got together more regularly, it would..."

"There's nothing wrong with meeting on a Sunday, like this. Weekends are always cool with me."

"Weekends are difficult for me," she replies, evasively.

"How? What's difficult about them?"

She pushes hair back off her forehead. "Oh, I'm so terribly busy at Whig Wham at the moment."

I stare back at her. Busy with what? Carrying crates of Paul Jacob's plonk? "Don't you ever wake up with a free day?" I wonder.

"Not if I want to succeed. Do *you* have many free days?" she returns.

I felt regret, induced by that global rock star's vintage, remembering how we talked about sharing a place once: my house together. Maybe she'd just been fantasising about the future, but she'd been fantasising in earnest. She'd made me feel fit and viable again; years still left on the clock; even though I was secretly breaking into pieces. She'd made me feel like Peter Fonda - even pillion on the back of *her* machine - but at the end of that holiday I felt more like Henry Fonda.

"There's a future in your kites? Why don't you convince me?" Corrina says, knife and fork crossed.

"Certainly there's a future. I'm really optimistic. About balloon travel. You see, when the skies are knotted with dirty jet planes." Our summer trip had definitely added to this sharp aversion.

"Who's going to fly away on a silly balloon?" she challenges.

"One day soon trans-Atlantic airships will return. Sure, because we have safer fuels... with higher speeds... Sure they'll be very hi-tech."

"You make them sound like space shuttles."

"Do I?"

So our conversation progressed. I was happy to rarely provoke her interest in the subject. After the meal we found ourselves standing back in the hallway; flirting evasively; both wondering which direction I should take next. A game of sexual snakes and ladders was on offer.

Movie dialogue is seeping around the living room door. Her flatmates are watching a rom com; determined to play hard to get with the most attractive young men in Bristol. Or is this another insecure older guy kind of paranoid episode?

As Corrina and I tramp upstairs - the apartment is split-level - I'm thinking why she bothered to look me up and down again. Do I suddenly look good on her CV? Can she be seduced by my new life situation? The tubes and stitches have hardly been jerked out of my body. Even if she assumes I'm repaired and patched - which I have been - she has to be more aware of my frailties. I've been through a bad trip; and there are consequences and effects that I can't hide. Except that Corrina isn't repelled by my operational scars - as far as she's been exposed. I've noticed that. She's seen the beginnings of those wounds; asked me about them and touched them; and she must know they're serious; she knows that the scars don't end there. She couldn't feign that. She's cool with that. In the most basic way Corrina isn't disgusted by those shiny worms down my arms and along the inside of my legs; as I assumed she would be. The prehistoric arrow shape that's cut down my chest. She overlooks them more easily than I do.

To me those scars are repugnant. They mark me out from mankind. I have that plague sign daubed on my body. I don't know how she can still find me physically attractive. I assume that she doesn't. Corrina herself has those scars along her belly, after she missed a bend in the Alps a few years ago; a teen making her first Continental biking tour. Against parental or even peer advice, of course. Sewn up and patched herself, she climbed back on to her motor bike, the day she was released from a French hospital. It made me jolt back when I first saw those scars: when we first made love that hot afternoon at the Whig Wham HQ. I have to admit that it didn't put me off.

She told me the story of how she'd ended up on the ledge of that mountain; trapped on that sill of rock for hours, over-night, in agony from a dislocated shoulder, with gashed thighs as well. She was afraid of passing out in case she fell. She was bleeding from a gashed torso. The next morning she was spotted, by the occupants of a car approaching on a facing hairpin. Huntsmen and their dogs. But they were unable to reach her or to help. She had to be lifted off the mountain by a helicopter. Only her appetite for motorbikes and adventure was left unscathed. She doesn't like to hear people moan or complain. If she is indifferent to me, then scars are all that we share.

Liz has a gash, over her eyebrow, from where I released a sprung branch, by mistake, during a woodland hike. The mark was merely a cosmetic nuisance to her, not anything more serious. I was not to blame in any imaginable way for Corrina Farlane's injuries or disfigurements. I have always been able to kiss and caress her along there - as if they are tracks to love or bliss: I'm not pulled up short, either from disgust or because these wounds provoke bad personal memories or associations. Her scars are entirely blameless, even innocent to me: they don't relate to me. If anything they are attractive and mysterious.

Corrina strolls towards her bedroom window and gazes out in a distracted way. As she gazes towards the dark hills she raises her arms to stretch. Before she looks at me quickly and wanders back towards the bed, finding one of those smiles, like a river getting born from the rocks.

Lately her comparative youth is a scurrilous satire on my looks. We could have been an item, if it hadn't been for the damn coronary. I can't keep up with her life style any more, or with her friends. It's hard to live without an impossible vision of the future.

She pushes a forefinger into my belly. "Are you getting back into shape?"

"Any ideas?"

"Badminton?"

"Not sure," I consider.

"You can't walk about like a lumpy potato," she insists.

"Apart from the slight spare tyre, I've lost a lot of weight, you know, since..."

Sweated on the beach and sliced off on a Spitalfields' slab.

"You've definitely developed a bit of a paunch," she confirms.

"I'm taking up yoga."

"Yoga? You need to burn off the calories," she argues. "Start running again."

"I'm developing a new fitness routine," I reply. Running didn't feature strongly.

"I can offer you a game of tennis next summer."

"Thanks for the offer. Let's see how it develops, shall we?"

"You have to draw up your fitness programme for the winter."

"Do you fancy coming out with me tomorrow night?" I ask - straight out.

Suspicion stalls her gaze. "What are you thinking of?"

"I'm going to catch some jazz. Over at the Old Duke Pub. Do you know?"

"That's too slow for me," she says.

I feel her muscles stiffen. How can I ever understand this woman?

"Too slow?" I protest.

"That really isn't to my taste," she explains. "I'm more hard core."

"Don't you think my musical tastes are hard core as well? You saying that my music is soft core, or something like that? Is *Blonde on Blonde* out of fashion, all of a sudden?" I object - stung.

"Thanks anyway." She taps together the ends of her fingers.

"Why don't we make it another day? Another venue or event?"

"Lets!" She gazes back towards the window, where she is unable to see anything.

"Classics never age. Next Tuesday they're promoting that American sax player? Did you see him mentioned in the media? He's a brilliant musician. He's got a tremendous reputation. What do you say about that?"

"I'll have a look through my organiser," she promises.

"All right, then, have a thumb through your diary." All the pages must be falling out by now. "Let me know."

"Let's see."

"Right. So am I as loathsome as all that?" I ask. If I'm really the Elephant Man then she should put that bag over my head. Not even Kate Moss could do anything with that.

"Don't be a pain. You're not the only guy I know here in Bristol," she rebukes me.

"Do you work in the global music industry? Can you remind me?" I comment.

"You don't yet have exclusive rights."

"Why don't you invite them too? Or you can invite me?"

"I don't want to."

"Are you ashamed to be seen with me, or what?" This was upsetting to a Sixties peacock. "Who are these trendy guys? That you hang out with?" I enquire.

Corrina doesn't like going around in circles. She prefers straight lines at high velocity, like a rocket propelled Roman. *Time is a jet plane - it goes too fast*, in Dylan's emphatic words. "Why don't you stop grouching at me, Noah? Just *love* me," she implores.

I stare back at her, uneasy and disconcerted as Caesar with a dull sensation between his shoulder-blades.

"Just love me," she repeats. "Why scold the little cat when she's sitting in your lap?"

"You think you're the bowl of cream," I say.

She wrinkles her nose. "I want to feel your big rough hands on me."

I stare at them; at these hands; suddenly outsized as if they never belonged to me.

"You work very hard don't you, with those clumsy fists."

"You know I'm crazy about you. From the beginning."

"Don't start to get all icky," she warns.

"Icky? Why don't you go out with me tomorrow? My invitation not good enough for you?" I prod.

"I'll never be your drinking buddy, Noah."

"You're special to me."

"How come?"

"I'm not sure. But you're a very sweet woman."

"I suppose that I am. The last time I tasted myself," she teases.

"You're important," I blab.

"You're important to *me*." She smiles at me lopsidedly.

"I wanted to talk about *us*," I point out.

"It's more fun when you're talking about me."

"Can't we have a serious conversation?"

"I thought we'd come up to my little bedroom to have a lovely fuck."

"All right, but you mean more to me than that."

"Will you say that afterwards? Is that a promise?"

Her voice had dropped to a husky timbre, causing her extremely generous bosom to rise and fall - as violently when she first landed on that Pyrenean ridge. She tosses her thick hair in a characteristic way. We're not sitting on the end of her bed to discuss our future together.

"You silly man, I don't believe you're not in the mood."

"Most women enjoy the art of conversation," I argue.

"This isn't the time for a little chat," she corrects.

"No?"

Her aroused breath bursts like an opium pod and intoxicates me. "Don't you want to get your workman's hands all over my delicious body?"

Her eyes, dusky blue as the dust on purple plums, consume me. I search their depths. Can I read a sincere expression? Or are they simply passionate? If we're back on that last minute break then I'm dead in the water. I observe myself floating upside down in the black dilated pupils.

"Don't you think I'm a complete dish?" she remarks, breathily. "Wouldn't you like to lick every sweet drop from the plate?"

I can't find the answers I'm looking for, but the answer is clear and simple. By now self-respect and intelligence are taking a drink in the lounge bar.

"You're a lovely woman," I tell her. "The loveliest."

"You can't turn me down, can you?"

I recognise the aggressive hunger of her kisses. What dissatisfactions or unhappy needs are sublimated there? I can only keep guessing. She's never going to confide in me.

"You're the most fantastic, lovely girl. You're the spring of life," I babble.

"What's the matter, Noah?"

"Love is all you need." I feel the need to say this.

"Oh god, just be quiet and love me up, will you."

"This is going to be the supreme moment....between us," I explain, freeing my lips for a moment. "Expression...of eternal love."

"Oh, such nonsense, Noah. Just bonk."

"Be careful. I've only just returned home from hospital."

"What's it to be? Relax and turn over on your back. There's a good boy. Let me do the hard exercise, if you're still fragile."

"When did I say that?" I object.

"How's your stiffy?"

I'm trapped between her thighs like one of her motorcycles. Just one strong flick of the wrist it took and we got from one end of the street to the other.

My desires embellish with these thoughts. Passion is trapped and howls inside me like a wolf. There can be no peace until we've savaged each other. I should be all right, so long as I stay on my back. That's the way she normally plays it, so I can keep out of trouble.

Straddled naked above me, she's cool and silvery as a fairy princess, tosses aside her bra, torn out of her glittery wings, heavy bosoms springing from the centre of her chest, with the fat lips of her nipples pouting.

I've always believed, since our radical hippie days, that sex has a quasi-religious power. Not even quasi, in fact, but the real McCoy. The McCoy Tyner of the life force. The spiritual powerhouse rhythm.

We're not just having a bit of fun, we're falling into the eternal rhythm. We're on a spiritual journey along the ancient path. I'm the chivalrous knight of yore setting off into the dense shadowy forest. Thick branches fall before me until I hack them away with my sword. I push deeper into the forest undergrowth; fighting for a clear view of the shining castle, that I know lies at the centre. My princess is imprisoned in her turret peak and I make my final assault on the gloomy tower. She is calling to me desperately from her high window, beckoning me with her wails and delicate outstretched arms. If only I can find the strength to climb up the snaking vines to reach her, where I have the power to conquer her oppressor and gallop away with her on my horse.

This entire concept album, worthy of Yes, in the original line up, or maybe ELP is flitting through my head. But these erotic ideas only show I'm *Thick As A Brick* and still a member of the *Lonely Hearts' Club Band*, despite my romantic heroism.

"I'm getting there. I'm getting real close, Corrina, darling."

"Not yet awhile, Noah, you're not."

"Lay off a bit then. Relax. I can't rescue you, otherwise. I'm climbing up the tower. I'm reaching you. We can escape."

"Save your energy. Don't chatter."

A very moving scene between us. Who's screwing who? I watch her sliding away above me, provoking pleasure from her folds. Her eyes are rolling, her mouth is open, building gradually to the last act and, she may hope, an encore. Perspiration sheens over her exquisite shoulders. She looks pretty adorable. She's going through her breathing routines. These are different to mine.

"You're going to save my soul, Corrina. You're really saving my soul now, darling. I'm not afraid of anything with you...I have no fear...here with you."

But I might check out with a hard on.

At the end she drags herself back up and grins. She rests her entire weight on me, dipping her damp hair into my face. The smell is fresh and flowery. She holds that distant, cynical smile, as she leans forward. I love the gorgeous sticky weight of her body on me. I could stay here for hours holding her close. There's a still peaceful centre to this crazy spinning world. But we know that nothing lasts forever - particularly this.

Recovered, Corrina disentangles herself and clambers away from the bed. She is pacing around like a golfer on the green. Keeping me guessing. Looking for her knickers, as a matter of fact. They're in a corner. How the hell did they get there? Before she pulls the scanty silk back up her legs and hides away her tender spot again. But how tender it is.

"You're still a great lay, Noah," she declares.

"Right, thanks Corrina." I'm stretched back with my hands behind my head, disregarding the momentary shock of finding bare scalp.

She strides back to her side of the bed, shakes my shoulder and grins slyly at me. "You're great value for a lazy Sunday evening," she enthuses.

"And you're the delight of my life," I reply.

"Do you know what I would most like to do now?" she says.

"No, Corrina, what would you most like?"

"I'd like to twist off your cock and stick it on the wall as a trophy."

# Chapter 21

A few weeks later I decide to make a long overdue visit to my mother. I was returning from the doctors' surgery, after locking horns with Voerdung again, the South African prop-forward with sensitive hands. This well-meaning, massive GP offered me earnest sympathy and baffled consideration. As for a rock star on methadone he refilled my prescription and promised to draft a letter to Wickham in London. Apparently he'd beg them to unstitch the dicey heart valve, regardless of risk. The thought came to me that Mum had been neglected by us for too long. I took comfort in the past, as the present has my balls in a vise. After Corinna had effectively shoved me off the rear of her Triumph, this was the moment to trundle down memory lane. That chick gives a whole new spin to the experience of getting dumped.

The plan was for Angela to join us for tea, after she finishes work at the café. There was a bit of fantasy involved with this invitation. It was like asking Andy Warhol to your party by off-chance, offering your exact time and address. I should write something about Mum and our early family life, before I depict myself turning along her street. To be honest, Grandma - to refer to her as the kids do - lives less than half an hour's walk from Big Pink: or that's how long it should take our kids, adding an extra five for Tim. Obviously following my coronary I could barely shuffle to the front gate - that's *our* front gate. Just a few years ago I decided to stump up extra cash and move my mother into an apartment purpose-built for the elderly. As I think about it, in my current state, I could move into the flat next door. I definitely imagined cosy family tea times, but never considered being her neighbour.

The big idea was for Mum to set up home around the corner, to be near to her family, or at least my branch of it, in case of any health emergency. Nobody envisaged that I would have to be wired into the national grid. After the break-up of my marriage and family upheavals, we haven't been seeing much of the old girl.

The kids haven't been popping by regularly after school or college as I envisaged. I don't know how to twist their arms. Big Pink is a gloomy haunted house these days. She can rightly consider herself neglected.

This is the unfortunate woman who had to endure my Hendrix phase as a teen; who struggled to make any sense of Dylan's adenoidal (and increasingly larynx ruined) vocals, never mind to unpack the meaning of his lyrics, their relevance and allusiveness. That isn't to begin talking about the revolutionary politics and hippie philosophy of the period, interspersed with Lizzie's alarming readings about female mystiques and eunuchs.

In contemporary times Elizabeth is more inclined towards the *Sex is Destiny* thesis. Man, she threw out all those rad-fems after she found that magazine husband of hers. Could you imagine Susan Sontag marrying a keen amateur photographer and reading romantic novels with pornographic angles? You can't help feeling betrayed and looking back at our joyfully subversive youth with some bitter irony. Mum's bewilderment at her behaviour - which is the decision to divorce me and throw me into the trash can of history - is still as thick as pea soup; because she adored Lizzie like a Victoria sponge from Marks and Sparks. She couldn't get enough of that clotted cream accent. She was flattered by Lizzie's guileless girly attention, those innocent green eyes, as she reminisced at length; going on about her past life and family history. These memories and anecdotes of hers would be as labyrinthine as a Brazilian soap-opera, yet Lizzie encouraged her into a fresh episode and couldn't get enough. Mum didn't realise she was being heard out of sisterly solidarity. She contributed to Lizzie's vox-pop feminist sociology project. It's true that Lizzie was endlessly sweet and tolerant. Obviously there's a limit to everything.

Constance is eighty years old already and has been in Bristol for half a century. Amazing statistics when I still remember her sending me out with a packed lunch for school. She moved to this city after my father's death. My Dad you understand had a lethal coronary, when my brother and I were still little kids. At first Mum attempted to take on Dad's old job to support us: to fill his bread earning boots, and go to work on the land. The yeoman farmer character, who seemed to own all the farms around there, refused her offer. Obviously this guy wasn't the Glastonbury Festival kind of farmer. He didn't want any Soviet style female worker heroes picking his strawberries or pulling up his 'tatahs. Not enthusiastic about sexual equality at work, this yokel blimp just turfed us out of our cottage. It was like the bad old days of Victorian rural poverty and starvation, when people dragged themselves on to ships to America. That's what the SS Great Britain was still like in those days, before the post war social revolution kicked in; before the Sixties shook up this society. It was a kind of class-divided military boot camp, with no social mobility, so the poor were ashamed of their station and unable to change it. Bringing us two boys up on her own, deprived of work or a home, Mum had no choice but to decamp to Bristol.

As Lizzie used to point out, they'd throw young girls into lunatic asylums then - as close to us as the Sixties - for getting pregnant outside of marriage. The authorities had the power, or the moral degradation, to say a girl was mentally unsound, if she gave birth alone. Single mothers were criminalised and social conformity was linked to sanity, Lizzie explained. So don't listen when they say the radicalism of the 1960s didn't change society. All our freedoms and liberties are as fragile as this bloody valve lodged in my heart, I'd argue. The forces of reaction and control would snatch them away if possible. Some days I think that John and Yoko had a point when they decided not to get out of bed.

Mum fell back on the generosity of an old friend, to lodge us in Bristol. Peggy fed us all for months until our mother could find employment. My brother and I stared out of the bus window on the way, with Connie gripping our one-way tickets as if setting off for Hong Kong. But Aunt Peggy was waiting at the station to greet us, with a bunch of tulips in her hand, cut from her own garden. Tulips had romantic associations for aunty, as they were the favourite gift of her first sweetheart, a carter who was holed in the trenches. For her they were a flower of sexual love and remembrance, rather than poppies. This woman was touching forty three and worked as a packer in a chocolate factory, but she was a fascinating and even alluring woman to me. She was all smiles, fancy gloves and pretentious petticoats, I recall. From the beginning she lived on a different planet in Bristol, more sophisticated and exciting than I'd known before. Somehow as we jumped off at Bristol bus station she was inviting us to this exotic new planet. Then the river and the waterways were heaven to my brother and me.

Mum's first job was cleaning the house of a glassware importer, here in Clifton. For more than a year she had to keep the guy at bay with a window pole. Eventually he lost his breath and decided to stop chasing. But Mum was out the door of course. Fortunately for us she was offered a job at Rolls-Royce. No, nothing to do with designing jet engines, just working in the canteen. Not a glamorous position over all, but certainly more glamorous than her previous one. After years of service and being a well-known character at the company, she was promoted to supervisor in the restaurant. She would bring food home some evenings. So there was no chance of us going hungry in those days. That danger started when Lizzie and I began a family and decided we'd better get married. This was when our saliva glands began to feel the squeeze.

My elder brother Oswald started work as soon as he left school. He was required to bring an extra income into the house, although I personally never enjoyed a penny of it. He would come indoors on a Thursday evening, grinning, putting his boots up on the coffee table, waving a brown packet in front of my eyes, which contained a worker's wages then. On the other hand, did he ever attend the longest party in history, did he hell. Mum took a mortgage for a little house in Bedminster, so she required my brother's contribution. I guess he was resentful that I'd stayed on in education; that I contributed nothing; that in fact I was a net-drain on national resources as a lazy long-haired student, listening to that crap music and sticking my nose into boring books, "talking shit".

Elizabeth enjoyed teasing me about my home situation. I was bound to get a degree of ridicule from girls - especially nice brainy girls like Lizzie - with a brother like Ossie. I still cringe at his misjudged efforts to seduce her - his man of the world walk and talk back then - though she just encouraged him ironically. He didn't get that of course, or didn't want to, that she found him as sexy as a baboon's arse. Lizzie wasn't a snob and she hasn't turned into one. That's in contrast to her parents, compared to whom the Nixons were a pair of free thinkers. It's become more acceptable to sneer at people who are poor or less privileged, but she never has. In that way she didn't live through those radical times without any effect or impact.

To be working class at university had some cachet for a guy then. There's only one class at university. At first we spent nights together, or just an hour or two between seminars, back at her shared flat. She comes from Taunton. She knew that the accent was seductive, not just for my Mum. By then every guy was out to impress her.

Mum needed a lot of persuasion to move into this place in Clifton. She regards the Clifton district as a little under Nobs' Hill, to be honest. It must be related to her memories of that volatile glass maker. I assured her that she'd be closer to Elizabeth and the children up here, as well as more comfortable. I painted her a picture of life here worthy of a biscuit tin lid. But it was another flat promise. If she wants to see Elizabeth these days she'd need a pair of binoculars.

Looks as if my account is also turning into a Brazilian soap. I guess it's something they do well, like the footie.

I await some response after plunging my finger into a rusty chime. I visualise the minor alert of flashing lights and sirens triggered within my mother's apartment, to alert her to the fact of a caller or, thinking darkly, a mugger. There's a security system for the building as a whole - as it largely shelters the elderly - but Mum is nervous and suspicious about technology. Lately I've begun to share those fears.

I expect to idle under the porch for a while, casting my eyes over the honeysuckle and rose filled front garden, which is aimed at pleasing them like a sentimental lyric. My mother's knees are not good and her hearing is less acute. I have to allow her more time to navigate the complicated emporium. At last, after a percussive interlude, she puts her features around the edge of the door. A fixed expression of dire suspicion changes into one of recognition. From her look she nurses a wound of neglect, but at least she still recognises me. She's definitely unhappy about the recent twists of the soap opera. Mum isn't old fashioned about these moral questions, she *predates* fashion.

"Oh, it's you boy," she greets me, unhooking chains. It's like Leeds Castle. "Come on in then, come on in. Don't hang around out there."

"How are you then, Mum?"

"I'm all right, Noah. Just battling on against old age," she informs me.

"You're looking well, at least, Mum," I observe.

"How are you these days, Noah?"

A quick inspection offers discouraging signs. Somebody definitely punched a hole through my portrait in the attic - this is written across her face. But even the Love Generation has to grow up.

"You're a bit pale and drawn, boy, aren't you? What's the matter? Don't you get any fresh air these days?"

"I definitely had the wind taken out of me," I reply. "The heart attack didn't help."

"You seem to be in such a mess these days," she remarks.

After shutting up she allows me to kiss her and trundles off, towards her own apartment. Navigating a musty, brass-fixtured, red carpeted hallway, I keep half an eye for Norman Bates or Edgar Allan Poe. Fortunately they don't jump out, although a few of her fellow tenants do a good impression. The space is cluttered with the excess heirloom furniture of residents. It's a type of warehouse for the autumn years, with enough timber to build a Tudor battle fleet.

Safely inside, away from any snoopers or psychopaths that might have inveigled their way inside with me, we give each other a bear hug. This is by way of apology for not calling by in an age. In the clasp I feel her sturdy, solid boned frame with its low centre of gravity, and she rests her large solid head into my chest. She's built like a gun carriage is my mother. I can't imagine having enough strength to leave an impression on her. She grasps my hands, squeezing and turning them over, as if trying to rub extra vitality into them.

"Let's have a mug of good strong tea," she suggests.

"You're the expert there," I joke.

"I've got a nice bit of cake for you as well. I baked it this morning, Noah. You need a lining for your stomach."

"Sounds good," I say. At least there's no need to worry about my cholesterol.

"You haven't visited for weeks," she complains. "What happened to those grandchildren of mine?"

"I'm expecting Angela to be here soon," I inform her.

"You don't take sugar, do you? Very sensible. You need to watch your weight. You being so thin and you've got a podgy tummy. No my love, I can manage on my own. I'm all right if I keep on my feet."

"Sure you don't need any help, Mum?"

"Sit down and relax, my boy."

Her glance is misty these days, but in youth it hypnotised like the exotic dark of a deep cave. Her once black hair is now candlestick silver, pinned tightly across her scalp in a bun. My daughter's inherited these tints and tinctures.

When I was young I wished to inherit such exotic darkness myself - it would have fitted into my own preferred image, somewhere between the Parisian left bank and alternative Hollywood anti-heroes. Unfortunately I take more after the Sheer side of the family.

Constance releases me and makes for the kitchen with poor balance. Yet she still has the solid deportment of a canteen supervisor at Rolls-Royce. I can see her bowling between the tables, barking encouragement through noise and steam.

The interior of her flat is crowded with furniture and heirlooms too. In the end we offered big money to a team of Sherpas, who had to ferry everything up Nob Hill. The rest of the family felt their rights trampled. So I didn't put myself at the top of the hit parade. My brother wasn't getting in close around the jukebox to hear my favourite tune. This was the kind of selfish and rash decision he expected from a long haired hippie with dicey views. Even though I have the signs of success, Oswald still regards me as a penniless student, with pockets as big and empty as my ideas.

Ossie continues to live in our native Bedminster district. You couldn't force him out of that area if you deployed a tank regiment. He'd probably die of exposure if you dropped him into Devon. Ossie and his family are still in their house, just one street away from where our Mum used to live, before Noah interfered and persuaded her to leave forever. Ossie was absolutely hopping mad, to be honest.

We arranged a viewing of the apartment together, Mum, with my brother and me. She turned the place over grimly, while Ossie conducted a guerrilla campaign against the agent. The guy was sound but Ossie felt he was dealing with a gentleman thief or a geriatricide, or is it a 'geriatriapath'?

As Mum had fungi blooms in her old kitchen, she decided to etch her signature into the contract, not surprisingly. She was moving on a promise, to see more of Elizabeth and the children, as well as Ossie's brood. This was like getting a wing of Kensington Palace rent free.

From the direction of the kitchen there's a clattering and breakage.

"You all right, Mum?" I call.

"You stay where you are," she answers.

"I'm not helpless."

"You're not a well man."

She's taking a different line from Corrina. Our mother's never had a light touch. She's lived in a comparatively small world, but she's ruled over it like Queen Ann.

I take time to recompose myself, casting my eyes over the reliquary. I'm left with my thoughts, but I don't like them. Corrina roars back into the mind's eye again. How could I pretend to miss her? I try to absent myself in the ticking of our grandfather clock. I attempt to relax within the sunshine entering through French windows. But I tend to sink into the armchair, as if into a depression. My loins still feel like a squeezed sponge.

"Are you still all right? I'll be with you soon, Noah."

If she breaks another cup I shall be drinking directly out of the pot.

Ossie's family allow Mum to feel loved and wanted. They always create a cushiony background of noise and vitality. My children are more often out of doors and our house is like a John

Cage piece, in which the environment and atmosphere forms the composition, so that you merely hear a door being slammed.

Luke gets along with Grandma better than the other two. It seems a bit of a miracle but they somehow mix well. Perhaps he also reminds her of Liz. Anyway he's rarely to be seen around Con's flat. You're more likely to see the Buddha jogging around the park. Angela says that she finds her grandma hard work - as if that is the ultimate negative. In truth they have a strong resemblance to each other. They are both stubbornly single minded; so loathe to hear a single word of criticism. Then there is the physical resemblance.

We're still waiting on Andy Warhol. I tell my daughter that Grandma can be good company, recalling childhood evenings of dance music. She doesn't listen; so a bloody mind and small dark features are not the only features they share. My brother and I were grateful for any high spirits in that house, I can assure you.

Finally Constance hobbles back from her kitchenette, clutching a tray holding a large cosied teapot, a couple of surviving cups and a plate holding breezeblocks of cake. The stocking bandages around her arthritic knees give her the look of a hardened rugby player, coming back for another punch up following a sin binning. But she ignores her doctor's gift of a walking stick. This varnished cane is propped in a corner, more used as a warning against a defecating moggy, which has stolen a soft spot in the old folks' back garden.

After she plonks down the tray, with a dangerous rattle and roll, and arranges our tiffin across a nest of tables, Constance begins to beat around in the undergrowth of my life.

"How are you bearing up, Noah?" she enquires. She groans with satisfaction and relieved effort, lowering herself into her formidable old armchair, which has travelled the many years and a few miles with her.

"Not too bad, considering," I answer. It is unlikely that I am going to confide in Mum, if I am unable to talk frankly with close friends.

"Taking all your medicine, are you?"

"Oh yes, Mum, I'm being a good boy." Neither of us is virtuous in that respect.

"That big house up there, with those growing children to take care of," she tells me. She arranges herself into an ancient dent.

"I keep my eye on them. Don't worry," I say.

She tugs her heavy cardigan closer and adjusts a heavy pin, which cuts through her thick tartan skirt. "I can't stop sitting here and thinking of you, all alone by yourself in that house, with nobody to take care of you."

"I'm quite happy by myself, most of the time," I assure her, taking a sip.

"Did you say that I should expect Angela?" she wonders.

"That's what she promised me. I've got every confidence..."

"Why doesn't that girl make herself more useful around the house? She's old enough to help you out. What does she do with herself? Why didn't she come with you now?"

"She's still at work, Mum."

"Did she say what time she's likely to visit me?" she persists.

"Angela's got a little job along there in Park Street. You should see her in her nice uniform, serving people with the tasty food and drinks they have, being helpful. Serving at the tables and taking money at the register."

"Is that the best she could find?" Mum asks, gripping the little teacup in her paw. "You told me that she's a bright girl. You said she's clever at school."

"She's working at the café to save money for university," I argue.

Constance isn't convinced or impressed by this explanation of Angie's determination. "You're the only one in this family who's been to university. Your brother never needed to."

"Then my daughter will follow in my footsteps," I reply firmly.

Angela could enter university as a mature student. She shouldn't count on her old man attending graduation. It hurts me to think about that.

"I walked all the way up to your house. It must have been Thursday evening. You should know how hard that is."

"I have to assume you rang the bell," I say.

"Couldn't get any reply from you or anybody. So in the end I had to walk all the way back home again. By myself," she tells me bluntly.

"Sorry about that, Mum. Let me think back. Try to understand what might have happened. I think I was working late that evening. So I'd guess there wasn't anybody at home."

"Then who was playing the loud music and switched a light on?" she asks. She's determined that I get the whole shot.

"I couldn't say exactly," I admit, hunched under the accusation.

"I wouldn't mind saying that it would have been our Angela."

I take a repentant sip of the tea, that's indeed strong enough for the bearded lady. "Your guess is as good as mine, really, Mum."

"What do you say to that?" she wonders.

"I don't know, but the kids have their own keys. They are free to come and go as much as they like. We don't try to lock them up, you understand. I don't always know who may be at home. You have to take your chances, I'm afraid."

My reassurances are undermined by this picture of latchkey kids, taking full advantage of a broken home turned upside down.

"You shouldn't allow your kids to run riot," she warns.

"They just want to do their thing," I say.

Her dark brow wrinkles and she pointedly slurps on her tea. "Keep an eye on those kids, Noah. You have to be careful in your position. You have their mother's shoes to fill these days too."

"That's something I wouldn't dare to try," I say. Would it be the pair of red high heels? It's sad that I still possess my boots of Spanish leather; if not the passionate, thoughtful girl who surprised me with them. Now she may as well pull them on and stamp all over my grave. I've no problem if she wants to wear *my* shoes in future.

"They have to miss their mother," Con remarks.

"They miss for nothing," I insist.

Mum doesn't approve of unkind thoughts about the sacred Liz. From her experience the departure of a spouse is shattering, be that through divorce or death. Take away the security and love of a family and children begin to run amok. Release them from that routine and discipline and your kids are as dangerous as victorious troops in the enemy's wine cellar.

"Fathers are always too indulgent to their children," she argues. "Mothers are more confident of their children's love."

"I'm fully responsible and caring for them," I reply.

"They need their mother."

"Not that they miss for anything." Then I change tack. "They're able to visit their Mum any time," I say. "They have their rights too. We recognise that. Liz hasn't abandoned responsibility for them. We just live separate lives now, that's all... our domestic arrangements have changed. But we're both the caring parents we ever were. We understand our role as parents."

"They don't know where they are," mother says. She edges forward on her throne and employs the lap of her skirt as a napkin.

"They'll get used to it," I reply.

"What a beautiful wedding Lizzie and you had, Noah. Such a lovely ceremony at the cathedral," she recalls.

"Me in my top hat and tails, she in her generous dress."

"You've lost a lovely girl there, Noah. What a shame."

I exercise the capacity of my lungs.

Constance focuses on breaking her hunk of cake into edible sized pieces, as if searching for ore in rocks.

"Maybe that girl was too good for you, after all. I thought so when you first brought her home."

She brushes crumbs from her large hands.

"Let me cast my mind back," I say.

"I always enjoyed listening to that girl talk. She had most interesting things to chat about. What a beautiful face she had, such lovely flowing hair."

"We're divorced now," I remind her.

"I always remember the way she folded her napkin?"

"Her napkin?" I declare.

"She was always so very graceful and dainty. Her manners. Our family came from that village as poor as the church mouse, after your poor father died. I wonder what she wanted with a lot of rough country people like us."

"I can tell you exactly what she got from *me*," I retort. "I don't know why you talk about Lizzie and me in that way. Lizzie and I were friends right from the first day she joined my school," I remind her.

"I don't know why she wanted to marry you," she admits.

The remark almost fires cake out of my throat, like a cannon ball.

"She was such a gracious and thoughtful girl."

"We had an awful lot in common," I insist.

"She came from a very nice family," she recalls, nostalgically.

"They forced Lizzie into a posh girls' only boarding school," I recall. "What's so nice about throwing her out of home and sending her away? At that age, when she didn't want to?"

"They were always very pleasant to me," Constance returns, stubbornly.

"Lizzie kept running away from that school so often, her parents didn't know what to do with her. That place was like Newgate prison for middle-class schoolgirls," I argue. "So finally they relented and allowed her to mix with an uncouth brute like me," I comment.

"She was so very well brought up and polite. So clever passing all those exams and getting on in life. Whatever got into her? So cheerful and chatty too. You won't find another girl like that."

"How do you know that exactly? Perhaps I have already met someone else," I say.

"A pretty girl always turned your head," she admonishes. "You've always been far too easily led. I'm sorry, Noah, but I miss her. It's so hard to understand."

"Incomprehensible."

"You need someone to look after you. Like all men."

Doggedly I stir my own brew and try to dissolve my shame; to break up a sludge of regret and bitterness that's left over, apparently, at the bottom of my existence.

Everybody says how much I resemble my father. They insist that I'm virtually his double these days. I inherited Dad's complexion and thick straw hair, what's left of it. My eyes are a dirty green. I haven't fallen far from the tree.

"She was a friendly, lively girl. We always enjoyed it when she came to our house. Remember when you first brought her home for tea? Those were the days, boy!" she declares, suddenly animated.

I look away gloomily, in the direction of the garden, through long rain-speckled windows between drapes.

“After that she’d come around regularly. We got along famously,” Con remembers. “Honestly, I could sit and listen to that girl for hours at a time, without getting bored.”

“We were students in those days.”

“About her funny ideas. She didn’t worry that I worked in a factory canteen.”

“Lizzie was never stuck up,” I say.

“I never knew her to go searching under my pillows,” Constance remarks.

“That’s all true, Mum, but what difference does it make now?” I comment.

“Well, I’d like to invite her to visit me one afternoon. She and I ought to sit here and have a good long chat together.”

About me? “Elizabeth doesn’t want anything to do with me.”

“With you, maybe.”

“It’s all over with us, don’t you understand? Why would she want to visit you these days?” I point out.

“Just because you don’t see much of her,” she tells me.

“She’d never agree to that.”

“Invite her the next time you see her. It can’t do any harm.”

# Chapter 22

There's a penetrating drilling noise and flashing of lights in the living room. As usual this shocking alarm makes me jump out of my skin. This has been set off by someone pressing the door-bell, either another visitor or armed intruder. Mum asks me to go out to investigate as the intercom system is not working properly - more loose wires. Does Elizabeth have a direct line into my brain? However I'm expecting my daughter to call around to see grandma.

"This will be Angela at last." In that split second I know that I'll be glad to see her - our angel.

But when I reach the step to investigate, our visitor is none other than my brother Oswald. Usually he doesn't go inside her apartment, but will wait in the car or van until she is ready, before driving her back to the family. He's equally surprised to find me here and even offers to go away and come back. I refuse to hear of that, because my reactions are on auto-pilot.

Ossie cried off from visiting me in hospital, citing his work commitments, which even incensed Elizabeth. Any talk of driving up to London sounded as unlikely to him as flying to Berlin, before the wall came down. But Ossie doesn't lack brotherly feeling, even if he didn't rush to my bedside.

"You look bloody tarrable, little bro," he blurts out. He deliberately addresses me in a rougher local timbre.

"Right, but I'm much better than I was," I state.

"Did they tell you that?" he demands. "Those doctors and nurses?"

I gesture for him to enter and he tries to adjust to the idea: the shock of my new appearance. Embarrassment forced out the comment, but he's not a bloke to hide his real feelings.

"You come from work?" I ask, sociably.

"What 'ave you been doin' to yourself?" he wonders.

We make our way through the museum exhibits towards Mum's door.

"Your heart goin' wrong again or something?"

"Maybe you've put your finger on it," I say.

I re-enter the apartment and we go searching for our mother.

"But you look tarrable, Noah, honest."

"Try to be more sensitive, Oswald," Mum implores, from across the room.

Tearing his eyes away from my mask he strides over to hug our mother and give her meaty kisses. "All right, Mum? How you been keeping? How are your knees?" he bellows.

"Not so bad, my boy, if I stay on my feet... if I keep moving," she informs him; though she doesn't risk them on this occasion.

Ossie falls back into an armchair and surveys her flat with displeasure. His work clothes make no concession to the neighbourhood. The sole of a boot is flapping at us. Just the garb when you're making a social call.

As I move between them to find my place, Ossie notices and observes me again, as if trying to square up a misaligned brick in a wall. "You're not looking good, Noah boy, are you. What you been doin' to yourself?" he wonders.

"I'm on the mend," I insist.

"Doesn't look like it," he states; as if I've been touching his wage packet again.

"It's taking a bit longer than anyone expected. There have been a few setbacks, but nothing to worry about."

"Aint they gonna do anything for you?" he challenges.

"They already have," I say.

"Aren't they going to put you right? What's happened?"

"What are the odds?"

He adopts a relaxed sprawled position, as if he's a kid again and just returned home from school. His work clothes are caked with sand, concrete and other materials from his trade. His strong face is permanently roughened and raw from the out of doors. The blue eyes are narrowed and hurt, paradoxical, as they scrutinize me, across the floor.

"So you're tellin' me you're gonna kick the bucket?" he asks.

"Please try to be more sensitive, Oswald," Mum protests again.

"Not if I can help it, Ossie, I'm not," I say.

But he knows this is not a certain bet. "Well I'm bloody upset to hear about that little bro." Ossie shakes his head at the terrible injustice. "I'm sure the wife will be upset too. But let's hope it never comes to that, shall we?"

"That I might not live long enough?" I say.

"You do look bloody tarrable though, Noah boy, let me tell you."

"I'm travelling light," I admit.

"How good to see you two boys together," Mum comments.

"You putting in some over time, Ossie?" I say.

"An extension," he fires back.

"I've already had one put in," I inform him. "Sorry."

"I didn't notice that. Anyway I thought your place was listed."

Oswald celebrates his origins and still lives proudly in that first house in Bedminster - with front and rear extensions. He had a one-handled wheelbarrow, two bags of substandard cement and a ton of stolen bricks, when he first started working for himself. Then there was a family of kidnapped gnomes which brought in a handsome ransom.

People say that we look alike. We're brothers. Or they did.

"Have another slice of cake with your tea, Oswald," Mum suggests. "Come on, boy, it's good for you." She starts to hew off another generous hunk.

"Hand it over here, Mum."

She may have got this recipe from Elizabeth, as she's been sticking to it for years. Liz is passing back into my body by a transmigration of ingredients. The cake is growling in my stomach like a villain trapped in concrete under a motorway bridge.

Ossie slides down further and fixes me along the sights of his cheeks. The old grandfather clock becomes more paternal. We manage some crumbs of small talk under the searchlight of Mum's attention. She's happy if we produce a good vibration. But we're not Dennis and Brian in their heyday.

"What exactly did they say to you, then?" he enquires. "At the 'ospital?"

"They said that my operation didn't turn out as expected," I admit.

"You don't sound very optimistic," he remarks, chewing.

"There's a complication with my surgery," I say. "There's no way back."

"You pulling my leg or what?"

Ossie never knew how to take me and I still don't slip down easily. Not like a few pints at his local, with old school mates every Friday night. They only know me in passing, and get any woeful news second-hand. I wouldn't really be welcome there anymore. It all dates from my university days. My brother has struggled with his feelings since that decision. Then there was the pretty girl I married; Lizzie with those strange and laughable ideas, who didn't take him as seriously as a luminescent piglet. He's never forgiven me, either for inventing myself or for marrying Lizzie; never has got over his shame and disgust about us.

"Shouldn't they take you back into 'ospital?" he asks. "What are you doin' out here? I've never heard of anything so ridiculous. What's wrong with the National 'ealth these days?" he declares, raising his voice.

"They can't help me," I say.

"Christ."

"I'm trying to adopt a more relaxed lifestyle now."

"Christ, you're not *that* old."

"Have another cup of tea," Mum implores.

My brother stares towards me challengingly, seeing a different guy. He rubs spiky blonde hair violently, releasing plaster dust into the atmosphere, and becomes disillusioned with my life.

"The consultant told me to eradicate stress from my life. To improve my survival chances," I explain. "I'm looking forward to sitting back and relaxing. Do a bit more gardening, fly my kites... that sort of thing. I've even joined a yoga class."

"A yoga class?" he replies. His sore bewildered eyes stick to me in astonishment. "What good's bloody yoga going to do you?"

"There's no harm in it," I argue.

He's unable to suppress rough, confused laughter. "Is that all the doctor orders?" he remarks. "Haven't they got any new drugs? Aren't they going to open you up again? To see what's wrong?"

"There are different paths to enlightenment," I tell him. Not along a gangplank. I toss back another chunk of cake.

Constance looks between us with helpless horror. But this argument is something for the boys to settle. She checks off the time, but there's still no sign of her granddaughter. I shall have to abandon that idea soon.

"When you came home after your operation, it was nothing short of a miracle. Wasn't it, Mum."

"I'll soon get my colour back," I insist.

"Weak hearts run in our family," Constance recites. "You have to look after yourself too, Oswald."

"What's going to happen to your kids?" he wonders.

"Sure, I think about them too," I say.

"Especially after that Lizzie went off and left you like that," he reminds me.

"I don't plan to burn out yet," I say. "I intend to keep rocking and rolling for many years to come. But I hope our kids will be tough enough to cope. They've had to get used to the idea of Liz and I being divorced. This isn't going to be easy for any of us."

"Bloody 'ell, Noah!"

"I don't understand children today," Mum says. "What are they looking for?"

"You let that Lizzie get off too easily," my brother tells me.

"How do you mean? You expect me to drag her back?" I wonder.

"For a start, you should have gone an' punched that bloke's face in."

"Which bloke? Do you mean Frank?"

"Who else?"

"In fact I did drive around to their place one evening. But they were out," I explain.

"Why didn't you call back?" he asks, amazed.

"Why do you think, Ossie? I'd cooled down. I'd thought better about it." Not to mention more obvious physical factors.

"Noah's been married to that lovely girl for over twenty years. Don't speak badly about her," Constance tells him.

"Well he's not married to her any more, is he."

"Try to be more considerate, Oswald."

"She divided this family from the start. You must know what she's really like."

"Don't talk about Lizzie in that nasty way," Mum rebukes.

"Go ahead and speak your mind," I say.

"Nobody forced her to walk out on you, did they. Always full of her own importance. Poking fun. Trying to cut our balls off," he recalls, bitterly. "But if she was much better than us, she should have proved it."

"She was such a happy go lucky person," Mum remembers.

Elizabeth is happier after finding her individual path in life. My own ideas about happiness have become more abstract. She and I used to enjoy looking up at the night sky. We'd stare towards the moon and the stars, as a newly married couple. But what do the moon and stars know about human feelings?

In an effort to get out of this negative groove I ask Ossie about his own family. He's recently become a grandfather, after the eldest daughter had a son. The infant resembled him from the beginning of life. His youngest girl, Martha, intends to go on to university. Oswald doesn't like the idea of further education, but as Martha is a girl, he reasons, she may as well study, because she will not be following him into the business. The poor girl's too weak to shift a bag of cement.

"My boy Mitchell's a chip off the old block," he assures me.

I can't quite keep the jealousy off my face. Man, he's delighted to notice.

"Where is Angela? Didn't you say she was visiting me?" Constance says.

"I expect she's caught up at work," I reply. "Always busy there, she is. Loves it." I shift my seating arrangement.

"My boy's doing a proper day's work in the building trade now," Ossie adds. *Sheer & Son. Cock a hoop.*

Oswald luxuriates in his own pool of ultraviolet light. To be so comfortable with life. So certain of circumstances. He expects his future to be as predictable. How can I hold this against him? Growing old has become much more attractive. I could envy old people. They possess a secret knowledge, which makes them fortunate and mysterious. When I notice them these days I look at them sadly.

No doubt Constance will be upset when I check out. But she'll have no need to reproach herself, as she's already given me a mother's love and a large part of a father's. I'm a big boy now. She already has grandchildren to think about. There's a great grandchild too. Human beings come along like tennis balls.

Admittedly her heart has become a bit leathery over the years. She's too familiar with tragedy. When you lose your husband, at so early an age, this has the power to dwarf any *further* tragedies. My own demise will remind her of my father. She'll spend some of her savings on a wreath. She's always been fond of flowers.

"Leaving us already, Noah?" she notices.

"Yes, sorry Mum. I should go and see what's happened to her. You know where I am," I say. "You only have to telephone."

"I want to see my grandchildren," she complains. "I don't want to speak to them on the telephone."

"I understand that. I feel the same way."

I wish my brother good health as he jumps to his feet. "You've got to stick around little bro," he tells me. "Do you hear what I say? We can't have you goin' off and leavin' us. We'd miss you!"

"Thanks, Ossie. Appreciate that," I nod.

He observes me with beer bruised brotherly eyes. "Why don't you come down and see me on the boat one evening? Drop down to the quayside when there's a big match on the box. You still enjoy the football, don't you?" he enquires.

"Right. You bet."

"Well then, bring Luke with you, if you'd like."

"Thanks, Ossie."

I hover awkwardly, until I stick out my hand to grasp his for a few seconds. Didn't expect this warmth or sympathy from him. I can take his bluff attitude towards my heart condition; in fact it is welcome after the evasions of Wickham. Concrete dust coagulates between our damp palms. We both know that I will never venture down to his boat. But we both wish to believe this. Another thing is that we both support different teams, and he can't forgive me for that either.

"So it's really true that you might kick the bucket," he says.

I experience a powerful desire to get away. If something bad happens to me soon, then his kids will get their grandmother back. They'll move her back into the old house or one nearby.

There's no reason for me to worry about this. I have a more detached attitude towards politics now.

Leaving Mum's building, turning back into the street, I think about never seeing my brother again, along with everyone else. I experience this sadness about him, regardless of our deep cosmic differences. I'd wish to find the sympathetic all-too-human aspect that he keeps hidden; that he's spent all his life trying to beat, to destroy even. Like unscrewing mirrors from your house because you find them too revealing. Enlightenment has never been part of his life journey. It's too late for him to begin searching now, in the troubled contemporary era.

I hesitate agonisingly on the pavement, thinking whether I should go back to talk to him; to ensure that we part on better terms, face the end of our journey in a more positive aspect. Why don't I invite him and the family back to Big Pink one weekend? He might accept under the circumstances. Ossie and I could wander into the garage to tinker about on my old car, which has always fascinated him; if only as Frankenstein has always fascinated the reader.

We're brothers after all. Isn't that what we're supposed to do? Hadn't we better arrange to have a heart to heart, while there's still a chance?

The answer to this logical problem doesn't come. Sadly I decide to continue the route back home with more determined strides. Maybe I will take up his invitation one evening. After all it wouldn't kill me.

# Chapter 23

In our cable sweaters Bob and I hook up to dig jazz at the Old Duke pub, which is a place down on the cobbled quayside, dedicated to this music. Dylan's tastes and mine go their own way here, as he would trash jazz as earnest elitist doodlings from a chin rubbing older generation.

I tried to make a date with Corrina, except she turned down my invitation. No good anyway if she just stood about glumly, being held prisoner next to me, openly sharing - for once - Dylan's (first) views on the early American music. At least her boyfriend didn't pick up my call enquiring, in an indifferent post coital daze, about who I was: although Corrina reached for her excuses and rapidly hung up. Man, she can get out of a telephone conversation faster than a motorway gridlock. But I'm glad to be here with Bob H, as he can appreciate the music, even if he prefers the British blues revival scene.

The Old Duke is full to the rafters this evening. The place is buzzing with bonhomie and conversation from a chin-rubbing, yet cosmopolitan and multi-generational audience. A New Orleans style band is getting into full swing, in homage to the early greats. If you want to hang out with a hep crowd and get hopped up the Old Duke is your joint. It's a great help to my state of mind in these modern times.

Bob H and I prefer to listen to modern jazz at home, post-bop and contemporary, but early jazz is more sociable. Experimental music demands complete attention and, for me, that encourages darker thoughts. I tend to avoid darker thoughts. They don't need any encouragement. Dark thoughts gnaw like woodworm.

I haven't seen Bob H since his annual hoot and he's telling me what an outstanding success it all was. Like the routine set from an MOR stadium band.

"We really enjoyed ourselves, man," Bob says.

"You did?" I shout above the polyphonic cacophony.

"Everyone left happy." He leans in with his stout strong body. "The crowd always enjoys coming around our place for our big celebration."

Didn't he notice Corrina leaving early, with a trail of smoke, from burnt fuel and me?

"Right. Everybody's still talking. We can look forward to next year, I guess."

"That's if we are still in the country, Noah," he explains.

This puts a jolt through me. "You two have more travel plans?"

"Sue and I have some travel adventures in mind. We want to offer the boys experience of different cultures...and there are good schools abroad, if that's a consideration."

"That's not travel, Bob, that's joining the armed services. Besides we've got plenty of different cultures here in Bristol. Why do you want to travel overseas?" I press.

He's grinning appreciatively at me. "Man, you must really enjoy our hoots. If we travel again we shan't be leaving forever. We can't predict what might turn up."

Bob is enjoying his post-party glow. He has delusions of being a master of ceremonies or a type of rock raconteur or promoter: Harvey Goldsmith style.

"Sue and I were so pleased that you came. You were on the roustabout, just like the old days!"

"You can't keep me down," I parley.

I remember Susan's shocked anxiety when she first set eyes on my new visage. I don't like to remind him how he was hiding in the kitchen, guarding his empties. When all the guests have safely left the couple's property they become as magnetic as Mick and Marianne again.

"You mentioned a complication to your health," he says. "Are you sure you're allowed to caper about as normal?"

"Doctor's advice is like a bad hand in poker," I insist.

"An evening out can't do you much harm, I suppose."

"This is the equivalent of a Sunday morning kickabout," I argue.

"Consider your complete health system," Bob tells me, getting closer. "Rather than focusing on one organ, relieve pressure at the vital points," he explains, "to help the healing process."

"Which points?" I ask.

"You can heal yourself by restoring balance to your life as a whole."

"Hey Bob, d'you remember that poor guy at university with blue lips."

Huntingdon scratches his coarse, greying dark locks, thinking back. "Blue lips? Why do you bring this up?"

"You know, the poor guy with a heart condition. That's why."

"The blue lips are a sign of bad circulation. Your body isn't getting enough oxygen."

"But we laughed at the guy," I remind him. "We made fun of him, didn't we?"

"Youth can be cruel when it comes to bad health. We don't want to believe in death."

"That's too right, man!"

"What was his name?" he wonders, still scratching himself.

"We don't even remember his name," I comment.

"He was always on his own. He had to wear a hearing aid as well. It must have been so humiliating for him. To feel so different."

"So mortal."

"Nothing seemed to go right for that guy," he remembers, saddening.

"We didn't make his existence any easier, Bob."

"No, we didn't treat the guy fairly," he admits.

"We were all bullies. That's what we were," I conclude.

"I suppose we were very young and thought we'd live forever."

"Lately we know otherwise."

We both muse on these shameful memories, dropping into our drinks. Somehow the immersive, raucous music is closed off to our brains.

"You know Bob, I'm going to clean out my total health system. Just as you say. I'm going to climb on to the wagon after tonight. One last pull on the ale, then I'm going to concentrate on my yoga class."

"Really, Noah? You serious about the yoga?"

"Maybe I'll meet a lovely divorced lady there, at the leisure centre, on a Monday evening...and finally settle down again for good."

"We wish you the best, Noah."

"I'm making a new life resolution," I insist. I'd probably shoot some video footage as well.

"It's never too late to find your life direction," Bob encourages. He swivels on the sawdust to raise his tankard of bitter.

"Enlightenment, spiritual balance, peaceful contemplation," I say.

"Susan and I think you're an amazingly brave guy."

A brave face anyway, I'm thinking. "There's a plastic valve in my heart that could break apart at any moment," I remind him. "I have the San Andreas fault line running across my chest."

Bob H is knocked back on his heels. "You're sure this is life threatening? That what you're telling us?" he challenges.

"It might have 'catastrophic consequences'. This broken valve in my heart artery may... to quote the specialist who saw me," I report. Finally I get this thing off my chest - the information that is.

"Oh, this comes as a shock," he admits. "We're grateful to have you around, Noah. Don't blow out just yet."

"I don't know if I'm coming or going!"

Bob raises his arms and squeezes my shoulders, as if he wants to dance. But arguably we've already had *The Last Waltz.*

"My nerves are strung out these days," I admit. "Don't think I am so courageous about this. I feel like the Telecom Tower struck by lightning. Believe me. It's all the drugs they foist on me. The legal drugs. I'm terrified to shave in the mornings," I say. "I'm reluctant to walk around town and bump into old school or university friends. I'm one gulp short of aspirin poisoning at any time of night and day."

"You're a survivor, Noah."

"At least I screwed up enough courage to meet people again and went to your annual hoot."

"We're grateful for that."

"I don't always want to leave the house. I feel like a ghoul."

"Don't worry about appearances. We're all past our best. Our generation. We have the best of us inside," he tells me.

"I can't tell if I'm losing weight or gaining it. The scales tell me I am losing, but then I have to look over my belly to see. I don't remember when I last had a healthy colour. I'd have to raid Corrina's blusher to achieve the effect. That poor guy with blue lips had a healthier complexion than I do."

My friend stares at me with intense concern. "It's the real man or woman inside that counts. Don't you believe that? Didn't we always?"

"You talking about the soul?" I reply.

"Where's the best part of a fruit found?" he suggests. "When I'm selecting pears from my trees I'm not examining them for their skins. I'm not climbing up into the branches looking for blemishes. Checking them out for blotches, bumps or impairments. Do you get me?"

"I get the analogy, Bob." I can't help thinking how unappetising I've become.

Huntingdon is pleased with my concession and allows space. Sagely he gazes away and takes fresh notice of the busy pub, nodding vigorously to the melancholy high spirits of the jazz band.

"What's your Angie up to lately?" Bob returns.

"I haven't seen her all weekend," I admit.

"I hear stories about the kids she's hanging out with."

"Don't blame *them*," I tell him. "What did you hear?"

"But don't let her get too far out," he warns.

"I think I'm out of touch," I say. "I'm no longer where it's at."

"We haven't been 'where it's at' for decades," Bob argues.

I ponder that. "How do you always keep so tight with Susan, as a couple? All these years together, so close, no tremors. I have to admire you guys."

"Wish I could put that into a bottle," he replies. "I guess it's about recognising when you are wrong. Knowing when you have to back down. Not sticking to your guns and trying to shoot each other's head off," he says.

"Difficult," I laugh. "I'd no business going off on holiday with Corrina," I admit. "The kids needed me at home then. I was lucky I wasn't in the bloody newspapers."

"Now you've hooked up with her again," he observes. "You were hanging out with each other at our party, weren't you? You disappeared together for a while. I think you made sure everyone noticed."

"We coupled and decoupled, if you're really interested." Bob H was talking about pears and now I'm dreaming about her perfection again.

"Is that such a clever idea?"

"Do you have any more obvious questions?"

"Is she really interested in you, Noah?"

"She's really into me," I assure him.

There's a sceptical ripple. "Aren't you laying yourself wide open?" he suggests, cradling his ale.

"We dig each other, as always." I knew this was shallow, but I couldn't help myself.

"She isn't going to burn you up and leave you behind?" he wonders. Maybe he really did notice her style of leaving a room.

"She's already left her Dunlop pattern across my rib cage," I recall.

"You sound disillusioned. That's a good start."

"What are you saying? You have a negative vibe about her?" I ask, struggling to pierce a high run from the trumpet player.

"You don't have a healthy relationship with that woman."

"I don't? Why should I care about what's healthy or not?" I argue. I rock back precariously as I take another flagon of forgetfulness.

"Go ahead," he tells me. "Get out of consciousness, Noah. But that's never been your philosophy in the past. So why adopt such a blind attitude now?"

"I went into that relationship with both eyes open," I say. With both feet would be more accurate.

"Since when did you get a fatalistic handle on love and life?" he challenges. Can't he take three guesses?

But he's knocked me off balance: I shrug and stumble for a disposable gloss and appendix.

Bob H is annoyed, animated, shuffling his sandals around the spit and sawdust. He gapes up at me with big bespectacled eyes. "Did you marry Lizzie from that negative spirit? Did you guys have those great kids for that motive? We know you for being an idealistic, conscious guy. Where's your positive take on the future?"

"Where's the future?" I repost.

"Cynicism isn't your style, Noah. Don't allow your judgement to slip now, man, just because your health isn't so great."

"Sorry, Bob, but maybe I don't deserve any better," I say.

"You got down on yourself? You don't know who you are? Is that why you allow Corrina to work her charms? That makes everything in your life all right? This excuses all the bad attitudes and mistakes you've made?"

"Corrina's taking me to the Chinese laundry. I admit that. Why should I worry? Maybe I enjoy it," I declare. It must be all that press and steam.

"As you already admit to that," he yelps above the trombone.

"She brushes me with her wing tips," I remark. She was travelling at over a ton - that was the problem.

"Don't let her drag you down, man," he warns, refusing to look at me still.

"She's gorgeous," I bleat.

"You're also coming from completely different generations."

"She's over thirty one you know," I point out.

"She's not so well past it," he says.

"Come on, Bob, you're not even speaking for yourself. She's a match for me." Do uncompetitive matches count?

"I was talking about generational attitude. Social and economic times have changed," he argues.

"It's been cool to hang out with her... with a younger woman. We've had our good and fun times." My youth went backpacking around the world. While I was stuck at home.

"You're not serious?" he protests. Maybe he'd seen a few of her holiday snaps. His brows lift like the suspension bridge, to emphasise critical points.

"Are you advising me to lay off? That could wreck my health even more."

"Corrina isn't the girl for you. Susan and I agree on that."

"Well, that's settled," I comment. "Whose round is it anyway? Shall we get another one in?"

Bob holds fire, allowing another crashing drum solo to progress, accompanied by whoops of approval from the clientele around the room.

He comes forward to tackle me again, scratching me with his coarse beard. At Uni he was an understudy in an amateur production of Hair; he had the most macho facial growth of any undergraduate in Bristol; as well as a reasonable contralto.

"You have a risky love life following your divorce," he says. "This young woman could push you over the edge."

"I've always been of that colour. That's the way I walk," I insist.

Bob's disgruntled with my offhand attitude towards modern love. He never likes to raise his voice or get annoyed, so he has to feel strongly about this. A very tolerant, easy going, peaceful kind of guy is Bob H. How else could he put up with me over the years? particularly over recent months?

"What happened to Rachael? She's a bright woman. Why don't you look her up again?" he suggests.

"Rachael? Isn't she! Sure, I may do that. Great idea."

"Seriously, Noah, you should think about dating a more sympathetic person," he argues.

"But I'm not a sympathetic person either," I say.

Bob puzzles it over. "How did you figure that one?" he asks.

"Years of exhaustive research," I argue, "leading to a deeper self-understanding."

"Corrina doesn't want to understand you," he says.

"How did you get that? You been putting me under surveillance? Sticking microphones up in her bedroom?" I object.

"You're got your own version of the truth," he comments.

"I realise we don't have the perfect relationship. Let me alone to figure it all out." Sitting on the dock of the bay?

The idea of Corrina and me creates an internal sea of strife. Bob tries to follow the complex train of music; a boisterous ensemble counterpoint. Yet, even as he's turned away from me, I notice that his facial muscles are in spasm. Sound advice is often painful to impart - as it is hard to accept. Hopefully he understands my eternal gratitude for enduring friendship. Especially during these anguished contemporary times. You can't buy that for love or money.

At the conclusion to their Tiger Rag the quintet meaningfully lower their instruments. As the musicians grin and gesture between one another, in mutual recognition of the music made together, the pub atmosphere returns to relative tranquillity.

In contrast to the band's harmony, Bob and I continue to pursue the argument about Corrina. I've told him that her bad attitude towards me is not the most important factor.

"She's an exciting woman," I argue.

"So you still need excitement," he notes. He's crossed his arms and set his stance against me.

"She was the closest I came to love at first sight." Just a split-second after uttering this, I realise that it's untrue. Couldn't I hear myself?

"You mean lust," he bluntly states. As with cupid's dart, he's not a feather-width off target with this shot.

Patrons are knocking our elbows, in a push for the exits, but we don't peel away.

"Just because you see somebody's hard side... that doesn't mean you change your feelings about them, does it?"

"She's definitely wasting your precious time," he says.

*Don't think twice, Babe, it's all right!*

Rotolo: does that mean completely broken?

The truth of his comment strikes me like a constant drip of icy water. "Sure, Bob, I suppose that she has wasted a lot of my precious time. But how much time do I still have left?" I say. Precious or otherwise.

He growls and considers. "You going to Rupert's dinner party next week?" he wonders.

"Rup' and I don't see eye to eye...or even eyeball to eyeball. But we're a group, aren't we? And he wants to watch me with a certain lady..."

"They've invited Corinna," he informs me. "She may be there, if she's really so much into you, as you claim. Or it may be wiser to stay away."

"She'll be there! We're still cool."

Bob H considers me quizzically again. "You'll have Susan and I, because we've accepted. Then what are you doing this Thursday evening?"

"Thursday evening? There's nothing scheduled," I say. Only a candlelit dinner for one as usual - you can't draw a pretty face on the wall.

"D'you fancy checking out a Truffaut, showing at the Arnofini?"

"Yeah, great. You're on. I noticed they had a season of French new wave cinema. I haven't seen them on a big screen for years," I tell him.

"So how much do you know about Corrina's background anyway?" he returns.

"Her background?"

"How much did she tell you about her previous life and origins?"

"Man, you're being mysterious. We've only been on holiday together," I remind him.

"You're never around when her friends are invited. So didn't you notice that she cuts you out of her life? The biggest part of her life that is most significant to her?"

"Cuts me out?" I say.

"I've listened to the way Corrina and her friends talk. They speak a different language to us, Noah. I don't like it."

"That doesn't sound like you, Bob."

"Susan and I bumped into her socially, at the Watershed. Just the other week."

"Oh yes, so she was with her friends, was she? As you mention it, I don't believe I have met any of her friends... not as such. Did she say hello to you?" I ask, more brightly.

"No. She didn't say hello. She didn't acknowledge us, to be straight up about it."

"Oh, well, that seems rude," I admit. "I know what I'm up against," I assure him. "I know she belongs to a tight set. I know she's jealous of my business. She wonders how a bloke like me could have started such a business...built it up over the years and made a success of things...at least until now. This makes our position vulnerable. She'd like to run her eyes over my order book and interview the bank manager," I explain.

"Takes a close interest in business, does she?" Bob points out.

We share a moment of insight. "They don't understand us. We followed our passions and interests and took them as far as possible."

"They're coming from a completely new direction," Bob observes. He shakes his greying locks, but he still needs a haircut. Space time is smoothing off my own scalp.

"You'd think love was something to be ashamed of," I complain. "To tell another human being that you love them. A dirty word, a sign of weakness," I muse. Then: "Are you going to get a last round in?"

"All right," he agrees. "But did she ever talk to you about her father?"

"What about her father? Do you mean she has one?"

"You sound like your brother sometimes," he notes. "Her father was an entrepreneur himself. Only he managed to lose all his money and most of his wife's too. So obviously Corrina hasn't discussed this with you," he concludes.

"What a terrible disappointment for her," I say. "No, she hasn't breathed a word."

"Listen, the guy went out and shot himself."

"He didn't," I observe flatly. Gravity tugs on me.

"Colin Farlane was a motorcycle engineer and designer, you see."

"Makes sense," I have to admit.

"Farlane decided to begin motorcycle manufacturing for himself."

"But he couldn't get the thing started. Is that what you're telling me?"

"He spent years in preparation, designing two models of innovative motorbikes. He got building permission and built a state of the art, for the period, factory. Unfortunately, months into start up, the currency shot up, collapsing his export market. There was an influx of cheap foreign machines in the UK at the time."

"It was a complete wipe out for British motorcycles," I recall.

"They actually turned out some of those Farlane machines," Bob tells me. "They could be valuable today. You know, collectors' pieces."

"They realised that motorbikes had already been invented."

"You didn't know about her father? She didn't touch on the subject? Then what do you guys talk about?" he asks.

"So you're telling me she was pushed into poverty?" I say.

"After Colin Farlane blew his own head off, the family lost everything. They were uprooted from their Oxfordshire home. She was pulled out of school."

"These experiences must have left a mark," I conclude.

"She was close to her father. They shared the same passions. For motorcycles. Her sense of humiliation and shame must have been sharp."

"Why did she keep all this from me?" Couldn't I guess?

"She must be aware of a stigma, in her social circles. She was glad to leave all that behind, when she went off to university and began work in Bristol."

"She's found an interesting career at Whig Wham," I consider. "Has to keep her mind and energies directed elsewhere. I only wish that my daughter had that kind of drive and ambition." But did I really?

Our experience is closer than I imagined - Corrina and me. But does that matter to her, even if she is conscious of our comparable experience? Are these the family secrets I failed to decipher?

# Chapter 24

After trying to return me to the road of enlightenment, Bob drops me back at Big Pink. Not before he's arranged my tour itinerary for weeks ahead. The Huntingdons always keep a handle on the big picture. But if they go away on their travels again, I'll be crushed.

After his snail Citroen rattles frothily down the street, red antennae receding, I note that there are lights blazing in our front room. Our kids have returned to the haunted castle. I won't be facing an empty dungeon tonight. Back in the hallway I discover something being passed off as music. I maintain a cool paternal mind-set, but for how much longer?

I blunder into the room to find a gaggle of youngsters sprawled over the floor and upholstery. Either from fright or amazement they freeze into attitudes of indifference. The sweet smouldering aroma of marijuana fills my nostrils and lungs.

"Dad. You're back," exhales Angie. "Where'd you come from?"

She's lounging on the floorboards against the bottom of an armchair. In appearance she is dishevelled, grimy from lack of sleep or showers. Her pallor has a greyish, twilight tinge, which doesn't originate from major surgery or anxiety.

"What's happening here?" I declare.

In an unnaturally loud and confident voice she says: "You been out on the town, Dad?"

"Aren't I allowed to?" I reply. "D'you expect me to hide up the chimney?" This draws ironic snorts of derision from the young people. I've turned myself into the establishment. The art of satire isn't dead.

"You been in this boozer tonight? Are you hammered?" she says.

"I've been down to the quayside listening to some classic jazz."

There's laughter.

"You think that jazz is funny, do you? What's the origins of rock music?" I challenge. Unfortunately this isn't the time slot for University Challenge.

"That's anybody's bloody guess," says this lad.

"You're not going to load me into the deep freeze yet," I declare strangely.

"Is it smart for you to get drunk like this, Dad?"

"Is that irony?" I object.

"No, this is pharmaceutical," she retorts.

Like getting chastity lectures from Anais Nin, fidelity classes from that Colette chick, this is hard to swallow. Angie's been raiding her parents' intellectual parlour. She's been reading the feminist writers that Liz used to quote. Except that her mother wouldn't be impressed anymore.

"You're not listening to doctor's advice?" Angie says.

"Are you thinking of a medical career?"

"I reckon you wanna look after yourself better...in your present condition," she informs me. Those black orbs turn up at me through smoke rings.

"I'm not drunk and I know my limits."

There's no miracle cure at the pub, but it certainly raised my spirits.

Her pack of friends eye me spitefully. Looks as if my rapport with the city's youth has broken down, since that morning outside Mike's café. I'm not a Guthrie, Kerouac or Ginsberg figure. I'm a scarecrow of yesteryear. I can't find the puff to talk up my kites and balloons again. It's getting late, I'm wacked, shattered. I'm not inspired to re-run my disoriented trip around Tokyo. Man, I was like a fly in a bowl of spaghetti soup.

"Angie, what happened to you this afternoon? Grandma was disappointed not to see you. She was worried what may have happened."

"Grandma wouldn't want me to miss out on life," she argues.

"You better tune into reality, Angie, or you're gonna lose the signal," I warn.

Angela rolls her eyes in teenage mock despair; except she's no longer a teenager. All right, she's fragile, adolescent in body construction, yet as Corrina pointed out, unmistakably a grown woman. Why can't she be more like Ossie's girl?

"You need to smoke your peace pipe," a lad comments.

"Does this need your contribution?" I retort.

I'm stranded on the peak of our alpine rug - inevitably a gift from our friends - which Liz chose not to pull out from under my feet.

"Where have you been all weekend Angie? Your brother and I haven't seen you for days."

"We've been to a field," she replies bluntly, in a wobbly tone of voice.

"A field?" I state.

"A beautiful field with a floppy fringe?"

"Can't you be sensible?"

"We like fields," her mate adds.

"We're field freaks."

"Does that pass for a witty remark?" I tell them. Maybe I've had a humour bypass.

"What are you like?" Angela objects.

"You've been smoking, you've been drinking. You don't look all that great," I argue.

"Solid. I'm really solid, Dad!"

"Don't worry, Mr Sheer, she's on the pill."

Elizabeth regarded her as a potential defender of the underprivileged, of the oppressed, *pro bono*. We dreamed of seeing her through university into an exciting profession with a radical edge.

They're passing around a bottle of vodka. I want to stand as firm as a column at the centre of the room. Instead I'm struggling to keep focus and I feel like a kicked spinning top. I can't blink away swimming vision as my daughter and her playmates get steadily blotto. What I've crashed into here is the last hooray from a weekend of excess.

"Have a pull on this, man," the youngster parodies, as he thrusts a vodka bottle towards me.

After palming the booze off, I back away. "So aren't you dudes gonna tell me where you've been?"

"Over the humped back bridge," this beefy boy says.

"Just down from the tractor," adds his mate.

"And the three legged cow," explains the other.

"Just outside of Chippenham," says another girl; Samantha, a bulimic redhead in narcoleptic shock.

“So what were you dong in Chippenham?” I wonder.

“Chippenham cows are the craziest!”

There’s a crescendo of hilarity. I try to hold my strong position on the woolly peak, waiting grim-faced for their joke to tire. Unfortunately it isn’t tiring, it’s extending every time they look at me. Until Angie catches me decisively by the wrist and pulls me down with her.

The kids’ mockery twists my heart, like a fraying rope in a tug-o-war. There are moments when you reach emotional breaking point. Your best efforts come to nothing.

“Get yourself another drink,” the agricultural lad suggests.

“Already had more than enough, thank you,” I protest.

“Go on, Dad, you can always sink another one.”

Her note of proud bravado is repellent. They might go back to their parents and brag about me.

“Look at the state you’re in!”

“Don’t stress, Dad! There’s nothin’ wrong with me!” she squeals.

“That was a decent skirt before you set out on Friday,” I note.

We don’t stop caring. The pain doesn’t cease. I’m still prepared to clean up, to rescue her after she has got lost on the beach or fallen into another hole.

Constance would be shocked at the acreage of bare flesh in my front room.

“You a fashion guru too, mister Sheer?” I hear.

“Didn’t you know that?” I reply.

“Nobody’s impressed,” Angela rebukes.

“You’re not looking great. I know that. It’s enough.”

“You’re not like your old photos either,” she retorts.

My ego takes a plunge. “Who’s your new boyfriend? Is he here tonight?” I press.

“Don’t make yourself ridiculous.”

“What’s the big secret about your private life?”

“*I* don’t keep any secrets, Dad,” she informs me.

Holding me in an intense stare, her expression shatters and she breaks out into a splitting, hysterical laugh. With no chance to plug my ears from the decibels I just slump into a resigned unhappiness, as reality knocks around a spin dryer.

"How'd you like this old boy as your Dad?" she declares, struggling to regain control.

"Something's giggling her gerbil," her friend, Samantha, comments.

"My daughter's mixed up in something dicey," I tell them. Definitely mixed up.

Angie's dark eyes struggle to focus through the effects of another wild weekend. "Why so concerned? All of a sudden?"

I find that my own telescope is hard to control, when I turn my head to meet her. "Haven't I always been?"

She chuckles at my seriousness. "We've got to be free, haven't we?" She sets off on more gusty laughter, seeking her friends' entertainment.

"Angie's gettin' hassle off her angry old man!"

As for the referee this Saturday, when City played Port Vale at home, someone doubts my parentage; another accuses me of regular sex, or self-gratification. Yet my daughter proves my point. I don't need to write a dissertation.

"Stay cool, man!"

"We've all been neckin' beanies, know what I mean?" this boy pipes up - like he's just got home from the shops to tell his Mum.

They savour a joke amidst the layers of blue - tobacco - smoke.

"What are you going to do if she cops out?" I wonder.

"She aint goin' to!"

"All right, man, don't be square! What's your problem, Daddy-O?"

"Huh?" I react.

My well-oiled vision locates and focuses on this particular guy. He's well dressed, neat, wide awake. Sat, almost sober, on the other side of Angie. You could almost put a scalpel into his hand.

"No harm droppin' a few tabs. Not if they keep hydrated."

"What's that?"

"You have to be in the right mood," he explains.

"Where did you meet *this* guy, Angela!"

"Has anybody got any more tackle on 'em?" she asks defiantly.

"Is this him? The new prince bloody charming?" I press. The new lad in her life - the evil genius or - more accurately - the numbskull bum, wrecking her future hopes?

He looks at me indifferently through long grey eyes. Like those through a slot in a painting. "What you got against people enjoying themselves?"

"Drugs are never as simple as that," I object. "Who said you could smoke in my house, anyway?" I query.

"I don't smoke anything. I'm clean," he informs me.

I stare across in confusion. With those clean chiselled looks I can see why Angie may fancy him. He's the young man I should have turned back into. That would have ended my troubles. I'd get the girl and live happily ever after. Although I'd never slather on the artificial tan, or go in for the body bling, like this guy.

"Are you my daughter's boyfriend?"

"I'm everybody's friend, know what I mean?" he replies, gazing away.

Despite going to a music festival over the weekend, he hardly has a swept hair out of place, a stain or even a crease in his smart casual wear. Must have spent last night off the ground. This isn't my idea of a decent free thinking boyfriend.

Angela rouses herself, subsides and places a protective arm around his shoulder. Looks as if her taste in men has done a complete round-the-world flight. When's she coming back to her family?

"What's going down with my daughter?" I say.

"Let her enjoy being young, know what I mean?"

"Is that your attitude to taking drugs?"

"No harm necking back a few cheekies over the weekend," he remarks coolly.

"Where did you meet this guy, Angie?"

I'm suffering the effects of a naked living room. I heard Liz's admonishments. She might turn up at any moment and tell him where to go. She's always the ghost in the house.

"You can't dig a great big fuckin' hole somewhere, and bury 'em all under the ground," he argues.

"What about all the damage they do?" I blather.

"They aint gonna change the world," he informs me. "Peace and fucking love. Know what I mean? The world's fucked up, but it's gonna *look* a better place. It's gonna *feel* like a better place. Let people forget their fucking worries."

"That's really fucking broadminded of you," I return.

"Look, mate, if there's a market then it has to be filled, know what I mean?"

"I'd still prefer to dig that big hole of yours, boy. Did you walk along *White Lady* Road or *Black Boy* Lane recently?" I suggest.

"I'm not talkin' about the fuckin' slave trade," he scoffs, lightly.

"There was a market that had to be filled."

"Better to trade drugs than people, isn't it."

"All kinds of people get hooked," I tell him. "You don't have to have an addictive personality. You just turn into an addict. Their lives begin to fall apart."

"Bollocks. It's all about personal choice and freedom. If you can't look after your own life, then you aint worth a fuck, know what I mean?"

"D'you want a puff of this, Mr Sheer?" Samantha enquires.

"This is the most drug addicted civilisations ever," this bum tells me. "We're chemical creatures, know what I'm sayin'? So we're changing our chemistry all the time."

"Your average junkie is just out of it," I retort, keeping slur away from my speech.

"We can't let the losers drag us back," he says. His nostrils flicker in aversion. "Can one of you open a window for me, or what?"

"Nobody needs these poisons," I come back.

"What do you mean by 'poisons'? That's just bollocks, that is," he complains.

"Right, well, if you're selling any drugs to Angela, I would certainly have your bollocks," I inform him.

"You'd stop people drinkin' tea, you would, if you 'ad your way."

"This isn't a cup of tea, boy. Do you look like her? After a cup of tea?"

His facial muscles taughten. "When you're looking at these kids, you're talkin' about a completely different scene."

"What kind of scene would that be?" I speculate.

"They just want to get hyper."

Angie nods her head and mutters in half heard agreement.

"They don't look hyper to me," I point out.

"Not right now. Last night and the night before. Know what I'm talkin' about?" he complains, with a first grimace. My leather couch isn't so accommodating for him at last.

"Whatever happened to youthful idealism? Dreams for a better future?"

"The future, man? You have to face it, life is a pile of shit, ain' it?" he disabuses me. "Haven't you looked into the fucking media lately?"

"You should stay away from these kids. What kind of message is that?"

"There's *no* message," he remarks. "Geddit?"

"Just make your money how you can? Is that it?" I reply, shocked.

"What's your problem? Know what I mean?"

"Don't you believe in anything?" I put to him.

"What d'you want me to believe in?" he wonders. Chemistry, the market, money - this is his culture.

"Dad, stop being a pain? Don't even talk to him, Adam."

I don't know him from... The guy shrugs and brushes his knees, as if plaster has crumbled from the ceiling. He begins to play with a gold bracelet. He allows the chain to rise and fall along his wrist, like a fretful tennis player.

"Drug addicts are just bums. When The Beatles went out to Haight-Ashbury they just found a group of stoned bums. Chasing after them in a field. Nobody reached utopia. Nobody was enlightened," I argue. "Your drugs just screw us up?"

"You a fucking hippie, or what?" he mocks, without looking at me.

"Do you have any skunk in the house, Mr Sheer?" that farmer's boy asks me again.

"Too late to change the fucked up world, Daddy-O," Adam considers. "The only world these kids can change is their own. Know what I mean? If you get soft then you get stomped on. That's the law we live under, know what I'm sayin'?"

"That's pretty damn depressing, boy," I tell him, gloomily.

*But one day, I know, I shall be released.*

As I telephone for a taxi the kids arrange themselves, waiting, around our staircase. To complicate matters, when I finally get through to the small-hours company operator, the friendly guy on the line announces he's South American and has difficulty in understanding my request.

Adam came with his own wheels. The kids came with him on the same set, but he doesn't want to run them all home. Angie's playmates live in different areas of the city from Knowle to Filton. The idea is too demeaning and humiliating for the guy: it would be like taking a job as a council driver.

Arguably I could now use some of those mind altering drugs, to increase powers of ingenuity and positivity. A lot of different things happened to me in that London hospital, as they hacked me open. During open-heart surgery they'll close the patient's brain down, for the course of the procedure. They put my nut on hold, killing off brain cells over the duration, whole universities of them. You can't ask difficult questions under anaesthesia. In effect I was lobotomised for hours, destroying grey matter like buckets of ice cream in a heat wave. When you come around you can only count your stitches and try to pick up the thread. They didn't warn me about that in advance, and it's hard to calculate any damage or limitation.

"Aren't you too old for this scene?" I tell Adam.

"You're never too old," he replies disdainfully.

"Never?" I consider. "You should stop making money out of these kids," I comment.

"You're in business yourself. Aren't you, Noah?" he returns.

"You think it compares? Maybe you should start a clinic," I say.

"I reckon the bank boys'd listen to you, wouldn't they... You'd cook up some fancy business plan an' they'd be throwing the loot at you. Know what I mean?" he sneers.

"A business plan may help, boy," I admit.

"I make a bit of bread outa the alternative scene. Without me there'd be nothin' goin' on. The plods would be hangin' around every slipway waitin' to arrest the little bastards, know what I mean. There's got to be a bit of brains behind the operation," he informs me, tapping his subtly bleached locks.

"You're Colonel Parker," I argue.

"Dad, don't be a pain," Angie objects, hanging off the cynic's shoulder.

"You can go to bed now, girl. The sobering-up begins here," I declare.

"Well, me, I'm getting' out o' this hole," Adam promises.

He buttons up his cashmere coat and heads off. Jauntily his sharp heels pick off our front steps and he moves down the street without a second look. Collar turned up, gloved hands dug into pockets - it's a cold night - a tall, stooping, gauche figure. At the end I see him pull out a hand, point ahead and bleep open his super-expensive new car, similar to one Liz owns, just a different colour. The guy's a dark horse, but how dark?

As he revs and squeals away, I notice many curtains being dragged apart, with bedroom lights falling on the pavement in cubist patterns. Do I know what I'm getting in to? This is more risky than throwing off your clothes in an anti-war demo. Illegal drug entrepreneurs aren't noted for their tolerance.

The ordered taxi arrives at speed, having chosen a narrow passage through the Andes. My daughter's young friends struggle into the cab, not without a last show of their hilarious antics. This scene is going to feed the neighbourhood's supply of gossip for months ahead. It certainly won't get into the entertainment section, and a caricature of events may find its way to my ex-partner. Many of these youngsters' parents are going to be shaken from their sleep. Assuming they ever got any. The problems of the world ripple back to your own front step eventually.

# Chapter 25

Along with the gas bill, the *Kiteflier* magazine and my renewed membership of the BBC (that's the British Balloon Club) I also find a thick document from the London hospital on our doormat. After I rip the seal on this envelope, and squeeze out the bulky scroll within, I find that there are two separate letters contained. One comes from the hospital management and the other's from the Marquis de Sade who operated on me, in the third person.

The hospital junta expresses regret over my setback; it wishes me a long life, while restating legal and ethical facts on the issue; that they bear no responsibility, liability or blame, in relation to me and what has happened. Call me paranoid. The other epistle - which is the best way to describe such a long and assertive letter - explains in great detail how I might claim financial redress in the States. Hired legal experts, on behalf of the surgeon and his hospital, referred me to identical cases in Japan, Australia and the United States. An international fiasco, it turns out. A whole global society of luckless cardiacs, coming back around after their major operation, hoping to stir back into a new life, with dodgy hearts finding a regular rhythm, only to realise that a vital component is breaking up. So instead of recovery and rehabilitation they face a precarious present, with a radically ambivalent future. We could all get in touch and form a bad luck club - a terrible luck club - keeping up with each other's news, like green bottles hanging on a wall.

A lawsuit was being drawn up against a certain Pearly Synthetics and Life Aids Incorporated, I kid you not, the manufacturer of these plastic beauties. The California victim support group has got a football team of silk-suited barracuda lawyers, scattering the medics with a powerful whiff of corporate blood. And these guys are prepared to allow a few limey victims to sit on their subs bench. Can you blame me for getting bad vibes? Man, those solicitors will be buying more beach houses and I'll be lucky to get a new hot water bottle.

I wander stiffly back to the kitchen, re-reading my correspondence along the way, chewing on a slice of toast daubed with blackcurrant jam, that resembles blood-cells separated from the plasma.

What does any guy with a faulty heart valve want with lengthy litigation? Do they have any awareness of our delicate position? Mistakes can be made in business, I'm ready to concede. Errors occur, in all spheres of life and business, not only in the medical profession. There are accidents, mistakes and blunders, in the nuclear, armaments or food industries; whereby safety checks are not made, workers fail to check on the production process, managers compromise with safety to improve profits and efficiency. Consignments erroneously or illegally transported, whether that be enriched uranium, armoured cars or baby milk. These blunders can have a catastrophic impact on our lives, individual or collective. Call me a bit paranoid, but I know how it all works.

An error of that nature obviously happened with me. And with all those unfortunate cardiacs around this great big onion, whose surgeon hit on the smart idea of fitting Pearly Synthetics' new artificial heart valves (having read the glossy brochure). I couldn't help reading those hospital letters over and over again, with their menacing tone of sympathy and warning. I chewed on further slices of crimson toast, pouring yet more cups of breakfast tea, leaving the day's newspaper for later. I understood very well that the heart attack machine had absorbed me: I had become no more than a single cell in a larger organism, of fear and paranoia, like a gnat squashed between train buffers.

How would I agitate my generation to protest on the streets about this? What was going to be my call? my manifesto? Nobody would likely come, but I still have those feelings of anger and injustice. One reason why we demonstrated at all was to get rid of unbearable ideas, which could torment the mind and conscience. Protest is a matter of personal healthy and sanity. It's critical to voice and to express such powerful feelings of disgust and outrage. Otherwise you are left feeling dirty.

These Pearly Synthetics guys are guilty of negligence or criminality - agreed. They deserve to be forced to stand up in a courtroom somewhere - or at least sit behind their silk suited barracuda - wherever in the world those broken-hearted coronaries may live. Some form of pay-out, in compensation for damage, sounds attractive and might heal the sutures in my own business. But it could never repair or recompense me for the physical damage it has created. A windfall would have a negative effect on our kids. They'd become richer than their wildest dreams, so then what would happen to their wildest dreams? Liz may or may not have lost her youthful ideas, but she'd never forgive me for that. Call us old-fashioned or moralistic. No, it's best to leave that Californian law suit hanging.

Decided on this, I scrunch up all that official hospital paper. When I have a moment I'll shred the whole thing. I slouch back at our kitchen table, taking advantage of the solitary silence. I think about those guys around the globe in the same delicate situation as me. As a saint I wouldn't wish this condition on anyone. As a flawed human being I can't help feeling glad I'm not alone. Everybody thinks about death. Premature death's the most unjust kind, because it catches us out, while we're busy doing other things. Suddenly you're not counting years off, you are peering around the next corner. Sometimes it's a blessing to worry yourself sick over your kids. If this life really is a test, as Lizzie and the Dino would have us believe, and all humanity is just messing about in the waiting room for a final interview with The Big Guy (the consultant in the heavens) then I'm happy to put myself in front of my kids. That's what you'd expect; that's regular, so I'm not asking to be canonised (or to be put into the rock 'n' roll hall of fame either) or anything like that.

There was a lead article in the Bristol newspaper this week that caught my eye. This concerned a well-known vicar in the city who tragically died of leukaemia. The guy was just into his forties, which isn't any kind of age. He was known as a hard working priest of liberal views that offended some - although this is an easy-going liberal city on the whole. He worked a lot with reforming prisoners, drug addicts and the homeless. We have plenty of those categories of people here. Built like an ox, a bearded charismatic, thick skinned and compassionate, married with three children.

In this photograph, reproduced by the newspaper, his eyes seem troubled. Evidently this shot was taken before lethal illness kicked in to annihilate red blood cells. What was the cause of his angst? If he didn't yet know about his illness? Could it have been the difficult individuals he worked with? Or maybe some doubts about his own faith? Or was it the lost faith of the society around him? What's the point of a priest without a decent congregation? As for a father without a proper family?

It's an injustice to be stolen away from this world too soon. If you love life and other people it is. So how am I coping with the idea? I know that self-pity is not attractive to others, particularly after they have divorced you. When that deluded fool gunned down John Lennon on a New York street, how can I have self pity? Lennon still had a love of life to go with his love of Yoko and his children.

*Lightning strikes.*

Yesterday morning, I think it must have been, I was listening to BBC Radio Bristol in bed, when they told the story of how a workman, out cleaning the Clifton Suspension Bridge (just a few streets away from us here) had fallen to his death. What a foolish if tragic step, to entertain the whole city over its breakfast table.

I walked around the gorge this week, as I often do, where I noticed that a temporary platform has been constructed under the bridge. It was from there that the guy went for a tumble. The workers stand on the platform and, as they finish cleaning one section and shuffle around, their wooden ledge is shifted along. Apparently this guy leant too far out with his mop, causing him to slip and to plunge, hundreds of feet down into the stinking mud of the Avon at low tide.

Do you know, the gang was back cleaning the bridge next day. They were all assembled high-up on the platform with mops and sponges, soaping the metal lattices and girders, just as if nothing had happened. You can't ignore that type of karma. They even went and replaced the light bulbs knocked out on his way down. They couldn't face the idea of not seeing the historic bridge lit up at night. They couldn't bear to leave any unsightly dark patches among the fairy lights.

But then again, why hang about? To be honest with you, most of the time, I try not to think about it.

By my reckoning Angie was supposed to be at work by eight. I check off Liz's pilot's watch gift again: It's already gone that. She's unlikely to reach her percolator on time. While I'm anguishing over my existence in the basement kitchen, she's upstairs, quietly buried under a duvet a few floors above my head. What should I do? Get hold of the bottom corners and tip her on to the floor? She'll reach the age of majority next year, whatever that means. Not marriage, I hope. Not to that spiv alternative music promoter. God help us. Seems unlikely. Will the Dino be giving her away one day in my place? The bastard's taken everything else.

Meanwhile, trying not to stress-out, I complete my application to join the Yoga society. None of the drugs work anymore and, anyway, they leave your head like a limestone quarry after a flash-flood. Satisfied by my efforts to explain my reasons - with no mention of pretty divorcees in leotards (though it's a legitimate reason) - I lick the seal and address the envelope, trying to feel pleased. I read in the Sunday supplement, health section, last weekend, that you can get an overall view of your health by examining your tongue. That was it; you stick out your tongue, get the end between your thumb and finger, to examine the colour and then, if you're an expert in tongue tone, you have the low down on any medical condition. That's great news for tongue solipsists. Most mornings I'm too nervous to even clear away the steam from my bathroom mirror.

I'll post that Yoga application on the way to work. No more loping about the squash courts now, two steps behind Rachael and her sister (the girl with the elastic elbows). I'll trust myself to a deep spiritual peace with the help of those chicks in tights. Those experienced ladies know how to move to a slower wisdom.

What if Corrina fails to show at Rupert's dinner party? How to drink that rich claret of total humiliation and save my face? if she stands me up again? Bob H warned me that she may not attend. She only treats me to private interviews, usually on a Sunday afternoon at her place. Many of our previous dates, as I think back, were accidental meetings, including the very first time we met at Whig Wham. But then so was the birth of the universe. So why bitch?

I think about where Lizzie and I were, when we got the news about John Lennon's death. That's right, we were down here in the kitchen, this same spot, in December 1980. The shock and disbelief on her face as she came through and announced the dreadful fact. But he wasn't a member of our family or a close friend. We couldn't blow it out of proportion. The posthumous album was released shortly afterwards, like a devil's marketing ploy. Lennon was singing on that album about watching his son Sean growing up. For a generation that had grown up with Lennon, as with the other Beatles, this was unbearably poignant and sad to follow. Yoko sang about middle-aged contentment, bad times (musical and personal) finally over, the chance to start life anew. A *Double Fantasy* cruelly ended. It was an empty elevator moment for our generation.

Arguably Lizzie and I have been through a similar annihilation. She decided to use the ultimate weapon against us, as if Khrushev insisted that his ships should get to Cuba or Nixon had got angrier with Ho Chi Mhin.

They say you can't erase the past. I'm haunted by her presence around the house. I'm rooting around the place, when I hear her voice, telling me something, or asking me to do something. "Did you say something?" I reply. "Did you call me, Liz?" I say. Occasionally I even rush into a room expecting to surprise her, as if she's playing some kind of game with me. Until I understand that she really isn't there, she can't possibly be in the house, even if I do pick up her voice and feel her presence everywhere. I remember that she is gone and the place is empty. When the silence is pressed up into my face, like a steel door in the dark.

There are numerous, particular places in Dylan's songs, which carry an impression of Liz's words - her voice and way of expressing herself - fused with Zimmerman's lyrics and notes. We've played those albums so often, that our lives are engraved into them. Sensory and psychic memories contained in that music. I guess that's more Lizzie's territory than mine. I can't help wondering if she's disturbed by the same. Except that she won't be listening to Dylan any longer, never mind keeping up with him. If they notice a picture of Zimmerman they stick their index fingers together and back away.

Going upstairs to investigate Angela's absence, I shout another wake-up call; trying not to strike the tragic note. When I get to the second floor balustrade I notice another sheet of wallpaper slowly peeling down from a corner. It reminds me of a giant tear falling down the wall. Can I safely get up on a ladder these days, or should I pay my brother to do the job? Angela's muffled groans and complaints tell me which way to go. This brings about more short-term memories of that attitudinal, much older boyfriend. So how am I thinking of straightening her out?

"Angela! Angela! Where are you?"

More ghosts rush into my head; as this time I'm yelling across the immensity of a Pembrokeshire beach, over a decade and more ago.

"Go and look, Noah! Didn't you notice her running off? Didn't you see anything?" Lizzie challenges. She's provoked to this by anxiety. My lovely young wife begins to get changed out of a polka-dot swimming costume, after completing another swim in the ocean. Apparently I'd been dozing amidst the dunes, lost in my own world as usual.

"Sorry, Lizzie, really sorry. I just closed my eyes for a moment, you know. Then she was gone," I explain.

"No good being sorry if she's drowned," Lizzie warns.

"She's just gone to explore. To buy another ice-cream."

"I can't leave you for a minute, Noah!"

"What do you expect me to do?" I object, struggling to my feet.

"We have to go and look!" she insists, shocking me with icy drops from her fingertips.

"Which particular direction would you suggest?"

"Let's set off... let's go in different ways to find her!" Lizzie says.

Babe, best you go your way and I'll go mine? Liz stomped away, holding the rim of a floppy hat with one hand. I set off through the sand dunes with trembling knees and tom-tom heartbeat, scanning that desolate sweep of bay for our errant child.

*"Angela! Angela!"*

Bathers of all shapes and generations played around the surf's edge where the waves rolled in, like cruel laughter. As panic rose in me, the shapes were no more than vertical blurs over streaming vision. I felt that Angela was dissolving in these acidy tears. How can a small child get so far away so quickly? There's no longer any sign of my wife - no polka dots or sun hat - as if we are not a young family of three, but entirely isolated individuals - man, woman, child - going in different directions, away from each other on that windy shore, lost from each other forever.

My drunken return the other evening was regrettable. Then, after Angie's friends had gone back home in a taxi, I had to put her to bed - as if she was ten years old again. Except it wasn't quite like that. We threw our arms around each other like a pair of drunken sailors crossing the swing bridge. Who was taking the weight? To make no mention of the fitful heart muscle. She twists that café owner around her little toe, apparently. Why can't she get to work on time? She's vending cappuccinos; she isn't running a public limited company.

Suddenly Luke edges out of his bedroom on to the landing. Unwittingly we are thrown into a conflict situation, when I least expected to see him. His school uniform has been pulled on any old how; half strangling himself with the school tie; a Formula One sports bag slung over his shoulder, containing study materials. I'm the last guy he expected to see through his windshield.

He's got into the habit of leaving Big Pink early, like he's a keen scholar. I realise that his weekly routine has been influenced by new mates and fresh interests. His return home times have become just as erratic and extended. We all seem to keep to a different time in this epoch. His behaviour has become alarmingly unpredictable, even allowing for ripping hormones and blitzkrieg growth spurts.

"You can't leave the house without breakfast," I warn.

He treats me to edgy eye contact. I step neatly aside to get out of his way.

"I'll be waiting in the kitchen for you," I say. Where else?

He colours rapidly and growls at me: a primitive throaty whine, like the angry throttle noises from the pipes of Corrina's motorbike, as she reluctantly lingers at the lights.

"An empty stomach leads to an empty head," I argue. I've certainly got a few holes in my own thoughts.

Luke cuts off the warning sounds. "I'll get somefin' on the way to school wan I!" he protests.

"Double death burger and fries?" I wonder.

"You checkin' what I eat now?" he says.

Elizabeth's original red hair - a dangerous electrical copper - is rucked up into alarming punkish spikes. It gives him inches over me and an alarming menace. He has her passionate, uncompromising eyes too.

"Go back to our room and fetch me your dirty clothes."

"What's that?"

"I'm not your bloody laundry maid, boy," I complain.

"Wait here!"

After a period of banging, dragging and dark muttering he returns. He thrusts a spilling bundle of balled clothes towards me. As I try to make sense of the tangle, I notice heavy grease stains on his best denims. "So where did these come from?" I say.

"Stop sweating me, Dad!"

"Don't run away yet, as I need to talk to you about..."

"What now?"

"I'm looking at your best pair of jeans... that you haggled out of your mother and...what are these stains? Can't you explain?"

"What are you steamin' over now?"

"These!" I tell him, holding up the offending garment like a crazed floor scrubber in a television advertising campaign.

"How the bloody hell should I know?" he objects.

"Tell me how you got grease on these trousers."

Luke's sore unfocused eyes narrow on me. He's trudged half way down the staircase and is glaring up at me - with those tigerish eyes.

"I told you!"

"You haven't been mucking about with my car again, have you?" I ask.

"I didn't touch your old banger," he replies.

"You need to ask me first, before we do any mechanical work together. All right?"

"I'm not interested in your stupid car."

"Last time I conked out on the motorway to Cardiff," I recall. "'Cause you'd loosened the fuel pipe. That's a vintage motor you know, which has to be treated carefully. Not that you did anything deliberately," I add.

"If you got me a motorbike, proper," he argues, "I wouldn't need to mess around on it, would I."

"You're still after that motorbike?" I say.

"What's the point of doin' bloody motor mechanics at school, right, if I've only got toy cars to practice on?" he tells me.

"You're not old enough yet. They're too damn dangerous. Do you want to fall off, like Bob Dylan? D'you want to risk your future career?" I say.

"Your girlfriend's got one, hasn't she," Luke reminds me. "That blonde bit you hang about with."

"That isn't relevant," I reply. "Don't talk about Corrina like that, please."

"In fact she's got more 'n one bike, doesn't she. She must have three of them."

"Ask me again when you turn eighteen," I comment.

Next thing I know Luke will be hammering through the city centre too, like Corrina Farlane on acid.

Smarting from our conflict, I take his straggling laundry into the wash room. I take another look at those soiled trousers. If these oil stains didn't come from my classic car, there has to be another explanation. Most likely he's got an old motorbike stashed away somewhere - in the garage of a mate - or he has a friend with a machine. I need eyes in the back of my head, but I'm just Cyclops with a squint.

Why is Luke so angry that I care? The idea's that we become closer friends in the current perilous epoch. We have to make up for lost future time. If I suggest running a movie in the evening - an action film that we can both take an interest in - he always turns me down. Suddenly he's lacking any concentration beyond the computer screen and is fixated on owning a motorbike.

Elizabeth has made the same observation. This type of behaviour isn't just confined to Big Pink.

When I make it back to our kitchen Luke is at the table, shovelling cornflakes. Like a visual gag he's missing his mouth. There's no point cracking open a fresh argument. I try to ignore his hit or miss style of eating. I studiedly pour myself another cup of tea, to keep him company.

Coughing and spluttering, swinging his bag, knocking over the coat stand, throwing aside the front door, Luke is ready to confront another school day.

This is as close to a traditional family breakfast as we get.

Angela appears downstairs finally, sporting her blue café uniform. I'm happy that she chooses to join me, as I continue to hang out in the kitchen. She's prepared for work, even if her skirt is crumpled and too short, while a sweater is twisted around her torso like a stocking. There's another ring of black under her eyes, I notice, which she hopes will evaporate by lunchtime. Doesn't she realise that there's a point in life where these marks begin to stay. You get to a stage when the body's ability to repair itself slows down.

She has an enviable ability to recover from her late night revels and chemical excesses. The nonchalance of youth that doesn't have to make an effort. Whereas in these contemporary times I have to scramble up an extended step ladder.

"You'd better get your skates on," I suggest. At least she's prepared to sit at the table with me and take in some fresh coffee and toast. Maybe she should have left home already, but I'm in no hurry to get rid of her. Not only this morning, I am talking about, but generally to begin her own life. Liz insists that I should be there for her, because they have a volatile relationship. I find that a gratifying observation, but nobody's saying it's easy.

"I'm not in the mood to argue with you," she warns, pushing streams of smoke into the space between us.

"Will you blow that pollution over your shoulder?" I say.

"What's the problem? You smoked once," she replies.

"I gave up. Are you suggesting I should start again?" I object, rocking on the back legs of my chair.

"If we're going to have another pointless argument," she comments.

I swear that I'm taking over my mother's role at the tea urn; or coffee percolator in Angie's case. Then if your father dies at a young age, how do you know if you're turning into him?

"What sort of condition is that, to be going into work like?" I state.

Brandishing the cigarette emphatically, she dismisses my question.

"You've got some difficult life choices to sort out."

"Oh shit, Dad, let them wait."

"What's on your mind?" I watch her nibble on the crust of dry toast. Calories are banned from her body before lunchtime.

"Did you really throw all my friends out?"

"I asked them to leave, at a certain point," I admit.

She funnels smoke back over her collarbone. She runs fingers through that spiralling tangle of dark hair. Screws up her small dark features for a moment, as if feeling the pinch of a hangover or a memory flash about my bad behaviour. "I don't believe that you really chucked them out," she moans.

"Don't you remember anything about that night?" I object.

"I thought I was dreaming that part," she explains, "when you got into a strop and pointed them to the door."

"They couldn't all shack up at Big Pink," I point out.

"So are you going to apologise to them?"

"Why should I do that?"

The focus of her glistening dark eyes sharpens. The hell raiser is coming back to the surface.

"Who was that flash bloke you were with?" I ask.

"Who are you talking about? Do you mean Adam Jakes?"

"That would be him," I recall.

"Adam's a bit of all right, wouldn't you say?" she grins.

"He's a bit of something, all right. I don't trust that guy as far as I could hop skip and bloody jump," I tell her.

"That's bloody open-minded of you, Dad, isn't it. You hardly know 'em."

"How well do *you* know him, Angie?"

"The guy isn't my boyfriend, if that's what you're thinking."

It's my turn to be surprised. "Are you sure?"

"Don't be fooled by the flashy exterior. You have to get to know somebody before you can make a judgement, don't you," she says.

"Are you saying that Adam and I should get to know each other? Maybe we can buy each other some drugs one evening."

"That's up to you, Dad, isn' it."

"Did he buy you that gold bracelet, by the way? Is he trading in precious metals as well?"

"Ha, bloody, ha, Dad. I bought this entirely with my own money, if you wanna know. Haven't you ever seen me cutting up the cake, for a living?"

"That would depend on the cake," I say. "But generally café work wouldn't purchase such an expensive item."

"You think you're a jeweller now, do you?" she laughs, moving the bracelet protectively around her delicate tanned wrist.

"Must have made a big dent in your savings," I suggest.

"Mum gave me some money. When we last met. She can afford it."

"Is that right?" I reply. Certainly I will put that theory to the test, next time I drop by at the Noggins' lair.

Angela ignores my investigation, takes another draw on her cancer stick and stares at the brick wall opposite between brass pots and pans.

"You had your arm around that creep. You tell me he's not your boyfriend? You're not involved with him?" I pursue.

"Our mate Jack's motor got stuck in the middle of nowhere, right? I don't know what was wrong with it. Anyway, it stalled and it wouldn't shift. Then Adam found us in his motor and offered to give us a lift back into the city. That's what he can be like, he's an angel," she eulogises.

She is the angel, I think, and nobody else - particularly that drug adulating scum - is going to borrow her wings.

"I wasn't impressed with that boy, Angela, to be straight with you."

"You wanted him to leave us stranded in the middle of nowhere."

"These days you don't have to be stranded anywhere. Hasn't this Jack lad heard about motoring organisations?" I remark.

Angela sluices black coffee around the bottom of her white cup. "I can't believe how you judge my friends," she objects. She peers at me through a dishevelled curtain of dark hair, trying to steady her internal compass against gravity. All her queasy feelings, so stubbornly suppressed, now interfere with her powers of reason.

"Some people can't be tolerated," I explain. In this case I'm not thinking about myself.

"Adam Jakes saved us from dying of exposure or hypothermia or something. Don't you realise I could have been lying in a ditch somewhere?" Angie protests, colouring.

"Not for the first time in your life," I remind her. "But I still don't like Jakes."

"Adam is well sound. He's solid, Dad. You can't censor the blokes I want to see. We'll go on seeing 'em anyway, just the same. D'you hear me?"

"I hear you, but this guy is involved in some dirty business. Your Mum would agree with me on this. You know that she would. You wouldn't dare to introduce him to her. I've got enough to worry about, to try to get off to sleep at night, without thinking of you with that drugs pusher."

"That isn't your business," she says bluntly.

I stare back unhappily.

"Look, Dad..." Angie struggles for the right expression or excuse. "Adam's already married with kids."

Suddenly I'm wide awake and don't need any stimulants.

"But he's not playing around, or anything like that. It's really positive that an older guy like Adam keeps in touch with what's happening. He understands the music scene and young people," she argues. "He doesn't look or feel out of place. Not to us."

"How can this guy understand you?" I wonder. This idea really hurts. Even though our daughter is already twenty-something, Elizabeth would still 'ground' her, there's no question. My former partner would have no qualms about the resulting conflict; she would face up to any drama of kicking, screaming, or outrage. But in my present delicate state, I am less fortified against family controversy. I have no strength to confront Angela in any such emotional battle or siege.

"At least Adam listens to me," she says. "He respects me as a free individual."

I continue to stare at her, stunned, as she pretends to be distracted. I can't believe that this prince charming is a better listener than me. Angela knows all my anxiety buttons and she's playing on them like the cathedral organist.

"The guy could be dangerous. He gave every impression of being a thug, with the breaking point of an old pencil," I argue.

She isn't impressed. "That depends on how you treat people. On the way you talk to them, don't you think?"

"You'd have to be an animal trainer to talk to that guy," I comment.

"Adam has a little boy. He's a father. He's got to earn a living. That's why he's involved with the indie music scene around here," she explains. Angie vigorously rubs her eyes, in an attempt to rouse herself.

"You're cool with that?" I retort.

"Why shouldn't I be cool with that?" she answers.

"This creep's taking advantage of you."

She considers the idea; shades of emotion fluctuating across the too bright surface of her deep eyes. "Do me a favour, Dad."

"This is way over your head," I say.

She forces a dry ironic laugh that turns into a cough. "I know what I am doing," she finally forces out.

"Is that right? I've seen people get involved with drug dealers before," I say, with distaste. "A best friend of your mother and me got caught up with some heavy handed guys. They have some charm at first. But then they get you snared. Then they end up trying to break your neck. That's what happened to a close friend of ours."

Angela no more believes what I am saying that she agrees with it. Her stubbed fag end makes a hiss in the saucer. "You can't restrict my life. You're just freaked out over something you don't understand," she insists, neck sinews tightening.

I try to relax into a more appealing posture. "You reject our experience?" I say. "Don't want to hear the wisdom of your parents, such as it is?"

"I'm old enough to look after myself," she tells me.

"That isn't our impression." Yet it sounds strange to be talking as a couple again.

"You looked wasted yourself the other evening," she points out.

"I just went to the pub with Bob Huntingdon. We went down to the Old Duke by the quayside. I told you. I didn't expect to come home and find the children of the Grateful Dead in my front room."

"You're not looking so great," she informs me. "Shouldn't you be getting better now? Didn't you go to the hospital, to have an operation? I thought they'd done the bypass and you should be on the mend."

"Just look after yourself, Angela," I reply.

"So when's your old self coming back?" she suggests.

"You tell me. Apparently he's not allowed to go to the pub."

"It's like everything Luke and I do and say has become, like, this big problem to you."

"I still have a few health issues to resolve," I admit, mysteriously. I dare to look across at the smooth young face of my daughter, as she questioningly attempts to hold my gaze.

"So you're still worried about your heart then?" she pursues.

"I'm not rubbing my hands together with excitement," I declare.

"You told Luke and me that you was feeling as good as new," she recalls.

"I was."

"So why aren't you getting back to your old self? Why do you look so pale and drawn, Dad, and getting so stressed out about, you know, what your kids are doing and stuff?"

"It's taking me longer than expected to get better," I inform her. Then why not tell her the whole precise truth?

"It must be harder to recover without Mum."

This shocks and puzzles me. "Where did you get that idea from?"

"I couldn't forgive her either, if I was in your shoes," Angie argues, gaining heat. "I'd have thrown her out immediately, knowing what was going on between her and that..."

“All right, Angie. No need to revive the old news stories. I’ve heard enough about that.”

“I haven’t got any time for the woman, to be honest with you,” she argues.

“She’s your mother,” I remind her.

“Yes, all right, but I take your side in all this,” she assures me.

“Do you?”

“Yes!”

“But you’re still her daughter.”

“How couldn’t I be?”

“So there you are, your mother still cares about you. What happens to you,” I add.

“But when I see the kind of a mess divorce creates. Puts me off the whole idea of getting married. What a terrible idea. Best to just muck in with guys you like... who you like being around. Don’t get attached, thinking it’s gonna be forever. Do you get me?”

“That would depend.”

“I wouldn’t want to live under the same *roof* as that person,” she says indignantly.

“Well, she isn’t expecting you back any time soon.”

No, they’re not making extra space for her, in the technologically well-appointed Jurassic cave.

# Chapter 26

Whatever the troubles at home, there's always a chance to escape to work. Most mornings I look forward to pulling on a pair of worn jeans and a Dylan tour shirt. The idea of turning back into that reckless young guy appeals to me. In those days I had a dream in my back pocket, and didn't have to keep searching for my pulse - or for my wallet.

Our factory is based around the ground floor of a huge red-brick Victorian construction. Those guys in stove-pipe hats knew how to work on an ambitious scale. The buildings were used as warehouses or factories. In modern times they've been left mouldering and derelict. Recently they've undergone renovation and rental space remains cheap. You don't need to be an academician architect to recognise an eyesore. Visible from the top rear windows of my house it's a suture across the city. These angry scars swell against the perspective, as you look out at them, as the sun's going down.

I'm addicted to the smells and sounds of our manufacturing process. We pass most of our days in this space; this gutted relic of 'pandemonium'; of the great industrial age, or is it outrage? But all that coal and iron, manufacture and empire, has passed away into the cosmic scrap-yard of memory. It's a postmodern trope in a Pynchon novel. Instead we make a modest profit from wind power - that original idea of humanity - as we flutter pocket-handkerchiefs in the air. Who knows about the future? We could be getting aboard giant balloons to commute between cities, as cars lock horns on motorways and trains get glued to the tracks. Man, you have to stay positive, although I can't read tarot cards, tea leaves or crystal balls, unlike my former wife.

My business was shooting up for years, so to speak, until we hit these turbulent times. My diversions around divorce courts and operating theatres didn't help growth. All those bright lights and pointed questions were not helpful to running a company. Character assassination and physical dismemberment eventually drags you down. This coincided with difficult trading conditions, competition and an economic downturn. Man, you've got to keep a weather eye.

I started the business with my close university friend, Stuart Maybridge. Stuart and I hooked up after a Pink Floyd gig. Syd Barrett was still in the group then. Stuart had his psychedelic period, although mathematics helped to clear his mind. I frequently drove Stuart and Lizzie crazy with my aeronautic passions. During the first two years they assumed that my interest in kites was merely a quaint hobby. He wondered if it was a pretentious, faddish hobby, meant to get the attention of the chicks. He doubted if my obsession was going to be successful on either count.

One weekend we were up in London together on a demo. Students were trying to force Wilson not to give any blessing to napalm. This was the day that Stuart and Elizabeth began to take my dream seriously. We were pressed into Hyde Park waiting to march towards Trafalgar Square. We listened in pained silence to garbled, tedious speeches from a far-off platform. Boredom wasn't the point - it was more burning bodies. During this wait I reeled a kite up into the London drizzle. I waxed enthusiastic about eastern spiritualism and pacifism. My best mate and girlfriend soon concentrated on how to raise some finance.

Lizzie stood next to me in that exposed crush of demonstrators, somewhere in the expanse of Hyde Park; itself the site of that famous Rolling Stones free concert. She was staring up at the kite's cheerful stamp of colour against the dull sky. She was wearing her characteristic red duffle coat, as I recall, fronds of drenched copper hair stuck to her rosy cheeks, large mineral eyes concentrating on the heavens. Later that day we found a coffee shop in Knightsbridge... I'm not sure what it was called or what street it was in. Lizzie asked for a dubious revolutionary mix from the menu, as she was already pregnant. It was here that we agreed to push my idea. She was trying to share my vision of the future. Man, she had no idea how difficult it would be over time. But that was one of the most memorable days of my life. In the evening we went to see Sandy Denny at the 100 Club along Oxford Street.

*Who knows? Who knows where the time goes?*

Graduation approached for Stuart and me. Colour brochures from anarchist cells and free communes didn't free our imaginations or turn us on. Lizzie grew visibly pregnant, exhausted by quarrels with her parents, who indicted her for sex and thought crimes. They still clung to the idea that babies were delivered by stork from Selfridges. Soon they were busy organising that white-wash of a wedding at the cathedral. They were sending her off to the dressmaker, to hide her bump in taffeta. Lizzie was the only reason I could go through with it - my feelings for her - as she was the pearl in this polluted ocean.

We put down a deposit on that first flat above a hairdressing salon. At least that fleet of energy-inefficient hair-blowers kept down our winter heating costs. We were struggling with our monthly payments and Lizzie couldn't afford to run down for a bouffant. Getting money out of the banks was like panning for gold nuggets in the Avon. They were not throwing money at me, contrary to what Jakes may think. In the Sixties bank managers were even less utopian than today. Stuart Maybridge was the least self-conscious dandy in Bristol. His favoured style was that of Jagger at his *Performance* peak, including make-up. We didn't need a large sum, but they were reluctant to dig into their pocket. I made concessions to the counting house; I was less outrageous. But I couldn't disguise my hippie wiles under that sharp weekend suit (borrowed from a reluctant brother). I couldn't hide long hair under an unfamiliar collar.

"Young man, what's your experience of enterprise?"

Did the guy mean a star ship? I began to stare at my feet.

"Do you envisage any profits from making kites?"

"That's where you will come in," I said, unwisely.

Stuart helped us to get a loan, with strict conditions attached. The bank manager was impressed by his first class mathematics degree and his business plan.

I remember how the bank manager began to sit straighter. Stuart's facts and figures were sinking in like fence posts. The guy put his eyebrows at a more relaxed angle. A faint smile cracked his thin lips. But we were planning to machine-gun him down, in the event of a refusal. I didn't have to throw myself out of the window like Malcolm McDowell during *O Lucky Man!* We both admired *If*, but we didn't know how to obtain any machine-guns; by chance we didn't move in those circles.

Lizzie's parents offered a loan or gift, to enable me to start up and become a respectable husband. They wouldn't refuse their daughter anything, other than her own mind and personal freedom. Turning down their dubious money was the best type of foresight. My mother emptied her piggybank on the bedspread, god bless her. But you can't live on next to nothing, not even during the Sixties. In the Sixties you didn't want to - that was probably the point.

Stuart brought mathematical genius and our financial worries vanished like teaspoons in a vat of acid. The incredible fear and excitement of starting your own business! But, as Angie would remind me, you can't live off the buzz forever.

"You have to start this business," Liz told me. "Why of course you do, Noah. What am I going to tell our child? How am I going to explain that her father abandoned her dreams?"

Stuart's passing was the cruellest blow. He had a condition related to MS. On the specialist's advice he took up pottery classes, to keep his fingers nimble, swimming sessions and comprehensive physiotherapy. He was a great fan of Spike Milligan, Kurt Vonnegut, Georges Perec, Lewis Carroll - interested in Dada and surrealism. But they couldn't find a trick in time to save him.

That was another empty elevator moment in my life. People said that it was a great relief in the end, but we felt terrible. Elizabeth and I could barely speak for weeks afterwards. I still miss that brilliant little guy. Sometimes the shy kid turns into the *enfant terrible*. One afternoon he climbed on the lecture hall roof and began to make absurd faces at us through a skylight. The profs couldn't fathom him, inside or outside of a paper. They wanted him psychoanalysed.

"You can't begin post-graduate work as a fresher. We have to warn you, Stuart, however brilliant you may be, that you have to conform."

We consoled ourselves (or tried) by arguing that his mind never lost its brilliance, even as his body folded. He was making mental arabesques to the end. His mother called me to say he had slipped away. We lost some of the glue that kept us together. At the end you realise how important close friendships are to a marriage. Without good friends you become sterile, you begin to gasp and stare at each other, like a pair of goldfish in a plastic bag.

For months I was forced to sweat over our company accounts. Lizzie wanted to find time to help, but again she was hanging nappy pins from her earrings. At times I rediscovered Stuart among the figures. Obviously he took his box of tricks with him.

"I couldn't explain what's going on inside my head," he would tell me. "But I try to relax and enjoy the party."

If it had been a party it was over. I was trying to remember.

James Nairn, his eventual successor as my finance manager, was introduced to me at a conference. I couldn't ignore the devil in the detail any longer. His approach is different to my tragic university friend's, but it sorted out the unholy mess. Typically James will apply himself to the job all working day. Then he will take it home with him, to worry over during the evening as well. To describe him as an obsessed man wouldn't really catch him. He enjoys living alone in that picturesque canal-side cottage with a savage cat and a pile of food cans. He can live in the woods, if he likes, because he rescued me from a financial bear trap.

"So what's the fall out?" I ask.

"Serious," he asserts.

"Oh?"

"It means that we have to make some hard financial decisions."

We are holding this briefing in Nairn's 'office'. He insisted on having his own private space from the beginning; and he doesn't much like to leave it. His office is no more than a husk of modern spacing within the empty cavity. The building still reveals iron accoutrements of heavy industry, such as hooks in the wall and rings on the floor, all pocked with rust.

"Go on then, Jim, spell it out." I drag my chair closer to him and cross my legs at the ankles.

Nairn arches tensely over his metal desk, clutching his stack of figures, elbows up on the surface. He's prepared the bad news for me, as Wickham had at the hospital.

"After I checked over these figures again I can only conclude," he explains, "that spending is exceeding our income."

"What are you trying to tell me?"

"You have to lose five employees."

"I can't do that."

"Otherwise you're going out of business in months," he warns, harshly.

I experience the shocked rigidity of our original bank manager. "You can't be serious, can you?"

"Don't I look serious?" he wonders.

"Right," I respond.

"It would be like bleeding ourselves to death."

"Would it?" There's no answer to that.

"If we don't drive down costs and expenditure..."

"It's against my principles." Nervously I play with the central button of my brushed cotton jacket. As if feeling the economic cold. The Dylan tee-shirt is showing through the gaps.

"You'll be lucky to have any principles remaining," he warns. "I've been going through these accounts, before the auditors can get hold of them."

"Never thought I'd reach this day," I wince.

"You have to make the decision."

"There's a lot more competition around," I say.

"Now they are breathing down your neck," he replies.

"We're long established and respected."

"Which makes the company more appetising for a take over."

"We'll survive. We always do," I assure him.

"Not unless you act."

"You really believe we might be taken over?" I wonder, alarmed.

"Definitely so."

"We're just experiencing some turbulence."

"You have to reduce your costs. Your staffing costs are most significant." Nairn grinds on his back teeth. "Or face a cash flow disaster."

"Can't we get along somehow?"

"Definitely not," he tells me.

"You'll have to explain this to them. To our people," I say.

"That's your job, Mr Sheer. I'm your finance manager, but you're the boss."

"Right."

I consider my prospects unhappily. I swing back on two legs of the chair. "How do you expect me to make these backward decisions?" I say. My chair comes back down heavily. "I'm going out on the shop floor again. There's an urgent order to pack. Somebody has to do something constructive around here."

"Oh, well, right," he retorts, distractedly.

I throw his flimsy door back with zero dramatic effect. But James doesn't look up from his print-outs for a Nano-second. He has to be deadly serious about his bad news, after all.

As I stroll back through the factory and vend myself another coffee, finding everyone cheerfully at work - who wouldn't enjoy working here? - I feel guilty about their prospects. This is a small power over other people that I don't enjoy. A small act of playing god that I hadn't considered during our protest against the Vietnam War.

# Chapter 27

The day soon delivers another jolt. My switchboard operator puts through the head teacher at Luke's school. Why is she getting into personal contact? Does she fancy me after spotting me at the last parents' evening? But if that's the case she's keeping her crush on ice, because she's talking about Luke's absences from school.

Luke's truancy comes like a news flash to me. Her report completely shocks me, as he gives every appearance of leaving for school every morning. My first response is that something must have happened to Luke on the way. I get tuned into these unconscious archetypes. The teacher proceeds to say that Luke has been playing hooky for the entire week.

"Do you have any explanation?" she quizzes.

From the period of dead silence, which follows her question, it's obvious I do not.

"Don't you talk to your son about school?" she presses.

"We talk. But not every day," I admit. Do hostile animal noises count?

"Have you any idea about his emotional condition? His attitude to study and attendance?"

"Why didn't you tell me about his absences before?" I reply. "Certainly I talk to my son."

The head teacher is addressing me, yet I sense Elizabeth listening behind my shoulder. I could hear her initial anxious concern. She and the Dino want to take Luke into their house on a permanent basis. To achieve that goal they have to depict me as irresponsible and unstable - a failed father. Those dreaded words 'failed father' that coil in a man's guts like the creature from Alien. If the Noggins couple learn about this development they will have enough evidence. This wouldn't look impressive in front of the magistrate would it? They've already worn my social graces down to a hair shirt. If they ever get the full picture on my heart condition, then they'll be able to stick a knife into our family portrait.

"Luke's teachers are concerned about his examination prospects. He's a clever boy, but his work has deteriorated over recent weeks. He has been missing after-school revision classes as well. He hasn't handed in essential assignments."

"Now you tell me," I remark. "Don't worry we'll get our heads around this. Yes, leave that with me. I will talk to Luke about these problems... whatever may be worrying him. Then I'll get back to you. He'll be in school on Monday."

So what's the not-so little devil been getting up to? Haven't we drilled into him - into all our kids - the vital importance of qualifications? We've preached the virtues of knowledge. Sometimes for its own sake. These may be the dog days of his school career, yet as the school mistress told me, with exams and assignments, the most important. This is the crunch end of the season for him, to decide those issues of promotion and relegation. Though he wouldn't appreciate the football metaphor.

Liz and I never faced so many school tests, when we were kids. There was more space and freedom for our generation. We took full advantage of that, spending the afternoons smoking and listening to music. We'd sit around at home chatting, playing Beatles, Stones and Floyd records, over a roll of finest Virginian. The school looks more oppressive under the new regime. Controlling.

Not that I mentioned these views to my son's Head Teacher. Best to keep my individual opinions out of this. She may be one of those power-dressing curriculum robots, with a Cyber-woman's piercing stare. Though she sounded quite pleasant on the telephone. *Concerned.*

Is Luke getting freaked out by his final exams? The big wide world's waiting for him around the corner, like the bully from the rival school. But he isn't the anxious type of kid. He's always completed his work confidently, comfortably above average, particularly in Maths and sciences. Takes after his mother in that regard. All right, he fritters away hours on those pointless computers. He doesn't have to sweat about finding a career. One day he will come into my company. That's a chance that any kid has the right to envy. We'll encourage him. With a degree of application and wit he'll make a success of his life. He's assured of my complete support. Even posthumously. *Especially* posthumously.

What's he doing while he's playing hooky? I've bumped into him around the city centre, hanging with a skateboard gang. They give every impression of enjoying illegal time in transitory places. The kids believe they are menacing, as they make noise and clatter around; hiding under long black fringes, presenting a rebellious image of ripped clothing and metal accessories; tee-shirts and sweats that ally them to rock groups fresh from the morgue. In truth I find something touching and comical about their teen and pre-teen desire to shock and disturb: it reminds me of being a kid myself and I'm sure many other grown-ups feel the same, when they pass by. The other day I was strolling along Colston Avenue and Luke came flashing past on a board, flying off the pavement and dodging between traffic on the road. Was he trying to copy my driving style or what?

Letting myself back into Big Pink, I feel the place's ghostly atmosphere and pick up its many echoes: that needle bumping around the grooves of our past. The house is extremely eerie at this afternoon hour, with no humanity to speak about. It's hard for me to even imagine that we shared a family life together in this place. The dream home is now the haunted mansion - a museum.

Then I plod upstairs and, after a moment's pause, decide to enter Luke's bedroom to investigate. There's a chance that he may be hiding out in his room, waiting for me to leave again. Otherwise I don't like to invade his personal space. I want to be close to his soul and to protect him. But once I let myself inside, I merely experience the exact weight of his absence.

He's started to vacuum his room, as a protest against the slipshod condition of Big Pink. Angela treats her space as would a Beat poet at an artists' rural retreat. Luke's reacted against his sister's untidy attitude. His bedroom is a games centre and computer laboratory. Our son passes a lot of relative time here. I meet the gazes of mean-ass rappers, new rock zombies and big-breasted babes, all pinned helplessly to the walls. The blind eye of the computer awaits his miracle touch. The set of mixing desks, that I got him under duress last Christmas, are not in their spinning mode. Carefully I begin to explore the bedroom, poking, lifting, and rummaging into every corner; as afternoon sunshine catches me through slatted black blinds, streaking across his Formula One continental quilt.

Not immediately finding anything, I get down on my knees and look under the bed. There I find motorcycle and soft porn magazines. Nothing sinister or unexpected there, you have to conclude. I will speak to him about them, if I can, the girly mags, but normally I wouldn't fret. They indicate that the sexual energies of adulthood are beginning to race through the veins of my son. I know all about the influence of sexual energies. They get us into all kinds of trouble. Sometimes it's like sliding down a ski jump with rockets strapped to your back.

Luke and I both enjoy the Star Wars series of movies and spin-offs. At least this shared popular-culture enthusiasm helps us to inhabit the same universe. For most of the space time. May some kind of force be with us now. May good triumph over evil.

Am I to blame for his truancy, by telling him to get out of the house? Has he taken up the challenge and gone on the quest for reality? What exactly might he be doing in that big wide world?

As I am about to leave his room, taking a final scan over the floor, I notice some glinting silver material on the carpet. These turn out to be several sheets of foil, which show narrow scorch marks and a gritty residue on the surface. What the hell? My heart inflates and pulsates, like a stiff hand that's been working a punch bag. My son's dropped these bits of silver paper carelessly behind him, under the windowsill behind his bed. Bad luck for Luke that he didn't retrieve them after cleaning his room; or that he became so slack after consuming the junk. What should I do with this stuff, this evidence? Simply scrunch it up and throw it away? It's very hard to come to terms with. Our son experimenting in this way. What's my ex (but litigiously alert) wife going to say and do about this, if she ever discovers the truth? How quickly is that magistrate going to get Luke out of Big Pink and into the Noggins' techno lair? Faster than you can chase the dragon.

To gain thinking time, to hit on an action plan, I occupy myself with small jobs around the house. There's a book shelf to straighten out, some dining room carpet to tack back down, a radiator or two to bleed. Luke doesn't return from school at the appointed hour and I'm suffering extremely bad radiation.

Meanwhile I dine alone on his favourite dinner. I prepared the meal for him, hoping to keep him happy during our urgent conversation about drugs and truancy. Though depressed by his no-show and by eating alone, I take the attitude that he can't stay away all night. Even if he suspects the Head Teacher has notified me, Luke has to return to our Hammer House of Horror. He's due to stay at his mother's this weekend. It's very unlikely that he'll turn up to their place early. What will Liz do if she gets any information out of him? I'm the guy who's really on the run. Except that nobody is out searching for me.

How does my former, very-much-living-and-breathing wife react in such a crisis? I can tell you, she goes into a terrible panic about the situation. She would have a dreadful wobbly when, all of a sudden, the accidental or the catastrophic happens; when life goes haywire. But that initial panic would quickly wear off, and then she'd turn raw energy to positive action. She'd be capable of rescuing the situation. She wouldn't just do nothing; sit in front of the television, hoping for the best. That's what I'm more likely to do. Mistake complacency for calm. Put my big feet up.

There was that notorious episode when Angela was a little girl. She failed to come back one evening from playing out. Lizzie sent me tramping around the park to search for her. Despite shouting her name for hours I didn't have any luck. On my return, a militant Lizzie decided to rouse the whole neighbourhood. Half the street went out searching by torchlight around that local park. They were yelling out and smashing the bushes like the living dead. Fortunately someone picked up faint childish cries, coming from one direction. Closing as a group into that area, we eventually located her at the bottom of an excavation ditch. She could easily have been lost and perished in that hole. Angie was miserable, wet through and bedraggled, squatting between huge exposed pipes - but safe.

After I had pulled her back to the surface, my wife, furiously upset, slapped the back of her legs. I didn't like that response, not at all, but didn't feel in any position to criticise. Our daughter might have died, if it hadn't been for her mother's desperate actions. What was a slap on the legs compared to a miserable death in a freezing, watery ditch? Who had the high ground there?

Angela regularly wandered off. As a kid it was her trademark trick. You'd just take some interest in the newspaper and, when you looked up again, she was gone. My wife would insist on searching the entire beach, including wooden changing huts, refreshment stands and amusement arcades. It could be a nightmare, but you can't live without experiencing a few of them. Lizzie resembled some flame-haired Amazon as she strutted over the beach, strong and bronzed in her polka dotted bikini. Until eventually she'd drag the child back - inevitably snivelling - to the safety of our windbreak. I wouldn't know where to look. She made me feel irresponsible and incapable. In those situations I would fight against my resentment, as if pushing back a poison that crept higher along the vein. But Lizzie wasn't too far wrong in her opinion, and the bad feeling between us soon wore off.

So what am I planning to do to bring our Luke back? I have to start thinking for myself. Where did he get the dope? Who was his sleazy contact? Adam Jakes looms across my thoughts, although he was only here for a few hours. Luke was upstairs asleep - there wasn't any go-between.

How would Bob Dylan handle this situation? He has enough children to populate the Old Testament and much of the New. Surely his eldest kids progressed through the terrible teen years. Jakob and siblings must have presented a few challenges to the great man. Even the voice of a generation has to bear contradictions, you'd assume. Even Zimmerman suffered backchat at the breakfast table from time to time. How did he respond when kids' ideas about the world, and the right ethical code, ran contrary to his own? Did all the blood run to his head while he hid behind his broadsheet newspaper?

All I can do is keep my investigation open. Forlornly I begin to flick through my telephone book. Unfortunately I don't have Dylan's number. Lizzie would always ring around all her friends and everyone she knew, covering all bases, in an emergency. What I'm doing is punching a few numbers and hoping for the best; already anticipating a new family regime, whereby Luke spends most of his time at her place. This scandal has to leak out eventually, like the smoke from Luke's nostrils. As I said, we live in hope, when optimism has died. Our generation could argue that drugs have the power to bring people together - the hippies said it and the ravers said it - so let's test the theory again. Even the druggie has to share his secrets with someone. Man, it's a beautiful but scary world out there.

This is grimy if essential spade work, digging around in the gutters of my son's life. Getting in touch with various Mums, Dads and mates, I certainly have a chatty hour on the blower. They'll soon have a few more colourful stories about Noah Sheer. Naturally I have a reputation by now. I'm listening to their theories about Luke Sheer; hooking up to the grapevine of school gossip. So far I don't have Luke's versions of events, but I intend to.

My son's a popular boy at that school, when he's there. Equally a picture develops of a kid who has become more unpredictable, in mood and behaviour. That must reflect his ugly home experience, it crosses my mind. Am I mistaking Calaban's wild spirits? Or is he Hal? He must enjoy getting this respect off his peers. They must have a lot to recommend them - in his eyes - drugs. Jakes argued that you have to create menace in this monetarist ego trip. A self-justifying drug dealer can never be a Confucius or even a Nietzsche. Luke's been put out on those mean streets to handle himself. Seeing the world through his eyes, it may seem as if he must. But isn't that still my job? Wasn't I the guy who first went missing?

Jahinder Singh is my son's closest mate. The Sikh lad's considered a wizard on the computers, if you'll excuse those mixed theologies. Jahinder isn't used to getting calls from me, or any other Dads, so initially he doesn't recognise my name or voice. When he's adjusted to the idea he doesn't want to tell me much about Luke.

"I don't know - haven't seen him for days!" he says. There's a hint of betrayed friendship in this statement.

"So whereabouts could he be? You know?" I coax.

"No."

"Didn't he mention anything to you? Where he may hang out? Different lads he's attached to?"

"Lukey doesn't say much to me anymore," Jahinder concedes.

"Sorry to hear about that. So when did you last see him?"

"Oh, it must have been last week."

"Really? As long ago as that? Did you two fall out over something?"

"Luke's got another gang of friends," he explains.

I feel the skin on my scalp shrink. "Can you describe these lads to me?" I press, scrunching the phone into my ear.

"Oh, well, not really," he begins. "But they are rough and tough."

"Where does Luke meet them? Is it in the city centre?" I press.

"They're on the Heartcliff estate, you know. Lukey takes the bus out there. They buy small packets of drugs and stuff."

"Packets?" I say.

The kid is opening up. "I don't know, a dealer. They spend the day getting a buzz. They go and slap a few kids. They ride about on motorbikes."

Luke gets his way, after all, at dangerous speed. "Do you think he's over the estate this evening?"

"Could be."

So I thank Jahinder for the dope and hang up to dry.

Heartcliff is a 1930s working-class estate to the south of the city. It has a tough reputation, built up by newspaper horror stories. My own experiences about the district haven't been negative. But then I'm not a post-structuralist geographer. My company employs a few people from the estate. Most of the houses are well maintained, with large gardens at the rear. There are also tower blocks there. Being situated on the edge of the city the estate has access to the countryside. A few years ago we gave a flying demonstration, at a bank holiday fete. Now my son could be running loose over there.

Then the telephones are set off again - three contradictory tones in different spaces of Big Pink. Jahinder calling back. Something more to add?

"Luke back yet?" he asks.

"Not yet."

"You could find him over the Heartcliff estate tonight," he tells me.

"Right. How will I ever find him over there?"

"He's hanging about bus shelters with those new mates."

"That's useful information. But which bus shelter do you mean?" I wonder.

"So haven't you seen the news on teevee?" he declares.

"What are you saying? I'm watching a Corman movie on cable. What news?"

"There's a riot going on over there," he tells me, with a slight Indian accent.

"A riot, are you crazy?" I declare.

"Between the local kids and the police."

"You're not saying Luke is involved? Or that he started this riot? Are you?"

"I dunno."

"Well I haven't heard anything about a riot. In Bristol? In these times?"

An occupation of the Dean's office did not constitute a riot. The Poll Tax riot was the last one I remember, but I didn't feel comfortable with that, the anarchists who'd never read a book. It was purely a distasteful media event for us.

The explanation strikes me that my prescribed drugs are inducing a heightened condition. Maybe these drugs are turning me jittery. My nerves jangle like Roger McGuinn's twelve-string guitar. But not as played by McGuinn.

As I pull on my black leather jacket, and shut off the house lights to leave, I'm highly suspicious about the side effects. There always have to be side effects. My thoughts may be affected. My judgement impaired.

# Chapter 28

There are signs of disturbance ahead, because the traffic out of Bedminster - my brother's homeland - is bumper to bumper. Vehicles coagulate within the narrow twisting roads of this area of the city. There are exhaust fumes enough to choke central Tokyo. I should know about that.

During this shunting and waiting I switch on the drive-time show and listen to reports about the riot in Heartcliff. An 'outbreak of violence' flared up following the death of two young boys, after they'd stolen and crashed a police motorbike. They were pursued at high speed until the cops lost patience and set them a trap. There was a set of impassable metal traps and spikes on the road surface as those lads hurtled along. The boys accepted the police's challenge but, recognising the impossible hazard in front, couldn't skid to a halt in time. They slid across the greasy tarmac like an ice puck. Until the bike and riders smashed into a wall, the perimeter of their local school, killed on impact, crushed into a knot of metal. In a split second the kids had escaped authority forever.

My initial reaction to this report is the most extreme. I imagine that Luke is one of the young motorcycle thieves. I'm trapped in the car, depressed into my seat, considering these terrible scenarios. How could I possibly face the future without my eldest son? Ironic given my health condition. How would I begin to explain my tragic negligence to Liz? Do I really believe that her grievances couldn't be any more serious?

My thoughts return to the oil on his trousers, that pile of motorcycle magazines under his bed. Chasing these motorcycle fantasies is more dangerous than merely chasing the dragon, I consider. I try not to avoid emotional meltdown, but my hands are shaking on the wheel already. If he's one of those motorcycle thieves, I don't want to stick around this planet any longer. I might as well snap that damaged heart valve like a cyanide pill.

Local knowledge is useful as I take a circuit of side-streets. The estate is on the edge of the city, integral to itself, as explained. It isn't a place that people normally visit in the evening, unless they actually live here. That is, unless they *have* to live here.

I lower my speed and begin to cruise the streets. On the look-out for my son, checking both sides, with a darkness on the edge of town. Soon I glide past groups of youths - gangs and gang members. They have clustered together, teamed up individualists, like wasps; menacing, out for revenge. You can feel the crackle of bad radiation in the atmosphere around.

I puzzle out the unfamiliar maze of this district. I'm still far away from the epicentre of reported violence. But the lower sky has an unnatural angry glare, outlining rooftops, chimney pots and side alleyways, exaggerated by a smouldering sunset. Sirens wail from indeterminate directions. Something's definitely going down in this neighbourhood.

As I approach a large group of youths, stood about the middle of the road, they divide slowly, reluctantly, around my car. Sullen, cold stares wish me harm through the side windows, as I chunter past in the vintage DS. One or two jaws drop in astonishment at the sight of me, as if ready to catch police helmets between their teeth. I keep them framed in the rear-view mirror, uncertain of their intentions. I don't expect these young guys have ever seen Jean Paul Belmondo cruising their district before. They wouldn't have encountered Alain Delon in *Les Samurai*, gliding through the side streets to another deadly assignation. Man, this is certain to attract curiosity in *any* tough neighbourhood.

Heedless of threat I keep my cool and accelerate away from trouble. Wisely I keep the Bogart-like sneer away from my lower lip. But it isn't clever to hook Ray Bans over your nose after dark. So I take them off again and place them in the glove compartment. This is no place for a middle-aged Dad, not even a cool one. Elizabeth will brand me an unfit father, if this comes back to her. Then we'll see her next move on the legal chessboard. But I'm not going to knock over my queen yet.

Before I can turn around, a pair of cops descend on me. One of them taps on the window to indicate that he wants an urgent word. I keep the car ticking over and up on its hydraulics, in case of a getaway.

"Hey, officers," I greet.

"Where you goin', sir?" he demands, leaning in. An experienced officer this one, who has seen many beats, going by the broken capillaries across his cheeks.

"There aint no way through," his young colleague adds. There's toffee on his breath.

"You telling me I'm not free to drive home?" I ask.

"You're a resident?" asks the mature policeman. He leans and peers at the interior of my car - *funny frog motor* written across his features.

"No, I'm not a resident," I admit.

"Then I'd advise you to get out of 'ere," he tells me.

Would Peter Fonda meekly assent to the intrusive questions of an aggressive cop? I don't think so. So I decide to end our conversation by sending the window back down.

"Do you hear me? Do you hear me!" is cut off from my ears.

The power steering is definitely *ancien regime*, causing aggravation to the surgeon's handiwork. I don't want to come apart at the seams. While performing this manoeuvre, a fire engine hurtles across my vision in full battle cry; like a disturbed scorpion; clattering past the opposite junction ahead of me, in a heart-stopping flare of noise and lights. The effect is to reignite all my fears about Luke. The dreadful idea that he may have been killed, smashed into a wall, as one of the two juvenile joy-riders. All my fantasies of riots and rebellion are extinguished.

The policemen were more contemptuous than suspicious. No respectable citizen should be wandering these streets tonight. Yet as a precaution I turn off the main-beams, as I nose into another road, melting into the darkness. Each street is hard to distinguish from the next. The estate has become a smoke-filled hall of mirrors. I can sense where the riot is happening only by trembling lights in the sky. I might be driving around the area all night, I realise, assuming I don't land in the arms of the police. Do I want to add a set of criminal lawyers to the family ones?

I decide to park the Citroen - its Gaullist nose rising into the air - and walk to the riot as if going to the football match. I dig my hands into my jacket pockets, keep my head down and step over the cracks. I don't get far before I'm sharing more eye-to-eye contact with the city police. No wonder that Marlene Dietrich was such a killer with men in uniform. This time my lines are better rehearsed, as I claim to be visiting a sick relative in the area. The cops agree to let me through while warning about rampaging youngsters.

"Hey, sir! Hey there! Not in that direction!" they shouts after me. "You're goin' in the wrang direction!"

But they decide that it's my neck. Let the idiot go where he likes, they judge, if he wants a close neck shave. Luke's putting himself through a risky rite of passage, but I'm not far behind him.

Are these streets ahead spookily dark or merely coloured by fear? Flashes in the sky make dangerous passages and walkways seem even darker. I sense the disturbance, feel it, like an electrical storm ahead. Respectable citizens have bolted their front doors and drawn their curtains for the night. I pick up their angry vibe against the cops. These guys are catching up with the latest news and debate their means to avenge the boys' death. I've been involved in demos and marches in the past, but nothing like this. I watch this guy come out of his garden carrying a crate of empty wine bottles and a can of petrol. There's no need to put two and two together.

Finding my broadest native twang I seek directions and information. The youths think I'm an ageing rubberneck spoiling for a fight. I don't mention that my son could be one of the destroyed duo. The gang's too agitated to offer full tourist information. But I get a better idea of my location, if not a free street guide. They don't take the chance to empty my wallet or work me over. All right, so I'm not a lusty student radical with flowing locks any longer, but that doesn't reduce my coolness. That doesn't affect my credibility, even if my street fighting days are over.

At least I'm dressed for the occasion in Levi's and black leather jacket. In fact I bought this jacket comparatively recently, after my marriage broke up, as a kind of ego lift. You have to stay true to your original image - even if it's taken a recent battering. Around that time I began to date Rachael - in and out of the squash court - and I was convinced this outfit took years off me. The opposite may have been true. Tonight I resemble the Elephant Man in search of female compassion. Do I really intend to make conversation with these youths, who enjoy resting their feet on policemen's faces? What kind of role model am I?

I'm formally joining the yoga society next week. The lady telephoned me and personally invited me along. Now I'm shaping up for an urban riot. You can't predict where you may be going in this crazy life. Makes little difference if you keep your eyes open or not.

Before too long I stray into festivities. The riot is no longer a nasty rumour, a sensational news report or even an angry glow across the horizon. One minute you are looking at a picture postcard, the next you're standing in the middle of the scene. I feel as if I've pursued Alice into her adventures. Fallen down a hole with her, then emerged into an orgy of violence. Is that the Cheshire cat grin hanging in the night sky below the moon? Could it belong to one Adam Jakes?

A huge crowd has gathered on an exposed concourse, between towers blocks, at the centre of the estate. It was here that we set out our stall and flew our gentle kites, on the summer day of their fete: A desolate strip tonight. A grainy wind blasts my cheeks, as people close around me. I'm locked in a nightmarish press of bodies. Pressure builds against my sore chest cavity. I'm forced to hold my breath, not to panic, feeling the overbearing crush. The under-class is coming back to the surface. The mob hurtles and lunges forwards, sideways, taking me with them like a tattered flagpole.

Faces press towards me, hardened with hatred. The front of the crowd edges into confrontation. I'm swept along with them like a hapless daddy-long-legs. I get glimpses of police lines, in closed ranks, further down the street - waiting to form a quick response. They have no idea they have a veteran peace protestor on the scene. In many ways this resembles past demonstrations, including torrents of missiles and abuse. Rocks and bottles fill the air above my head, as if a rubbish collector is switched into reverse, to spew the crap back out at high velocity. This storm of glass shatters on the road ahead, as a jolly thud of police shields cuff aside rocks and bricks. Finally the truce is broken as the cops make their first charge. The front of the mob cuts back through the mass, like a huge wave hitting a wall.

With panic, screaming and shouting, people trying to escape the suffocating crush, to avoid baton blows and arrest. Somebody's elbow catches me on the cheek, which knocks me to the ground. I'm astonished to feel the grit and dust on my face, on the palms of my hand, broken winded, trying to struggle to my feet. I picture those waves of police bearing down on me. Thank God I'm not trampled. My luck's holding out, my heart's still beating, for the time being.

These moments of scrambling isolation give views of the cops, advancing visored and truncheon wielding. They're protagonists in a malign Spielberg. I take my cue from the other protestors, getting back to my feet and peeling away to reach cover. My famous past as a student radical could re-emerge if they capture me. All my youthful misdemeanours will return to my dusty record, up for reconsideration, like the official release of a legendary bootleg.

For the first time since heart surgery I break out into a full run. The hegemonic muscle bulges like Fat Boy, the first atomic bomb. My limbs melt together like sticks of seaside rock left in a hot window. It's a bad dream. I try to imagine myself scampering back to the base line, playing tennis again, trying to intercept a lob, but it gets away from me. My opponents approach the net just in case, waiting to kill off any reply.

As the riot police hunt down rioters, the mob disintegrates entirely and people are running away along alleyways. Truncheons seem to float in the air before coming down on heads in ruthless thrusts. I watch this and, to my horror, a cop singles me out and pursues me. The policeman is chasing after me, with the intention of cracking my skull and taking me into custody as well.

"Hey, officer!" I shout at him. "Let me explain! Don't do that, right?"

He's breathing like a Star Trooper. He has the collar of my jacket, jerks up his truncheon, waiting to strike me at the least resistance. That is what happened to Rupert Lloyd in fact, when he was invited to Paris by a student committee. The French riot police got him into a tight corner, while he was trying to show solidarity with Parisian students and workers out on the boulevards. This was completely unexpected to Rupert, but the ferocity of that squad is legendary and they were showing no special favours to British tourists. Speaking for myself, I was too stunned to fight back, so they didn't require tear gas or water cannon against me.

Astonishingly, as I resign myself to getting arrested (facing the resulting scandal) some youngster steps up and bludgeons the cop. The kid smacks the riot officer across the shoulders with a lump of timber; what could be a requisitioned fencepost. The cop crashes forward on his knees, under this heavy blow, eventually crashes forward, until his helmeted head bounces on the concrete, as if a poison dart has pierced his armour. For a few seconds, what feels like an age, I stare down at the inert law-enforcer, stupefied. My rescuer fixes for a moment, elation in his eyes, before scampering away. Sometimes you don't need to drop any tabs of acid.

My left eye is swelling up, I feel, after having received that crack to the cheek. I haven't had this kind of vigorous exercise in months. My Brando style biker jacket is scuffed and scratched. Blame *The Wild Ones*.

My delinquent exploits vindicate Hoggart's tracts about dissolute youth, in the early 1950s, when lads had regular punch-ups around the milk-bar jukebox. I'm a mothballed version of teen rebellion. What am I still rebelling against at my age? In my condition? *What have you got?*

Corrina Farlane is not so easy to impress, whether I'm in or out of the biker's jacket. *Oxford town, Oxford town. Everybody's going down to Oxford town.*

I fall back into my labyrinth.

Before I lose myself again I try to find the spot where, according to Jahinder, my son hooks up with his new mates. A signboard says that the drab construction ahead is really a maternity unit. It resembles a military hut. I wouldn't like any child of mine to get a first taste of life here. It's like a barracks with teddy bears. Then there's a bus shelter and a block of public toilets, as master Singh informed me. You don't want to hang out there either.

Smooth faced tower blocks loom up into a dead glow of faint orange light. Sixties brutalism doing time. They're compensating for all that love and flowers gone to waste. Like a hasty marriage. For once those flats are the safest and cosiest places to be inside. Certainly you don't want to be caught out here between rioters and police. I'm still afraid that Luke was one of the motorcycle tearaways. I struggle to keep that image out of my head; concentrating on immediate threats. Luke was always an easy going kid, he'd never wander off or get into trouble. I must search every place, looking into every corner, just as Lizzie and I did for our daughter.

Maybe Luke is sheltering in a friend's house. There's nothing to suggest he's involved with the riot. What are the odds of finding him here? I'm the guy who's leaving town soon.

As I wander uncertainly, alert for potential dangers, some youth steps up and hurls a petrol bomb through a window of the maternity clinic. There's a smash and then the fire begins. I have to rub my eyes to make sure I'm awake - I am. He completes this move with the easy practised manner of an angler casting off. The young guy's a loner type, laconic, with straggly hair and a sagging parka. He's making his own nerdish contribution to the mayhem.

The blazing maternity clinic is a spark compared to the shopping centre. This was meant to be their community pride. I can see sheets of flame pouring from roofs, as the structures beneath groan and ache with intense heat and chemical change. Thick smoke billows out into the paved areas around; noxious threads of blue and green smoke in a heavy metal light show. Stuart Maybridge would have found this more awesome than Floyd among the ruins of Pompeii.

Advertising hoardings, public seats and litterbins sear into weird contortions, as if they are wodges of bubble-gum chomped by crocodiles. A squad of riot police emerges at the end of this thoroughfare, stomping at a canter through flaming shops, trying to deal with looters. Hopefully Luke has beamed up to his mother ship. The new community policing policy has gone up in smoke. Anyhow, I don't hang around to do any window shopping.

The cops launch a baton charge, amidst screaming and shouting, the sound of things breaking and falling. The previous street fight has dispersed over the estate, flaring up in those scrubby desolate areas that only locals know. From these margins the youths ambush the police and hurl missiles and debris. No doubt the cops will lick the rioters eventually, but they aren't having an enjoyable evening. Obviously the riot act has become too predictable.

I trot by the shell of a jacked-up car, its windows smashed, the tyres disappeared; burning like a Christmas pudding. Thank goodness it isn't a vintage Citroen from the old movies. A swarm of little kids is cycling around this relic on their bicycles, whooping up a festival atmosphere. Man, this is the kind of party I'm happy to poop. I'm all in favour of early bed times.

Plastic bags from disturbed rubbish bins float off, sail past my head - strangely peaceful, almost spiritual. They remind me of kites, but I'd prefer to take Luke to fly them on the down with me. The cops have seized back control of the shopping arcade; though not many people are going to be doing their Christmas shop there. The riot cops march back down the tarmac esplanade, like a contemporary version of a Roman legion, banging their shields and shouting in unison. But I'm not going to wait to salute them as they pass. They wouldn't understand where I'm coming from.

Bewildered by my futile search, I stray across another, very unusual gathering. These are mostly women, with pushchairs and little kids, around the entrance to a school. The kids look as if the excitement of bonfire night has turned against them. There are newspaper reporters hanging about - I recognise one of them - as well as a television crew killing time between shoots. What is this, Vietnam?

A female photographer moves around in various positions, showing off her long jodhpurs, whirring off images. There's a guy with a shoulder-held camera. I'd hold on to that if I were him. Luke isn't around here either. I'm getting deeper into my nightmare movie. He may have taken that chrome horse into the sunset.

These women look dignified, although many of them are crying. And they chat fiercely between themselves. There's a bitter sting of threatening conversation. What's their grief about? I notice that a display of flowers has been banked against the school wall. When I move closer my stomach churns at the sight. There are splotches of dark red, turning brown, splashed against the pale brickwork. Chunks and gouges too have been taken out of the surface. I conclude that this damage was caused when the young motorcyclists veered off the road. My liberal heart begins to bleed. Not if it was my son killed! Graffiti has been sprayed over the wall in tribute to the perished youths. Luke? No. Sean and Harry. So my liberal heart relaxes like a boxer in an ice bath. No need for any formal identification.

The police wisely keep away from the grieving mothers. They triggered this riot by pushing those boys to a premature finishing flag. A young Bob Dylan had an infatuation with motorcycles and Che Guevara went on a motorcycle tour of Europe, not only South America. Despite my poser's leather jacket, I've never been a motorcycle fanatic myself. The jacket isn't just to look cool on the back of Corrina's machine, it was to protect me if she ever threw me off: that was a definite risk when she cuts the corners. Corrina's bad accident in France wasn't a discouraging factor. Maybe it should have been. Motorcycles are seductive icons. But I'm never going to turn the ignition. Neither will Luke, until he's old enough to buy his own. Then he'll need a powerful engine to go against the wishes of his mother.

I've got some vital dope on my son's safety. Nobody takes any notice of me as I slip away from the school, despite my jacket and boots. I'm invisible as the ghost of rebellion past. Nobody looks twice at a sad skinny man. So I decide to feel sorry for myself. The angry hushed voices die away from me. Warily and disgustedly I walk past the burning community and youth centre. Maybe I should have introduced myself to the ringleaders of this protest. I know how to formulate a manifesto; I have some ideals and convictions; I understand how to get the media working on your side. I was the secretary of the Uni debating society for a year. That was all many moons ago. I don't need to point that out.

I refuse dangerous shortcuts. I dodge away from another gang, like a rabbit getting the whiff of gunpowder. I can't identify with any nihilistic group here. The idea is to get my kite tail out of here. No time to ask directions from police or thieves. I even saw an ambulance crew being stoned by youths. As were the firemen. Apparently firemen ruin everyone's fun. A riot without a fire is like a wedding without a bride. These days the thought of storming the Winter Palace just gives me heart burn. There I have a psychological connection between the red flag and a bottle of ketchup.

Giving up hope of ever finding Luke, what should happen? I see him walking on the other side of the street. You just can't predict. Moments later he notices his old man - or does a double and triple take - and suffers a horrible hallucination. A mescaline hallucination. His own eyes can't be trusted. The look on his face is a picture but not a beautiful one. So I cross over to speak to him, while he's too amazed to run off. I dig my hands back into my Levi's pockets, gazing down at my boots, trying to keep cool.

"Hey, Luke. What's happening?" I blab.

"What?" he challenges. His large green eyes round in disgust, like a bushbaby caught in a lamp. The spiked copper hair seems even more startled by my appearance.

"Out for a walk?" I say.

The puzzled expression doesn't tone down. "What the fuck!"

"That was going to be my question," I tell him, stepping closer.

"What?"

"This isn't your quarrel," I tell him, referring to the disturbances.

"I wasn't in any fights," he assures me. He eyes my riot gear contemptuously, as if I'm out of the wax works. But you can't say his dress sense is any better.

"Why get involved here, Luke?"

"Who said I was?" he ripostes.

We stand having this crazy discussion by someone's front wall. I notice a curtain twitching from the house, and the people inside observing the dancing apes outside.

I root about in my jean pockets, before pulling out that bit of scorched silver foil. It's still there. I rustle it accusingly under his nose.

"You been pokin' about?" he accuses.

"Come on boy, turn all your pockets out," I insist.

I prefer to think that his high colour comes from all that fresh air and running about.

"What happened to you?" he wonders, inspecting my shiners. I haven't yet prodded them in the mirror, but his reaction tells me a lot.

"Never mind all that. Don't get sawney with me now," I encourage.

"You got a couple of bruised eyes," he says.

"I know about that. I was chasing after you, wasn't I," I tell him. "Shouldn't I take any notice? What you get up to? Let me see what you're carrying."

To my surprise he begins to empty his trouser pockets. What emerges is the typical youthful bric-a-brac, but he also pulls out a small plastic bag of junk - heroin.

"What do we have here?" I remark. "Come on."

Luke responds as if he doesn't recognise this, or know why it is on him.

Don't ask me exactly how much junk, or what it could be worth. I've never cut anything in my life, especially after we lost friends that way. Adam Jakes offered to fix me up, to smooth away my troubles, a kind of bridge over troubled waters, although I'm way beyond that. Elizabeth could snatch Luke back after this, using her oddball lawyer as a getaway driver. She'd be justified in strafing me from a helicopter gun ship. Luke would sign up to her liberation army.

"So where did you get this stuff?" I enquire firmly.

"What's the big fuss?" he objects, colouring deeply - rage and humiliation.

These scenes are not positive, nor are they avoidable. "Who sold you this shit?"

"It's only a bit, aint it? For personal use. I'm not selling stuff."

"I bloody well hope not," I tell him.

"What do you care?" he bellows suddenly. Voice box cracking again.

"Pretty stuff isn't it," I comment, rubbing soft powder between my fingers.

He stares back at me trying to second-guess.

"Expensive shit. It could certainly be costly for you, Luke." Does he have a life to spare?

Luke shuffles, impatient and aggravated. He has a heavy chain pulled through the loops of his jeans. Neurotically he spikes up his burnished locks: hair, eyes, complexion identical to his mother's. I have another double vision. I falter as if he's expressing *her* rebukes. My head totally screwed up, not just the beat box. There's a battery of heavy chemicals surging around my veins - messing with my thoughts. I don't know who and where I am.

"Where are your mates then? The ones you came to see here?" I ask him.

"Don't know."

"So you were just hanging around the street corner."

"Guessed in one," he replies.

I consider the unfamiliar irony of his response. "You were out here buying drugs?"

"No!"

"Joy riding?"

"We were just playing about and then the filth arrived, didn't they...out of nowhere."

"Then you ran off, did you? Where are your friends now?"

"The next I knew," Luke explains, "they'd got 'em into arm locks and slammed 'em in the meat wagon, didn't they."

My bemused expression gains in concentration. Although the purple rings around my eyes may give me a clownish appearance. "How long have you been out here? Wandering the streets?" I wonder.

"They're good mates of mine," he insists.

"Why don't you keep me up to speed?" I suggest.

He shrugs his shoulders and looks into the distance.

"Two boys were killed here tonight," I remind him.

"I know that," he comments.

"*They* don't," I retort.

He scowls and slumps.

I regret being such a smart arse with the young generation. "You're messing around here, hanging out with these new mates, riding on motorcycles, chasing the bloody dragon," I lament.

"I was just looking for the bus home," he argues.

"D'you think your mother and I work like harnessed mules just to provide you with drugs money?" I complain.

"No, Dad, but it's my money, isn't it? When you hand it over to me?"

"You think you're the Chancellor of the Exchequer? Your mother will have a blue fit if she finds out about this evening. How do you think she would react to this?" I argue. Maybe he can tell me how she would react. I need a better idea of the consequences.

"I don't know. She wouldn't be happy," Luke admits.

"Too right, boy, she'd go into orbit."

Our son laughs in recognition, despite himself.

"Come on, Luke, we're going home. We're driving out of here." A resource not available to everyone. I have to assume that the vintage Citroen remains in one piece and with all four tyres.

"No, Dad, I have to go back and help my mates."

"That isn't possible, Lukey. You can't do anything for them now. You going to chase down the police wagon or blow off their cell door?" I suggest.

"You can't tell me what to do. Not any more," he objects.

"I had a call from your head teacher today," I say, gripping his arm.

"What about it? She doesn't know stuff."

"You have exams to pass, revision to catch up with. You want to ditch that?"

"No, but I'm old enough to look after myself."

"Maybe," I tell him. "I'd like to think that. But it's getting dark. You're expected at your Mum's place tomorrow evening. You up for that? Can you get yourself clean in time?" I say, only half in jest.

At this I flick open the packet of junk. I shake the package and empty it, as if mixing with the background of shouts and smoke. The shit disperses and drifts through the air. Luke's outraged at such waste, but he isn't an addict, thank goodness. Thank God he doesn't offer violent resistance. He's almost as tall as me now. And my over-boiled muscles have run out of stamina.

"You throwing money away?" he complains.

"Whose money?" I counter.

"Who told you where I was out here, anyway?" he quizzes. His voice slips down the scale like an elephant losing its footing.

"That isn't the point," I say. Why doesn't he queue up at the popcorn stand at the nearest multiplex?

"Why don't you get your fucking hand off me? Dad?"

"Do you know where heroin comes from?" I ask him. I lean forward, placing my hands protectively on his shoulders, looking into his soul.

"What does it matter? Who cares?" he retorts, with an anguished expression.

"On our drive home I will explain everything. You'll be a wiser young man when you return."

"No, Dad, no talks."

"That will give you something to brag about to your mates. Your real friends that is." The one who grassed him up, for his own salvation.

Alternatively, he could ask his mother, if you see where I'm coming from.

But hindsight's like a successful career in show business.

To my considerable relief, we set off and head for the car, away from the fires and violence. Luke smells of smoke himself. This doesn't prove anything, although it doesn't dampen my suspicions either. Why does he hang around this neighbourhood at all, coming from a comfortable and loving home, as he does? I'm not trying to play the angry old man, but Liz and her legal team will rebrand me as a failed father.

Her chief lawyer is a broody guy in nylon shirts, who reads popular novels by his American counterparts, I noticed. He sought me out at the adjournment: "I've been watching you carefully, Mr Sheer," he told me, shiftily. "I've listened to all your statements. Watched the way you conduct yourself. I have to say that I've really been admiring your guts." He offered a quick ambiguous smile before hustling away from the building.

But I fought him all the way and will continue in that battle. I've always tried to do my best for the kids. Suddenly your best is not good enough. Times may change, but attitudes shift even more alarmingly.

Luke and I leave the temporary stage of history. I suspect that he's secretly grateful to escape this scene. We had a few problems trying to find where I left my car. Neither of us has a good mental map of the area. Just a few mental scars.

# Chapter 29

The following evening I drop Luke at his mother's second-home as scheduled. Our son is scrubbed, changed and perfumed, with no whiff of street disturbances about him; just a few scratches and bruises which he has to keep to himself. Since that notorious evening his gaze has clarified and balanced, broken capillaries erased. Opiate alkaloids are water dissoluble. He was pulling glass after glass of fresh grapefruit today.

"Remember what I told you, Lukey," I say, on the drive over. "Play your tarot cards close to your chest. Nothing about your off-the-rails doings?"

"Or-right Dad. I heard you, didn't I?" he grumbles.

That way we both keep our heads on our shoulders. Like a couple of airmen in Colditz we've discussed the dangers of his stay; we're rehearsed all his lines and moves. Even in an open prison you can't do exactly what you please. I'm all in favour of personal liberty but loose talk will cost custody - not just my private life.

I'm not negative about putting Luke into captivity this weekend. The way I figure, allow him to reconsider his actions on the estate; let him meditate about his behaviour while hanging at the Dino's mausoleum. He'll be lucky if they allow him to pop out to the newsagents.

I pull up on the opposite side of their lair, with a sharp view up their driveway. There's Liz's dinky red convertible under the port. I'm cast into the role of seedy private detective again. I'm the marriage killer as divorce victim. Luke and I allow ourselves to sink down into the cracked Gallic upholstery, overhearing our own thoughts and expectations. He's hanging loose for a minute, taking advantage of the whining heating system, as the engine turns over.

We've been more relaxed with each other post-riot. Companionably we listen to the Beatles' greatest hits in another repackaged shuffle. The tape whines to a halt during Love Me

Do, requires a pencil shift, but you can fast-forward to the more interesting tracks. The lad doesn't express any approval of the Mop Tops but he can tolerate them. Even his mother hasn't repudiated the nostalgic power of the Mersey sound. She and I both listen to their lyrics with some bitter irony, in the contemporary era.

No need to let the Noggins' imagination run riot. Such as it is. Don't blab too much about hurling missiles at the police and escaping arrest. Even if they bring the topic up, having followed all the media reports. We don't want to give bad impressions. All those solicitors' fees must be a drain even on Frank's pockets, be they as deep as the coalman's (who came to our little house in the old days). I don't want that sweaty little lawyer of hers, with his pencil moustache and nylon shirt, insinuating himself, while clutching on my sleeve, again.

Eventually Luke drops out of my old Citroen. Tosses back the machine's deep clunky door with a practised parry. After scrutinising top and bottom, slinging kit bag over a shoulder, like little orphan anarchist, he skulks off over the road: Pretends that he's not conscious that I watch over him. I follow his reluctant lanky progress along their driveway. Luke takes a moment to admire her Merc. He rides an imaginary wave on a surf board, stubs a thumb into the brass bell and lurks around the porch with bored anxiety. He gets in a surreptitious parting shot of me, checking that I am still there waiting and not about to dash off immediately. I'm heartened and touched by this hesitation and solidarity on his part. You'd suspect that such a delicate feeling would perish in that bonfire. I'm the guy who needs reassurance. It's a beautiful and scary world out here.

A brief delay until the hallway light comes on. As the front door opens this light falls on one side of Liz's face, the plump healthy cheeks, on chemically metallic curls. A smile, a kiss and a hug and she pulls him inside after her; half raises a hand in my direction - to the assassin in the banger - but there's no need for chat or even eye contact. She won't be asking me inside for a beer this evening - one of her new hubby's stack of iced lagers. It's strictly hello, thank you and goodbye, tonight.

Deal done, as I build revs and begin to pull away, who should approach but Frank in his tank. Their street is already choked with parked four-wheel drives and family saloons, compelling us to nudge carefully through the gap. Therefore we are forced to cross precious vehicles with extreme care. We both have a vested interest in avoiding any nasty scrapes. It wouldn't be accurate to describe a car insurance dispute as a cherry on any cake. Consequently we both stare ahead, rigidly concentrating on our driving skills, struggling to trundle to safety. I do notice that his jowls turn a succulent red, his neck creasing down into a tight office collar, as he exercises a misguided but compelling curiosity. Hello, it's Noah.

He may believe that I'm more accepting of his domestic arrangements lately. He thinks that the past and the future are consigned to their places. That a broken heart is now coming before an ex-wife. That I must have lost all my ambitions.

Think again, Frank. Some people have their heart in a different place. Mine should be dropped into a preservation tank at the university, for future generations to splice and study. But if you're looking for my opinion the seat of our emotions can be traced to the appendix. They should put a picture of an appendix on Valentine's Day cards, all greetings cards, and the like. Appropriately I don't know what shape the appendix may be. I've never handled one, have you?

Having left Luke to his Mum's - and possible interrogation - I head off to Rupert Lloyd's dinner party. I've been sitting on the invitation card for weeks and the expectation to see Corrina again. I want to express my desire to mix. Here's further evidence that human feelings can be found in the appendix. Or maybe I've just had a bad experience.

Apart from Rupert and his fiancée, there are three couples at the gig, and one gooseberry. That's right, Corrina Farlane doesn't show, but merely has her excuse broadcast to the company, where it falls on my ears: she's been called to an emergency meeting on Pacific instruments. I have to leave that one open to interpretation, but it defeats me and I'm eating my heart out again. Once again I'm hearing that door slam in the middle of Cage's silent piece. Man, it's like an old steam train pulling in to Waterloo, as all the passengers alight to the platform.

Nursing the centre of my hurt like a hot cannonball, I'm left tongue-tied, humiliated; as well as sporting bruises around each eye, where that lout smashed an elbow into my face. Just as well that Lizzie didn't invite me indoors this evening, forcing me to explain. They all ask where I got these black eyes from (or really a pair of purple spectacles by now). Swallowing disappointment I describe a trip in the garage that brings frail flesh to hard surfaces. They may think that these black eyes are another sign of cardiac arrest. Everything else is pure paranoia.

Guests get through initial drinks and introductory chatter. We're all gathered by candlelight around Rupert's dining table. Not sure if the dimmed romantic lighting does anything for my eyes: it hadn't been Rupert's intention. The atmosphere does nothing to soften my divorcee status among these hitched people. The room is large and high-ceilinged, decorated with East African artefacts, against huge bookcases and whitewashed walls. We pick our way through a menu of unidentifiable courses and zinging sauces. I know that it includes a few animals and birds that I haven't tried before. Not to consume, to eat that is, though I may have visited a few of these creatures in the zoo before now. Cuisine is the only way I get to travel the world really. And this is 'white water' cookery.

Ostrich was one of the courses. If somebody was quick enough to kill one of those birds, you have to pay tribute to them and ask how Rupert prepared the dish, attentive to the herbs and sauces that have been added: Unless of course it was burying its head under the sand at the time.

A smart cosmopolitan guy, Rupert Lloyd, except something went sour in his mind, if you're looking for my opinion. Despite falling in love and planning to marry, somehow that idyll only confirms his past mistakes. I'd describe this as his equivalent of the coronary, even if his pulmonary muscle is going harder than ever. Like Jimi.

Sheila and he have been talking about their time in Kenya and their experiences around the globe. Bob and Susan are able to participate in this subject and discuss travel writers and writing. I'll never follow in anyone's footsteps except my own, even if I do own hot air balloons. Rupert avoids talking about our past, our youthful passions. For him those days are a smelly-cigarette mirage of headstrong fantasies. Yet the topic of those riots on the left bank of Bristol soon comes up. Even more reason to keep my head down at this party, hoping that they don't notice my embarrassment; or, in recognition of that pair of shiners, connect a past radical with current events.

"British people are disgustingly greedy and selfish," Rupert argues. Again his disillusionment is revealed like a metric measure hanging in an empty reservoir. But his rhetoric always had a hollow ring.

"No, they're certainly not grateful," his friend, Farley, concurs.

"And an edgy district of the city like that," his wife Daphne says. Where did this girl come from?

"As far as I understand," Sue recalls, "Thursday night's trouble was caused by the deaths of two boys. They were knocked off their motorcycles by a roadblock." She is stung by the uncharitable opinions of the neo-conservative consensus.

"The motorcycles didn't belong to them," Farley corrects.

"What were those youths doing on the streets to begin with?" Rupert wonders.

Enjoying a free country?

"It was just awful...that they were killed," Susan declares. She turns to her husband for support.

"Awful," Bob echoes.

"What are their poor parents going through?" she says, inviting us to sympathise.

"Who can possibly imagine?" Bob contributes. "Shocking. Hard to bear."

"Think of the poor police," Farley suggests, piqued.

"Those children were running wild... out of control," Daphne says.

"Serves them absolutely damn well right," Rupert tells us. "What do they honestly expect?"

"They were somebody's sons," Susan objects.

"To older hooligans, do you mean?" Rupert counters, with a dry smile.

"Come on, Rupert, have a little human sympathy, will you," she suggests.

"Do *they*?" he muses. "Do these hooligans have any decent humanity?"

"Does anyone know what a police car costs these days?" declares Farley. "We're the guys paying police salaries with our taxes," he states. He's a fair haired, trim chap, with darker moustaches and a constantly amazed expression. I don't know what's so amazing to him. His own stupidity maybe.

"No child deserves to die in such a horrible way," Susan continues.

There is a kind of triumphant ironic laughter between Rupert, fiancée and friends.

"What are the parents doing?" Daphne asks, throwing her shiny fringe across consulted cosmetics.

"Giving birth to more screaming brats, most likely," Rupert suggests to her. Bitterness and resentment takes away any mirth.

"Scum," Farley observes.

"You're a charitable guy, aren't you?" Susan tells him.

"You should bring back army service," Sheila tells our party. "Martial discipline."

This brings the liberal elements to a stop.

"They are not up to it, darling," Rupert informs her, squeezing her long arm.

"If I was the mother to that murdered boy, then I would be forced to make a protest as well," Susan declares. This is shaping up as an old-time shoot-out.

"That would be socially irresponsible and I would condemn you outright," Rupert retorts. He wriggles his shoulders inside a colourful pyjama suit. Flicks his dramatic fringe, gold frosted with iron, while tackling another slice of fruit tart; it is fruit of some kind. This doesn't feel like the moment to enquire.

"I can make up my own mind about social responsibility," Susan tells him.

Bob offers her an uneasy look, utters an involuntary queasy noise; his pointed expression urging her to avoid further conflagration.

"You British should just flog them," Sheila suggests helpfully. "You're too soft in this country! My family knows how to deal with this riff-raff."

"Many decent thinking people would agree with you," her fiancé adds, lending moral support. "I'm afraid the leftists have made us too squeamish about justice, crime and punishment."

Damion and Melanie, meanwhile, listen to the dispute uncomfortably. They are hearing about the behaviour of the bad people. They are among the good people and so it is difficult for them to comprehend. I know that their pink little ears are constantly tuned in to my life, so let the riot news keep them distracted.

"People in this country don't take responsibility for children. They're allowed to roam the streets without any control."

"Our love is exhausted," Melanie declares, face flushed with innocence.

"They have lost the meaning of love," Damion adds, not wishing to be excluded. This evening he's wearing some kind of silk blouse - maybe borrowed from his wife.

They used to be against hanging and all forms of corporal punishment, but apparently these methods only hurt the wealthy.

"Tough love at the point of a water cannon," Farley argues, raising eyebrows above a stunned expression.

"That's the only gesture they understand," says his wife.

"What can parents do?" Bob says.

"What would you think they should do?" Rupert retorts.

"Hard to keep teenagers locked in doors all evening, wouldn't you say?" he suggests, anxiously.

"What I mean, Bob, is these chavs should teach their kids civilised social behaviour."

"They should stop ragging each other?" I add.

Rupert glares sideways for the first time this evening. "Whatever happened to the traditional family unit? Don't people have any pride in keeping a good name?"

"Kids have a mind of their own. Didn't you, Rupert, once have a mind of your own?" Susan argues.

Rupert focuses his thoughts irritably. Doesn't Sue know how weak and irresponsible she is? "If these people haven't experienced discipline or control, then they are never going to learn responsibility," he says. This statement makes me think twice, because it's an echo of his former views about the CIA and the Pentagon, or the Kremlin and the KGB. He was an intimidating student agitator.

"You're talking about discipline and control. The revolutionaries must be turning in their graves. Am I hearing right? It would be like an ice pick through Trotsky's heart," I suggest.

"Nothing fans the flames better than a lot of bleeding heart liberalism," Rupert argues, pointedly. Apparently we didn't grow up with him.

"Gorgeous fruit, Rupert!" Davinia declares, in an elaborate scooping exercise.

"Do you really think so, you're too kind," Rupert tells her.

Damion and Melanie fidget nervously with their own desserts. Not only is the fruit unrecognisable, but these negative thoughts are playing havoc with their digestion. They didn't come to this party expecting to talk about riots or working class insurrection. Only that full fat cream is more distressing to them. It comes from Channel Island cows - it's very special. I should be bothered.

"The problems of parenthood must be doubled on an estate like that," Bob considers.

"What do you mean, Bob? The problems of parenthood?"

"Well, you know...it's very isolated and bleak there... there's not much for these kids to do. Even the movies aren't a cheap night out any more," he reveals. "Sue and I were out on the town the other night, and we were really taken aback by..."

"Do you imagine that justifies yesterday's scenes?" Rupert returns. He's leaning back from a great height, as he once appeared on a lion in Trafalgar Square. "Because these people can't afford to go to the pictures?" he says ironically.

He made comparable speeches about Kissenger. The city council members and MPs of the period were in fear of his opposition. He was the guest of a Parisian student committee and addressed a crowded theatre audience, in fluent fiery French, to declare that bourgeois democracy was bankrupt and had to be faced down on the boulevards. Goddard shook his hand and Rupert was an extra in the movie, reading a radical paper at a café table behind Jean Seaborg.

Bob has taken off his spectacles and is cleaning them vigorously with his handkerchief; which shows some evidence of his back garden. Bob's easily intimidated by egocentric Europeans, which is why he travelled to meet gentler peoples around the globe. Or is it a matter of culture?

Rupert puts his elbows up on his huge mahogany dining table, risking the rough stitches of his flax suit. "If these chavs had any intelligence, or resourcefulness, they would create their own entertainment," he suggests. "Whatever happened to their sense of community?"

"British Marxism comes full circle," I observe.

"What are you talking about, Noah?" he returns.

"Would Raymond Williams, for instance, have ever argued that popular culture should be something that people *made up*?" I ask him.

"Except that the new underclass has no sense of community," he counters.

"So they simply invent a sense of community and shared culture?" I say.

"The very notion of popular culture is absurd in their case," he insists, again inspecting my mysteriously blackened eyes.

"Isn't that because it has been degraded if not destroyed? Wouldn't we once have argued that?" I argue.

"The working class has lost the plot of history," he tells me.

"Ah, so you think it's their fault, do you?" I conclude.

"Look, Noah, the fabric of British society is falling apart. There's nothing keeping this country together. It's disintegrated. Anarchic. Nobody's prepared to stand up to these scoundrels and face them down. We have to hit these people hard before they attack our houses too."

"Best pull down your shutters and make a cup of cocoa," I suggest.

"We should make an effort to understand their problems," Susan says, backing me. "Do you know the frustrations of being poor? The sort of anger and confusion that's going to create in their minds? What's happened to our old radical sympathy for the underdog?"

"You suggest that we put an arm around these people, do you?" Rupert replies.

"These scum are beyond understanding," Farley remarks.

"They've all lost touch with their feminine sides," Damion tells us.

"That would include some of the girls," Melanie says.

"So would that include you as well?" I ask her.

"What are you talking about now, Noah?" she rounds.

"But you can't condemn these people entirely," Bob returns. "Not an entire section of our society. Their aspirations and, even, their self-image. Frustrated. Damaged."

"That's the whole point, Bob, we should condemn them. Or their behaviour at least. There's no excuse for it."

"No, I believe that if you are talking about Britain, the United Kingdom, then we all have a responsibility," Bob returns, screwing up his courage to be heard.

"They're all our children," Susan adds supportively.

"I can't agree with you there," Rupert reflects. "They are no children of mine. They've put themselves outside of society."

"But you don't have any children, Rupert, do you. Not yet awhile."

"Rupert wants to make sure they all stay in their place," I comment. "Even if they don't know what their place is anymore."

"I wouldn't have any of these children," Melanie insists. Not even in her crèche.

"They live in one of the wealthiest countries in the world, with an abundance of everything. If they knew how many people in this world live, they would feel humble," Rupert argues. "Truly humble and *ashamed*, I can tell you."

"If you want people to behave well, then don't you need to treat them well?" Susan argues. "Don't the poorest people in this society deserve to be treated with respect...to have their problems and frustrations addressed?"

"They make me truly ashamed of this country," Rupert tells her. His tone is lowered to one of near silent despair. "Morality isn't an issue to be debated," he informs us all, his large troubled eyes swivelling around his company.

"But you're keen to have it branded into them," I suggest.

"Really, Noah, that's a fine recipe for the future, I have to say. Personally I couldn't go along with it."

# Chapter 30

After my just desserts I get a chance to put my head together with Bob. He kept an eye on my house and garden while Jekyll plugged me into a chemistry set. You need somebody to hold your suitcase while buying your ticket for the last station. Just because we suffer pain we can't always be blamed for our injuries. The world's a beautiful but scary place and we'd like to stop it with our finger for a while.

Raw with shame and embarrassment, I tell my friend about Luke's involvement in an urban riot. When Bob's boys have grown up into their teenage years, I hope that drinking lemonade and ballroom dancing may be fashionable again. Either that or society will be returning to the coliseum, for more fun and games. You just can't predict fashion - what comes around goes around, but does the world spin that quickly?

"I wish Rupert the best with Sheila," says Bob H. "But his views can be extremely aggravating. Why must he express himself so aggressively?" Despite an outdoors complexion he looks ruddy cheeked from Roop's intellectual abrasions. He resembles a hardened hedgehog in a fisherman's sweater.

"It feels like being strapped into an iron-maiden," I concur. At this time we are safely in Lloyd's backroom. Here we find nothing more tortuous than a pianoforte and a Meissen porcelain clock.

"You'd think the guy'd have mellowed by now," Bob smarts.

"Rupert's politics have changed, but they're as red and saucy as ever," I muse. Or maybe I just had a traumatic experience.

"Did you hear the way he rounded on Sue?" my friend says, indignantly.

"The French riot squad is more liberal these days," I comment.

"I thought you were unusually quiet on the subject," Bob H tells me.

"I decided to keep my head down...in the circumstances."

"Is that where you got those two black eyes from?" he wonders. "Aren't you going to tell me?"

"When I got caught up in the mob...there was a police charge.... everybody scattered pell-mell..."

"Not to blame you. No need to be ashamed. You should make a formal complaint and bring them to book," he argues.

"Don't start that legal business again, Bob," I object. It isn't so much litigation fatigue, it's collapse.

Bob is cautious about my riot report and doesn't believe Lukey could have taken part. "Your son's not one to look for trouble. The riot just happened to him, most likely."

"I found a packet of junk on him, after I got up to speed," I explain.

He jolts backwards. "Did you really? Luke?"

"But he's not a junkie," I insist - backtracking from bravado.

"Where did he get the stuff from? Do you know?"

"Not exactly," I say. "Have a few guesses though."

"What did you do?" he wonders, shocked.

We gaze about the incongruously comfortable room, as if checking for wires.

"I gave him a lecture on the drive back home. But I was so angry I almost whacked him," I admit, "at the time."

He blinks hard as if fumes are smoking his vision. "What got into you, man?" he declares.

"I know, I'd lose his respect as well as my own. It was a tense moment. It was a hard call. Luckily I pulled myself together...and I didn't do something that I've never believed in." Raised my hand to one of our kids that is.

"Crises reveal our strength of mind," he argues. "I believe that. Crack up and you begin to fall apart. Then, what kind of influence does his sister have?" he asks.

"Lukey hasn't been himself lately. Maybe the drugs thing explains it. Not only the divorce and disruption to home life. He's a bit unpredictable, even troubled. Something's going on with him. Then I have to chase his tail."

"What about Angela?" Bob persists.

"Where to start?" I admit.

"You able to keep up with her?" he presses.

"There are car loads of revellers in the small hours. Incoherent accounts of dance raves, stalks of grass in her clothes, empty plastic impressions in her pockets..."

"So you've got some idea," he concludes. He zeros in on my reaction, rises on his toes, braces his short stocky legs, and bristles dark eyebrows in anticipation of more. He's so close that I can smell the sea-proofed resin from his jumper.

"What are you driving at, man?"

"Do you know a guy called Adam Jakes?"

My hackles rise spontaneously like a toothless porcupine dropped into a snake pit.

"Ah, right, so you already know about him," he immediately sees.

"My daughter brought him home one evening," I remark. With an unintentional picture of family convention.

"This young guy has become a hero to the young," Bob explains. "You can argue he's damaged goods, but she's at the head of a long queue."

"We all know what's for sale," I comment. "He organises these raves and hands out sweeties. No surprise that he's so popular, is it?"

"He's a Peter Pan figure," Bob says.

"For real? Well he definitely flew out of Big Pink the other night," I recall. "How's Angie ever going to straighten out her career, if she falls under the spell of this creep? No doubt she regards me as Captain Hook in this adventure," I realise, agonising. "How am I going to explain this to Liz, if she finds out?"

I feel angst gnawing my guts like a starving shark at a metal cage. I can't get my head around Angie's tricks and deceptions, since all the drugs have side effects. Just as relationships do.

"His fashion sense reminds me of a born-again Christian," I say. "He's selling narcotics but he never takes them. Or so he claims. He could turn up at Lizzie's place with a guitar and she'd welcome him into her church. They'd have a picnic and gather round for a singsong. She'd see him as a perfect future son-in-law and partner for our little girl."

"Until she finds out the truth about him," Bob H reminds me.

"If she could overlook his bling jewellery, I guess, that Angela's been wearing lately. So," I persist, "what else do you know about this creep?"

"Left school at fifteen and parked cars at the casino. Have you seen the cars he drives these days?"

Am I supposed to be impressed? I'm sure not to look it.

"He fell out with his father, who was the notorious haulier," Huntingdon persists.

"Right, is that the same Jakes? Son of the 'haulier'?"

"Yes, the same. You remember that drama?"

"Jakes senior turned the motorway into snipers' alley. It was a dispute with a rival firm, wasn't it? I definitely don't want to bump into his father," I say. Certainly not at a family wedding.

"No, you don't really want Angela to be hanging about with Adam. They aren't a pleasant family," Bob considers. "Adam was supposed to take over the family firm, the fleet of trucks, but the pair fell out."

"Must have been feisty, as family rows go." Makes the Oedipal struggle resemble a pillow fight.

"I've seen Angela around town with him, Noah," he informs me.

"Out socialising? A few weeks ago, but Angela promised me that she wouldn't see him again."

"I noticed them today."

As if Tyson put his paw into my cheek, my expression changes. "You're certain?"

"They were going up Park Street together. Angela works along there, doesn't she? She was in uniform. He was... never mind, she must have been taking a break."

"I'd put my faith in that." Whatever faith remained.

"Well, I was strolling down on the opposite side, when I recognised her. I greeted her and waved. Reluctantly she waved back. After all I'm her god parent! But she was embarrassed... didn't want to be seen or acknowledged."

"What about that little criminal?" I wonder.

"He didn't take any notice of me. He didn't even look."

"What did he want with her? What was he talking to her about?" I think out loud.

"I don't know about that, Noah," he admits

"Maybe Jakes called into the café to see her...twisted her arm and compelled her to leave with him."

"I've noticed her sitting with him outside the café," Bob says.

"For real? I visited her at the café one Saturday myself."

"All under the awning."

"But he wasn't with her that time. I'm quite sure about that."

"Angela seems to be caught up with him. She raised a hand to wave to me, but her other arm was around his shoulder and...the body language."

"What other choice would she have? She couldn't get away easily. She had to distract him. She had to stall for time."

Bob thinks about my optimistic picture of this relationship. "I don't know where they were going, Noah. Just for a walk maybe."

"He's meant to be Peter Pan, so maybe she flew out the window with him," I complain unhappily.

"Do you know Pete Sparks? My friend, the accountant? He helps to fiddle Adam Jakes' taxes. No point trying to fudge the issue. Pete says that Jakes is a player in a drugs ring. Evidence is hidden from Pete. But the police keep a watch on Jakes."

"Such a clean cut young guy," I remark.

"Jakes even has a power launch moored inside the plimsoll swing bridge. Did you notice?" Bob asks. "He has other boats in harbours around the coast. We're not talking about the grass I smoke by the compost heap." To disguise the aroma from Sue, he means. "That year-round tan doesn't come out of a bottle after all. It comes from the Iberian Peninsula."

"Our Angie's hooked on this character?" I declare, in revolt.

"You'd better check her out, Noah," he warns.

"Don't worry. That big boat belongs to him? There are Royal Navy vessels in that dock. I take Tim to explore the quays many Saturday afternoons. We've spent some time looking at them. I would never have guessed this. But if he's selling hard drugs to Angela...or to any other member of my family."

"You've got the info on this guy's background," Bob tells me. "You've been filled in about this character...got some idea about the allegations against him."

"*Some* idea."

His eyes gleam encouragingly.

I can only stare back like a moron, struggling to fill the grey gaps.

"His business methods are less than friendly, it's rumoured. Jakes is reckoned to have beaten up a few business rivals, if that's how to describe them. To within an inch of the guy's life, in one case. He's able to draw on his contacts," Bob suggests.

"No need to call a lawyer in that situation," I say. Not even Lizzie's lawyer.

"Then there was that ugly incident a while back...when he assaulted his girlfriend."

"Girlfriend? Wife, don't you mean?" I declare. "Angie's already admitted that the punk is married."

"Mm, well, it wasn't his wife. She seems to be happy in her big detached house on that new estate," he explains. "With a couple of kids and a few fluffy dogs. No, not his wife, it was definitely one of his girlfriends, that he attacked. I mean, one of his previous girlfriends. A while ago, it would have been. A few years back, I'd reckon."

"Our sweet lord," I retort.

"This unfortunate girl's family brought charges against Jakes... initially...for assault or grievous bodily harm...a charge of that type. She eventually took the whole story back and those charges had to be dropped. The police were frustrated, but there was no case to answer."

"She tripped at the top of the stairs, did she?"

"Something like that," he says. "Either she was intimidated or thought better of the prosecution."

"Angela's impressed and she's dating him," I bleat.

"Don't panic or fear for her yet. Not until you get her version of events. Perhaps they aren't an item. He's got the influence to make these illegal raves happen. He's good looking and self-made, I suppose. Young people get passionate about these confident and powerful individuals. To them he's a kind of rock star."

"If he touches Angie I'm going to put him into the charts," I promise.

"He's done a lot for young people. We don't like the look of him, but is that the point?"

The image makeover doesn't convince me. "Flogging designer drugs to our kids?" I ask.

"Nobody has any proof. Anyway we experimented. Are you going to prohibit?"

This throws me to the back of my mind. "I have to catch up with Angie... she and I have to put our heads together ...I feel completely out of phase with her. You should worry about your own kids," I argue.

"So then, what are you two men plotting about now?" Susan asks. She slipped into the room without us noticing. "You're making Rupert nervous back there."

He isn't the only one.

Locked up in Big Pink next evening. Placed into solitary, again, putting down another mental track in the basement tapes. Thrown back into my own thoughts and memories; taking leaps into the dark. *Lo and behold! Lo and behold!* Regrets like fumes in a wine cellar.

I recalled the week Liz and I separated and sorted our personal belongings and possessions. We were busy disentangling our life as a couple, untying that marital knot, before she lived under another roof. Roaming about the house, avoiding conversation and each other's eyes; except when unavoidable; shifting boxes and making a final search of the attic, down into the basement, pulling our life apart like a wishbone.

She left the complete Dylan collection to me, without a moment's hesitation. Dylan, Cohen, Buckley, Young, even Mitchell and Baez - any artist of any significance to our youth and happiness.

"You love completely, or you stop," she told me.

She intended the epitaph to burn in my mind. Sure enough it continues to smoke through my thoughts. Unerring as cupid's arrow in the first place.

No indication of Angie returning to Big Pink, tonight or any night. I'd happily entertain the children of the Grateful Dead. I stay up late - four in the morning at last look - slumped in front of the telly, goggling a god-awful dubbed crime movie. Following the lip movements like an idiot. I've lost the spirit to switch off, as if to admit that Angela is never coming back home.

I tense with anticipation at every jerk of headlights around the room. Her Renault already has a crumpled front bumper and a taped plate. Finally I extinguish my reading lamp and recover a spilt book. Let the bats have full play in the belfry.

She hasn't made it back for breakfast either. Not that I was really expecting her. She may be chewing pieces of hash cake washed down by neat vodka. She could be referring to some of her mother's old recipes. Or maybe I'm just victim of paranoia.

Stood up over cornflakes, I slip out into the naked city. There's no good in hanging around this lonely old castle. The obvious place to find Angie is at her job; Mike's Café; the nerve centre of her existence. She's due to go into work today. She has some milk to froth. If she doesn't serve her future well, she can expect complaints. I could even have some luck - or is it luck? - and find Jakes hanging out under the café awning.

I rediscover my DS and enjoy a magic carpet ride to the city centre. The journey will be less smooth from this point on. As I push through into the café I spot owner Mike busy with tea things. I scrutinise his movements carefully, yet he doesn't seem a suspicious character. Obviously he doesn't always keep track of his waitresses and waiters. But he's not a drugs baron. Hard to keep a check on your cholesterol levels in this hideout, I note.

"Has my daughter turned up for work this morning?"

"She's not turned up yet," he replies. He's preoccupied with his work and doesn't look at me.

"Any idea where she might be?"

"No. Do you?" he retorts, organising his crockery and condiments.

Mike can't tell me where she's getting her kicks. Obviously she can twist this guy around her little toe. When a girl goes on a trip with Jakes you know they are going for more than a country ride. You only have to ask his wife and former girlfriends.

"Jakes could be dangerous," Bob H had warned. His warning reverberates like this morning's alarm.

Not a smart idea to discuss Angie's movements with her boss. Must remember I am on her side. I don't want her to lose this job.

She's saving up to pay academic fees. Or supplement them: Lizzie will cough up the lion's share. Can't depend on her old boy any longer, with his suspect plumbing system. Mike is too hassled to tell me more, as customers tuck into breakfast specials. So I have to chat up one of the waitresses instead. The kind of beautiful girl who makes you regret your youth is gone. This young woman is able to confirm that there's a rave happening, this weekend. She doesn't want to tell me the precise location, or logistics, as they keep rave details secret until the last moment, to evade the cops. The police try to move in to break up illegal festivals. That's always been one of their traditional duties. The police commissioner gets as excited about breaking up parties as Warhol's stars were eager to find them.

I get in customers way, as the waitress abandons me. She's considering her options, anxious and preoccupied by my questions, as she serves around the café. She squeezes her box trying to understand why I need all this dope. Is she getting Angela into more trouble or rescuing her? Obviously this girl doesn't know Jakes well enough either. She may be in his fan club too.

"Will you excuse me, Mr Sheer," Mike says. He pushes past and glares. When am I going to order or leave? But I'm resisting the fresh pastries on principle. Liz is the bread-maker, recently, but I refuse to wake up and smell the coffee.

At last this gorgeous young woman, friend of my daughter, tracks back to where I stand (like an incongruous lemon). She relieves this misery, while continuing to wipe at the table and gather plates into a pile. Her ethereal face has a tragic and distant look. Ophelia. Is she ever going to open her trap?

"The rave's going on near Bath," she informs me. "At the hippie festival this weekend." She avoids my eyes and speaks softly, as if encountering a ghost. At the sharp end of contemporary culture I hardly count. "I don't know the exact place, sorry, but it's happening. Is Angela there?"

The information comes without commitment, as if giving a stale cheese scone to a vagrant intruder. This is what it feels like to fill those boots of old Spanish leather, in the contemporary era.

# Free Festival

# Part 3

# Chapter 31

I knew what to expect long before I reached any 'alternative dance tent'. Driving out of the city I soon encountered traffic jams. A rainbow of anarchy is spreading across the land.

The first encounter with hippies is on the A39, as they follow a yellow brick road out of Bath. The whole snaking charabanc is smoking down the slow lane. That's in the sense of thick dirty fumes from exhaust pipes, not so much Californian slang. There's no hint of Tim Leary or Ken Kesey, spreading the word from the acid love bus. At this end of the line the cuckoo is extinct and hippies are an afterthought written in smoke.

These are the stragglers of the convoy, trying to bully and bluster their jalopies into movement. These scruffy outsiders are desperate to reach the festival before a police swoop, as if fleeing towards Kyiv after Chernobyl went up. Like a monster irradiated snail meeting a wall, my inflated French motor bumps against their rear. Not sure if it's good or bad radiation. Angela's got herself into an evil atmosphere. Jakes' malevolent magic. Right now she needs a snake charmer. Not a father. Not even a concerned father. She's a caring person irresponsible to herself. That's how I'm trying to figure her out, fighting the lonely road.

Tempers are warming up in the sunshine, between respectable people and refuse-niks. Tax paying motorists are involved in shouting matches with drop out hippies. For sure they're not comparing map references. I decide to put an elbow out and remain detached. But for how long may I keep a laid-back attitude?

This year the hippies have outsmarted the cops, capturing some land for the festival, after feeding them false information. A convoy has already gathered at a spiritually important site known as Old Lime Hill. According to ancient legend a Mercian magician was beheaded by Celtic warriors, after the sage was mistaken for a Viking spy. Celtic crosses at the top of Lime Hill mark the junction of lay lines that intersect three counties.

Stalled vehicles have made the route impassable. After a lot of revving and blanking, rolling car wheels into ditches, scraping chassis over bumpy ground, I forge my helter-skelter way. You'd think that my vintage car is a part of the procession. Already there's another dent in the front side panel, which I'll have to knock out later. The adventure encourages nostalgia about my own exploits as a young man. I think of this, dream on the festivals and concerts that we attended. For a while I sit back with one hand off the steering, enjoying my memories. The body's engaged in a sit-down protest these days. My hair follicles are committing suicide in public. Why should I worry about gravity or the speed of flight?

What am I going to achieve by chasing Angela? I should give pause to consider my motives. She's in danger but does she want to be *rescued*? By her father? Not a handsome prince or a rock singer. I'm struggling to recover, but my life already went over a cliff. Am I trying to get back to Elizabeth? Is this an attempt to put our marital mistakes behind us, like poor quality service stations along the motorway?

I can't enjoy these reveries much longer, since I notice hippies indulging in fist fights with cops by the hedgerows. They're taking swings at each other between truncheon blows and rolls in the hay. How much do they understand about our generation anyway? Do they know we were almost incinerated in our push-chairs? In our state of terminal decline can we be of any interest? Is there anything creative and progressive in our place? We're in the dustbin of history; we're the flowers of protest, dry and faded on the compost heap.

I struggle to bump and jump the car up this damn lane. Leafy shadows dance on a dusty track, unravelling over farmland ahead. Dark blue uniforms tussle with tie-dye in fields around me. Sylph maidens, with rich braided hair and smooth bare bellies, swig from jugs of cider. Machete wielding Morris Dancers are turning up in troop carriers, I fancy. This is a typical rustic scene from our West Country.

I lose tree cover as I run out at the top of the lane. I've avoided fights and kept my head on my shoulders. Gaining in confidence, gaining on the festival, getting back in touch with my daughter. I spot a settlement ahead, temporary structures, that must form a festival village. Soon I'll be writing postcards and sending them back home to my mother.

Before I can find a suitable place to park - intending to continue on foot - I rattle into another battalion of Somerset and Avon coppers. My wheels are up on the bank and they see my old car ploughing a field. Consequently they pour around me from their roadblock. Some of them are carrying firearms. If I want to reach Angela I must volunteer the truth. Sharing the truth has become painful.

"Do you live around here?" the policeman asks.

"I'm here to find my daughter. To bring her home," I explain.

The officer examines the interior features of my vehicle and considers his response. "Your daughter, do you say?"

"What's your daughter doing around here, with these drop outs?" demands another.

"She ran away from home," I dramatise.

A cop with sergeant stripes takes his own viewing.

"I'd say that these kids are all somebeddy's sons or daughters," he eventually remarks, in our lingo.

"Only one of them is *my* daughter," I insist.

"Thank God none of 'em belongs to me," he comments. He coldly weighs me. "You took it in your head to find her, did you?"

"Haven't your kids ever got into trouble?" I ask.

"When their father is a policeman?" he replies. "I'm asking you to turn around and leave this area. Immediately, sir. Do you hear me right? In the direction you was headed from."

"What were you intending to do here, sir?" asks his constable.

"Put yourself in my place. Do you want me to leave her?" I plead.

The look of my car, and my attitude, is not appealing. I'm old enough to know better and I'm suspicious in this garb. But the coppers are reassured by my comparatively respectable appearance. I may qualify as a bit of a crank.

"You're wasting our time. Police time."

"I really have to find my girl," I tell them.

"We can't allow that. Turn this boat around."

"I've got proper reasons to be anxious about her."

"I wouldn't have any fears," the Sergeant says, chuckling.

"She's mixed up in a bad scene," I argue.

"All of 'em's in trouble!" he guffaws.

"You must leave this area immediately," warns his colleague.

The group of police is gathering tightly around me in the car, like a range of blue mountains, blocking out my view.

"I'd advise you to turn around and drive home again," a young policeman tells me. "Between you and me there's going to be a disturbance here today."

Tension builds as I consider my options, unable to break my resolve to find Angie. In the background there's a harangue between a knot of hippies and the police. The guys are bare chested, drinking and smoking, carrying supplies, like outtakes from the Woodstock festival.

Eventually I press the button to send my side-window back up. I stare contemptuously ahead, refusing to recognise my opponents, like Fonda dealing with a traffic cop. I have calculated the risks: I realise there's little chance of breaking their lines. Silver bracelets never suited me. Not wise to play *Easy Rider* in this situation. They already have my name down, on record somewhere. In court they don't accept stage names. I don't want to get too far out.

I observe in frustration as squads of policemen advance across the land and form a cordon around the illegal gathering. I can't leave Angela to make her own luck. How should I move from here? I'm not going to rescue Lizzie or our first child.

Our angel.

On returning to the factory I have difficulty concentrating. The Whig Wham order this year is a priority and we need to work up the job. This will not be enough to keep Corrina sweet, as a lingering bitter taste informs me.

After lunch I go out on the shop floor. Wanting distraction from mental vibrations. James Nairn jumps out of his office to round on me. He has a further shock to add to our troubles. I was beginning to relax with our company's finances, when I was really having a smoke over a fuel dump.

"If we don't face our problems, it'll be the end of the road!" he warns. Always coining a phrase.

"Don't worry," I promise. Aiming for a friendly chat with colleagues, I attempt to palm him off.

"All of them will lose their jobs otherwise. You have to take these decisions," he insists.

"All right, man, I'm cognisant," I reply. "No need to rush me up to speed."

"You can't put this off, as if there's no tomorrow."

"Later."

"You oughta know that your company is ripe for take over," he says.

"Oh, really? Take over? Who's going to take over this company? Not while I'm still at the controls," I inform him. "Or afterwards."

"At your own peril," he warns.

This gives me pause. Over the years - decades - the company has been the object of generous offers and bids. Millions of pounds to sell up and rest my bones in a hammock for the remainder of my days. Too much money to count, even as my hands shook. Why didn't I buy myself a mansion in the Black Hills somewhere? I don't know if Luke will resist these temptations. He's the son and heir.

"Did we have any new approaches, then?" I enquire.

"The company is small to medium size, with stagnating profitability...they see opportunities there!"

"This business is my life time's passion," I remind him, tetchily. "This was the dream of three young people."

"Be that as it may," he comments.

"Definitely they would like our mark, the established brand," I conclude.

That way my name could last forever. But would I recognise myself?

James' next warning carries a more personal note. "In the short term you will have an individual acquiring a majority share stake."

"For real? Who could that be?" I reply. "What are you warning me about?"

"Shareholders are disgruntled by your performance," he says.

"Is my performance the issue?" I challenge.

"They may be tempted to sell," he persists.

"The traitors!"

"There's a chance that somebody will get their hands on a block of shares."

"Who has the motive to dominate this little company?" I quibble.

"Your girlfriend, that's who," he states.

I form a tense smile of disbelief. "My girlfriend?"

"That's right, Mr Sheer."

"Which one are we referring to?" I want to know.

"Ye'know, Freda. What's her name? Freda Fardine?"

"What about her?" I retort.

"Miss Fardine..."

"Farlane," I tell him.

"Well, that bosomy lassie... the one on the bike... she's been purchasing shares."

"Has she?" I remark.

"In a fury, Noah," he warns, with emphasis.

"In a fury?"

"That's correct. In a positive fury."

"Then we've got to stop her," I declare.

"As many shares as she can get her hands on. They're only too glad to be rid of 'em at the present time."

I wince. Have we become so devalued? "After everything we've been through together," I consider. But you never can predict.

"At present her stake is just below thirty per cent," he instructs me.

"Not a controlling stake. But we can't have too many private shareholders left can we?"

"Mrs Regina Hargreaves at fifty three York Terrace," he informs me. "I was just talking to the lady this morning."

"This is bloody outrageous."

"But what are ye goin' to do?" Nairn challenges.

"You're the money guru, aren't you?"

"But then you're the boss, Noah."

"No point arguing," I say. "My idea has always been to bring Lukey into the business...eventually...when he graduates. As soon as he develops an interest in kites and balloons."

James makes an ironical expression to himself.

"Does Corrina know what she's doing? The consequences to me and my family? Putting my son's future into danger? Taking away their inheritance. Man, we're not exactly the Murdoch family."

"Are your kids prepared to sell their shares?" Nairn presses.

For drugs? For porn? "I don't know...only Angie's old enough to sell at present."

"If your kids agree to sell then Miss Fardene will have a majority stake," he pronounces.

"Our sweet lord."

"If you don't move and take these hard decisions...to make people redundant and to reduce costs...overheads...the girl is going ta succeed!"

"She'd love to take me over," I declare.

"Then I would have a sharp word with the lassie," he advises.

"What happens if I should leave the scene, any time soon?"

"I don't know," he tells me. "We have to form a strategy."

"I'll tell you what happens," I say, "this company will be handed over to the famous Farlanes!"

"What's so famous about them?" he comments.

"She'll never get her oil stained fingers on my company. We'll go through those accounts again. We'll get an accountancy firm in to help. I'll get in touch with my solicitor," I say, moving resolutely through the building. My heart rate climbs. My eardrums are thumping.

"She could find herself an extremely rich young woman," James warns.

"Don't worry," I vow.

Nairn and I discuss Corrina's probable moves. He vends me yet another coffee as we talk. We take refuge in my office, trying to form a plan. Fortunately I still have one. An office.

I mention my daughter's escapades. My self-confidence has been shaken, but I've not yet gone completely to pieces. I want to remain on speaking terms with James. He's as easy to shock as my mother though.

"My family's breaking off into so many directions, I don't know if I'm keeping them together or chasing them away," I say, in navel gazing mode.

"Don't fret, Noah," he consoles.

"Maybe she's too far gone," I consider.

"Did you think about ballooning into the music festival?" he suggests.

"That's a bit far out."

"Fly over the top of them coppers. Are ye afraid they'll shoot you down from the sky?" he chuckles.

"How many miles d'you think that will be to fly?" I consider.

"About eleven miles, from take-off point."

My eyes narrow and my mouth contorts.

"You've flown that far for a cuppa tea b'fore now," he reminds me. "Well, for a pint of beer m'be!"

"There's no law against high spirits and balloon flights," I remark.

"This morning we had a brisk south easterly...so presuming there's been no shift, from the last reading, wind direction oughta be favourable."

"Do you think? What about wind speed factor?"

"Good question. That would be fifteen knots."

"I may find myself in New York for breakfast," I comment.

He shrugs, looks past me, with nothing more to add. The final decision to fly rests with the pilot.

"In these conditions, tricky to reach the festival location," I argue.

"You're the guy with a runaway daughter."

"How are these hippies going to react to my arrival? Landing at their festival in a hot air balloon," I say.

He shrugs again.

"The machinery we have to buy for ourselves. It isn't cheap or disposable, you know."

"I don't see why these scruffs should want to vandalise your machine. See how this balloon flight will solve the problem."

"You'll have to follow me on the ground. Take my car. I'll try hard to touch down near the festival. Then Angie and I can rendezvous with you later, at an agreed grid reference."

"There you have it, Noah," James concludes, crossing his arms; deal done.

# Chapter 32

Ashton Park is a large estate, formerly in the aristos' hands, a stone's throw from the Pirates' football ground. In those good old days the aristos were involved with coal mining, forestry and commissioning designs from Inigo Jones. In these duller days the estate belongs to the council and the grounds are a favourite launch site for Bristolian balloonists. I count myself among those Bristolian balloonists.

After we park and get out to look around, James surveys weather conditions ruefully. What is the flight plan this afternoon? It's a calm and pleasant afternoon at the moment, but the forecast isn't encouraging. The sky already has a tortured look, at the edge of a storm, air temperature falling in relation to the setting sun. But as an experienced pilot I should be able to cope, even as the atmospherics change. The most awkward stages of a flight are take-off and landing of course. This applies as much to airline pilots as to human cannonballs, to swans lifting from and landing into lakes as it does to gliders on the end of a line or coming down in silent isolation.

I have to get up to speed. James and I waste time bickering as we debate the most favourable take-off area. Finally I go along with his suggestion of a clear patch by Church Wood. A feathery tree line offers protection from the wind. Trying not to delay further we unpack our equipment efficiently and begin to assemble rigging. I ensure that the propane tanks are securely strapped to the main frame: then I attach burner hoses. Pre-flight checks take longer with just the two of us. We spread out the massive colourful balloon envelope across rough grass, ready for inflation. We run through further safety checks with great concentration. James is a man capable of such deep concentration and focus; valuable qualities both for a finance manager and an engineer. The only conversation between us is technical, purely related to the task ahead. Personal differences and past arguments are behind us, as if we're preparing to escape from Colditz; at times Big Pink does feel like Colditz, when there's a lack of other prisoners. This is how we work at the factory, despite our high jinks.

James takes special care examining a deflation panel. This mechanism is a vent at the side of the envelope, that the pilot can open and close to stabilise altitude and position, by trapping or releasing the warmer air that provides lift. As I adjust the pilot burner and check fuel pressure, the envelope is already, gradually, by increments, puffing out into the atmosphere before us: Like a grumpy giant clambering back on to his feet, the material begins to move and spread. Lazily at first but with increasing vigour, the giant sock fills and inflates.

Preparing myself for the adventure, I clamber into the carriage basket at this stage. This isn't the simple leap that it used to be for me. I have to be careful not to tear stitches or muscles - especially the master muscle. There's enough lift in the craft to raise an edge of the basket from terra firma; to tauten guide and anchor ropes. At this moment I can feel the 'artificial lift factor', which is a phenomenon in which the crown of the balloon is pulled up by warmer currents above. The problem is that the balloon quickly reaches colder currents on top, which has the effect of switching off your lift. In this situation your craft hasn't built up enough heat and lift to get up to a safe height. The danger is that the balloon will begin to pitch and fall at a hair-raising horizontal in that situation. This is a false persuasion, as the feeling of ascent comes too early. The danger is that the pilot is deceived into setting off. I've seen many balloons ripping through tree tops, tearing holes into materials and wallets.

Nairn and I check our flight plan and arranged references. He will track the craft along the way and zoom in on me if need be; if my flight shapes like a Brazilian free kick through thin air. I've burnt enough gas to warm the envelope to a full vertical. The dirigible is nudging upwards with determination. I catch the main line as James throws it towards me in the basket. Gently the wonderful bulbous contraption lifts, takes off majestically from the earth - awesome as a space ship, quiet as a dream. James gives the traditional lavish wave as a send-off; before rushing back to my car and starting off in hot pursuit. No way to recapture an errant daughter without defying the laws of gravity. Man, you need nerves like electrical cables.

Dragon fire leaps up into the void of the envelope. Storm clouds race across the horizon in front, lead-bellied as the old blues singer, resembling furious warriors in full armour. Psychedelic images are sliding and reconfiguring in front of my eyes. The fiery noise of burning gas compares to terrified amazement. You feel so perfectly - or imperfectly - alone. The gods have me in the palm of their hand. I am gripped by a fifteen knot wind, as strong as the jaws of Rachael's bull dog when he got hold of my trousers.

I get a picture of the patchwork of fields, hills and estates. Unfortunately the craft has only found a low altitude as it scuds down a slope towards the wood. The aerostat loses shape as it pushes out warm air and takes in cold. I'm shaping up for a fiasco in the tree tops. It's a perfect illustration of the manual's "don't do"s. What am I going to say to the other guys in the club, if they find out?

I think of Nairn grinding his teeth below, as he struggles with the Citroen's unfamiliar controls. I should have enough flying experience and miles in the logbook. But here I am skimming tree tops. I could be sharing my supper with the crows this evening and offering a few titbits of my own. I hallucinate about Angela throwing herself about at the festival, while I'm pulled limb from limb by hungry buzzards. To escape that horror I burn fuel like a Texan tourist in Alaska.

As a consequence the craft surges up into the sky like a plunger on a test-your-strength machine. The earth reduces below me as if I am watching camera shots from the side of the Space Shuttle. To counter this dangerous ascent I'm forced to tug on the deflation panel. This is misleadingly called a 'parachute'. After wasting so much propane I hope not to run out of fuel later on my return trip - assuming there's going to be a return trip. Jim Morrison didn't come back to reality after climbing into that final warm bath. I peer up desperately into the heavens of the balloon's interior; feeling like a midge in the great web of the planet. Where's the escape strategy?

While I vent warm air, that feels like steam from the pipes of a dragster, I manage to stabilise the craft. Excessive lift factor is removed as I level out at two hundred feet. We're still in one piece, despite my pantomime efforts at a bump and tangle. I'm on my way at last - to rescue my hedonistic princess from the tower of song.

Worse luck as wind speed picks up; cross currents distorting the shape of the balloon envelope. On any normal day the pilot doesn't hear the wind, doesn't feel the speed, as if the world's slipping away under your feet. This afternoon the balloon is crumpled in its trajectory - a paper streamer in a fan. Menacingly there's a school of cumulous clouds waiting in the distance, with the impact of bored and hungry sharks. From the ground cumuli are puffs of cotton wool. In fact they're created by vapour rising in warm air and then freezing in the middle atmosphere. If your balloon gets caught in this convection you'll finish up a cork on a Roman fountain. But there's nobody around to coo and point at the delightful trick. The pilot may get a kick out of the rise, but then he or she will freeze and asphyxiate in the stratosphere. After which he or she will plunge back down to earth, blue faced and bug eyed. Don't let anyone persuade you that balloonists are wimps or eccentrics. Man, you've got to be like Arnie when you consider leaping a'ship; particularly if you're an android with a dodgy component, no fault of your own.

The exhilaration of flying hasn't diminished. Hundreds, sometimes thousands of feet above the ground, sometimes with breathing gear. Even today, buffeted and sick with worry about Angela, I get a kick out of it. The mountains of the mind are invisible. Except for that trip to Japan, which turned my mind to Sushi. It's a big regret that I didn't travel the world, encounter different cities and cultures. Liz and I had that hunger and curiosity, before life intervened. I could only leaf through magazines and think what could have been. Somehow that desire became lost as we grew apart. My own sense of adventure comes from flying these balloons. They keep me to my commitments. They don't take me far away from home.

Liz can be dismissive of my sport. We used to play tennis together. At one time she was a good club player. I can still think of her stretching to the net. She never approved of my weekend vanishing tricks. She knows that I'm happiest at a thousand feet in a picnic basket. In her view it's a way to avoid real life. That's her critique of the sport. But then it's my look-out. Ironically she's the person I'm most eager to avoid these days. Not exactly the love of my life, but the alien with hostile green eyes, that she has turned in to, in contemporary times. Previously I was happy to come back down to earth, to hitch up with her again. So to speak, my *clear-eyed* lady of the lowlands.

High altitude was more appealing after marriage break-up. In this era Liz doesn't care what I do. In our youth we were regarded as the stellar couple; we were watched and followed by friends and associates, even when we ended up in a domestic horror of premature nappy pins, while cooped up in a fungi box. Our love was written up in the stars until we crossed each other. This was the biggest hangover in history and nobody else was invited. She can hardly bring herself to look at me, but I'll never see sixty. As long as she can write a deepest sympathy card. That'll be the last bouquet I ever get from her.

Only four miles remaining to Lime Tree Hill, if James' map references are correct. I'm out of radio communication. No sign of the French nose slugging its way along the lanes in hot pursuit. But I've no reason to question his lore. Checking off the charts, taking my bearings from landmarks, I find that I'm bang on target. Then again so was Apollo 13. I can't fly too low for fear of turbulence around buildings and of the buildings themselves. You have to be foolhardy to fly today - even to get your girl out of a fix.

The festival site comes into view as I pass over the next hill. This is where I drove earlier and was turned back by the cops, with fist fights breaking out in the fields. At a lower altitude I can see the broken lines of hippie convoys. The land is rushing under my feet; my heart is in my mouth. Is that why I keep it shut these days? I force myself to keep calm. There's an amazing incentive to keep calm. I can hear Wickham, my consultant, jabbering again, like the Old Testament God:

"Avoid situations of extreme stress. Learn to take life sedately. Don't overtax yourself," he urged.

Does Wickham have any ideas how to get this balloon down safely?

"Change your ways. Make sacrifices in your life style."

Don't enjoy my sports, stop listening to music, give up sex, abandon my roustabouts? I didn't take any notice.

Within another mile I notice the contours of Lime Tree Hill. This ancient landmark emerges through metallic sunset hues.

The balloon is sweeping over the top of woodland in a green rush. The craft swings out lee side and finds cool currents. In this context cool does not mean hot. Man, I can't claim to be fully in control. I'm flying by the seat of my pants. It's like plucking guitar strings with loose teeth. I can distinguish police columns and further snarl-ups of hippie and traveller vehicles, as well as the weekenders and pleasure seekers trying to join in. In the further distance I notice the music festival itself has got underway. A screech of white noise, a shaken blanket of wiry sound, greets my ears at this height. Man, I'm serving myself up to them like Captain Ahab to Moby Dick. I peer down from my basket to see police running and waving their arms at me. The balloon and I are breaking their checkpoint. They are demanding that I come down and report to them; offering my details. They couldn't have anticipated some guy arriving by hot air balloon. They may believe I'm a hippie crazy enough to attempt this. Now that's what I call a love of music.

Nairn's strategy is working like a dream. The law of lift has beaten the constabulary. I'm having a good trip so far. The big nosed car may be left far behind, so hopefully James will avoid a police interview himself; circle the festival site and find our rendezvous reference for later.

"Ahoy there coppers!" I call down. "How high's your conviction rate? Ha, ha!"

If they notice my awesome movements, they can't hear me. They merely stop to observe the antics of some lunatic balloonist. I'm well beyond their reach. A new dimension comes into play and leaves them baffled.

The sound of freeform noise grips my eardrums like the incisors of a Rottweiler. My phantasmal machine continues to drift and tug towards the musical tempest ahead. My feet surf over the roofs of hippy charabancs like the slippers of an Arabian prince on his magic carpet. Then, while I'm fearful of crash landing into their mobile homes, the wind drops for a spell, into a type of mid-ocean lull. This leaves the Ancient Mariner dangling in his rigging; his paranoia fully dramatized.

The young savages hail me with waves and squeals from below. I have become a major attraction. Why do people always react in this way to a balloon? Big deal, this is how I chill out in my free time. Angela must have noticed me in the sky too. Aware of commotion, she would have looked up, and realised I was coming to save her. I assume she would get away and try to reach me, so that I can lift her out of that gangster's dubious clutches. We deliberately chose an aerostat with a bold and colourful design, so that Angie couldn't miss me. She's always kept us guessing. Your own imagination is most shocking. Some days you had better keep the theatre dark.

Meanwhile I continue to drift over the village, pursued by a horde of children and yapping dogs beneath. I reach for my bottle of aspirins. Not only to keep my blood from freezing. The cardiac patient more or less keeps afloat on warfarin and aspirins.

Like the hyperbole of fantasy, the huge aerostat floats over the landscape.

You can make your dreams come true, but often the nightmares take over.

My glorious balloon descends - no use burning more fuel - finding warmer faster currents. I'm uncomfortably near to the ground and, skimming at knots, a violent encounter with youth culture is imminent. These perils are confirmed when I come out into the festival area. I'm headed directly above the action, with rock groups thrashing, kids throwing themselves about in ecstasy, primal hunters fuelled by their magic mushrooms. My craft always follows the breeze and there's nothing I can do to change direction. At one point I am no more than ten feet above their heads in the arena. Hairy is the word that comes to mind here.

They believe that my arrival is a deliberate stunt, as part of the entertainment. But I'm not the Trojan horse I'm just the matchstick man. Many of them jump up trying to touch the basket. A carpet of astonished and delighted faces unrolls beneath me, as if I am sailing on a sea and leaving a wake behind me. People raise their arms to greet my journey, as the balloon is a beautiful dream to them. I continue to peer over the side of the basket at them, up here, on Desolation Row. It isn't necessary to drop any tabs of acid in this life.

The current moves me. I don't crash into the stage or those stacks of speakers and bins. I pass fully over the flying hair of those four guys on stage. Long hair looks as incredible to me now as the thought of deep pockets. The band is definitely whipping up a storm, whoever they are. Finally I ebb towards the shore of this wild scene. Angela couldn't overlook me. Ironically the festival is safer than the narcotic charms of Jakes. The guy needles me.

I need to decide on a landing point. I dampen the burner unit, cut off fuel, preparing to kiss grass. The craft is descending responsively to below tree top level. Speed increases as it sweeps down: land slants menacingly towards me. It's coming into the area that James intended. That's good news. But the landing isn't.

Obviously it's dangerous. It's essential to pull on the 'parachute' at this moment, to deflate the envelope. In preparing for ground zero I get a grip on handles inside the basket, bend my knees into a strong posture. In moments the basket comes into juddering contact with the slanted field. The basket rips over on its side and drags me over the lumpy and stony earth. This isn't a beautiful experience. I'm going to get a shock as well as cuts and bruises. I don't want too many of these experiences. But my ticker's still working and that's the most important thing.

Rough landings are a typical indignity with this sport. You can understand why Lizzie preferred an armchair. I stay where I am after impact, perfectly still for a while. Check out the potential damage, deep breathing, checking on my ventricles left and right. Ballooning equipment is strewn around, as I wait for the inner mechanism to regulate. I cradle my knees against nausea, while the colourful balloon envelope deflates around me, like an enormous piece of gift wrap. So what happened to the gift? I'm completely still even while the universe continues to spin.

Staggering up, brushing myself down, there are no hippies or cops in view. Not even an irate farmer with a shotgun cocked. The craft drifted about a half mile away from the actual festival. That's a good hiking distance for a guy in my condition. The distance will safeguard my equipment, which I quickly conceal, ready for a return journey. I can't be too fussy about losing gear. There are more troubling issues to look at. Such as where is Angela at this time? Why isn't she striding out to join me?

Where are you at this moment *'Queen' Elizabeth*, when I need you most?

# Chapter 33

By all appearances I'm the biggest taxpayer in the area. But I'm not the only middle-aged fossil. I look like a member of the Caravan Club on the roam for a shower block and a supermarket. The street plan of the festival has the complication of a Middle Ages town. I notice that a good portion of the citizens are in the fourth flush of life. In contrast to me they have never *stopped* being hippies or alternative, in terms of dress and lifestyle. They haven't compromised *ever*. This wouldn't recommend them to the affections of my former wife. I even bump into hippie grandparents. They're busy looking after hippie grandchildren.

Not that I'm rigged out in my dress suit, you should understand. I was hip enough to dress down for this jig. Problem is that I could never dress down far enough. Definitely not, if Angela is going to recognise me, or take me seriously. No matter how disorientated, I shouldn't lose context with fashion sense. I have to admit that I'm out of touch with the youth culture scene.

I fall back on my idea of Bob Dylan exploring the lanes and alleys of a North African coastal city. He was a solitary man in that period; he was down to his faded embroidered jeans, with a soft cotton shirt billowing in the dry and spiced air. There was a lost and confused expression as he looked back over a shoulder. Man, I can see where that feeling came from.

The festival doesn't radiate a hostile or aggressive vibe. Despite a police cordon and intimidation around the site, there's a peaceful and cheerful vibe. They could have suspected me of working undercover - an under-kaftan man - if anybody saw me stepping out of that balloon. Even if I am smart-casual or even bourgeois-rock 'n' roll, nobody hassles me around here. No one confronts me about what I am doing here. They leave me to my own cloud: which isn't cloud nine. But can I make out where I'm going to?

There's a rainbow of tie-dye on show; a revival of the whole show of hippie display and paraphernalia; some ironic some straight-up. I'm too hung up about Angie's immediate safety and future to have my fortune told. Certainly I will need a clairvoyant to locate her. Elizabeth's supernatural pretensions would fail me here.

After that I intend to burn my way out of here. Before Angie swallows more uppers and downers and gets laid by some guy as wide as the Bristol Channel. All I can say is that Daddy's coming in with the tide. My only concern is to steer her away from danger, before Jakes gets ticked and blackens her eyes, for all his outlaw charisma and good looks.

A police helicopter clatters over our heads. This could be a response to my high jinks in the aerostat. Man, I'm just trying to find a direction home for Angie. The hope of finding her becomes more ridiculous by the moment - as distant as that helicopter. I waste limited time and energy by losing orientation. I trudge through crowds of rough humanity. I caught up with Luke in a riot, yet can't always fall back on coincidence. There must be tens of thousands of souls about the area. I know that I don't really belong here. I'm out of character.

But I can't allow that girl to escape from us, even if she is some kind of artist. Rebellious daughters aren't easy to bring back. Or should I understand that she has her own life? This concept frightens us, as it is very different to what we experienced, but should we intervene? She's put another crack into my thermometer.

Did Angie miss my arrival? How could she? My entrance was more colourful than the national folk culture of Uzbekistan. The idea was that we were going to find each other. So what's the big draw of that dope fiend? No sign of her here. How could there be? I have to keep some irony between me and the stage. Another rock band is going out of its collective heads on those boards. They send tidal waves of skull-splitting feedback ricocheting about the surrounding hills, to roars of approval from the audience. Man, I doubt if the wildlife shares their enthusiasm.

Hard rock, metal or thrash, isn't Angie's scene. Her musical tastes orient around songs and dance style: often artificial heartbeats.

da dah, da dah, da dah, da dah

When she's at home with me she laps up Sixties and contemporary pop and rock. We coincide there. I don't know which tribe or youth movement she belongs too in this era. I have faith she'll keep to the edges of extremes, if not exactly completely out of danger.

There's a big market day atmosphere at the festival; a buzzing trade in everything; food and clothes, pots and pans, face paints and body piercing, bootleg music and incense sticks: not just narcotics. This place reminds me of the West Country gypsy fairs of my childhood. That's back on the planet Zog of course. The summer of love's been through a hard frost since then. Don't know if we'll see the flowers bloom again.

Temporarily the search for my daughter is abandoned. I decide to hang out for a while, to get my head around the situation. All that stress and sport has made me hungry and I snap up two 'veggie-burgers' at one of the food stalls. Not sure what *kind* of vegetables went into this concoction - or *herbs*. My meal is served up by an alarming girl in a leather bra. She thinks that *I'm* the startling misfit. I feel no nearer to the situation between Jakes and my daughter. There's a grungy guy selling pots of home brew from a plastic bucket in the back of his camper. A few mugs of pokey tackle help to calm me down. All great minds drink alike.

If you can get your head around it there's plenty of good weed. I sit on a cushion on the top of a box and watch the sun set behind woods. Lime Tree Hill is crowned by a spectacular cloud formation. Like God blushing. What's he embarrassed about? Plenty to choose from, I guess.

This ancient, resonant area of England has a mystical beauty and powerful draw. While this flaming western sky is developing I experience a strong connection to place: I go through the experience of my hazardous balloon flight. That's where I feel most fulfilled. I can imagine myself up there still, caught by the powerful forces of those elusive elements. There's a mystery in that, which still makes sense.

As I sieve the swampy beer I grow conscious of an observant presence. There's a crawling sensation where the guillotine should come down. I realise that a festival-goer is studying me, although

I don't immediately turn to find out who. Anyway I'm occupied in my head, trying to ignore pictures of Angie with that fastidious thug. You've got to stay cool, I tell myself, because you don't know what kind of psycho is wandering the fields.

I'm not used to attending music festivals alone, as always I'd be in company with Liz and, very soon after, Angie strapped to my back or to Lizzie's back. It was even known for Corrina and me to camp out - albeit in relative luxury - at the Whig Wham world music weekend last summer. But there's nothing more dismal than being solitary at a festival. Looking like Jean-Paul Sartre on a package holiday. All I can do is stare ahead, rubbing my grey stubble, running fingers through phantom floppy-fringe. Well, I'm glad that somebody's taken an interest in my existence. Otherwise I could have melted back down into the ground like an old mushroom.

The curious bystander is a distinctive girl. I've been chasing after beautiful girls all my life - why pause now? She stands there watching me from the edge of the trees. Lovely as a deer, though not as shy. She's got a whippet dog on a string, that's all eyes and sexual organs, skinny and bent backed. Maybe the unfortunate mutt has a heart condition, though it must be a natural look. This girl's an absolute stunner, I realise, even if she's tortured her hair up into ratty plaits, dyed green and red. She's decorated her face with painted circles, in the fashion of Native Americans or Stone Age People; or even Joni Mitchell escaping into the wilderness to escape fame and fortune. She has a silver ring through one nostril. So who is this warrior queen?

Her native dress is too thin for the chilly evening conditions. Really Native Americans would run for their lives. She weighs my mood and presence carefully; she tries to place me in her universe. Exactly like a deer scenting seductive danger. Then her curiosity becomes too much for her. She has to check out this peculiar beast caught in the trap.

"Looking sorry for yourself," she declares.

My gaze back is ancient in origin. "Am I?"

"Not enjoying yourself then?"

I grin unhappily towards her. "Not especially."

"What's wrong with you then?"

"Feeling like one in a billion chance," I comment. Defensively I cradle the pewter of bog water.

The girl approaches on soft feet - leading the whippet - and circles around me, amidst clouds of frozen breath. She takes in all my freakish and unexpected contours. The pooch switches his glance between her and me, a thin tongue hanging out, showing studded canines. Maybe he's been drinking some of this beer too.

"It's a beautiful sunset though, isn't it," I observe.

She follows my gaze heavenwards for a moment. "Awesome, mate." We share a West Country twang.

"Can you tell me something?" I call.

"What's that? What can I tell you, mate?"

"I'm just curious. Do you believe in any kind of afterlife? By any chance?"

"No chance, just this one," she replies.

"Only asking."

"But I completely believe in this one," she emphasises. She takes a firmer stance.

"Right, thanks girl. Crazy idea really isn't it."

"Doesn't have to be," she says.

"Many rooms in the mansion?"

She allows herself a smile, as if the soft face is made of rock. "Why not."

"If only there's a spare one," I add.

Far out thoughts. Powerful to pharaohs and medieval field-hands. Not only to contemporary computer nerds in tanks. Stonehenge wasn't a picnic site. I don't have a sky gazing character. I'm a sportsman, or used to be, and I recognise the world around me. We all have to battle with the forces of divine exasperation. Frank Noggins actually told me that humanity is part of a computer programme. We're a circuit in the mind of an original creator. Reality is the consequence of a big bang in the head of that giant Geek. Frank really believes that. Right, so now he's got his thumb on the delete key, this Geek. Mister and missus Noggins and the Geek.

We get to talk this woman and me - overcoming initial suspicion. The big music festivals gave this opportunity to interact with many people; for an exchange of contrasting thoughts and experiences. Away from the tall buildings and confined spaces, the mind can open up; dare I say 'expand'? Even when we returned to our regular lives, to humdrum existence in conventional society, we were never quite the same. I wonder if my daughter will have similar experiences here. I couldn't begrudge Angela that - I couldn't deny her the chance. But, I guess, I'm just wary if she wants to open up the doors of perception.

"Yeah, I was always hanging out at the big rock festivals," I tell her. "You know, in a younger incarnation. That was the authentic period, you know, when we turned machine guns into ploughshares."

"What, like a youth opportunity scheme," she retorts.

"Authority branded us a bunch of dangerous weirdoes," I say.

"Are you a weirdo?" she wants to know.

The idea causes me thought. "We were proud to call ourselves freaks. Misfits of conventional society. Hopeless idealists," I blab. I've probably got Stuart Maybridge in mind. "Sit down here next to me. We can put our heads together," I suggest.

"I'm cool standing," she tells me.

But it isn't a chat up line. I'm not scheming to conjoin anything but our thoughts. "Don't worry, that's cool," I assure her. "The name's Noah."

"Pru," she returns.

"Great name, Pru. Excited to meet you."

"Cool."

"So what's the hippie movement about in this era? Is it a lunatic fringe or merely a fashion statement?" I blurt out. *Something's* happening.

"You'd better cut back on the grog," she advises. She continues to watch me carefully. Her tender face too healthy, too ruddy from the out of doors. "Don't we have a right to exist?" she challenges.

I shuffle on my cushioned crate. "Tolerance is essential," I say.

"You're *tolerating* us?" she wonders. She whisks back the braided hair, while adopting that firm posture. Striking looking, yet not a girl to tangle with. She reminds me of Lizzie in her youth - Amazonian.

"I don't agree with the cops," I assure her.

"But you're disapproving of us," she concludes.

"From my angle you're trying to escape from reality."

"Don't you know how to enjoy yourself?" she wonders.

I furrow my pale clammy brow. "There's nothing wrong with a few home comforts, from my..."

The girl scoffs.

"I'm just squaring up to these contemporary times," I argue. "I can't turn back the clock." If only.

"My generation has the right to live how it likes," she declares. A flush comes up through the war paint. "You're well out of order," she growls. The whippet turns up his eyes, nervously adoring.

"Well girl, you're entitled to drop out of society...if that's what you want to do."

"There's nothing to drop out of is there!" she argues.

"Then there's no chance of changing things, is there?"

"Change what?" she wishes to know.

"The world, the future, society," I reply.

"We don't belong to society."

"More than your hairstyle or your consumer choices. You know where I'm coming from," I say. I take another swig of the swill. Lord knows what was in this or those burgers.

"You're arguing to me, are you, that your generation was more political?"

True or not, I'm just trying to survive, in the current historical epoch. "We were more conscious," I argue. Often barely.

"So what did you do to change the world?" she retorts.

"What did we do? It was more a case of what we aimed to do."

"So you just talked about it and jumped into bed together."

"At least we cared." For comfort I take another slurp of radical homebrew.

"Bullshit," she replies.

"I've got to admit that, you know, many of the radicals lived in suburbs."

"You're fucking up your image now," she says.

"You kids are living like this, naturally, outside of conventional society," I drawl. "Yet that isn't a decision, a political choice...a principled choice...it's because you don't have any choice."

"Bullshit. We *choose* to live the way we do," she replies hotly.

My bottom tenses on the brocaded cushion. "Fair dues, girl. Straight up, it isn't meant as a criticism."

"There's always been alterative people, travellers and hippies. We're as old as the land."

"But you're regarded as a social problem," I risk.

"We're not any kind of problem. Social or otherwise."

"Right, so you take the idea of freedom at face value?"

Pru considers the issue, shifting her elegant weight from tuft to tuft.

"I've never wanted to work in a factory or an office, Noah. That's not in my nature," she confides. "Makin' small talk and waiting for the next tea break. And I could have had that kind of life, you know."

"Depends on the type of office. How do you mean?" I wonder.

"I was engaged to this guy, see. More'n three years ago. It was difficult to turn him down, because he was a real sweetheart. But he had this really horrible idea. Which was, that I was gonna stay at home. It was me who would look after our kids. Yes, and I would be having them too," she agrees. "When they came along. He was talented see. And he was going to have the fascinating career. He was going to achieve and discover. I was going to tag along and applaud. Only I wasn't gonna do that," she explains, puffing clouds of ice.

"You couldn't put your trust in another human being? To bring kids into the world?" What have I been dragging on? I pull my jacket tighter around me. The shadows are long.

"I'm gonna have a tribe of kids, and they're gonna be as free as I am," she insists. She runs her hand up an ear of long grass, while scratching an itchy calf with her boot.

"Why does straight society hate you so much?" I consider.

"I don't know, we just get on with it, to tell you the truth."

"What you represent is a danger," I say. "The danger that there could be something else out there for people...if only we had the guts to follow."

"We don't want to get too popular," she says.

This could be more proof that reality is getting away from me. We'd better summon a magistrate to find out.

"They persecute you, not to mention prosecute," I say.

"Then they can sleep peacefully at night," Pru agrees.

"We say we believe in freedom, but when radical politicians ever get into power, what do they do? They create extra police powers and knock people around their heads," I argue.

"Why don't they leave everyone in peace?" she says. Frozen air billows from her delicate nostrils. Revolution is in the air.

"That's right, leave people in peace. Live and let live."

"This land doesn't belong to anyone."

"Doesn't it?" I reply, bewildered.

"No mate, why should we be pushed off the land? I was raised on this land and it's always belonged to everyone."

"If only," I say.

"If the 'cream crackers' lose their rights, then so does everybody else."

"Sorry, what's that?" I reply, leaning forward, fearing the influence.

"We're making a stand just by being here. There's a new type of enclosure going on in this land. Know what enclosure is?" she asks.

"'Course I do, girl. I took a minor in History."

"If we lose our freedom then the rest of you do. Do you get me? We're a thorn in their side. Otherwise there's no point to any of this." She spreads her arms to embrace the horizon, where the ashes of the sun are going out. "We might as well run about topping each other," she continues, "stealing and robbin', d'you see?"

"Which is exactly what's going down," I concur. "When my generation was young we aspired to Woodstock ideals. In this contemporary era my son aspires to being a hoodlum in downtown Los Angeles or wherever." What did I know?

"There are millions of egos colliding, looking for the advantage, refusing to take any notice of each other," she tells me.

It's music to my ears. "I see where you're coming from."

"It's a gi-normous fuck-up on the grandest of scales," she concludes.

"Right. Now we have the job of repairing the damage," I philosophise. "We've got to straighten out this twisted planet, before it's too late."

"It's all about get rich quick, find the perfect partner. Absolutely fucking bonkers," she offers, in her fruity tones. "They think a soul is something you sell."

I think about the idea and like it.

"There's no valuing people's true spirits. It's more about how much money we can screw out of them," she says, animatedly.

"Right, we're in the same place," I say. "You and I."

Mind expanding stuff. At least it was expanding mine. The girl and I drop into companionable thought. Sid the whippet - as he's named - continues to shift his weight nervously between delicate toes. I get to the bottom of my brew, without finding any interpretation to the dregs and believing that Angie is lost. Lost from me at least.

# Chapter 34

Prudence observes me warily at her distance. A flow of lumpen humanity passes beyond us, resembling the citizens of Blake's London taking the poet's advice. It isn't hard to interpret this chick's thought patterns - 'so you think *we* are weird!'

I definitely have the smack of a worried parent, even if I could be a maverick pot-holer with a taste for radical rhetoric.

Uneasy curiosity gets the better of her. "What are you doing here anyway? For the music?" she enquires.

"Do you call that music? Aren't I allowed to enjoy myself?" I counter. "I was one of the original hippies. I've got all the Dylan bootlegs," I brag.

"This isn't a bootleg, this is our way of life," she insists. If she had her bow and arrow she'd run me through.

"I've come out here to rescue my daughter. If you want to know," I say. "She ran off with some dodgy druggie bloke."

"Wouldn't that describe most of them? So how old is this daughter of yours?" Her alarm bells are synchronising.

"Does that matter? She's still only young. In her twenties."

"Ha, ha, that's a laugh," she cracks. "I thought you meant she was like twelve or something like that."

I stare ahead, blankly disillusioned. "She's still putting herself at risk," I argue. "Even if you believe that twenty-something is mature." Maybe it's old enough to drop out of society.

"She'll be really pleased to see *you*," Pru remarks cuttingly. She tilts back her warm rosy face and treats me to a filthy cackle. She's got a sense of humour this girl. "What a lovely surprise your little girl's gonna have. *Hello Daddy!*" Her laughter goes on a long run like Art Tatum in a joyous mood.

"Right, have your fun, girl, but she scrammed to this festival, you know, and I don't have a clue where she might be," I bleat.

"Can't she look after herself?" Pru tells me. Mixing satire with a statement of the obvious is devastating.

"That would depend on the company," I say.

"Is she a hippie? your daughter?" A free spirit in common?

I consider. "No, she isn't a hippie. She just came here to enjoy herself. There's a rave going on."

"She's a cheesy quaver!"

"She's a wotsit?" I ask.

"A cheesy quaver. A raver. Stinks of perfume and she wouldn't be seen dead without a slap of Number 7."

This character sketch takes some while to decipher. "No, you haven't caught my Angie very accurately there," I conclude.

"You said she's not a hippie or a traveller, didn't you?"

But my life went electric years ago and I've learnt to withstand audience jibes.

"Well, I'm not going to find her in this crowd," I lament. "What hope is there?"

"Why don't *we* go and find her? If you want," Pru tells me.

My glance returns sceptically. "Just like that? That's hardly likely," I say.

"Trust me because I know my way around," she insists. "Come on."

"Oh yes? You sure about that?" Blood rushes to my extremities, as I struggle to my feet.

"Don't worry. Follow me," she says, waving me towards her.

"You've got my daughter all wrong. She's just mixed up in her beliefs."

"Who really understands themselves?" Pru remarks. "We just limit our potential, when we think we have." Potential, or *meaning*? "We have to remain open to everything. See what's around the next corner," she argues. Not too many corners about this place.

"If there's anything there to be found," I suggest. The more you love life the greater your sense of loss.

Angela struggles to find purpose or direction to her life. Sometimes I worry if that isn't related to her upbringing. That's complete rubbish of course, yet this concern plays on my mind.

"So are we setting off to find this sweet little girl of yours?" Pru calls to me. "Come on, we'll follow the trail of puppy dog tails, sugar and spice."

Pru's invitation couldn't be turned down. This lost balloonist needed a festival guide. She leads me around the makeshift lanes and paths between hippie home-from-homes. She cuts a tall and striking figure in the twilight - as if it is Lizzie walking ahead of me; guiding the way, taking command. My mind should be focusing on the search for Angie - my errant daughter - but it's wandering towards Mount Venus again, if you catch my drift.

The girl's lithe waist becomes traced into my senses, like a lost comfort - the lost Lizzie. She's tangled in the lush beauty of this landscape, provoking fantasies of permanence. I thought about sticking with Pru and her friends in the convoy. What if I spent the rest of my limited life-span travelling with them? Going from town to town, hedgerow to hedgerow? *Super Tramp* rides again.

The travelling people are tough to endure these privations. Yet they don't have strict residential qualifications. Anybody is welcome. Life has ruined my reputation and these are tolerant people. I can pitch a tent with Pru and adopt the easy riding freedom of the open road again. What do I have to lose? More to the point, what do I have to gain?

If this has the ring of ridiculous fantasy, nothing was holding me back. I was convinced that their way of life could make me happy and forgetful. I could make this radical gesture to obliterate the question "why me?" This question came up regularly in the small hours of every night and my brain never found an answer. This question left me soaked through with terror and confusion. How many cold sweats can you get through in a single night?

For months I've been dicing with death - shaking under his bony grip and cruel glare - and now I prefer human company and spiritual fulfilment. You may say that I just seek escape - don't we all? To know there's something out there greater than we are. It's the comfort of knowing that we're something more than just the passengers of random chaos. You've got to serve somebody, in the great man's words. If the surgeon had taken this attitude he would never have fitted the faulty heart valve to my existential pump. He sliced me open, pulled my ribs apart and inserted something alien and lethal inside me, likely to split into infinity at any second. Call me squeamish or ungrateful, but I don't regard that as the gift of life.

Shack up with this sexy child-of-nature woman, my inner voice urged. Snuggle down under a patchwork quilt in front of an open caravan fire. Share a hearty breakfast with her on the step between an open door. Maybe she wouldn't be freaked by my operation scars and slack muscles. What bliss that could be, I thought. She'd help me to feel young again, with the past reimbursed. This beautiful hippie girl would be my companion. She'd prompt me to drop out of society again, just shy of my forty ninth birthday.

This fantasy lasted for a few minutes, as I stumbled after her. What caused the alien to drop down to Earth? When did reality check me out? It could have been the look of our neighbours, the quality of living quarters, or the packs of dogs and uncool clothes. In truth it was Angela's likely reaction to any decision to drop out - as well as the urgent need to find her. I couldn't insist that she go to university, if I went to live in a gypsy caravan with a chick half my age. Man, it would be a hard sell. You can only fit so many crazy daydreams into a single lifetime.

On the other hand it was a *beautiful* daydream.

Pru serviced as *agent provocateur*. If she was sexy she was also incredibly high. At this point I saw myself as an ageing rambler, trudging back to dull suburbia. She could never guess the ideas percolating in my brain; arguably the dregs from a bygone era. Then I came out with the dumbest chat up line of the festival.

"You're such a gorgeous girl, Pru," I declare. Hard to believe that the daydream was this crazy, but here it was, vocalised.

"What?" she declares, stopping to face me.

"I said that...I've met some gorgeous chicks in my time, but you're one of the tops."

"*Chicks?* You want your head examining, don't you?" she spits.

"If you changed your cosmetics a bit," I say, taking in her vivid war paint. "Modelling agencies would pay a fortune to take you on."

"You're haking me on, mate!" she searches my drained features, aghast.

"You look like a Shrimp' girl," I say.

"Why are you being so fucking offensive?" she wants to know.

"Don't be offended, my ex-wife also looked like a Shrimp' girl."

"Did she? You told her that? You think that helps?" she retorts.

"Why ruin your looks?"

"Do you want me to ruin yours?"

Her attitude is really puzzling to me. This is meant to be high praise. She should be flattered.

"I'm not so self-obsessed," I tell her.

"Your sexist bullshit just makes me puke," she complains, turning the words over like cowpats.

"Is it? Is it sexist?" I wonder, baffled.

"It's to escape from the shackles of fucking patriarchal fucking propaganda, that's what I'm talking about!"

"Right, sound," I tell her, enthusiastically. "That's well put."

At this stage self-respect has gone back into the bar and is slumped across the counter.

"Amazing you found some sorry woman to marry you," Pru tells me, "if that's the best you can do. Do you really have a daughter? I'd guess you must have adopted her as a single parent or something. Compare me to a fucking shrimp and think it's a tremendous compliment," she sneers.

"No, you don't quite get it," I bleat.

"That how you treat your precious little girl? Is that why she decided to run away from home?" she wonders.

"No... Great! Yes." This was getting weird.

At this she skips off again. Even Sid the whippet snarls his disapproval, from the end of his lead. Fortunately I'm thinking for myself again. Totally stable people don't normally drop out of society and go live in the wilds.

Perhaps sexism has always been my Achilles heel. I should never have married Elizabeth. That is I should never have married a girl *like* Elizabeth. The relationship was never going to work out long term, even if she hadn't become pregnant. Even if we were the *Jules et Jim* of our set, Lizzie, Stuart and me. We should have left it there. Even if I agreed with 'women's liberation' as they called it then, I kept these unconscious prejudices. I went to Rupert Lloyd's party meetings and to his ideological study groups, making wise cracks from the corners. Did I really take any notice of Lizzie's ideas and convictions? These sound like extreme statements about our past. God knows if there's any truth in them.

We guys made the girls sing backing vocals. They did a great job, but it was never enough for them. We prevented women from writing their own songs or playing their own instruments - with a few exceptions. Guys got worked up about the injustices of society and governments, while treating their girlfriends badly. What was wrong with us, that we treated them so meanly? *Tough guys*, we thought ourselves.

When girls were willing to sleep with you, this was a big change in consciousness. If by some chance they got pregnant, many of us guys were not interested any more. Lizzie would take care of everything - including the baby. This was just before the pill was widely available. But I was proved wrong about that, wasn't I? Lucky we really loved each other - we were passionately committed to one another - and felt that we could deal with everything. Or Lizzie did.

Even during the excruciating divorce hearing I couldn't express myself properly. I couldn't express my feelings and opinions as I wished - adequately. I can't identify exactly what went wrong. I generated enough bad radiation to power a submarine on an Armageddon mission. There was something wrong about my way of expressing myself; as expressed on the faces of everybody else present in the room. That's why her greasy lawyer was admiring my guts.

Anyway she had me done and dusted before we reached court. Way before the cold fishes were slapping me about. Judgement in relationships is taboo - a big no no. Judging the person you love brings catastrophic after-shocks. When the big criticisms start it's the beginning of the end. Divorce courts are exactly in that business. Man, suddenly judgements are all you get! After she chose to use the ultimate weapon it was impossible to forget.

From that point on I knew that it was more than just a simple twist of fate. A simple twist of the knife more like.

In relation to Angie I'm aware of double standards working in me. Double agents of the unconscious.

"Why are you so desperate to find your daughter?" Pru asks.

We are striding side by side now. Not sure where we are headed.

"Where should I start? She's hanging out with a guy who beat up his previous girlfriend."

"Doesn't sound any good," she admits.

"None whatsoever."

"Can't she look after herself? Wouldn't it turn out better that way?"

"Can I leave it to chance, with such a guy?"

"Do you know the bloke's name?" she asks.

"Will it help you to know his name? You think you may know him?" I comment.

"Try me!"

"Jakes. Adam Jakes."

"Him? I know Jakes," she says.

"He's running this festival," I tell her.

"Hard to avoid in these parts!"

I return her gaze with tense inevitability.

"Right, I'd guess so."

"He sent the pigs in the wrong direction. So this festival could happen. He set up a power generator. You know, *for the music*? And he spoke to the farmer bloke about using his fields."

"The farmer doesn't mind about this?"

"Yes, he does mind, but we asked him first."

"Thoughtful wasn't it. But what do you know about Jakes?" I press.

"Not so much, mate. But if he organises our festivals, I don't ask too many questions."

"That's a bit cynical, isn't it?" My turn to be critical.

"All right, mate, if you're so worried about your sweet little girl... If she's with Jakes then there's reason to be worried," Pru warns. "We'd better do summat about it hadn't we? I don't know anything about the bastard's love life. I thought he'd already got a mirror. He doesn't have much love for us hippies and travellers. He exploits us really, but we get something out of him too," she shrugs.

"I have to get to our Angie fast," I say.

"All right, he isn't going anywhere fast," she replies.

"I wouldn't bet on that," I comment.

*Tough guy.*

# Chapter 35

There are bonfires circling the festival as if to ward off evil spirits. As we pick off the path I notice the trees are moving; the woods are filled with people collecting timber, caught by flickering heat and light, resembling wood sprites or scouting soldiers. Pru leads me up the next incline, from where we stop to gain the vantage, not just to get my puff back; she guides my eyes down towards the lee side, to the sight of a futuristic silver trailer, like a prop from *2001: a Space Odyssey*. This caravan definitely isn't another hippie charabanc. The whole rig is stationed to escape any sign of a dark blue uniform or the machinery of law. This capsule has a sinister metallic cast that makes me jittery.

Pru points a finger at the end of her stretched arm. "I'd reckon that's where you'd find Adam," she suggests.

"Should I expect our Angela to be keeping him company?" I speculate.

Pru and I observe the activity around the trailer; the various comings and goings. We see a pair of strong armed guys stepping out, apparently disgruntled. There are more heavy vibes going down there. A sense of danger pervades. In an angry mood the two heavies walk away, seeking other diversions. I'm happy to stick to the festival fringes, assuming there's no agitprop.

There are thousands of youngsters bopping around in the fields to our right. They are worshipping before a massive stack of speakers, booming a massive electronic pulse, that's affecting my own heart rate - triggering a background of physiological panic. Those kids will keep up their manic dancing until the small hours, if not to the break of dawn, stoked up by truckloads of uppers. In our youth it was amphetamines and speedballs at first. We'd be wide awake at some folk or jazz club in Bristol or London until the milkman arrived; so that often we'd buy a bottle from him. These kids have come from towns and villages far and wide to dance like this, from ordinary caring families, so why should I worry? More positive to think of my daughter enjoying herself in such a cheerful crowd of her peers. I try to identify Angie or any of her playmates. That's an impossible task from this distance. Except that it's unlikely she will be with them. It's more cheerful if she's dancing with friends but I believe she's with Jakes. Despite here presence at the festival she doesn't really like dancing. She prefers talking and socialising as a pastime. She can talk the back legs off a millipede. But not relating to anything crucial in her own life. She prefers discussing other people's troubles, including her father's. Her own life has turned into a taboo subject.

"Want to go down and take a closer look?" Pru suggests. "If you're crazy enough to rescue your princess."

"All right, girl, let's go," I resolve.

When we get down the vale I have some luck. I bump into a mate of my daughter's, a girl called Samantha. This teen lives in the Eastville district with her three siblings and her mother. The mum drives a warehouse forklift for a shipping company. We try to make ourselves heard above the din. Then after finding the right volume I struggle to get any coherent answers out of her. This chick's on a high and the sudden appearance of Angie's Dad proves that anything is possible - any miracle, wizardry or horror. I'm the genie that came out of the bottle - or capsule. I gaze into the looking glass and see our generation as if the party never ended.

"Aw-right Noah!" she screams - exhilarated, astonished, happy.

"Sam, do you know where my daughter is?" I yell. Man, this is the mother of all sound systems: rigged up by Jakes.

"We're buzzing, Noah!"

"Right. Any ideas where our Angie is?" I shout again. Percussion shreds my inner ear and thunderous bass lines rattle my skeleton. Like a nuclear war starting in my head.

"Menace? D'you know where Ange 'as got to, mate?" She's addressing a skinny lad in a baseball outfit, number seven, who looks frankly out of his nut. Grinning at us like a loon, eyes rolling back into his head, struggling to get any vibration out of his throat, waving a beer bottle towards us, losing any powers of speech.

"Never mind, boy!" I tell him, disconsolately.

"Dance with me Noah! C'm on!" Samantha urges.

"Not in the mood!"

“Dance!” She begins to shimmy around me, waving her arms in the air.

“Trying to find Angela. My daughter? Did you see her?” I bellow.

“*Where* did you see her?” Samantha shouts, puzzled.

The gap between my front teeth is bigger than her attention span. There’s no point shaking my hands and continuing our shouting match: Susan and Bob H got better communications with that lost hill tribe in New Guinea.

Pru and I exchange ironies, understanding there’s no more info on offer. I decide to hoof it towards the silver trailer, rather than to Fred and Ginger with this girl. Pru’s whippet’s still following her on a piece of string, flickering his ears in pain, with a morning-after-expression, unaware of his heroic role in events.

Our hunch is that Angie is with her drug dealing dandy. This is the moment to go trick or treating, while praying that his bouncers are looking for some doors. So I follow my companion across the boggy ground, battling to swallow my heart. There are no more Bungalow Bills to lead enquiries. But if Jakes respects other people’s rights then Norman Mailer was a legendary ballet dancer.

“You seriously going in there to find her?” Pru warns, as we approach.

“Do I have another option? If you get any brighter ideas throw the switch.”

Pru and I stop before the high-tech vehicle. It resembles something to be shot into space. That’s where I’d like to send Jakes. Sadly my daughter’s part of the experiment. Now I’m volunteering as lab monkey. Arguably that’s the right role for a guy who’s been operated and experimented on.

My legs have turned to overcooked spaghetti. No good trying to think of being Alain Delon as the samurai, or any other counter culture or rock heroes, ‘cause it doesn’t help. No brighter ideas arrive as I stand on Adam’s step, knocking on his door as the angry father. This is as smart as I can do. A heavy rap has minimal impact in this environment. I discover that the two guys were careless in leaving the mobile unlocked. Prudence decides to keep away and offers to stand guard. She's got a wise head on those young shoulders.

"Watch yourself, Noah," she says, shedding her toughness.

But if I refused my ex-wife's advice, I'm not going to heed this girl. They'll have to drag me off the world stage, as I'll never retire gracefully to the wings.

Jakes' rigout is swanky enough to make any gangster drool. From experience I recognise quality materials and metals, manufactured for strength and lightness. The interior is finished to high standards, with fitted extras such as carpets and leather upholstery. It's a dream mobile for seaside holidays of the kind our family once enjoyed. We could have traded in our VW *Caravanette* for this beaut.

I don't pick up any voices or movement in here. Am I fully prepared for a scene or confrontation with my daughter and her latest flame? Life is what happens while you're busy making other plans - true enough. My heart is banging like a kettle drum played by Keith Moon. What is there left to be afraid of?

My fingers drag over the surface of a fixed table. As a result I notice fine powder sticking to fingertip perspiration. But I don't make any assumptions. I dab the granules on my lips. Then a sign goes off inside my brain - heroin. It's a candy-coloured motel sign, I recall, flashing neon over the empty lanes of the freeway, promising refuge to the shattered traveller. This is Jakes' game and it doesn't come as a shock. We tried smack once I have to admit. That was after Stuart died. We didn't become addicted. It was only an experiment in desolation. Maybe that was just our luck.

Trying dope begins as an experiment, often; but we watched people getting hooked, gradually. Then trying to kick the habit. It's like falling in love. Fortunately not any of my close friends. So I didn't watch them doing cold turkey. I drove straight past that motel: I refused to break my journey back home. I was afraid that if I checked in I'd never find the strength to leave. But here I am again, decades later, edging towards middle-age, getting the same bitter grainy taste. I know that Luke already called at reception. Had my daughter refused to take the key to that luxury room?

Surely it would look enticingly comfortable to her, in the face of her many problems and dilemmas.

There are other substances, powders and detritus, less familiar to me. I don't know my way around the contemporary drugs scene. I'm stuck inside the mobile with the Memphis Blues again.

It's a given that Jakes uses this vehicle as his control centre. He's dealing, and doing business, around the whole region, and beyond, while keeping his operation highly mobile. I hate to concede the point, but it's clever; cynical. It takes nerve when there's an army of police around the site, ready to sweep in. Bob already told me about a boat moored in Bristol in the wake of Royal Naval vessels.

The trailer contains a fortune in electronic equipment. There's a wall of sound outside, but I pick up snatches of conversation. Locating those voices, reaching a further compartment, I turn a door handle carefully, then put my whole weight against the divider. Which leads me to hurtle inside and, after staggering to keep on my feet, I notice that my daughter is within there. I see her stretched out on a bed with him. They're more or less still dressed, but I get the idea of disturbing them at the start of a new fitting. Man, just wait until her mother gets up to speed with this one.

Angela's first reaction is boggle-eyed amazement. She's convinced that this is a doppelganger or a living nightmare or even an overdose. Moments after, when she realises I am not a ghost or a wraith - just my usual imitation of one - but really her Dad in Technicolor - she jumps up in a panic, bare footed, and begins to rearrange her scanty clothing.

Bristol's young entrepreneur of the year - son of the psychotic haulier - is stretched out on his own side of the bed, hardly stirring a limb, eyeing me ironically. As if he's used to having girls' fathers burst into his boudoir at the fateful moment. Like it's a sexual problem but not the most serious.

But I haven't dropped by to expose Angie's sex life. It was never the idea to humiliate either of them. Or myself.

When Lizzie was a similar age she considered herself a sexually liberated woman. She'd read all the classic feminist books, gone through a reading list, attended lectures and meetings. Her friends and she, including Susan Huntingdon, would share sexual secrets and discoveries. Lizzie would talk and joke nervously with them about 'sleeping around'. In reality this was confined to regular boyfriends. Trustworthy guys like me. She was cautious if bravely outspoken. Elizabeth would be scandalised by Angie's permissive behaviour - by the sleeping around. Let's face it *Andrea Dworkin* would have been scandalised by Angie's exploits.

I puff myself up in front of her, trying to put her criminal into the background, as if I have some authority and can cope with the situation. "Are you going to explain yourself?" I'm fighting for my breath. I should have been prepared.

"What the hell?" she counters. She's padded towards me on her bare feet, dressed only in a long tee-shirt and underwear. Or am I adding underwear for reassurance. But she only takes seconds to recover from the shock of my entrance. Cynicism wins out. Memory is burning bright but her secret life remains under wraps. She isn't thrilled to see Daddy. Prudence was right. Absolutely the opposite. I crashed through the scenery before the vital act.

"What are you trying to do?" she growls.

"I'm here to take you back home. Get your things," I suggest.

She is puzzled as she is amazed. "No, no," she mutters, stepping back. "I'm going nowhere with you." She shakes the goddamn bracelet for strength.

"You're not hanging out with this sleazy lizard," I remark.

"What gives you the right to judge him?" she retorts.

"Even if he does wear silk boxers...and a Brooks Brothers style shirt," I add, noticing this garment over the back of the chair.

She looks genuinely puzzled by my attitude. "You're completely out of it now, Dad!"

"Straighten out your life, while you still can," I say.

"Why don't you give *my life* back?" she says, dark eyes blazing within bruised rims.

"You're well out of order, know what I mean," Jakes declares.

"This has nothing to do with you, boy."

"What do you think's wrong with her life? What's it to you?" Jakes wonders.

“Why don’t you concentrate on your own bloody family?” I tell him.

Jakes stretches luxuriously and shuffles slowly across the bed. I realise he’s trying to cover the sting of my comment. “There’s nothing wrong with Angie. What’s eating you, *man*?” he sneers, finding his feet.

“I’d suggest you keep out of this,” I tell him.

“Dad, you’re mad coming here. You shouldn’t get involved.”

“You’re my daughter. You’re getting into a bad scene. ‘Course I’m involved,” I insist.

Jakes pulls his trousers back on and pushes his feet into a pair of sneakers, without having to untie and tie the laces. “What’s so outstanding about your life, anyway, Noah?” he wonders, sauntering across the space.

“Compared to your life it’s outstanding,” I say. Looking back caution has never been a characteristic. “Your business is wrecking people’s lives and exploiting people. Don’t hassle me about personal ethics, man. On that subject you’re about as credible as a dirty bomb.”

“Look Noah, I heard your business is going down the shit hole, know what I mean? Why don’t you take a loan off me? Even better consider it an investment.”

“Over my dead body, am I going to take any dough off you,” I say.

“Why are you telling ‘em all this, Dad?” she pleads.

“Just relax Daddy-o. Why all the stress? Know what I mean?”

“She and I are just getting out of here, all right? Then you can enjoy your stress-free evening, okay? Pick up another girl at the rave and take your coke or whatever,” I suggest, dismissing him.

“You know I’m clean. Let me find you something to relax. That’s it, you need something to take away the anxiety and tension. Forget all your troubles, granddad, do you hear me?” His sly, slanted grey eyes are still shining from his sensual friction with Angie.

“You seriously trying to push your products with me? You think I’m going to get hooked up with your candy?” I say.

I’m continuing to teeter on my Sergio Leone legs.

"What I'm sayin' Noah is like, are you getting enough?" he asks.

"Excuse me?" I reply. I'm trying to concentrate on my daughter; to persuade her to accompany me from *Apocalypse Now*.

"At your age. Know what I mean? In your condition," he persists.

"Don't worry, boy, I already have a girlfriend." Sort of.

"What's your taste? Little blondes? Know what I mean?" he grins.

Bridgitte *Bard*ot - Anita *Ek*berg - Sophia *Lor*en.

"Go drown in your hot tub," I suggest.

"Come on, you angry old man, don't play innocent. I've had enough news bulletins from Angie. I know what you're about. Do you get me? *Man*?"

"Even Bob D was the victim of the legend makers," I argue.

"Get out of here in good health, do you understand?" he suggests, adopting a masterful posture. "You may have been screwin' for kicks but for us it's just business." He straightens the seams of his designer trousers. He trusts them.

"Stop interfering, Dad. Call quits and leave the same way."

"Angie, how much stuff did you bring with you? Get all your things together, will you? You came here with your mates, did you?" I ask, attempting to hurry her.

"How the hell did you get here?" she wonders.

"You and I need to put our heads together," I insist. Then considering her question more attentively, I can't resist a chance to boast. "I dropped in to your festival by balloon. Are you saying you didn't notice my aerostat? I caused frenzy - it was like Godzilla in New York.

"Listen to Jules Verne," she remarks, with a snigger. There are moments when we resemble each other. Most often in a crisis it seems.

"Never mind my heroics, Angie. Let's go home!"

Her gestures of helpless frustration are bemusing and shocking. Jakes grows edgier and restless; he bounces nervously, angrily from one sneaker to the other. "Angela? Do you want to run back home with your Daddy?" he declares, gesturing.

She rushes towards him and winds an arm around his waist. "Adam, sweetheart, I want to go to Paris as you said."

City of romantic love and revolution in communes. "What are you planning on doing there? In Paris?" I blab. Watching them together like this I'm as stiff as one of those old aristos.

"What do you think, Daddy-o?" Then to my daughter: "We'll see, won't we Angie...if you're a good girl. Know what I mean?"

"There's no way you're going to Paris."

"How are you going to stop me?"

"How are you going to tell your mother? That's more to the point."

"She must have been in love once," she tells me.

Jakes scoffs at my predicament. "You're making a total arse of yourself here, Noah, know what I mean." He holds me in a mocking twinkle. "Do you want your daughter to see you like this?"

"You're so cool, man, aren't you," I say.

"You said it, know what I mean."

"You've everything under control, don't you, eh?"

"Like a fucking Swiss army watch, know what I mean," he snarls.

"Like the powder on your table top...that I just ran my finger over and put to my lips. I may not have my taste buds back, but I'm not a bloody idiot, boy."

"Why do you have to interfere here?" Angie objects.

The revelation makes the trendy trafficker start. Rich colour spills along his high cheeks. "Let's not make any stupid assumption, Noah, right?"

"You've been spreading some of your magic, Adam?"

The handsome young face is puckered and distressed. "A lot of geezers come into this vehicle, know what I mean? Can't always vouch for what those fuckers are up to. I'm clean, do you understand?" he insists.

Jakes cools his spine against the metal wall and observes me through narrow ancestral eyes. My daughter still has her fingers around his supple waist, either in protection or restraint.

"Save your memoirs for the prison library," I advise.

My pulse has already been set off: blood beats at my temples harder than the amplified rhythms outside. No sign of heaven's door when you've been dropped into hell.

"I don't have to listen to a pathetic old dope-head like you," he quips. His pronounced Adam's Apple is bobbing emotionally.

"You've no right to make wild accusations against Adam," Angie tells me. "How do you know what goes on here? There's a lot of people coming around here, as he told you. Why should he check up if they are using?"

"You've already taken enough of my time, Noah," he says.

"Are you involved with his business, Angela? You taking part in his operation?"

"We're just seeing each other, Dad," she argues.

"Did you encourage your brother to try smoking junk?" I challenge.

She stares at me numbly. "Don't be so ridiculous. I don't believe this."

"I'm sorry Angela but I don't believe *you* on this issue," I reply. "You're giving me some heavily negative radiation about this."

"Are you accusing me of lying to you, Dad?" she crassly objects. She glances slyly, distrustfully at me: assumes a more protective posture towards Jakes. Man, she's going Patty Hearst on me.

"Let's all chill for a while, know what I mean," Jakes declares.

He circles the room - the living space of the trailer, shall we say - like one of the trapped leopards in our zoo; abundant hair spilling about his irregularly good looks, falling over his narrow forehead and slit gaze in these moments of crisis.

"D'you know the kind of damage dope can do?" I blurt out.

"Dad! Please! Have a heart," she implores. "What's he like, my Dad?"

"Spare me your moral lectures, *man*!" he retorts sarcastically.

The wrecked lives, the smashed dreams, the broken relationships on every level. And a hard rain's gonna fall.

He stops his prowling circle and brings his face close to mine. "All we're doin' is treating the side effects of this sick world," he argues.

"You're *making* them sick," I tell him. It can never be a cure, except maybe for a guy in my position.

"Soothin' the aches and pains of society. If these sad fucks want to fuck up their lives, that's their choice. They can have as much shit as they want, as long as they pay. If they want to end up in the gutter I can make it comfortable for 'em. D'you get me?"

Perhaps it's the roaring intensity of his snarl that encourages this: I know about your boat in the closed harbour."

"Is it your business to bring this up?" Angela asks. "What's the matter with Adam owning a boat?"

"What about my boat?"

"More about what you do with your boat. Let's say that I heard from a friend. A friend of a friend," I brag. But playing private detective wasn't a clever move. Not that I had much inside-info from Bob H. But I gave a dangerous contrary impression. I can't handle myself anymore with this heavy handed crook.

"Did you bring the fucking plods with you? Got the drugs squad following you, Noah? Waiting to break into here or what?"

He peers nervously through a porthole, trying to find these cops amidst the throng and the woods and the dark smoky fields. The camouflage has become a threat.

"You've changed so much, Dad," Angie informs me.

"What are you saying?" I return. Taking a moment to consider. "No big surprise, you know, that I may have changed a bit. My health's taken a big fall."

"You're not the same bloke, Dad," she says, gravely.

"Right, Angie. There's been an earthquake under my feet...a few of them... and obviously I'm not the same guy...the radical experience has marked me."

"You can't always hide behind your health problems," she argues.

"You call this hiding?" I say.

Her black eyes flash at me again. "Why don't you keep out of my life?"

"That's beginning to sound like good advice," I admit to her.

"Leave me alone," she insists. "You liked to talk about freedom...discovery...finding our own way. Now you come here and try to drag me back. If you're so confident of being yourself, why do you make me into a copy? I'm not even a boy," she reminds me. "God help my brothers. Do you understand me?"

When I try to touch her shoulder she pulls away. My intention was to reconnect, to reassure, to comfort, but she doesn't get this. She thinks I'm trying to constrain or even to hurt her. She should know better. I've never hit a girl in my entire life and that includes her. Jakes can't say that about his own personal history. In that way he considers himself a tough guy. In terms of violence he doesn't discriminate.

Next thing we know, as Angie is backing away from me, Jakes has pulled out a gun. I have to scrunch my eyes and open them again, believing that I am hallucinating the shooter. This proves that drugs are useless. He's pointing a weapon at me. How can I escape from this little red neck? Suddenly I'm in the movies and wish to cut the scene.

# Chapter 36

This is another big Zen moment of earthly existence. The kid wants to take a shot at Pops. And if he confuses me for his real father the odds are narrow. I've never had the experience of anyone pulling a gun on me before. When my brother and I were growing up, certainly, the village men all owned firearms, and they would brandish them during the season. But not even my brother ever played around with a gun. So I have never looked down the barrel until now. After our father died the gun was given away with all his personal property to neighbours and friends. Jakes holds out a shot-gun, which has sawn-off style short barrels, to the side of my head. He's got a glint in his eye like a malevolent doctor. One false step and I won't have any mind to change. He'll put my intellect through a liquidiser. Man, you don't need to drop any tabs of acid in this life.

"That's right, granddad, not feeling so clever now," he jeers.

His quick colouring face creases and flushes again, as if the hot colours of the bonfires have leaked inside.

"C'm on boy," I urge him. "You're taking this too far. No need to lose your cool." Unfortunately I can't feign empathy with this guy. There's an instinctive hatred between us, as between a freedom rider and a race school bigot. You can't beat that.

"Just do as I'm telling yer, yer old bastard. Or I'll blow your sorry arse into the third dimension, know what I mean?"

It looks as if he's got a mechanical hand, as the bling on his fingers clinks on the gun handle and coils over the trigger; the weapon resembling a metal scorpion. Adam Jakes is a young guy living on his frazzled nerves, exhausted by deception, worn down by anxiety. He's paying a psychological price for his illegal fortune.

"Put it down, Adam, and we'll think no more about it," I suggest.

"No old bastard's ever done me any favours," he remarks.

"Firearms don't make you smart, mate, believe me," I tell him.

“Keep your back against the wall... face up, granddad,” he warns, waggling the fire stick about.

“All I’ve got to say is... if your intentions to my daughter are honourable... don’t invite me to your wedding, boy,” I tell him.

“Where are the goons?” he calls to Angie. “Why aren’t those mutts back here yet? What do I fuckin’ pay ‘em for?”

“You told them to put their ugly faces into the next county. As I remember it,” Angela informs him. “You can’t expect them to be loyal, if you’re constantly insulting them.”

“Shut up, will you? Who’re you talking to, Ange? You turning into my fucking wife now, know what I mean?” Jakes snarls.

“See how your private life is gonna size up with this dude,” I say to my daughter.

You might argue that I’m already running on limited time. That I’m practically pencilled into the register of deaths. So why am I so terrified of being shot? Anyhow my heart thumps like crazy, so that a bullet could be an irrelevance.

Jakes picks up my negative vibrations. His face breaks out into a rudely triumphant grin. He could have been up against a steely guy. He’s no crime fiction psychopath - thank god it’s not as simple as that - but my fear makes him brave. My picture of terror reflects a flattering image. Hard not to be flattered by this powerful self-image.

“You’re taking this too far, Adam. I already told you Dad has a dicey ticker,” she reminds him. I don’t know what she’s been taking if anything. She isn’t exactly jumping out of her skin at the scene.

“Just get your glad rags back on, do you hear me?” he tells her.

“You don’t have to share my medical history with him,” I complain.

Angie is trying to second-guess her lover’s ideas. I’m holding up my arms as if taking the acclaim.

“You suggesting we go outside?” she asks. Rapidly she pulls on a dress over the teeshirt. “For god’s sake Adam, leave Dad alone. He can’t hurt you. He can’t *damage* you,” she insists.

“So why is he threatening me?” Jakes tells her. “What’s goin’ to happen to my wife and kids if I get banged up or something?”

"Listen to Scarface here," I say, impatiently.

"Leave this to me, will you Dad?" she says sharply. There's something of her mother in this tone. Nervously she twirls her gold bracelet around her wrist - his gift, his love token.

"I heard you was a bit of a sportsman," Adam says to me. "Didn't you play a bit of tennis in your youth?"

"I've retired from the game lately," I inform him.

"Let's see how your fitness is holding up," he suggests. As if holding a tennis racquet himself - as if suggesting he's my next opponent - Jakes is swishing the shotgun around my nose.

"They told me to lose weight and get back into shape," I consider. "Most likely nothing so radical as you suggest."

"This is fucking hilarious," he says. He's entertained and surprised by developments.

"Let him be, Adam!" she declares.

"Come on, Noah, lets see how quickly your dodgy ticker can run."

"Don't hurt him!" Angela warns.

The creep's pointing a gun at me and she asks him not to hurt me.

"You keep away from my son in future," I warn.

"Your old bastard already knows too much about us. We've got to be realistic Angie. We can't let him walk away from here, straight to the Old Bill. You hear me? I might as well think up my own sentence," he objects.

"But what if he goes and snuffs it?" she points out.

"What about it? Know what I mean? We've got to be cool about this. Face it, the old bastard's got it in for me, hasn't he?"

"You're not worried about shooting him?"

"I'd be more worried if he walks away from here," he says.

"For real?

"For real."

"In that situation how would you dispose of the body?"

"Nobody gives a toss around here...what's going on. All they want is a place to park their grotty caravans and broken down vans, know what I mean? They're too terrified of me and those goons...and the plods are like their enemy...know what I mean?" he considers.

My Über-muscle is pumping away without too much protest. The fragile pin regulating the reservoir of my life, for the moment, is holding in place.

"That's another brilliant plan against the cops you have, isn't it?" Angie comments.

"What are you talking about? Which plan?" he says.

"To get yourself a stiff on the carpet," she replies. "After that you'll have to carry the weight outside, in front of thousands of witnesses. Do you think they're gonna look the other way or what? They're not so scared of you," she tells him.

I can only hope she's bluffing. It's hard for me to hold my tongue during this lovers' tiff.

"What's your idea then, Angie? Stop giving me mouth girl. No woman talks back to me, know what I mean?" he fumes.

The clunky weapon grows heavier at the end of his arm and begins to pull on his mind.

My daughter smarts at his attitude - her chin bobs into her neck - but it isn't enough to alienate her. "You can't pull this one off," she insists. "You're taking it too far. If this becomes personal then we risk everything. You're breaking all your own rules, Adam!"

"I can't let this hypocritical old bastard walk away. Do you get it, Angie?"

"Then you don't have a lot of choice, boy," I bluff.

"Keep out of this, Dad!" She casts a desperate look.

I stare horrified, dejectedly, into her passionately outraged face - radiant and lovely as a youthful Grace Slick, though I could be biased as her father.

"Why don't we take him out into the woods?" Jakes declares. He shakes the two hollow fingers of death at me.

Angie's attention dashes back to her boyfriend, this druggie degenerate. "What do you mean by that? Take him out into the woods?" she asks - in drained voice.

"You'd better wise up on reality," I suggest.

"What do you think I mean," he tells her. "We'll give him a good clean kill, d'you get me?" There's a brief snaggly grin.

"Adam, this is my Dad," she reminds him. Her hands fall and she looks wide eyed and desperately between those dark bangs.

"I didn't think he was your fucking ex, or something like that," he tells her.

"You believe you can blast him and get on with our relationship?" she says.

"Do you want your own life, Angie? You said he don't understand you...or give you the time of the day. What kind of father is that anyway, do you get me?" he says.

Jakes is staring at me with one slanted eye, as a tumbled fringe conceals the other. As far as I know that's all you need for a good aim.

"This guy makes Hannibal Lector seem a romantic," I remark. "Just don't expect a card this year, Angela."

"Dad!"

"So he's your Dad. Are you going to let that affect you?" he suggests to her, while watching me.

Angela balances miserably, intensely nervous. You can tell that her soul's been shattered like a windscreen, to paraphrase Paul Simon.

"How can you let this creep sell dope to your own brother?" I complain.

"I'm a better mate to that lad than you are, Noah. Do you know what I mean, you useless old granddad?"

"Best keep a grip on that firestick, boy, 'cause otherwise you'll find roles reversed."

"Hear that, Angie? According to this old bastard, it's either me or him, know what I mean?" he argues.

"Adam, you can't just shoot him and get away with it." She's doing her Simone Signoret impression.

"What do you think your mother's going to say?" I declare - outraged. Clearly I'm prepared to take a gamble.

"Why don't you stay at home, Dad? Tinker with your motor? Potter around in the garden? Like most fathers?"

"We'll have to get him out of here," Jakes decides.

"Just let him run away back home," she suggests.

"How long is your luck going to hold out?" I say.

"I make my own luck, Noah," he retorts. "I'm not superstitious."

"The whole site is packed with these travellers and hippie people," she warns.

"You're losing your fucking nut, Adam," she protests. "You want to get the police on you?"

"Listen to yourself, Angela," I tell her. "Do I even exist?"

"Not for much longer, granddad," he cuts back. "Anyways chances are you'll drop dead before then."

"*Adam!*" she squeals; sounding a decade younger than her actual age. Is she afraid of growing up? Even more so than her parents' generation?

Jakes doesn't take any more heed of her. The narrow eye concentrates on me - I can feel as it bores into me - as the bullets (or the shot) that may pierce me.

"Stop waving that thing at me," I argue. Yet I'm running through the hots and colds as if running through a sauna on speed.

"Get the fuck out of here, you old bastard," he snarls, and kicks me in the small of the back.

"Don't be an idiot Dad. Do as he tells you."

"Even Mum's going to be shocked if one of your boyfriends blows me away," I say.

How in hell did I stray into this nightmare gig? It's like the Stones at Altamont, mixing up with the chapters. This could be my final roustabout.

"You're responsible, Dad. I didn't ask you to chase after me. Come looking for me," she seethes. "I would have come back home tomorrow. You wouldn't have known anything about this."

"Are those your expectations of me? We bring you into this world just to abandon you?" I reply.

"You shouldn't hold me back...disapprove of everything I do."

As the hoodlum jabs me through his mobile vehicle she hovers indecisively. I'm certain that he's killing off her feelings with that gun. This is going to be lethal to her affections. But if the guy shoots me, what do I care if they break up?

"Just give me the back of your head to aim at...know what I mean?"

“How do you intend to dispose of the body?” Angela asks ironically.

His manic eye flickers to her reluctantly. “None of these ragbags is gonna look for a corpse.”

“They don’t have to search dummy, they’re just going to find it,” she says.

“Nobody interferes in the business and threatens me.”

Angela struggles to relieve her tired astonished eyes. “But aren’t you forgetting about something else?” she asks.

“Forgetting what?” he answers - contemptuous. He takes a sprint back through his hardened mind. “Like what?”

“Like me,” Angela suggests. She opens her arms slightly towards him.

“Like what about you?” he throws back.

“What’s going to happen to me after this. If you go through with this...I know what you’re doing...I may see what you do... So do you think I’m going to watch you shoot my father and forget about it?”

Our charmless Jean Paul Belmondo gives a dry noise of amusement. Leaving my daughter in no doubt. Looking at me in panic, she knows we’re closer than she thought.

“He’s only trying to scare us,” she insists. But her trust has taken a lethal slug.

“Either he kills me in cold blood or he comes back to his senses,” I say.

Edgily Jakes adjusts his grip. He tosses the weapon about in his hand, to allow the blood to circulate back into his fingers.

“Keep your back turned to me, granddad,” he instructs. “I’m taking you out to bury your generation.”

We walk over the living space of his mobile home - or office, control centre, or other function it gives - past the dusty surfaces and bags of what looks like expensive bath salts but really isn’t so harmless.

“He doesn’t have anything against you,” Angela tells him. “He’s going right back up in his hot air balloon. You’ll never see ‘em or hear from ‘em again!”

"Let's all get some fresh air, know what I mean?"

"Tell him Dad!"

"Tell him what?" I declare.

"That you're not going to make any hassle with the pigs or anybody."

"I'm not going to make any hassle," I parrot.

Her dark emotional features crumple in frustration. Instantly she turns into an old lady. "Tell him you just want to go home and forget about everything."

"You want me to beg for my life, with this creep?"

It's exactly what I'm tempted to do; to get down on my pressed Levi's.

"You want to live don't you? You don't want to throw your life away, do you?"

"D'you believe this two-bob con is hare-brained enough to shoot me?"

The intensity of her look impresses the gravity of our situation. Not many people are going to hear shots. You'd already think a war was going on. We're held in a throbbing womb of rave and heavy metal. There's nothing left but the Memphis blues again.

My James Dean pose has lost cultural significance. What are the rules for this monetised contemporary society? Put yourself ahead. Don't let anything or anyone get in your way. A computer game existentialism.

"Your old man's trying to buy his life," Jakes tells her. We stand at the exit to his capsule, wondering about his next move. "He's a crafty old bastard, know what I mean? Let him walk now and he'd go straight to the pigs."

"Why don't you believe us? Let him go."

"No, Angie. I'm not going to spend years in prison. It wouldn't be enough. I didn't come this far with business to let your old man... to allow somebody to ruin it. My old man never gave me a chance either. Am I going to let Noah do the same to me?"

Angela turns away from him in despair. "What about all those people out there?"

"What about them?" he returns. "I don't give a pig's poke for all those sorry arses."

"They might kick the shit out of you... even if they *are* a bunch of hippies."

"Know anything about the American Democratic Convention of 1968?" I tell him.

"Fuck off," he warns.

"This is my Dad."

"Go and stand over there with your Daddy. There's a good girl," he orders her. He waggles the gun until she complies. "Get out of here slowly."

Jakes picks up a sweatshirt - not a cheap one of course - which he places over his arm to conceal the shotgun. Bizarrely he finds a golf glove which he hurriedly pulls over the fingers of his right hand. Does he want to club me into the next world with a seven iron? Man, you can't predict this guy's intentions.

"What are you doing with that?" Angie wonders.

"Stop asking questions, will you girl? Always questions, know what I mean?"

"You know Angie's answer if you ever pop the question," I tell him.

"Get out of here you sleazy hypocrite," he replies.

I feel those steel tips between my shoulder blades. "What's the hurry?"

I negotiate the steps first. Angela gingerly follows, on her heels. She's wearing an almost perfect replica of late hippie fashion. A leopard-skin pillbox hat can't change its spots.

The outfit reminds her of her mother. They must have compared wardrobes. Strings of beads swing from her neck, that she grabbed with her as if for luck. The cut of clothes is too exact, as if copied from an old Vogue anthology. But there's a resemblance. Our youth comes back to haunt me once again.

Jakes clambers back outside after us. As we three - the hunter and his prey - blink and adjust to the atmospherics, I'm surprised to see Pru still waiting. There's not much she can do to help. I came here to save Angela, not to mix it with Jakes. Angie with her young and healthy heart.

It is hard to adapt to the open space and closing light. Such was the mood of tension developed in the confined space of the trailer. A chill wind chisels into our ears - a distant bugle call of doom. The sky isn't out of reach to the balloonist. It's criss-crossed with potential highways of freedom. I can easily place us up there. It's a wish to find the safety of that poetic epiphany. Arguably I'm happiest up there. But there doesn't seem to be an obvious take off point.

"Where are you three off to?" Prudence asks, approaching our trio. Even in her universe this is a strange assembly. What's going on in contemporary society?

"Adam wants to go for an evening stroll," I say.

"Pru? What do you want?" he shouts at her.

"Adam's preparing for his trip to Paris," I explain.

"Not any more, I'm not," he tells me.

His nerves are exposed in the open. We're into the migraine of a free festival. Maybe tree cover is further away than he imagined, in his rush to push me into a shallow grave.

"What the fuck are you doing with them?" Pru asks. She's alerted by the Strangelove posture of his arm, under the shirt, with leather fingertips exposed.

"This isn't your argument, Pru. Just keep out of my way, you unpleasant hippie bitch, and you won't have any problem. That goes for all you head lice," he declares. He's referring to a gathering crowd of festival goers. They sense that something's badly out of phase.

"You've got a fucking shooter on them, don't you!"

"Out of my way, Pru. Go and trim your dirty beards, hear what I'm telling you?" he calls to the group.

The dishevelled bunch looks indignant and begins to call back.

Jakes reveals the shotgun - his deadly racquet - and scans for potential threats. More hippies and travellers are gathering to check out the fuss. There's a feeling that Jakes is losing control. There are many off-screen distractions. Yet it's too perilous for Angie and me to break for the trees.

"Give up your crazy ideas, Adam. Let us go!" Angie advises.

"None of these fucking skunks is gonna help you," he tells her.

"Don't be a total wanker, Adam!" Pru warns. There's more West Country flavour in this than a bottle of Somerset cider brandy.

“Fuck off, Pru, you skanky little whore.”

“You’re best shot of him, Angie, didn’t I tell you,” I confide to her.

In the heat of the moment Prudence let’s her whippet go. The skinny creature is picking around nervously in the space between us - the no-man’s-land between Jakes and the hostile crowd.

“Put away the shooter. Have you lost your fucking marbles,” Pru asks.

Angela and I glance uneasily within nozzle aim. You just can’t predict.

“Keep your hole closed, do you understand?”

“They’ll throw away the key.” Pru tosses her multi-coloured braids; hands on hips thrust defiantly forward. “They won’t let you out into the prison yard.”

Jakes taunts, waving his weapon. “I’d waste the whole lot of you. All you do is sponge up the mud. You fucking paupers.”

People shout back at him, but the gun keeps them at a physical distance. Pru’s doggie has wandered right up to Jakes, oblivious to the dangers, and is sniffing at interesting odours around his priceless sneakers. Then, at the signal of a mysterious intense stimulus, the dog lifts a thin leg, secures a good straight aim, looks up at the sky and urinates prodigiously over Jakes’ label trouser leg.

After a few seconds the liquid seeps through the fabric. Jakes lowers his aim and stares at the doggie in disgust. It’s a miracle that Sid the whippet doesn’t get it between the eyes immediately.

“You dirty little fucker!”

Sid cringes guilty away, back to his caring mistress, as Jakes flaps his designer threads. In a split second a sizzling noise goes directly past my ear, practically burning the hairs of my lobe on the flight path. Like an intervention from an irritated divinity. A bolt from a crossbow, I gathered; the shaft embedded in Jakes’ left shoulder. The sawn shotgun has fallen to the muddy floor. He’s not surprisingly lost his grip. When I look at him Adam is staring rigidly ahead, a white mask, everything falling away from him. His fingers - including the right with its golfing glove - are clawing at the wooden stem of the arrow, trying to dig out the pain; only succeeding in pulling out a few of the decorative feathers.

Angela is horrified and wishes to comfort him. But I get hold of her and prevent her running back to him. He could pull that projectile from his shoulder; retrieve the weapon. His heavies are somewhere not too far away. They may return when their feelings are repaired. So I pull Angela after me and we cut through the crowd. Fortunately she sees my side and ends her resistance. We make our tracks on gossamer wings. A ragged legged William Tell has saved our skins. Or it might have been William Burroughs taking another misaim at a spouse with an apple on her head. I don't hang around to watch the fall out. I've lost all curiosity.

# Chapter 37

This time I ride the crowd with my mixed-up daughter.

On balance I prefer to get crushed than to pose as a plastic duck in that gangster's shooting gallery. Don't ask me what make of gun he was aiming. I may have grown up in a rural community, but I'm not Heston. I assumed the thing worked and was loaded. I showed courage but I'm avoiding playing De Niro in *The Deerhunter*.

The huge chaos and noise of the festival overwhelms us, as we battle to find a path through: friction pulls at the wiring around my upper ribs and aggravates old wounds. Endless weaving, pressing and pushing through the gathering, as we try to get clear. This obviously reminds me of the music festivals Liz and I went to - later with Angie of course - although I don't recall the experience being so raw. This one is in conflict with the police, directly against authority, and there's a vibe of fear and anger. Maybe that's a consequence of being in danger, an effect of paranoia, or fibrillation.

I'm giving myself a hard time again. I should take up my daughter's advice and become a divorced househusband. There are rose bushes that have to be trimmed back. The front panel to my DS has to be taken off, the dent pushed out and then resprayed. That's thanks to my recent trips into the countryside. No pun intended.

Angie and I can't hear ourselves think for noise. If Jakes is making a live album out of this festival he'll just get a concept album. Not even Floyd would have released that one. At this moment he's more concentrated on pulling out an arrow head. But you can't pin the blame on Cupid this time.

We meet such a variety of human faces and bodies along the way - as we retrace my steps and retake the rural ride. Rough and tough faces on the whole, etched with exhaustion and heartsickness many of them. Yet with such character and resilience; the living and breathing descendants of the great rural population of these isles; what could be described as our *rich culture*. Man, it's a beautiful but endangered existence.

Angela and I try to keep to our path. Finally we emerge from the crowd, where the land has an 'edge of festival' look. From this point we can read our position and walk with some freedom. We develop Byronic clubfeet in traditional festival mud though.

We still have a hill to climb and a mythological feature or two, until I have rediscovered the track to my arrival point. The ancient land is playing its melody on my nerves. Recollected from boyhood, even from when Dad was still alive - those cobwebby memories. This compels a joyful response and is difficult to resist. Could Dad and I have visited this area, even though it's lost to immediate recall?

Angie is complaining about the pass she's come to. She's not happy about the gruesome injury to lover boy. But he hasn't endeared himself. She isn't any longer lovestruck. She pulled out that particular dart.

Much to my relief my flight equipment is still behind the dry stone wall. The constellations are beginning to unfurl over our heads. I begin to consider our return journey. I may finally have left my hippie days behind me. How can I read the runes? How can we predict the energy waves?

Next up Angie notices movement in the distance; furtive change. She leads my sight to spreading dark shapes over the fields and hills. She gets herself into a tizzy trying to make me see anything. My eyesight isn't so sharp. Police operations are an optical effect. But the force is advancing on the festival. They're starting a star-ship ambush against travellers' vehicles. There's going to be an alternative Jean Paul Gaultier choreographed finale to this concert, looking at all the uniforms and boots on show.

Angela and I share looks of disbelief and horror as the ambush begins. We can only look helplessly over the scene as the law enforces. Everybody knew that the cops would turn up to collect the glasses. They were enthusiastic to do that, after the original festival convoy evaded them, with help from Jakes. They were calling in the cheque and sending around spiritual bailiffs.

As we stand there on our peak, wind riffling us in fading light, there's nothing we can do to alter destiny. We can only visualise the destruction and mayhem going on, as windscreens smash, nuts crack, small children and their pets scatter.

"Don't ever take a trip on violence," I advise her. She was much too impressed by Jakes - tough guy.

I've had a good helping of violence lately, but it's beginning to rust my soul. At this hour it's too late for the cops to stop the festival from happening, as there are thousands of cheesy quavers, cream crackers, hippies and travellers over these acres of land. You'd need a large scale military operation to suppress a festival like this. That's something you don't want to witness in your life time.

So we drag our eyes away from the concealed violence. I try to distract Angela by asking her to help me reassemble the craft. Once she's up there with me in the night sky, I reason, she'll forget about that thug and all her worries.

She didn't have the luck to watch my spectacular arrival. She was too busy with Adam at the time. The first thing she knew I had burst into the bedroom - as if summoned by the first illicit kiss. Is that the kind of paternal attention that any girl would envy? I didn't regret interrupting their love match.

The immediate task is to reflate the dirigible, with only a single inexperienced ground crew woman. I get the charts out and understand that the wind direction is as predicted. It's a matter of ballooning pride to take to the air again. James should have reached our prearranged location; on the assumption that he hasn't driven my old Citroen into a ditch somewhere. I assume that Angie is going to take the bird's eye view and accompany me. But eternal optimists always take the hardest fall.

Fire arrows into the fragile dome around my head, as I get the propane units going. Flame builds to a sustained ferocity - awesome and angry. This fire always sends a shiver along my spine. The stars appear to scatter in fright at the intensity and noise of the burning. Stephen Hawking might offer a bigger picture. At the best of times life resembles a Panavision roller coaster ride. It's a beautiful but scary world however you care to look at it.

Angie shapes to hold open the mouth of the balloon. The poor girl isn't used to this and she's afraid of being roasted alive.

She stands in an attitude of frozen terror as if miming a scene from the Pompeii catastrophe. She's more afraid of this situation than when Jakes was pointing a weapon at us. Man, you can't always try to second guess female psychology. As it turns out I've got even more wild guesses than Freud. Man, at least we never believed that coke was going to save our souls.

Eventually as the massive lozenge of the balloon begins to puff and fill out, Angie can duck away to the side. She gets well clear as if the globe is going to collapse back on her head. At this point I stop burning any more fuel, afraid that such fuel breathing will draw a crowd. Jakes might go searching for his runaway girlfriend, if only for revenge. I don't want any ravers, hippies or cops to join us. We can't take any hitchhikers tonight, not even Kerouac or Ginsberg.

The mystics claim that everything in the world must come to an end. I wouldn't like to make any predictions.

After running through the sequence of pre-flight checks; in another parody of my prime; I complete a scissor kick back into the basket. Angie watches this move in perplexity, even without a full prognosis. She doesn't yet take up her own position in the craft. I soon regret such bravado as I lose the tab on my heart rate. Man, I could yet land flat on my face. I feel tied to my heart as to a panicky companion.

Recomposing myself, I adjust the equipment, check logistics and anticipate flight time. Not the most favourable time or conditions to make a balloon flight. But I've been here before. Or so I believe. Then I urge Angela to follow me into the carrier but, though body posture is hard to call, she isn't shaping up positively. She's expected to fly away with me out of danger, into a positive future of university degrees and idealistic fiancés, as the western sky collapses on the horizon like a fire gutted terrace. Her gun-toting drug dealing mistake is going to catch up with us, if she hesitates much longer, I fear.

"Come on, Angie girl! Jump in! Take off time!" I declare.

Her poigniantly hunched form is heart-breakingly unmoved. "Sorry, Dad!"

"What?"

"Sorry, I can't come with you!"

"How are you going to get home?"

Not by hot air balloon clearly. I struggle to make out her facial expression, as her figure is increasingly obscure. Night is pouring deeply into the vales, like crude. The last burnished rays of a sunny day slant around the rim of Lime Tree Hill, resembling lasers at the finale of a Queen gig.

"I'm not going back home yet," she tells me.

"What are you going to do then?" I cry from my wicker basket.

"There's a festival happening this weekend," she explains.

"Right. You telling me I have to leave you behind?"

"I'm old enough. I can take care of myself," she affirms.

The rigging groans and creaks and pulls around me. "Jakes isn't going to leave you alone," I warn.

The only way I can see Angie's facial expression now is to burn more fuel. If I do this too much I risk a premature take off, or even sending a personal message to Jakes, written in fire.

"You saw the agony he suffered," Angela replies. "Do you expect me to run away and leave him?"

"Why not?" Good riddance to bad rubbish.

"I know how to deal with him."

"So do I." It was either him or my health.

"Adam is misunderstood. I like him," she insists. "I don't like big softies. He's a challenge. You don't understand him. Nobody does."

Is that what they were doing on the couch? "I don't have the least desire to understand that creep," I admit.

"I care about him."

"God help me, he pointed a gun at me," I remind her.

"He was angry...definitely."

"Right. Try to calm down," I suggest. "He could start to knock *you* around," I warn.

"It just won't happen, Dad," she claims.

"You're brother's been experimenting. Chasing the dragon and stuff. Did you know about this too?"

She denies it. There's a noise to contradict me.

"You haven't been sorting him out, have you, Ange? Doing him a few favours as every big sister does?"

"No. But they're bound to be curious, aren't they? It's as I say. It's normal at that age, isn't it? If you try to stop 'em they just want to experiment even more."

"Listen to the drugs tsarina," I comment.

"That isn't fair, Dad!"

"Your brother's at an awkward stage," I tell her.

"Don't worry, I'll take care of 'im!"

"Everything's been tough on him...these last few years. He's taken it the worst...out of all of you...maybe."

"It was hard on all of us," Angela tells me.

"I realise that," I say.

"You went and hurt us, didn't you. With those other women of yours," she says.

"Right. I'm not going to give you my reasons for that again."

"Not that I ever want to judge you, Dad. I couldn't and I wouldn't... I backed you up."

"I never forget that, Angie. I'm grateful."

Take off is shaping badly - delayed by our conversation. The craft is losing lift and shifting about, riffled by the air. Fuel pipes are hissing as I choke them off. The gaping mouth of the envelope pulls me into the promising void. Into the velvety, warm folds of darkness.

"Are you going back to that creep?" I wonder.

It's a devilish type of charm he possesses. He pushes girlfriends down stairwells and fathers to the end of their wits.

Angela poses me some questions in response. "How many things in life are safe? Talking about meaningful experiences?"

"I could tell you a few," I insist. It's possible to attach danger to many of them.

"Adam's got a lot of ideas. To become a promoter, open a recording studio, a men's fashion chain," she says. "You want him to surrender quietly? Where'd you be without your business, Dad?" she challenges me.

"I don't know, maybe something in the music business," I reply.

"Just being alive is dangerous, isn't it... Do you call this a safe world?" she argues.

"Which is why we need to protect," I argue. "It's why we need to look after each other."

"You've only got to walk around Bristol at night," she suggests. Paranoid.

"Jakes has you in his sights, don't make any mistake, girl. As for me I'm top of his hit list." Thinks I'm going to sing to the police like Pavarotti. "This is Bristol, not Bogotá. Take my word for it, Angie, hard drugs knock you down. There's no sense cosying up to him." I grip the rigging as if surrendering.

"I can't ignore this man," she returns.

"Our sweet lord, I can't believe my ears!"

She's stood across the lumpy field. I can't see her expression. She has a hand on the top of her head to keep the floppy hat on. Giving a great impression of the vulnerable young woman in great peril. Jakes and his henchmen are closing. How close are the railway tracks? I'm Fatty Arbuckle. In disgrace.

"Don't you care about your life?" I call.

"That's my affair. That's why it's called my life," she formulates.

"You don't seem happy with your life right now," I observe.

"Why not? Why shouldn't I be?"

"You could finish up doing time."

"Don't be ridiculous."

"One false move and they'll bang you up."

"No, that's never going to happen." Did she know more than I did?

"You Mum would have to go to Holloway jail just to visit you," I warn. Obviously I'm not up on the location of female prisons.

There's dark girlish laughter. "There are always drawbacks." Drawbridges.

"You're confident about that?"

"Pretty much."

"And you're wrong about your Mum. She really cares about you..."

"Is that right?" she declares in a cynical tone.

Yes, I say.

"I do have a few issues to sort out with my life," she adds.

"Sure enough. I'm not going to be around forever you know."

"Are you sure? It bloody feels like it."

"Not according to the medical boffins...who experimented on me." So is this the moment to bring her up to date with my service history?

There's a hesitation. A breezy interregnum. "Oh well, Dad, they're probably just trying to scare you," she states. "I reckon that's half the job of these medic blokes."

"They succeeded with me," I say.

"How do you mean? You're not in good shape? You're not serious?"

Sometimes we are kept in the world by the force of other people's wishes.

"The truth can be scary," I reply. At least I have found this recently.

Angela falls into longer reflection. I feel the cold creeping into her limbs. she doesn't immediately react to the strange concept of paternal mortality.

"I tried to warn you, Angela. I hinted."

"I didn't get it then, Dad."

But I didn't tell her, or any of our kids, outright. This is hardly a golden moment. I've gone missing on the shore.

I could hear Adam Jakes taunting me: "Looks like you've been stitched up, granddad. Don't go looking for our sympathy, know what I mean?"

"You were the one who said how disgusting I look."

"That was only a bit of teasing," she ticks me off.

"Sure, I realise that."

"I expected you to get better. *We* did. Obviously I worry about you, Dad, and...then I can't lie to you about your appearance...or pretend not to notice the changes."

The flouncy hat has gone to a jaunty angle. She's twisting bead necklaces, in parody of the love generation. Arguably my generation has gone to seed. I'm plucking the old tunes with arthritic fingers. I'm in a purple haze, sicker than Hendrix.

"I never meant to upset you, Angela," I assure her.

I can't read her emotions. I can only make out the Carnaby Street pastiche. Reminders of Lizzie. Pressed flowers in my books.

I wonder if Liz experiences these recollections, despite my misdemeanours, even if they arrive against her will.

"You're not telling me you're a goner, are you Dad?"

I remember the night I came back from London, after my second check-up in London, *knowing*. When I returned to the house to find Angie alone, reading in the living room for once, with a chance to explain to her. But I chose to stay secret.

"I thought you'd had an operation...and they'd put it right." Yet she had noticed the physical and other changes and fluctuations in me.

"The hospital... My heart... They said I could... because there's... They put in a faulty heart valve into the aorta artery," I try to explain. "They didn't order the proper product." But she could tell an aorta artery from an electrical flex.

"I don't understand, Dad."

There's a stunned silence as she processes the hard dope. The eternal father is failing.

"You don't believe him, do you?" Jakes is speaking into her ear. "Noah's trying a last gamble. He's trying to get back your loyalty. He's a crafty old bastard your Dad."

Silence ravels with the air across empty space: it sings through the rigging and riffles the fabric of my balloon.

"The medics can't just abandon you, Dad. Why can't they operate on you again, or give you some better drugs?"

"There's nothing more."

"Why can't it be done?" she demands.

"Everything gets to a finite, I guess."

There's a glint in the corner of her eye, or so I imagine. Do we understand each other at last, my daughter and I? Or is the final report on my health just another stern paternal demand? Can we get the view of my ex-wife's solicitor? The legal one, that is.

Angela drops into silence, under a sliver of moon like a scalpel's edge. I can't offer her much for the future, but she's pulling for me.

"I find you hard to work out," she says.

"Don't listen to that hypocritical old bastard," Jakes argues.

"Are you looking for our sympathy?" she wonders.

"If you're offering," I reply.

There's an abrupt laugh that concludes as suddenly.

I burn upwards again, ignoring the risks. I hope to catch her expression by the flare. The searing light reaches out in an arc across the fields and woodland. The fleeting intense light turns her face blank as an ancient masque.

The burner unit peters out again. The illumination falls back, so that the night looks darker, and the stars and moon weaker. I get the idea that Angela is lost to me. As lost as Lizzie.

# Chapter 38

"You didn't get an approach to sell your shares? *Did you* Angela?"

"*Shares*? What are you talking about, Dad?"

"You know, the shares in our *company*, that I gave you? You wouldn't be tempted, would you? If someone offered a higher price?"

"That would depend on what they offered," she says. "I haven't given much thought to it. Haven't needed to."

"So you haven't had anyone approach? Recently?"

"Into your company?" She is considering hard.

"Yes, that's it. You haven't broken into that stock already?"

"I know what the company means to you," she insists.

"Right, dead on. So you didn't get any phone calls from Corrina Farlane?" I come out and say. Best to level with her on the issue.

"Who is she? Never heard of her."

"You did. She's a girlfriend of mine." Sort of.

"Do you mean the bumptious one on a motorbike?" Angela wonders.

"She owns a couple of bikes, yes," I admit. "Bumptious?"

"How did she get her hooks into you anyway?" she remarks.

"Angie, my taste in women isn't the issue." At least she didn't drug me up; if only because it wasn't necessary.

"I wouldn't speak to that bitch anyway," she tells me.

"That's encouraging to hear," I crow. I can overlook the insult to Corrina as long as the company's safe.

"What's going to happen to your company anyway, if..."

She cares more about my health than even her own prospects. There's nobody else in the family who so readily puts themselves last. This was touching, but it's a form of self-harm. She could evaporate like a rock of crack. Her misjudged love affair has only encouraged the girl to be even more self-effacing.

"So have you told my brother about this? You know, the stuff about your heart valve? That your health isn't good?"

"Not a word. But he surely guesses something. Tim went with Mum and me to the hospital. He must have a good idea, even if he's the tiddler of the family. He's a very perceptive kid that one," I say.

"Good job Tim's not in our house, isn't it," she says jokingly. Her silhouette shuffles before me. Then she hits a more serious vibe. "How about our mother?"

"Not in so many words," I admit. After divorce emotions turn into volatile compounds. What's the problem you have to deal with? You have to maintain a front of strong health, just to cope with your divorce conditions. The relationship - what was your love affair and your marriage - has suddenly gone under laboratory conditions. It would be advisable to put on a full space suit, if that was feasible.

"Mum will know that something is up," Angela says.

"Well, she already has a good idea, don't worry."

"This is hardly commonplace, is it. You had these operations and you didn't get better. Your secret will come out in the end," she warns.

"You're right," I tell her. "She'll piece it all together eventually."

"Why didn't you tell us? Doesn't your family deserve to know?" she challenges me. "What is it, that stops you from trusting Mum and us?"

"I was trying to protect you," I bleat.

"Were you thinking of giving Mum a good shock?" she wonders.

I deny ever having had that intention. Anyway she stopped being shocked years ago. Or so she told me.

"Then why did you keep the truth to yourself?" she wonders.

"Right, Angie, but we're sharing now. You've always been our priority," I remind her.

"Too much, sometimes," she retorts.

"Your future," I stammer. So the old guilt leaks out again, thick as blood.

"Nobody's telling you to get into a sweat over me," she says.

"Somebody has to."

"Why's that? I'm not going to be pushed around by you."

“You let Jakes push you around, because he’s got a handsome face and a wad of notes. Is that it?”

“Mum and you can’t dictate what I do with my life. Even if it’s the only thing you can ever agree on, it seems to me. I make my own decisions, when I get up in the morning.”

“About when you get up, yes,” I comment.

“Times change,” she ripostes.

“Mum and I gave you those opportunities,” I argue.

“Like my brothers and I owe you a big favour?” she replies.

I take a draft of the cooling evening air to consider this. “We took a chance to make something of ourselves.” Now she’s making more than me.

“Your generation’s running the world now. So what are you doing with it?” she shoots. “Grandma would never agree with you.”

“Let’s leave Grandma out of this.” That would be far too complicated. “I can only answer for myself.” And Lizzie.

“It’s my right too, that’s why they call it my life.”

I stiffen in my picnic basket. “How can you be so indifferent to your future? When Mum was your age she was excited about going to Uni. Every bright girl then aspired to get a university education and a professional career.”

“You stopped being a rebel?” she says. “I don’t want to go to Uni.” Angie’s tightening her small fists and pointed jaw against me.

“Is this for real? I can’t believe my ears!” I protest.

“I’ve no wish to join that club whatsoever!”

“What kind of club?” Night clubs?

I’d guess that her boyfriend has a stake in many of the glitzy new establishments around the waterfront.

I tighten my grip on the rigging; holding on for dear life.

“Look, Angie, university is to do with sharing ideas, expanding your mind, networking and, yes, there’s nothing wrong with this girl, enjoying the parties and the clubbing.”

“I’ve heard this one before,” she complains. “The way you talk about yourself at Uni, it sounds like it was Prince was taking that degree,” she remarks.

"Which prince?" I say. "Since when do I consider myself like that!"

"Oh god, Dad."

This reaction is puzzling to me. "You meet all kinds of interesting, hip dudes from all walks of life."

"I already have interesting friends."

"Oh right, yes, I met some of them!"

"If you're so broadminded and up for it, Dad!"

I'm disillusioned. "You've spent too much time out, Angela. You've lost the learning bug." Did she ever have it? "You talked about a gap year...then it expanded into another gap year...now it's turning into a PhD of indolence. How much longer is this going to continue? Your Mum's worried that you work in that café. When we talk about culture, we didn't mean café culture," I say.

"Better to learn the hard way. It's a high tip place. What's Mum complaining about now? That's what I enjoy."

"I can imagine the sort of tips you pick up there."

"I read what I like, watch what I like, meet the people I get a kick out of. Do you understand?" she appeals. "You shouldn't force your ideas on me."

"You have to relate to society. Nobody should exist in a vacuum, do you agree? You need to consider contemporary issues and struggles. Put yourself into a wider context and understand your place in life."

"All right, Dad. You told me to make a careful decision about university. Well, I'm letting you know...that I've decided not to go. The PhD has finished," she remarks.

"This is really going to cheer your mother up," I tell her.

"No need to begin sulking, Dad. You're not going to force me to study. I'm sorry if Mum is going to be disappointed. I didn't set out to hurt her."

Where did I hear that one before?

"I'm embracing life...I'm excited about that," our daughter informs me.

"I know all about your life now, girl. I've been introduced to your exciting friends in the university of life... sometimes at the end of a shotgun."

Of course it wasn't the first shotgun that had appeared in my life.

My girl's a true rebel. This isn't related to clothes, hairstyle or even jewellery, as so often rebellion is linked to identity politics, fashion statements or even a haircut. No, we have really produced the genuine article. Angela was born into adverse circumstances, although loved. She was very much loved: By youthful parents not expecting responsibility or commitment. Now she is prepared to risk everything. She's shunning the safety of convention. I fear for her but I can't help admiring her. She has guts. Maybe the guts that Lizzie showed.

"Right, Angie, can I ask about your plans for the future?"

"Dad, I really hate that kind of question. What do you expect? Become a secretary? A lion tamer? A pole dancer? That just shows such a numb attitude," she argues.

"I already dismissed those ideas, Angie," I tell her.

Does she have any plans or even dreams about her future? At this moment her life stretches ahead like a desolate beach, or even a flooded trench in the park. Man, there may not be anyone out looking for her.

She's restless, our daughter, Angela Constance Sheer. Hankering to escape the eternal mother and father.

"I'm out on my own now, Dad." As if she gets my thoughts and wishes to underline them.

"Should we abandon you?" I ask.

"You have to let me go."

"Maybe in the future you'll find the perfect pill, to make all your problems and issues disappear," I complain.

She probably sighs and makes a face. "You always talk about life, but what about living?" she returns.

"Is that your philosophy? No thought about a career...what you're going to work at?"

"I have to get back to the festival soon," she warns. "My friends are going to worry. I have my friends, you see." But she faces awkward questions, that she clears out of the way. "I don't have any job or career in mind at present. I'm happy where I am. I'll get in as much great music as I can this weekend," she offers.

Not exactly music to my own ears. *She's Leaving Home* - we've been on the side of the unfortunate parents for years now. But what's the point in generating bad radiation? Her mother and I are consulting about her future while the Dino lives off commission.

"Maybe I'll find something where I'm in charge," Angela comments.

"Is that right?" She's going to be the second female Prime Minister? Or the first feminist one, even better?

"Where I can see results? Something tangible. Something interesting and surprising. God know's what that's going to be," she admits. "Let me know."

"We've just got to put our heads together, Angela."

"I don't know, Dad, maybe something in business. I've been saving up some money. I'd be good at that...making deals, negotiating and stuff."

"Really? That sounds cool. But if you're going to succeed in business you've got to be focussed and hard working...around the clock...like Branson and me."

"But let's talk about it later. I've got to find my mates. They're gonna be out of their heads by now." With worry, she means.

"Right, I don't want to keep you," I say.

The balloon has begun to sag, after all this filial chatter. The skin of the envelope has lost tension and energy. I risk being grounded if we continue this conversation. I burn again to avoid such a miserable fate. Sometimes, even as an experienced pilot, I suffer sensations of vertigo. Everything spins. I allow another burn, another long tongue of flame reaching into the vault; another hiss of fiery pain. The bottom of the basket lifts from the rough grass. Air currents draw me up into the atmosphere, as if Adonis has gripped me.

"Away you go, Dad. Have a safe flight. Enjoy yourself!"

"This is your last chance to join me," I tell her.

"No, I'm staying over."

"So you should take care of yourself, Angela. Do you understand?"

"No need to worry."

"You're not running back to Jakes?"

"Only as a friend," she tells me.

"Excellent news." This is the best melody I've heard in years. I compromise on the idea of friendship.

At this point the machine is going up and there's no means to hold back. I feel a corresponding uplifting wave pass through my heart. The ascent has always gladdened me.

Angie has presence of mind to loosen off the guide rope. I gesture for her to throw it up to me. I successfully gather. Internal pressure and temperature builds. The machine continues to rise. Angie's wide hat resembles a flying saucer: her fingers grip the brim. The faint oval of her face turns up, as she follows my progress from below.

"See you Monday, Dad!"

"Monday morning?"

"In the café. Why not? Have some breakfast. Before you go to work."

"You have a date!"

"See you then!"

"Great."

Their menu isn't ideal for my cardiac waistline, or cholesterol level. But you shouldn't avoid a little of what you fancy.

"Keep out of trouble!" I shout down.

"Don't worry about me!"

I've the powerful mystique of fire in my hands. The awesome lantern glides up, the world eases away in a hugely impressive silence. Angie offers a double-armed wave by way of send-off. She acquired this traditional gesture from a very early age.

"Keep away from that gun toting loony!"

"Bon voyage!"

I notice Angie backing away from the site, as I peer over the rim of the craft. For a short while she leans back to follow the balloon's lift. Take off is a magnificent spectacle. Although, after the sun has set, the craft must only be noticed as a barely perceptible shape, against a slightly lighter sky.

Finally I see my daughter bounding away across the field. I distinguish the pantomime hippie hat, moon-dust flickers of arms and legs - until she vanishes. Our angel. Back to her friends, the free festival, a night of getting cheerfully stoned; and what else? With a certain exuberance of new-found freedom, I suspect.

# Chapter 39

I drift at unfelt speed, at a hundred feet in altitude, tugged by a ten-knot breeze: Aiming at the coordinates agreed with Nairn and to our rendezvous spot.

Leaning over the basket, the bonfires, the stage lighting, the patchwork of illumination from the temporary settlement, slowly diminish to sight. Until everything approaches vanishing point and is sucked back into darkness.

How did I put myself into this risky flying position? Having a metaphorical shave with a slashing open razor? Why try to find a particular mistake in my life that caused this? I've never consciously attempted to look backwards. Try to stay mellow with experience. I'm the sum of all the mistakes or misdirection that ever occurred during my life. You can either see life as a collection of greatest hits or misses, or as a *Blonde on Blonde*. I'm not the guy I originally set out to be and paid insurance to become. Man, there's no use giving a reverse peace sign to the whole shebang.

I know that it isn't only fear of death that pushes us towards religion. It's losing everything that we love. Even if I did have religious convictions I'd keep quiet about them. So that would make a change, you might argue.

Always plenty of time up here to think.

The Robins are playing away this Saturday. Tim and I could take in the rugby this weekend. It's good to have him around Big Pink sometimes. Just like the old times. I really miss those fatherly satisfactions. Often I hear Elizabeth's voice about the old haunted house, as I explained. Like a groove cut into my psyche. You get used to the sound of a woman's voice. Man, it's hard to train yourself out of this.

As usual I have to go into the dinosaur lair on Sunday; this time to retrieve Luke, assuming he's going to return and hasn't been interviewed by that oily solicitor creep. There will be tough decisions to be made at work on Monday. There are figures to torture, letters to compose, faxes to send and maybe doors to hammer. This has urgency as Corrina is trying to buy up all my ordinary shares. That girl's never had the reputation of being a slouch. Her idea of hanging around is a paraglider. I'd like to forget about Corrina at this point of history. Recent romantic memories - or are they merely erotic? - aggravate old wounds. From the other point of view, total romantic amnesia is difficult. Her beauty often comes back to haunt me. You could say that.

Finally I let Angie into my secret. This came as a terrible shock, but it wasn't something from an adult bookshop. She has every right to beat her retreat. We couldn't drag her back if we tried. She's always tugged at the baby reins; she never liked being buckled into the sling on Lizzie's back. In these ways, your kids never change. You have to accept that. Otherwise? My last wish as a condemned man could have sounded like an order. It's a beautiful but scary world, it's understood. Nowadays, the young have different struggles.

I don't know if Angie is trying to deceive me, saying she will treat Adam Jakes as just a friend. She thinks she has escaped me finally. I'm not the only parent on guard duty. Elizabeth is going to be suspicious about her highly sociable life. Lizzie's senses have always been keener than mine. In and out of the sack.

The girl's very dear to us - special. We don't talk about that much, Liz and I, but we understand the reasons why. My ex-wife can't dream about any degree award ceremony in the future. It would be better than a parole board.

Angela said that she's interested in running a business. She didn't specify which type. She'd like to run a company and feel the responsibility. She's been saving up some money? I recall. What is that for? How?

The problem occupies me for many flying miles; as I skim the atmosphere between the stars and terra firma.

Then I have an idea, of that type that strikes when high in the sky. Maybe this is only another mental disturbance. I'm gazing down at the moon dusted woods and fields, when I have the thought that Angela could become the managing director of Sheer Dirigibles. She can take over when I leave. There's a nice euphemism.

Luke's indifferent to my kites and balloons. Angie is the eldest. I was getting primitive on primogeniture. Forgetting that eldest daughters can be born leaders. I was trying to make the girls sing backing vocals again. My own girl's lead guitarist and vocalist. What took me so long to recognise her abilities?

When I've landed this machine and reconnoitred with James I'll brief him. He'll not be impressed by the idea of a twenty-something boss. But he's come around to my brilliant brain wave. He'll see this as a positive outcome and absorb the radiation. He's a good friend, with a good business brain and financial judgement; and I offered him a similar opportunity once. Man, he'll be excited about this smart young girl at the helm.

Angela hasn't expressed much interest so far. The last time she tried flying a kite there was more ribbon in her hair. She's street wise and able to think on her feet. We'll put our heads together and discuss the idea, after she returns from the festival. No point hanging around in Mike's café, with only a serviette tucked into her strings.

What will my former wife and living breathing woman have to say? I'm looking forward to telling her. I can already imagine Angela making revolutions in my swivelling chair.

So maybe I didn't make a wasted journey after all. When we imagine we are in a dark and hopeless situation, we can take ourselves by surprise by finding solutions. I wouldn't change or take anything back in my life experience. Love is the most powerful and creative force that we know. In love there's happiness unimagined.

# Daughter's Epilogue

My name is Angela Sheer, a thirty-something lawyer in Bristol, married for the past five years, with no children at the moment but considering, with my husband's participation, the strong idea of starting a family in the next year or two.

Don't begin assuming that you are reading my story though, because I'm the daughter of the writer. It feels strange to be footing up the narrative in this way. That first paragraph sounds really like my Dad, and it's scary; maybe we've got similar thought patterning, who knows? I am featured in this book. You might say I am a character in this story. That feels strange too, but then it's my Dad's account of his life, which includes his family and me, his eldest kid and only daughter, too. So I am "in it" if you like, along with my two brothers and my mother, Liz, who has these days retired to Bournemouth.

The point that Mum's now a pensioner, will give you an idea in which time the story is set, which is at the end of the 1990s. So you can tell that a few serious events have taken place in Britain since then. As an immigration and asylum specialist my job in the law often touches on those big events, but I am not a big shot involved with international issues. It is merely a decent length of time to pass before I thought about publishing my Dad's writing: his autobiographical story. His account gets close to his own ideas and attitudes about life, and particularly his family and friendships, during those years, that culminated with Maggie moving into a suburban new-build; although it was not budgerigar sized like the homes they were building for ordinary people around that time.

There we are again, I'm sounding like my Dad. Does this happen more obviously when I am writing something? I'm not so aware of that when I am speaking, or living my life. For one point, I voted Tory last time, and he'd be upset and horrified by such a statement; although he understood that politics doesn't say everything, or even very much, about somebody, or hardly anything in terms of general elections. He would say I was deluded and brainwashed, but I make my own mind up. Dad came from that generation that wanted to change the world, but I have different views because I know that the world does constantly change, not to how you would want it.

You'll find out about my Dad, Noah, soon enough as you read on. He was writing this account for the months before he died at a shockingly early age. I feel that I am fast approaching that age myself, and it seems strange to get there, as if he's going to show up again, just long enough to wave at me as I pass by. Don't begin to get squeamish at the prospect of reading about a man's death. There's nothing gory or mawkish about the story, I hope you'd agree. It's not possible to offer a rolling news story about your own demise; so Dad couldn't play god to himself either. Although I should say we get close to Dad's last hours, because he was writing constantly, almost up to the end. Dad knew that he was unwell and wished to leave his voice behind, while he hoped or expected to recover from his heart problems.

Dad kept his writing journal with him all the time. Maybe that was a characteristic of his generation too, as they were eager to create, to make their mark and to have their voice heard. He was to be seen scribbling away in the park, or in a café, or at his desk at work and, obviously, at home. He used to carry a stylish bag over his shoulder, in the times when a 'man bag' was not an acceptable masculine accessory. The bag was famously with him and he grew frantic if he left it behind somewhere, in one of those middle aged male moments. I didn't realise that the panic of loss was directly linked to the contents of his writing.

Sadly in those months he had plenty of time almost alone to compose his book; with only interruptions from my little brother Tim, who was only a little kid then. I definitely feel some loneliness of a divorced guy, not only a guy who understands the fragility of his health. These days my youngest brother isn't so little and drives HGVs across Europe for a living. Not maybe the intellectual job my parents would wish, but he does have partial ownership of the company.

So Dad was continuously adding to his story during that period, in fascinating folios he got from a specialist shop in Bristol; now closed and forgotten. He'd write segments and fragments in these notebooks and, we assume, transcribe them later into a better draft, before bashing them out on his old typewriter (these were still old technology days: Dad once tried a computer but packed it back into the box after half an hour).

The emergency services found a notebook in his rucksack on the day of his death; along with his Walkman device and navigation equipment, among other personal objects. That last notebook was inevitably rough in its jottings. He'd not written up his thoughts entirely for that day, or had any chance to smash them into a final form on the old typewriter. But for the sake of this book, I have put them into a better form without, be assured, trying to change his ideas or style.

It was incredibly traumatic for me to go through those testaments, into that journal again; to fold back some of the pages and to recognise his writing again. The final book was worst, as it was clearly folded and creased, suffering the trauma of his last fatal heart attack and crashing back to earth. But it wasn't easy to read through any of them; never mind to try to edit and prepare for publication. But I didn't change much, as I've already assured you. There are some gaps in the narrative. In one or two places he must have torn out pages, or he scribbled a paragraph out, thinking of going back. That irritation, or self-censorship, was quite rare though, as he knew or feared there might not be time to go back and rewrite or rephrase. I had to tidy up in places and change the sequence a few times. Some of the stuff that he wrote made me want to censor him. But I restrained myself.

The notebooks have been at the top of our wardrobe for many years. I haven't known what to do with them. Except that I could never bring myself to throw them away or to condemn them. This was the voice of my Dad; his account of his life and his view on the world. I went back to our family home in Bristol, on the day we lost him, and I found a stack of writing folios. Glancing through them I understood what they were about and I decided to take them away with me: at first I took them to my own room in the house and then they left home with me.

I got some insight that this was Dad talking about us, about his life. He had left behind his thoughts, without understanding the purpose. In particular I knew that Mum would wish to destroy them, or certainly never allow me or anyone else to read them. She was angry with my father, in the various ways that disaffected wives become angry. Maybe she had good reason for that antagonism towards Dad. Men often pretend to be forgiving after divorce, while really they are even angrier than their ex-wives and just hiding their emotions. But I'm not interested in family law - not as a solicitor anyway. Mum still sniffs through her nostrils at the mention of Dad, after all these silent years, so I'm sure she would have cremated his last thoughts along with him.

Yet I knew that I shouldn't want to broadcast his memoirs immediately. I hardly thought about my reasons at the time, but that's why Dad's notebooks gathered thick dust in our main bedroom: Who regularly dusts the top of their wardrobe? Those writings just stayed there for years, forgotten thoughts or experiences of long ago - which is exactly what Dad's writings were. When my partner complained about the old dusty notebooks, as he did about five years ago now, I refused to throw them away or even to move them; it was painful to discard or to stir these memories. He insisted that I do something with them, but it was years before I finally did. Maybe that was the reason: these were ghost books full of cobwebs and hauntings. Eventually these books did find their way down. My interest and courage revived, so that I was able to smear away the grime and to turn the yellow pages again; finding my father's thoughts as fresh and funny as the day he penned and typed them; but more crucially returning me to that time, bringing my father back to me, when he is no longer here in body; hearing (or imagining) his voice again, long after he was lost to us.

While I stayed up through the night, re-reading them, spilling coffee drops and cigarette ash on to the foxed sheets (sorry Dad, I still don't want to kick my nicotine habit), tears dripping off the end of my chin on to the paper, laughing in places and complaining in others, I knew that I wanted to type this up into Word and allow other people to read too. So I hope that you get some pleasure and entertainment from this account: some sense of who my father was, the times he lived through, how he felt and thought about life. Publishing the writing in this way isn't easy for me, even if a decade and a half has passed; even if patches of my hair are silver now and I keep up my own household; even if my partner and I are beginning to think of my most fertile days and trying to snatch breakfast before he has to jump into the car and snort his way to Templemead: the poor guy has to wait for a temperamental fast train to London, and I have to get my head around that stack of documents balanced on the far left edge of my desk.

Then our mother is still alive and we have to consider her feelings (if not all her thoughts about our late father). Ultimately I decided to go ahead and publish before her end, as she's probably as long lived as her name-sake Queen Elizabeth. I would like people to read our family story before we - my brothers Luke, Timothy and I - are pensioners ourselves (although working pensioners no doubt). Liz is unlikely to read about this book, but she will hear about it before too long.

Aside from that issue, of Mum's offended feelings, there are other issues that made me think again about publication. My brothers had to agree, as they eventually did. Luke is a successful gaming engineer, who hardly reads a book in any form, even electronically. If he does read anything on his device, it is usually a military story or an adventure story based on true facts and events. In a way you could say this book is based on facts and events, while covering the emotional territory that soldiers and explorers tend to avoid. My brother is blissfully married and has three sons of his own. He can afford to. Luke was annoyed by some of the things Dad said and thought about him, but there is nothing here to offend him. They were definitely close, and Luke remains close to Dad (even if Noah didn't always see that). Even less to offend our little brother, who never really lived with us. There's more in here to offend me; which was one of the issues for me, as I was reading, re-writing and preparing Dad's account. I kept saying to him "are you for real here? How dare you?" I felt young again. Or young*ish*.

I ran a helter-skelter range of emotions as I was reading and working on these memories.

Dad had his own way of looking at the universe, as do we all. He was outspoken and controversial at times. Partly that's because he was talking to himself, not expecting anyone to read. There is a lot of criticism in here about me, as I already mentioned; over the way I was living my life and conducting myself at the time. It wasn't all about smoking, drinking and staying out late. Dad was aware of his contradictions, a man with radical views from the Sixties who was fearful of his children's freedom and nervous about their personal behaviour. Maybe he was justified to be worried when I had a very dodgy boyfriend. I can see that now. But what father actually pops up in the middle of his daughter's bedroom when she's making love? Aren't there boundaries for parents too? I don't want to spoil anyone's pleasure, but that was hard to take. Over fifteen years later it is still difficult to accept or to forgive everything. Still, there it all was, and remains, in his own words, uninterrupted by my own!

He didn't need to worry as much as he did. Finally it was only a bit of drinking and after-hours misbehaviour, as with nearly every young generation - when they get the chance. It's interesting now to look back and see such panic and paranoia towards the young. Let that be a warning to us. Noah should have known better himself, but I understand that it was just his love and concern. Perhaps I will go through the same syndrome myself, if and when we have kids. Hopefully I will keep a tighter grip on my fears. I wish Dad could have seen the way we turned out -how I turned out. It was definitely a phase. It wasn't too bad finally.

So, yes, I had a theme-park selection of emotions while reading and working on these memories. I've already admitted to being surprised, hurt and, at times, even offended by Noah's remarks. But the book wouldn't have been published if that had been my verdict. However difficult his attitude towards me, he was always honest and caring. I felt as if I had come close to my Dad again. It wasn't hard to imagine him being in the room with me, as I listened to him, feeling his hand on my shoulder again as he followed my activity, even as I was considering his thoughts. I love him for all his faults, as I hope he loved me for mine.

Lightning Source UK Ltd.
Milton Keynes UK
UKOW04f0608190215

246506UK00001B/1/P